CODE NAME SEVEN

THE STARSTRUCK HUNTERS TRILOGY

CODE NAME SEVEN

BOOK 1

SUINNE CLARA LEE

Code Name Seven
© 2024 by Suinne Clara Lee. All rights reserved.
Independently published December 25, 2024 via KDP Amazon and IngramSpark
Paperback edition published via KDP Amazon and IngramSpark
Hardcover edition published via IngramSpark
Kindle edition published via KDP Amazon (pre-released December 24, 2024)

Cover illustration by Alexia Studio
Cover design by Nabin Karna
Illustrations and scene break designs by Suinne Clara Lee, with the assistance of
OpenArt AI
* No AI was used in the writing of the text, up to and including texts presented as
images.

ISBN: 979-8-348-21763-1
For permissions, inquiries or more information about the author, please visit:
https://suinneclaralee.com/literature/publications/

To my beautiful grandmother Young Oak Kim,
as I am made mostly of her Kimchi stew.

Chapters

Preface i

Chapter 1   The Golden Lioness 1

Chapter 2   The Gem Test 32

Chapter 3   Pierced 80

Chapter 4   The Starstruck Hunter 102

Chapter 5   The Emerald-Eyed Panther 128

Chapter 6   Princess Rena 144

Chapter 7   The Fair 175

Chapter 8   Vanna Daya 194

Chapter 9   The Cocktail Party 218

Chapter 10   The Beings 245

Chapter 11   The Plan 260

Chapter 12   Lillian Emmaline Shaffer 273

Chapter 13   The Night Before the Opera 292

Chapter 14   The Sire 321

Chapter 15   Mock Carnival 346

Epilogue 353

Author's Words i

Acknowledgements iv

Preface

The evening was still and strange. Serena perched lithely on a rugged boulder by the creek, her feet dipping in the stream. The soft chill lapped at her ankles, and her eyes wandered to the orange sun that glinted off the capering water. Many things had crossed her mind that day, among those a faint idea—a little ray of light, one could say, cast through the bars into a deep dungeon. Perhaps this could end the war, she'd thought with a swirl of sorrow. Perhaps this was the way. Serena picked up a small pebble and tossed it into the creek, and watched as the current swept it up in a soft embrace and carried it away toward the unknown.

The man walked over and seated himself on the rock beside her. Serena watched silently, her head tilted to the side and resting on her hand. His attire was somewhat erratic; he had been dressed this way since the day she'd met him, in a box-shaped coat the color of damp earth after the rain, and loose hanging breeches that draped his ankles.

"Are you going to tell me what's on your mind?" The man whispered softly.

Serena smiled, watching the swirl of colors in his eyes as the lolling sun flooded his irises. "The same thing that's on my mind every day," she replied. It wasn't a lie. She'd never stopped thinking about them. She couldn't sleep soundly knowing they were out there, those who had mercilessly killed so many, and killed for the sake of it, only because it was right for them, because they sought to make real their hatred; because they knew they could do so without dooming themselves. Because they *so falsely* knew. Each night she would close her eyes, and the image of Harvey's lifeless body would come back to her—draped over the back of his stallion like a rag doll, soaking its pearly coat in blobs of scarlet. No, she hadn't forgotten, and it had been the crux of her consciousness for the past years.

"Love, it pains me," whispered the man. His brows began to bury his eyes as they gazed intently into hers.

Serena looked at him. "It pains me also, Thomas," she said quietly.

"It will end, and it is my duty to see to it," Serena added. "But you and I both know that it can't end before it starts."

The man looked at her a while before he nodded.

"Those things know no pain, no sorrow..." he said.

"And no death," Serena replied. For a while her eyes darted between the man's eyes, only to set softly behind her eyelids like the evening sun. Hands, dainty and scarred, caressed the man's face, and her head rested against his.

"But they will end, Thomas. If my blood's what is needed to do the deed, then I shall give it."

Chapter 1
The Golden Lioness

I find myself, sixteen going on seventeen, in a dark, shadowy hallway of J. Kingsley High School.

No. Don't get the wrong idea. The hallway wasn't always dark. As to why it was pitch black, or if it had anything to do with the whispered gibberish I'd heard a while back, I still hadn't figured out.

All I knew for certain was that this blackout wasn't an accident. The girl stood in front of me, still and gorgeous, much like a hunter in the presence of prey. A strange sound came from the distance, flittering through the darkness as if it were coming for me. I then knew very well that the three things were somehow connected.

Something was about to happen.

Sarah Verona at sixteen years old was an interesting concept to think about. That teenage girl I was stood teetering at the edge of a giant divider, like an acrobat quivering on a rope. I stood on the border of ordinary and extraordinary, the good girl who knew everything on the test and the vice-captain of the girls' soccer team. School would end, and I'd jam my books into my backpack and head to the field. I then would transform gloriously into the ferocious attacking midfielder, tackling the defenses, dribbling the ball through the gaps like a comet hurtling through asteroids. Back in those days, I could not seem to find a way to define myself. No one word, nor a single alias, could describe me. It all came down to a bunch of words that did not go along well together, balled up like bits of crumpled confetti.

That particular September afternoon, however, a busy Tuesday in the second week of my junior year, may have changed that for good.

I groggily made my way through the hallway from Physics to English. The crowd had piled out from the classrooms and filled the halls already. The air was dense with the smell of sweat and unending chatter; school seemed to prove that humans were after all animals, flaunting their presence like dogs in the wild. I found my locker and mindlessly dumped my physics books into the top shelf, along with a pile of paper.

It had been my ongoing theory that humans did all sorts of magnificent things for the most futile of reasons. As I stood staring mindlessly at the messy interior of my locker, and the sheets of physics exercises lying about with A-pluses scribbled on each corner, I could not help but acknowledge it again. I thought back to a year ago when I'd seen this boy sitting under a tree in the courtyard, a physics book open in his hands. His name was Brian Harold, which to me sounded like royalty. I don't know if it was that ruffled dirty blond hair and those glasses sitting crookedly on the bridge of his nose, or that physics book, or even that crimson knitted sweater he like to wear with tightly rolled up sleeves, but at that moment he'd somehow turned into my hero. In my mind's eye I could see apples bloom on the branchlets, and Brian, lifting his eyes to land a childlike, marveling gaze at the merry fruits— a spark of deep understanding forming in those pupils as he conceived the treasured decrees of nature. Right that day at lunchtime I ran to the office to sign up for AP physics.

The history, however, would be better unsaid. I'd gathered up the courage to ask him out last winter, and we'd gone ice skating. Both of us were terrible skaters, and the afternoon mostly consisted of screaming in terror at charging toddlers and landing awkwardly in each other's arms, after which we flailed like baby birds learning to fly and went crashing down onto the ice. Afterwards I hadn't heard back from him, until I'd heard he was going out with this girl who read Heidegger in her free time. I might have shed a teardrop or two.

Strange as it may sound, it was these random sequences of events that led you where you were. Something so small as seeing the boy under an apple tree had led me to the depths of science, and little did I know at precisely that moment, that I would emerge on the other end of the tunnel defeated, the science I knew broken and transfigured—for I was about to enter a world where the rules no longer held.

In that moment, however, I had no clue. I simply took my English textbook and jabbed it under my arm. It hadn't been long since the semester had started, but I had already had enough—the kids were loud and obnoxious, the classes were mostly lame. I closed the locker, let out a little sigh, and started down the hallway, wishing one could have five Saturdays a week instead of one. And just then, without so much as a warning, the hall plunged into darkness.

Chaos unfurled. Murmurs became heightened cries. Somewhere in the distance sounded a clash of metal and paper as something knocked over. I dodged a cluster of frantic boys pushing and bouncing against one another. Amidst the riot my eyes fell on a figure in front of me, standing still as a statue; my footsteps slowed and stopped altogether.

Light leaked through a window in the far east, half shuttered with blinds. It cast an ominous halo around the girl's silhouette, bedecked with jittering flakes of dust in the weak pale glow. I blinked as recognition hit me.

Her name was Lillian Shaffer. I knew her. Pretty much everyone knew her. She was a grade ahead of me, former captain of the girls' soccer team, a legendary center midfielder. Each time she played she would tear the field apart—and each time she did, she would do it looking stunning.

We'd trained together, but barely talked. In fact I'd never heard anything more than strategy or criticism come out of her mouth. Sometime last spring she'd gotten into a fight with the vice-captain and quit; I hadn't seen her around much ever since. Although that did make me the new vice-captain, to this day some part of me still missed seeing her tear across the field like a cocky goddess of war who had just descended onto the face of the earth.

I'd been quite certain *she* had only a faint idea who I was, even though we'd been doing laps, drills and practice matches for half a year. She didn't really care to remember anyone else's name—from what I remembered, she'd referred to everyone by their positions. And yet, this moment, it was almost evident she *did* know me. She was everywhere today, everywhere I went. I'd seen her standing there every time I'd turned. It wasn't once, it wasn't twice; it was in fact multiple times—that I had felt a penetrating gaze on the back of my head. And at this moment, as soon as the lights had gone out, she had appeared right in front of me. She didn't seem the least bit surprised by the sudden blackout; my eyes adjusted to the find her simply watching me, calibrating, plotting. It was though it were she who had cut the lights out, and as though—I thought with a dawning sensation of dread—it was her pushing me forward.

A set of jingles sounded, then escalated. I looked around to see the kids huddled together in confusion. The hall was still full of whispers and occasional cries, but the chatter did not grow—it seemed, somehow, that I was the only one who could hear the foreign noise in the air.

It was a strange sound, with no pattern or order. It resembled notes of wind chimes, quaking in violent wind; my stomach twisted and turned as the sound grew, as if it were my own body that was being rocked by the unseen flow of air. My head began to spin, and dots began to form and swim in my sight like a swarm of bumblebees.

Then it came.

A rush of wind poured into my face. My hair did not fly back like a runway model's, neither could I feel it on my skin—but it was there, without doubt, a flow of foreign medium, rushing up my nose and mouth and blocking off my breath. I gasped. It was getting harder to breathe.

What is happening? I thought to myself in panic. *Is Lillian trying to remotely kill me?*

And something incomprehensible happened. My mind cleared, a bubble of calm forming amidst the chaos. I assessed where I stood, the spot in the center of the darkened hallway, surrounded by murmurs of complaint, curses and bewilderment; and something told me that this wasn't the place I should be.

Instantly my feet carried me through the crowd. I was led through the little openings between the oncoming groups of kids, hopping from one to another like a bug searching for air bubbles in the water. I could tell, with strange clarity, that Lillian was behind me, tracking me—her footsteps sounded evenly behind me, keeping distance, and I could easily distinguish them from the others.

Hastily and instinctively, I raced down a flight of stairs and to the basement. I found a room in the corner, from which came a low electric hum. I then threw open the door and plunged into the room.

I had not been in there before, neither had I known I would find such a room in the basement. I looked around, trying to make sense of what was happening, but with the jingles growing ever louder it was impossible to focus. My head rang terribly. The sound began to dominate my hearing, slowly drowning out the other sounds. The last thing I heard was a voice just outside the door, a high pitched, urgent rapping, but I couldn't make out anything except one word; something that sounded like *'change.'*

It wasn't a command, but my body was obeying it. As though a whirlwind had grabbed me and flung me into its depths, my feet left the ground, and I was thrown into a dizzying spin in the air.

I felt my body penetrate an unseen ripple. A loud set of jingles echoed through my head; it was as though I'd broken through a surface made of a thousand wind chimes. My arms were thrown out as the twirling took speed, and something seemed to tense in my chest, making it harder to breathe— and then in all stopped.

I lifted my head. I was still dizzy, but the ringing was gone, along with the strange sensation and dizzying momentum. But it wasn't quiet. It was quite the opposite. I could hear the murmur of conversations overhead, along with hundreds of footsteps, scurrying rodents... passing traffic, chirps of birds—probably coming from outside. I looked around, perplexed, and discovered I could see perfectly in the darkness—every corner, every dent in the wall, every dimension of the pitch-dark room. I could see wires, scorched patterns and mold on the ceiling, scattered gum wrappers and cigarette butts, along with the drying ashes scattered from their tips.

What's going on? I thought to myself. *It's as if I have night vision...*

And the realization that dawned on me almost stopped my heart.

I did. I did have night vision. I pulled myself up to realize I was standing on four padded predator feet, and that I had implausible night vision, insane hearing, and outstanding sense of smell that tortured me in this murky basement. I glimpsed a glass pane leaning on the wall and approached it. And to my endless awe, I found the reflection of a majestic animal staring back at me.

I had changed, and I had changed into a stunning golden lioness.

I had, for a bit more than a decade and a half, been living in a placid, slightly boring world. My biggest adventures happened in front of my desk, toward the end of a test when I'd come across the first tricky question I'd seen in months, and juggled two likely answers again and again in my mind before I'd settled on one. My biggest despairs happened in the field over a lost soccer match, my greatest sorrow over the death of a pet dog in books. I was living in an ordinary world, guarded, I thought, and real. What kept me in this world were not limited to laws. They were also rules, morals, expectations... and most importantly, the laws of science I'd grown up mesmerized in. They kept me in my world, where things made sense, and things did not shift much from its bounds—where people, by no means, turned into animals.

And about a week ago, it seemed, something had happened. Something had been tossed into a still lake, creating ripples in the fabric of reality. It was then, I thought in hindsight, that reality had begun to crack, soon to be broken open—I would, unknowingly, be spilt into a world of wonders I could not fathom. The boundaries I knew would be gone, and the perils I faced would come from outside my imagination. But at the very moment that the first stirs of wonder had begun to wake the airs of the unfathomed, I knew nothing of the sort; it had not even crossed my mind as a speck of fantasy that I would leave the life I knew for a new, great, perilous one.

It was a fairly ordinary Tuesday, a week before the bizarre turn of events. I was in the library at lunchtime, having found a cozy carrel in the corner between the shelves and the window. The usual chatter drifted in through the windows, along with a truckload of unwanted stories on everyone's social lives. Apparently whosit had broken up with whatsit, and wackamole cheated on nwackamole. I soon tuned my ears out of the gossip—those were meaningless stories anyway, and piqued no interest in me. I looked instead at the physics textbook that lay open on my desk.

Conservation of energy. Pffft.

For weeks we had been on the same topic in physics, dropping balls after balls from slopes and towers. I pulled out a packet I had to read for a quiz, along with a fat notebook, and made myself comfortable. I couldn't keep myself focused for long, however—I had begun to wander off to realms of thought. I doodled absently on my textbook until all the balls wore smiley faces—and thought, inanely to myself, that somewhere off in a distant world there might be philosophers who deemed this concept odd. How far did these laws stretch? To what barren edges of physics were these truths indeed truths? Was energy conserved even when it felt more natural not to? It would for sure be funny if, for instance, you had to make water crawl up a wall to conserve energy. It seemed for a moment that the world was made up of seemingly arbitrary laws, some patchwork of ambiguous concepts and wayward statements that somehow, coincidentally, explained everyday occurrences. I spun my pencil around on the palm of my hand, wondering if there were things out there that evaded these laws. Maybe you could read minds. Maybe telepathy was real. Maybe if you fell in love, something changed within you.

And it was at that moment that something curious happened.

A little fluttering shadow appeared on the edge of my notebook, dancing brittly in the rippling sunlight. I looked up to the windowsill and gasped. On the edge of the windowsill sat a butterfly the size of my palm, and by far the most stunning one of its kind—its wings were clouded with a swirl of foreign shades I had yet to come across. It traveled through depths of violet, through it surging drops of molten, metallic magenta. Then the tips were gilded with fair gold, wrapped in a halo of flaming orange, which then faded into a deep sunset red. The faces of the wings were then topped with cream white spots in the shape of waterdrops. I peered closer, locking eyes, perhaps, with the creature—and with a shudder, thought that the strange bead-like orbs were staring back at me, *studying* me. I blinked.

And the butterfly was gone.

What had I just seen? I thought to myself as I closed my book, craning to look around the carrel, in search of the creature I had just laid my eyes on. It was strange; for one, the color—I had never once seen a butterfly with such colors—and for another, the way, although I'd probably mistaken it, that it seemed to look at me, with its intelligent eyes, its fixed gaze. I briefly wondered if I was losing my mind, but a part of me was sure that I had not imagined it.

Had this been the last of the strange occurrences, I would have brushed it off as a figment of my imagination. But it wasn't. I was on my way home a couple days later, taking a shortcut through the park. Not much had been on my mind; I pranced through the shrubs of azalea, my feet patting the little dirt path in a contented rhythm—when I saw it again.

I held my breath. It was undoubtedly the same butterfly; everything from the size, the swirl of colors, to the little waterdrop patterns on its wings was exactly as I remembered. Before I could think, I reached for it.

In an elegant little dance the butterfly flew swiftly out of reach. I reached again, this time taking a timid step toward it. The butterfly fluttered out of reach once more, and I continued to follow the creature through the paths. Then something even more curious happened. The butterfly seemingly disappeared—it was nowhere to be seen. I looked around, dumbfounded, and found no trace of the magnificent creature. The only thing I could find was a shiny golden beetle the size of my thumbnail, buzzing off and away; and when it finally occurred to me that it might be worth taking a second look, it had disappeared into the distance.

These were the only disturbances in my life, and ones which quickly receded from my mind. I quickly returned to my ordinary life, going about my days just as I'd known them. Only when I'd stepped out of a stall in the bathroom and found Lillian standing uncomfortably close had I begun to suspect something was happening. The girl would then be seen watching me from a distance in the hallway, or sitting in the library—which I'd never seen her do—without so much as a book on the table. But nothing happened; no attempt at murder, no attempt to talk, nothing. She would always be gone before I could approach her. And when one day, out of the blue, something happened, it was the last thing I expected.

The door opened. I turned immediately to see Lillian in the doorway. I tensed, bracing myself for a fight. She approached me slowly, and I kept myself completely still, watching her every move.

What is this? I thought. *If she was trying to kill me, why did she turn me into a lioness? Did she find big predators easier to kill? Without a single weapon?*

"Easy," she said.

Easy! I've just been turned into an animal, for god's sake.

"I can help you change back," she said simply. She continued to approach me, ever so slowly. My hind legs dug into the ground.

"You have to do as I say," she continued in her husky voice. She had a strong Australian accent, which seemed somehow to go well with her aura.

I weighed my options. Trusting her was the last thing I felt like doing, but physically I was at an advantage. Lillian was terrifying, but even she would not be able to fight a lioness. I made a nod-like gesture with my head.

"First you have to stay still and close your eyes," she said quietly.

I closed my eyes as she said. In the stillness I could hear the rush of blood in my own veins.

"Now I want you to forget everything you see or hear. You just feel to your left with your whiskers. If you do it right you're going to feel a wall."

I did as she said. Nothing. I looked at Lillian, who was leaning against the wall staring blankly at me. I growled.

"You're the one that's not trying hard enough," Lillian said simply.

I let out an agitated breath. As much as I wanted to charge at the girl, it did not seem to me like the best idea. She was, after all, the only one who could help me change back.

I tried again. At first I felt nothing, but as if my brain was playing tricks on me, I could soon feel it. It was a rippling surface, like water; and it jingled like wind chimes at the slightest brush of my whiskers. I nodded again.

"Now I want you to spin to your left and break through it," Lillian said again.

Spin? I flinched, remembering the terrifying spin I'd just been thrown into. But if it was the only way out of this—unbelievable—situation, it was worth a try. Reluctantly, I found a sturdy footing, and took myself to a spin.

It was no use. I seemed to pass through the surface as if I were a specter passing through a wall, and with a painful thud I landed on my side. I let out a groan, which, surprisingly enough, sounded like a beastly growl. Lillian stood watching calmly as I gathered myself and tried again. It was, once more, no use—the surface had felt so real one moment, but phantom the next. Again and again I took to a spin in the air, learning to land less painfully on my feet. At something around the fifth time I felt myself brush the surface, narrowly—and I knew that on the next try I would succeed.

And I did. On the sixth jump I felt something lift me, like an updraft—and it was, although not physically there, tangible as anything else in this world. When I spun through it, I heard the same burst of chimes as before.

With a pain radiating from my side I stood up. I spread my hands before me, and saw they were my own, the same freckles, the same little bump on my middle finger where I held pencils. I was back.

Lillian strode over, her arms folded over her chest. She watched me as I regained myself. I did a terrible job—my head was completely blank, and I failed to conjure up even a single word. I staggered.

"Now you're back," she commented nonchalantly.

At that moment I was certain she was playing some sick joke on me. I threw myself at her.

"*What did you do to me?*" I snarled. I managed to tackle her to the nearest wall, but she was incredibly strong; she locked her hands around my wrists and pushed me away from the wall.

"I didn't do anything," she replied calmly. "It's not something I did. It's you. You're an Enricus."

"I'm a *what?*" I breathed, thinking this situation felt oddly familiar.

"You are... gifted with an ability to take another form."

"Gifted," I muttered as I yanked my hands from her grip. "Stop playing around and tell me the truth, Lillian," I snarled. *"Did you drug me? Am I hallucinating?"*

Lillian sighed and brushed her hair back with her fingers. "As much as I understand that's what's easiest to believe, no, it's very real." She said simply. "What kind of drug makes you feel like you've turned into a lion in some old cellar? With perfect, biologically accurate lion senses? Change again and change back, or don't and just go out the door as a big old cat. Try to walk past the Secrecy Committee and have them put a bullet through your head. Then you'll know it's real."

Dumbfounded, I peered outside trough a crack in the doorway. About a dozen hooded figures stood, with a strange looking cylindrical device in their hands in place of a scythe that would have easily suited them as well. I flinched and sprang away from the door.

"Who are they?" I asked, terrified.

"The Secrecy Committee," Lillian replied, as if they didn't scare her at all. "They'll leave if everything goes the way it should. They're here in case one of us is stupid and people end up seeing what you are."

I stood there, my head ringing. Lillian went in and out of focus. Her expression remained indifferent as I opened my mouth to speak, and closed them, then stood gaping like a fish.

"I'm... not human?" I whispered after a while. My head swam. The ground was tilting.

"You are. We don't really say we aren't human," she replied. "We're just something else as well."

"We..." I repeated, dazed. "Something else..."

Lillian stood with a calm, crooked gaze fixed on me, waiting patiently for me to say something.

"It was—it was you with the lights," I said. I meant to ask a question, but it came out more like a statement.

"Just in case you don't react fast enough to find a good place. I can't let you change in broad daylight."

"As if it's going to stop people from seeing what I've turned into," I muttered.

"No. But it does give me enough time to get you out of there before they start to believe what they see," she said.

The world started to spin mildly. "How many seconds do you need to get me out of this building?"

"Not many," she replied.

I staggered. Lillian didn't seem to care much—she watched me coolly as I backed away to the nearest wall. My head swam, worse than before; I let out a wispy breath as pieces of the puzzle began to fit together in my mind.

"The butterfly, the beetle..."

"Not me," Lillian replied simply. "You'll get to meet her soon enough. Although if you noticed her forms, I'd better tell her she needs to be less creative with colors."

My face contorted into a deep frown. There were so many things... so many things that needed to be straightened out.

"Anyway," Lillian began casually. "Calleigh's going to be here any minute. She thought she needed to congratulate you on your FT."

"Who? My what?"

"First transformation," she replied.

I stayed silent for a while, trying to process everything. *Congratulate me*, I thought silently, repeating what Lillian had just said. *Congratulate me for what? Losing my mind?*

"Meanwhile I think we have time for one question. I know you have many," Lillian said.

A whole bunch of queries popped out from the back of my head like moles out of their holes, and I found myself voicing: "How did you do it?"

I shook my head. That was what I was least curious about, but so many questions were swimming in my head that I couldn't get them out in the right order.

"Technical stuff?" Lillian snorted. "I'm just good."

Before Lillian opened her mouth to say more, the door squealed open. A tiny, frail girl walked in. She had messy ashy brown hair that ended at her chins, floating by her delicate face like little black clouds; it seemed to suit her eyes, which wore a dreamy expression. *She looks kind of familiar*, I thought, *I must have seen her somewhere—*

"You guys are talking a little bit too loud. They'll be here to fix the transformers, and they'll have no trouble hearing you if I can hear *every word* you say from the other side of the door. *Please* pipe down a bit, Lillian, not you, Sarah. I sure didn't mean to say anything of the sort to you, you're doing a great job already, but Lillian! You got to be more careful. Just because *you* didn't have your FT anytime recently, doesn't mean you can act this careless about anyone else's. I just thought you needed some experience of it as well, because I did Andrew's, well, you have to do it as discreetly as the Unit does. If you and I do the job it's going to be way more comforting for Sarah than the Unit, but still we can't risk exposing ourselves, Lillie, can we? You don't want to get directly involved with the Secrecy Committee, really you don't," whispered the girl, without stopping for even a short breath. "And cutting the lights out! What do you think you're doing, Lillie? This created a *commotion*. You're supposed to have led her out of the building *before* it happened. You know, approach her, comfort her, and take her somewhere else! And see—you could easily have sensed she's fully capable of guiding herself to a better place to change," *Her lungs must be filled with an awful lot of words*, I thought. *And speaking of leading me out of the building, no, thank you. If Lillian Shaffer tried to approach me, comfort me, and take me someplace else, I would have been terrified.*

"You're Sarah Verona? I'm Calleigh Russell. Senior. Enricus from birth." She added in swiftly whispered words.

"The butterfly," I ended up saying. The girl peered at me a moment, a look of confusion in her eyes—then it cleared up and her half moon eyes turned to crescent moons as she smiled.

"Oh, no," she said. "That wasn't me, although she does look a lot like me. Now that you've had your FT, there's many things you have to do... you have a long day ahead of you, Sarah."

I breathed. It seemed I had been forgetting to breathe for a long time, and I was a little lightheaded. "How did you know who I am?" I asked. My voice came out wispy like a wind.

"Of course I know who you are. Everyone does. I'd say you're kind of famous. You're smart, you're vice Lillian in the soccer team, I think people idolize you," Calleigh exclaimed.

I grimaced.

"I have literally never heard that in my life."

Calleigh peered at me with a genuinely interested look, and I blinked stupidly.

"Curioser and curioser," Calleigh whispered softly. "You'll learn in due time how much influence you have over that pack of rascals out there."

I looked at her, unsure how to respond. I could not tell if this was part of her character, of if I'd somehow fallen into a strange alternate reality.

"Oh," Calleigh exclaimed suddenly. "And don't get the wrong idea about the Secrecy Committee. They're not as bad as they look. All they do most of the times is to just wipe out the little bits of memory of things people shouldn't have seen."

I shuddered. "Thanks for *another* nightmare," I whispered, eyes closed, trying to gulp down the nausea that had just come back. "I hope they can wipe *this* from my head."

Calleigh laughed like bells. "They really aren't bad. They keep these masks on at all times and even use this device that changes your voice, 'cause they're not allowed to let anyone know they work in the Committee, but once you get to have a coffee or two with them you realize they aren't as *villainous* as they look," she went on. "Well, anyways. Enough of the chit chat. We need to get her out of here, Lillie. They're coming. The janitor and everyone, I mean. We can't just stand here looking like a bunch of idiots that's trying to cook something they shouldn't. Let's get going now, shall we?"

Calleigh walked out the door and I followed suit, trying to keep my balance while my head swam. A train of thoughts seemed to drift around in my head, without order, without mercy—and among them the least useful one took the spotlight. *I have a class left*, I thought suddenly. *Right. I have a class left.*

"I need to get back to class," I found myself saying stupidly.

Lillian let out a snort. "Really? *This* happened and you're going back to *class*?"

"Yeah," I breathed.

I had no clue why I said that—perhaps I simply needed some time to process what had just happened—but I did as I said. Leaving the two speechless girls behind, I headed to the classroom.

I had quite a lot of respect for teachers, but there were exceptions; and Susan Grebler was one of them. She had every trait of an undesirable teacher, from an irritable personality to childish talk of other students she'd run into the other day. She would always find an excuse to digress from the class, sometimes to give heated speeches that sounded a lot like propaganda, sometimes to lethargically talk about the weather for a full ten minutes, and sometimes to squawk like an angry wild goose that some girl's hair wasn't 'school-appropriate.' Those were some of the most lamentably spent minutes of my life, but there was one trait even worse, and it was that she was often wrong. And to top it off, she seldom admitted it.

I still did not want to miss any knowledge she might accidentally convey. On any ordinary day I would diligently take notes, scribbled in a messy way that only I could decipher. But that day was not an ordinary day. As I absently copied the contents of the lecture down on the margins of my books, my mind began to wander, ferociously, to what I'd just been through.

Had I dreamt? Was I hallucinating? I looked around at my surroundings and at Grebler lecturing loudly—well, I already knew everything she was talking about. There was nothing new. I might as well be dreaming.

But If I was, I thought, it felt like I would never wake up—whatever reality I had outside of this was far out of reach, intangible, forgotten; the only one I knew was this one. And in the only reality that mattered, I *had* changed into a lioness.

The world had, for all I knew, just broken apart. There was a range of things I could have expected to see in daily life, something close to a spectrum, things in the middle being more probable and things at the far end less so. But the reflection I had just seen of myself, the robust legs I'd felt my weight on, were nowhere within the spectrum. It was a sole little surge far outside of the bell curve. It was a fairy tale, engulfing my science and ripping it to shreds. I closed my eyes and tried to fathom what lay ahead of me. Would I see the hooded figures again? Would Calleigh introduce me to a secret society of shapeshifters? Would we meet in a murky little underwater room past a labyrinth of riddles? I wondered how many more of us there were in the world, and how they had kept themselves completely hidden for however long they'd roamed the earth. What else was involved, was there magic? What about the butterfly? Were there limits to what you could be? Was there anyone, far off in the coasts of the old world, spinning and turning into dragons at this very moment?

And at that moment that new reality gnawed at me so hard that everything else hardly seemed important. Before I could stop myself, I rose from my seat and left the room—and took the very first step of my adventure.

Lillian was waiting outside, sitting back in her dark blue Ford Mustang. The bumpers were weathered with age, but sleek and polished—I wondered how old it was, and what stories it had lived through. I hopped in. There was a can of Red Bull sitting in the cup holder, and a soft, worn leather cover on the dash, imprinted on which was the letter C.

Lillian practically teleported me to a giant house on the outskirts of town, something that would have been twenty to thirty minutes' drive if she didn't speed like a bullet that had just left the barrel. Without a word she jerked her chin toward the door, and I instantly hopped out of the car to be met, startled, by an excited Calleigh. Calleigh stretched her arm toward the house, and with a giant smile, voiced shrilly:

"Welcome to Vanna Daya."

It was the most stunning house I had ever seen. The facade shone a brilliant titanium white, and the blackstone roof met the sky like the tip of a distant mountain. The house had two stories and an attic, a solitary vine of ivy climbing past its window all the way to a little chimney atop the roof.

I followed Calleigh through the porch, around which were beds of cosmos growing up to my knees, swaying lightly in the wind. The girl looked like a little bluebird, prancing merrily through countless colors. She led me through the flowerbeds to her doorsteps. On the ornate alder door was a bronze knocker that resembled the head of an eagle; above it hung a beautifully engraved sign on coated bronze:

Vanna Daya

R. & S. Russell

R. and S. Russell—*Russell*?

"You... *live* here?" I whispered.

"Yes. We live right above the headquarters. We named the house Vanna Daya."

With that simple answer Calleigh laboriously swung the door open. I followed her in.

Somehow the house looked bigger on the inside than on the outside. The living room was a pleasant blend of antiquity and modernity; a stone fireplace sat in the far wall, lined with coffee-colored bricks, and opposite it was a long velvet couch glinting welcomingly in the afternoon sun. The living room extended through a little archway to a little gathering room; the place was lined with tall tables on the side, lit mirthfully by a rays of light scattering off a suncatcher on the window.

I followed the girl around for a while. Calleigh excitedly went on about where the furniture came from; who had gifted them this, who had carved that, and where they'd ventured to buy this. She even went on dramatically about the one time they'd gone to a lighting store and narrowly missed a shooting in the street. I tagged along, studying the dainty details of the interior, when a sudden movement caught my eye. It took several seconds for it to register; but when it did, I flew off the floor yelping—by the fireplace, sitting on a wooden branch, was a full-sized eagle.

"What the—" I exclaimed. The eagle stared back at me with its eccentric yellow eyes.

"That, is my pet eagle," Calleigh said casually, before turning toward the hallway. The eagle cawed, its burnt-gold feathers rippling lightly, vibrating like an engine coming alive. The bird looked nothing like a pet. It was untamed as could be.

"No, it's not!" I protested.

Calleigh shrugged. "Well, he is."

I raised an eyebrow.

"Okay... that's my brother. Chasey, you're freaking her out. Change back."

After another lazy caw, the eagle spun swiftly back onto his two feet. I stood stupidly, trying to catch my breath; although I had just done it myself, I had never seen it happen. Right there, in place of the eagle, was a boy slightly taller than myself, with a broad build and cropped ashen hair.

"Chase," said the former eagle, extending his hand with a warm smile. I finally realized why Calleigh had looked familiar. Chase was a phenomenal defense on the football team. Although very different in aura, the siblings shared a certain resemblance, from the heavily freckled cheeks to the dimples—and most prominently, the way their eyes crinkled into happy little crescent moons when they smiled.

"Hi," I greeted him. "I swear Calleigh looked familiar. It was you."

Chase smiled smugly. "So you've seen me play."

"Mostly at practice," I replied.

"Oh, yeah, right," Chase exclaimed. "I completely forgot. Athena."

I smiled self-consciously. "We hate sharing the field as much as you do," I replied.

Chase chuckled. "We probably don't mind as much as you do," he said.

"So... I heard Cal talk about you last night, and knew you were going to have your FT. How was it?" asked Chase.

I groaned. "Terrible. I thought Lillian was trying to assassinate me with superpowers."

Chase laughed. "I'd be terrified too, if I had Lillian on my tail when I changed. Thankfully this was the only life I've known. I've never been..."

"Human?" I suggested.

"I mean, *we're* human, too. We kind of unofficially call them Blank, the non-Enricus, but we're beginning to think that the term is offensive."

I nodded, contemplating. Calleigh had disappeared, saying she needed to fetch 'S Russell.' The sudden absence of Calleigh made the room painfully silent, and with questions swimming in my head, I felt as though I could faint any moment.

"So," I began, trying to regain my composure. "How did you guys know I was going to...?"

"Because... I don't know if you heard the sounds—when someone is going to have an FT, most of us hear it."

"Oh," I sounded. "But not the, the... *Blank*... I mean the others."

"No."

"And your whole family were always...?"

"Yeah, my whole family are Inherited Enrici."

A whole family of Enrici, I thought in wonder. What was it like? Were there family dinners in the Alps, where the four of them feasted on goats?

"Uh, Sarah, you look kind of sick," Chase said after studying my face.

"I am... a bit tired. You know," I gulped. "A lot happened today..."

"Can I get you something to drink? You can have a glass of water and when you feel better I'll show you around the house."

I smiled wearily. "That would be great. Thanks."

Chase walked into the living room a minute later holding a glass of water, and let out a chuckle on seeing me gawking at the living room wall. Over the fireplace hung a painting of the house—the bright white facade bathed in the soft light of a late fall afternoon, reflecting the gold of fallen leaves as if the house itself were swimming in a golden river. I turned to see that the walls were lined with more paintings, of animals, plants, and landscapes. It was then, when I turned windowside, that I noticed a stool and a drawing board.

"Does somebody paint?"

"Calleigh does," Chase replied.

Calleigh. It wasn't hard to imagine her behind the drawing board, a pencil stuck up behind her ear, her delicate hands a mess of paint; but it wasn't easy to fathom that—

"She painted... all the stuff on the wall?"

Chase nodded. "I admit she's kind of good. But don't ever act like you notice when she's around."

"Why?"

"She'll talk about it for like five hours. Seriously, three years ago I had my girlfriend over..." Chase looked aghast. "And I don't do it again."

I let out a little laugh.

"Calleigh's more of an indoors kind of person," Chase went on, "...an indoors *extrovert* kind of person. Naturally I don't get a lot of peace at home."

"Well, she gets a lot of peace," I said, looking up at the paintings.

"Because I'm an outdoors extrovert kind of person," Chase replied bitterly.

Chase handed me the water, which I gulped down in seconds. He led me around the gathering room, which seemed to serve as a homely gallery. It was reminiscent of the early galleries of the European aristocrats, where homes were in fact the most elaborate of art museums—but heavily different in nature. Calleigh's paintings weren't put on these walls to flaunt wealth; they had simply grown all over it like vines of ivy. It seemed that for Calleigh, creation was the most natural thing.

When we emerged back out the archway, we were met by two Calleighs— one exclaiming 'I was looking everywhere for you!', and the other who introduced herself as Sophie. Sophie had the same smiling half-moon eyes that Calleigh had, as well as her freckled cheeks with dimples and thin smiling lips. Her hair was up in a neat little bun instead of the happy little mess Calleigh had around her head, also a softer auburn instead of Calleigh's ashen brown.

"I know, right? I know what you're thinking, that I look exactly like my mom," Calleigh began with a big smile.

"For sure," I replied. "You really took after her."

After a little talk, the four of us made our way down the stairs to the basement, which, according to Sophie, led to the headquarters. We climbed down flight after flight of stairs and arrived at a corridor, at the end of which stood a sealed metal door.

I watched awestruck as Sophie punched a series of numbers into some sort of keypad. With a short whine a little slit opened on the metal door, followed promptly by a flickering honey gold light. Sophie gazed unblinking into the light, which flickered green in approval. Then she changed. I felt a tingle in my limbs as Sophie spun swiftly around into a glimmering gold spiral, which produced a sumptuous golden doe. The door adjusted itself to her, producing another slit at the doe-Sophie's eye level. She stared into it again, and with a final flickering green light, the door unlocked. What was beyond it was, if possible, even more spectacular than the rest of the house.

I gawked as I set foot in the gigantic hall. Chestnut and white marbles lined the walls, and three enormous chandeliers—each one shaped slightly differently from the others—filled it with a warm gold light. Across from us was a giant gold emblem on the wall, where under a spiral divided in half by a sole, thin line, were the words:

CABINET OF ENRICI, UNITED STATES OF AMERICA

"The Cabinet. They have branches everywhere," Chase whispered behind me.

"We would like to welcome you to the Lincoln Headquarters, Sarah," said

Sophie with a proud smile.

And I replied with:

"...*This* was under your *house*?"

It turned out the headquarters was strictly hidden from anyone outside the Enricus society. It was built under utter secrecy, the construction directed partly by the Secrecy Committee itself. It was with the aid of what Sophie called the *Traveler's Pocket* that the underground structures were made; all the pieces were smuggled underground, exploiting a very strange physics of the *interdimensionality* of Enrici.

The hall was where meetings were held, regarding all sorts of important, administrative matters—from what items to put on the curriculum for young Enrici to discreet matters involving the Secrecy Committee.

On each end of the hall were, according to Calleigh, little rat-sized secret passages leading above-ground, put there in case there was no other means of entry. I'd asked what happened to those with much larger forms, and Calleigh's eyes twinkled before she looked to Chase and replied; "There's always a way."

On either side were two arched doors, one of which led to a giant library stuffed with bookshelves after bookshelves. Sophie scanned her eyes on a little screen again, and once more as a doe—and to my amusement, one of the bookshelves rumbled out of its place, revealing a small room packed with dusty crates. In one of the larger crates something was whirring, its hum resembling that of a powerful computer but not as mechanical. Nearby, another crate sat twitching, or more like, absentmindedly rocking side to side; I wondered what they were, or if they could be opened—but now was not the time for those curiosities. Taking my eyes off the queer crates on the floor, I followed the mother and daughter through another doorway into a cozy sitting room.

"This room is called a Phonogral, Sarah. We share messages in videos and abstract projections with others in the CE," explained Sophie.

"This could scare you a bit... here, hold this." said Sophie as she handed me a small wooden medallion. On its face was an intricate carving of a bird with outstretched wings.

"This is a Phonogral Chip. This will allow you to slip in."

Slip in?

Before I could ask, Sophie had begun to speak.

"Sophie Russell," said Sophie into the air. The walls lit up with hazy images—I gasped aloud as the face of a plump, balding man appeared in the haze.

"And our new Original Enricus—code name?"

"Seven," Sophie replied.

"Perfect," said the man. I only learned later that the uttered words were codes of some sort, devised initially to keep information private. The code names were randomly assigned and, according to Calleigh scarcely used.

The man took a step forward, his face lighting up in a smile. He then spoke, his voice excited: "Nice to finally meet you, everyone! I'm Arnold Hoffman, the Original Enricus Instructor."

I gasped again as rows and columns of confused faces appeared around Arnold, greeting him with murmurs.

"Today there were seven FTs reported in the Cabinet. I prepared a little walkthrough for all of you.

"And by walkthrough, I mean *literally* walkthrough. We're going to transform now, with a quick spin to your right, angling it so you break through the surface. Please recall the moment you changed back after your FT, and do it again—"

I didn't wait for him to finish.

I did what I'd done earlier. I braced myself, throwing back my legs in preparation for the jump—and spun into the air, folding my arms onto my chest to give myself more momentum. I took flight, spinning violently, and I felt my body touch a wall in the air. It was made, not of any known medium, but of something out of this world—I felt it not with my skin, but in my head. I was drawn to it as if it had a pull of its own; and with a sudden gasp of bliss, I broke through the surface, the jingles resonating from somewhere deep within me into the fabric of space itself.

I did not turn, however. To my surprise, I found myself in a different place, an unending golden meadow I did not recognize. I looked down at my hands and saw much larger, dark-skinned ones. Past my hands I saw huge feet that also weren't my own—both bare on olive green grass. I was in someone else's body.

"I hope you aren't too alarmed by the transformation. This is a Phono-graphy—well, the closest word would be a *simulation*.

"As you probably heard, you are an Enricus," Arnold began, summoning a tall human figure out of midair who transformed into a black rabbit. He waited silently for the haze to die away.

"An Enricus—plural Enrici—is a human that can transform at will into a certain animal," explained Arnold, looking at the bunny. The bunny hopped around both of us in a messy scamper. I stared, amazed.

"But it also refers to other animals—" he said, this time conjuring a snarling panther. The black rabbit squawked. "—that can transform at will into another animal."

I watched in amazement as the panther spun into the haze, reforming itself as a white rabbit.

"When we say Enricus, however, it's usually only the former.

"The name was given after the founder of the old Kingdom of Enrici, Queen Enrica," Arnold began, conjuring yet another cloud of mist in the air that turned into a portrait. "You'll learn about the Kingdom in your history classes, so I'll be brief—Enrica was the daughter of an Italian prince. She was sent to Scotland to marry the Earl of Panmure, who looked to find ways against the Union with continental alliances. She was an Original Enricus just like you, and later when her husband lost his title after the Jacobite Rising, she ran off with her family and founded the Kingdom of Enrici."

I listened as if to a fairy tale, watching in awe as the face of a woman appeared in the frame, long dark hair, furrowed brows, exquisite and elf-like—yet bearing a deep-rooted resolution in her eyes. The portrait of the woman faded from the air as the short story came to an end, and I noticed that the bunnies from earlier were still scampering about in the grass. Arnold waved his hands, dismissing them; and they hopped away into the distance. I stared after the little creatures for a while before something popped into my head.

"Arnold?"

"Yes?"

I grimaced as I thought back to the strange butterfly in the library, then to what Lillian had said—*although if you noticed her forms, I'd better tell her she needs to be less creative with colors*—and asked;

"I remember Calleigh said that the butterfly and beetle I saw were Sophie, and then I saw her change into a doe—can you have multiple forms as an Enricus?"

Arnold smiled enthusiastically, like a geologist who had been asked about a certain rock.

"Excellent question, Sarah," he commented. "The short answer is no—we can only have one form, unless something leads you to change forms. Now Sophie's ability to change forms has something to do with her *gem*, which is something we'll take a look at a little later."

I mouthed the word *gem*, letting the word linger on my tongue. Something about it was sweet and appealing, like a distant birdsong from the land of your dreams.

"Now," Arnold said, steering us away from the subject. "We're going to look at what brings us into existence." The man twirled his hand at the air. The plains disappeared into a swirling mist, and the background slowly turned darker until it was pitch black.

The disembodied voice of Arnold continued: "This may be something that modern science forbids you to believe. But it's still the most likely theory on the origins of Enrici."

It was quite a moment later that I noticed a faint, opal dot appear in the distance.

"This theory claims that our universe is only a surface of a certain multi-dimensional body," explained Arnold as the dot approached us, growing into a giant sphere. "More like a star. The early scholars named it *Alpha Enricus*. This is a simplified visual model of the star."

The sphere now filled my sight. It was overlapped with a translucent image of a complex cosmic web. As the sphere came closer and closer, the web lost its density and instead turned to sparse collections of galaxies. Only when the star came even closer, and scattered dots showed themselves in place of galaxies, did I notice something change in the surface. The surface wasn't smooth. It had countless faces. It was like a brilliant-cut diamond, only it seemed not to belong in this world.

A closer look told me it wasn't obeying the laws of our geometry, and was instead subject to otherworldly optics; the way the faces intersected with one another, the way the light scattered and dispersed over the facets—none of it worked the way I knew. I marveled at the countless shades of white, the crystalline facets concealed in the surface of the star.

"Right here—" Arnold pointed. The image of the universe, overlapped on that of the curious star, had zoomed into a picture of our solar system. "There is something like a hole on the surface of our universe," said Arnold. "Through that hole comes a type of cosmic ray—like the solar wind—from Alpha Enricus. And that changes us. It changes humans, animals, plants, and also even caves and waterfalls. It gives them alternate states and unusual powers. This is what leads to the transformation of an Original Enricus.

"If whatever's affected by this stellar wind is a living thing, changes are made in their genes. This change is then passed on to their children. But the Enricus trait is *recessive*. It means both your parents have to be Enrici for the child to be one," Arnold continued. The surface of the star had come close enough to touch. I found myself extending a hand to touch it.

"If only one of your parents was an Enricus, then you would not be one. Not unless you were an Original."

It was the weirdest thing ever. The surface looked something like the inside of a gigantic geode, shimmering with shades of white—but when I touched it, it felt smooth as stone.

"But if you have strong emotional bonds with an Enricus, it becomes much more likely for you to become an Original Enricus."

The star then retreated, becoming once again the opal dot, and then disappearing from sight. The darkness receded and I found myself on the same plains as before.

"If you remember what I said about unusual powers," said Arnold. The black and white bunnies had come back, and were scampering about in peace. "Each Enricus has one given ability. It's called a *gem* and can be used only in our secondary forms.

"Gems come in a great variety, ranging from the very common Nonverbal Communication Gem—a.k.a. the Silent Whisperer—and Strength Enhancement Gem—a.k.a. Warrior, and recently also called Hulk Hands—to extremely rare ones like the Augmentation Gem—also known as the Fighter's Beacon."

Powers. Gems. My heart began to race, and a tingle swept through my body. I inhaled.

The talk continued, and with a thunderous heart I listened. Arnold went on for several minutes about different sorts of gems before he flicked his hand to conjure a mist-wrapped night sky.

"I'm sure some of you already can't wait to know what your gem is. The gems however take several days from the FT to develop. You will come back to the headquarters with a supervisor in a week to get your gem tested."

"Until then, you will all be attending to mandatory classes and stabilized transformation training."

Arnold conjured a cabinet in midair, on each drawer written names of courses.

My eyes caught some names off the lot. *Controlled Transformation, Special Case Transformation; Transformations in confinement, Emergency Transformations.* In the far left there seemed to be classes related to gems. I mouthed to myself the names on the drawers, such as *Gem Identification, Controlled Use of Gems,* and *Fortification.*

There also seemed to be theory classes, covering the laws and policy of the Enrici and the history of the Enricus society. One course covered the ancient and medieval era, and the other the modern era.

I studied the boxes, walking toward them and opening them, as Arnold explained each of the courses in detail. Each of the boxes opened into view of a room below, or a field like the one I stood on—where you could see twirling little figures performing various tasks. In the Controlled Transformation box I could see a rabbit Enricus turning back and forth from rabbit to human, and in Gem Fortification I could see a toad with its arms outstretched, conducting an orchestra of currents on the edge of an angry sea. In the history box I could see a small miniature of a crystal castle, along with little soldiers twirling simultaneously into a pack of wolves.

Arnold went on about the courses, explaining what order they should be taken, and when; apparently someone with a full time job, or someone at school, would be able to finish the primary courses in a year.

There were, I learned, private institutes for Enrici, disguised as private institutions for normal humans. They covered each and every one of those courses, and did it much more intensively. The idea was astonishing, a dream school perhaps—the nearest one, I learned, was in Lyons, Colorado. But unless you were an Inherited Enricus, and lived in a very extraordinary environment ever since toddlerhood, this was not an option. Most of these courses were taught through the Phonogral—I pouted my lips, wishing I could personally be in this field, twirling in midair into the majestic beast I'd become.

As Arnold went on to describe the courses in detail, I wandered off for a closer look. I crept around the drawers in awe, opening and peering inside, making mental notes of things that looked interesting. Some subjects in the upper shelf—secondary and post-secondary subjects—boasted fancy titles. I read through a list of Advanced Gem Training subjects: *Fortifications II, Extensions II, Basic Beaconing Stabilization* and *Secondary Gems*. A current of excitement shivered through my body. I stood still, contemplating the strange feeling, the strange exhilaration, until much later—by then I found that Arnold had moved onto elective theoretical subjects. I quickly paced to where he was, on the way peering inside a drawer labeled *Enricus Mythology,* in which stood a little dragon, its tail curling frantically as a gust of flames dissipated from its mouth. I quickly closed the drawer and hurried toward Arnold.

There was much more; something called *Dimensional Operations and Special Tactics* had a long list of interesting concepts in its box, and something about a certain *Void* also caught my eye, but Arnold waved off the boxes, which disappeared in the blink of an eye.

"I know you want to see more, but sadly our time is up. All these courses are waiting for you, and you will be able to learn as much as you want, so no rush."

The background soon faded and turned into the field I originally found myself in. Arnold stood there with a warm smile.

"This is it for today. Once again, we welcome you."

And without understanding how, I found myself back in the sitting room. There was a faint ringing in my ears. I pressed myself into the armchair, eyes firmly closed, swallowing, trying to regain myself.

The door creaked open, and Sophie walked in.

"How are you doing?" Sophie asked.

"I think I'm okay, thank you," I replied, pulling myself up from the armchair. The world spun lightly, and in a second Sophie was holding me up.

"Easy. You just had your First Transformation, and it was also your first time in the Phonogral. It's perfectly normal that you feel like this. Now would you give me back the chip?"

I did.

Sophie led me out, and Calleigh joined halfway up the stairwell. Calleigh went on about how something called a Memory Gem was used in the making of the tutorial, that whatever it was I'd just experienced was constructed with the collaboration of an expert lucid dreamer and what they called a Memory Gem artist. I could not pay much attention, however, as the words continued to swim around my ringing head. I held onto the railing like it was a lifeline, trying only to steady myself.

We emerged back in the living room. Calleigh had prepared a cup of tea on the coffee table, and Chase had morphed back into his eagle form, perched on the arm of the couch. The eagle spun elegantly back into his human body and offered me a seat; I staggered, feeling somewhat nauseous.

"Thanks, Chase, but I think I need to go home. I can't—I need some rest."

Chase looked at me sympathetically as Calleigh pulled on her jacket.

"Right. Come on, I'll drive you. You did great for someone who just FT-ed."

And at that moment I could not answer; I had, at last, fainted.

Chapter 2
The Gem Test

On Wednesday morning, I woke to the brilliant blue sky dawning over my window. My body was stiff as though I were in a suit of iron-clad armor. I lay still in my bed, my eyes halfway closed, as the sunlight grazed my cheeks and shimmered over my eyelids. It was quite like waking from a long dream. All of it felt unreal, from the blackout in the hallway to the transformation, that intense, powerful yet bewildering feeling of having the body of a ferocious lioness; from the smell of stank air in that dusty cellar, to Lillian, Calleigh, the majestic white house and the incredible sight I'd seen in the Phonie. Did it really happen? Had I really turned? Was I really *an Enricus?*

There was one way to find out. I climbed out of bed and stood up decisively, clenching my teeth and both fists, and began to take off in a quick jump spin—

"Sarah!" My mom's voice hollered from the other side of the house. I stopped at the last minute, slamming painfully into the footboard.

"*Ow,*" I muttered. "Yes, Mom!" I yelled back.

"You're going to be late for school!" She called.

I smiled. It was like any old day I'd grown to love—well, except for the unmistakable ripple of exotic medium, fluttering into my face like a spring breeze; followed, distinctly and undeniably, by a soft jingle of windchimes.

I walked through the school building with an intense sense of power up my shoulders. With each step a tingle shivered its way up my fingers; perhaps I couldn't spin webs from my fingertips, but nothing could stop me from shifting into a deadly, beautiful creature. The line between science and folklore had long since crumbled, and although nothing had changed in the atmosphere, nor in the drowsy, blank or excited eyes I passed in the halls, my world had shifted.

School, however, seemed to be someplace at a different dimension than me. It all whizzed past like the backdrop of a ride at the theme park. Limits, continuity, the teacher casting me a somewhat expectant glance as she briefly mentions something about the epsilon-delta definition; a demonstration on the limit of one over x as x approached zero. Some comment about the Oxford Comma which was obviously wrong—it was Grebler, for god's sake, I didn't expect solid facts from her anyway—as Peter Sutcliffe wasn't the person to come up with the idea of it; then an afternoon of Catherine struggling desperately to open the window and clamber through, the great depression and the New Deal, yellow sodium flames and teal green blaze of halide copper. The little details reached me and sank into memory, but in a strangely foreign way; it was as if they belonged somewhere else, on the other side of a thin flask wall, in the world of ordinary humans, where I no longer belonged.

I later found myself in the great white manor. Once again I gawked in awe, my eyes drawn like magnets to this part and then that. Some things caught my eyes that I hadn't noticed before—a small bronze wall stood at the side of the living room, ripples of water flowing down its surface, laying a soft background ambience. At the bottom of the waterfall were several fish of bright colors, dancing among the soft bubbles glittering like otherworldly opal.

Just as she'd done the day before, Sophie led me to the basement. We descended the endless flights of stairs—something like seven stories, I estimated—and walked through the corridor to the door that guarded the headquarters. It clicked open after scanning Sophie, both in her human and doe forms. The magnificently carved gate revealed itself. *I'll never get used to this,* I thought to myself as we entered.

The bookshelves came into view, and I marveled again at how they never seemed to end. I'd always dreamt of seeing the world's most majestic libraries, and it seemed a small portion of my dreams had come true—those aisles after aisles of old wood seemed home to half the world's knowledge.

"Why did they have to hide the Phonogral behind a bookshelf?" I asked, suddenly curious.

Sophie looked thoughtful. "The Phonogral is not just a small theater room. It's a communication device and much more. It stores a lot of information that should never fall into the wrong hands.

"That's the interesting thing. At first we thought it would be impossible for humans to open up a Phonie, and that to them it wouldn't be much more than just a room with an unknown purpose. But some decades ago there was a case where a passerby on the street accidentally activated it. Ever since, we made sure to take precautions. If the Phonogral falls into the wrong hands, more like the wrong hands *fall into the Phonogral,* then they will be able to reach millions of Enrici out there. We don't know what might happen then. Maybe they'll find out something they shouldn't. Maybe authorities would use them to extract information, plant the wrong ones, or send messages they shouldn't. You've already heard that there's a secret passage leading from the ground. But it's for Enrici with smaller forms. In your case or mine, not very effective. So we don't disclose the location of the secret entrance unless absolutely necessary." Sophie replied seriously, holding open the door to the Phonogral. "Tell the Phonie who you are. That will be enough. If you need help, I'll be in the study."

"Thank you." I replied before I walked in.

I looked around the room. To the eyes it was no more than a cozy sitting room. On one of the papery walls hung a small framed picture of a gray mouse. A red armchair sat in a corner, one of its legs sitting idly on a woven rug covered with colorful furballs. A soft buttery glow lit up the room, emanating, gently, from a moon-shaped lamp at the far corner. As I carried myself to the armchair I could feel with sudden clarity how stiffly my legs moved, and how the wooden Phonogral Chip pressed against my left buttock in my back pocket. I took out the chip to hold it carefully in my hand, I couldn't erase the thought that it wasn't just me in the room. Something about it was alive, as though made animate by some unknown enchantment. The Phonogral seemed *intelligent*. It seemed to be awake, it seemed to listen, and it seemed to question. It seemed to ask: *Who are you?*

"I am Sarah Verona," I whispered.

The atmosphere tensed. But nothing happened. No image appeared, nothing transported me to a grassy meadow. I sat blinking a while, and reached for the doorknob to go find Sophie in her study, and suddenly remembered how Sophie had brought me here the day before.

Well, maybe this was some sort of bug, like one in a computer program. Then perhaps—

I declared, a bit louder: "I am Code Name Seven."

Without warning the world jolted, and I was thrown into the middle of a grassy field.

"A savanna," came a voice, which nearly sent me flying off my feet. I turned to see the familiar figure of Arnold, in overly enthusiastic savanna attire.

"Today we will be training in the appropriate habitats of your Enricus forms," said Arnold.

It was strange—the world was painted in a different palette of colors, made from shades of yellow, gray and blue; it seemed as though the red had drained from the world. I looked around. The tall golden grass formed a plain that spread way beyond my range of sight. Sparse trees, short and slender, bent in unruly shapes to decades of wind, provided shades for resting animals. I could see a pride of lions resting under a large, flat tree, adolescent lions with prickly manes beginning to form, licking leisurely at one another's heads. The breeze was cool against my skin, soothing the blazing heat from the sun. It appeared to be sometime in the middle of winter, where rain was scarce but lakes and ponds have not yet drained.

"Today's lesson will be on changing, and equally importantly, *not* changing," Arnold said.

I made a puzzled face.

"Now how do we change?" he asked, holding out a hand as if to say, *we'll get there in a bit.*

"You spin to the right," I replied. I was surprised to find that the voice was mine. I looked down at my hands. It was me; this wasn't some generic tutorial body.

"Oh, in case you haven't noticed, this is different from the tutorial video. This is real, just gem-augmented," Arnold said. I rolled up my hands into fist and opened them back up, again and again, mesmerized.

"So if we go back to the subject of changing," Arnold continued. "As you pointed out, correct, we spin to the right. But do you always change when you spin to the right?"

I frowned. "No?" I guessed. I felt like it would be quite a disaster for some people, for instance ballet dancers.

"Correct again. We don't. So what makes us change and what makes us not?"

I thought back to the moment I changed. There weren't so many instances, but I remembered every detail. I could hear the jingle, the feeling of a melodic, satisfying shatter of the rippling surface.

"The windchime sounds," I replied in a hushed whisper.

Arnold nodded. "That is right. Before I go onto that part, we're going to look a little bit at the theory. I hear you're taking AP," Arnold said.

I frowned. "How did you—"

"Sources," Arnold replied, "The CE has sources. We would normally not go into detail about the theory behind it with our average young Enrici. But I hear you take some interest in science. What do you think, would you be interested?"

I nodded fiercely. "*Yes.*"

"That's what I thought. Feel free to let me know when it gets too excursive. We can then skip a few pages, I mean, parts of it."

With that the world faded.

In the darkness a sphere appeared. I recognized this sphere from earlier. *Alpha Enrica*, I thought to myself.

The sphere once again grew larger, and I could once again see the millions of facets, overlapped, interlocked and coexisting in intricately curled dimensions. A voice began to sound, not from one distinct source, but from everywhere; I could hear it in front of me, behind me, and all around me.

This is Alpha Enrica. It has never been fully observed, and to fully observe it with our limited senses would be impossible. We have, however, visited a part of it. It was thought that the portion we were able to reach was the surface of the star itself. But in fact, it was only a surface of the surface. The surface of the surface, as we know it, is called the Alpha Enrican Highlands, or the Highlands, and you can find out more about it in the book The Greatest Discovery.

If we return to our original topic, Alpha Enrica is a star-like entity theoretically existing, and partially observed, in the five dimensional universe. It releases spurs of energy, something analogous to the solar and stellar winds in our universe. That energy exists in lumps called quanta, and when transferred to individual humans, it brings us to a new state. As elementary particles jump to a state of higher energy, the inflicted humans become one of us; an Enricus.

Seen from the higher-dimensional world we are only the little bugs crawling on a piece of paper. In fact we are less. We cannot be seen, or observed, the same way we cannot see Alpha Enrica. Conventionally thinking, any flux of Alpha Enrica's energy passing our realms would be null even when integrated. But modern science discovered by our own kind has shown that this is in fact not the case in reality. Because of the fact that they are transferred in quanta, that energy can still affect us, change and alter us, even in the infinitesimal realms of our paper thin world.

The star faded away, and was replaced by a weird wire sculpture; a pair of cubes, one within another, with their vertices connected with one another.

A hypercube, I said to myself, smiling in self-satisfaction.

The cube spun around dramatically, fading into the distance and turning instead into a morphing cube, suspended in midair.

The hypercube is a four-dimensional cube, made by adding a dimension to a cube as a cube is made by adding a dimension to the square. Our eyes perceive objects in the three-dimensional space, albeit as a two-dimensional image. As a result, we would see different objects depending on how the hypercube is placed in the four-dimensional space.

I listened with my ears perked up as the voice boomed on. The cube morphed, edges and vertices forming on its body, into a strange polyhedron; only to turn, back once again, into a cube.

Now we take the analogy of elementary particles. A pair of elementary particles rest on something very closely resembling stairs. Just like quarters placed on a flight of stairs, there are heights the quarters can come to rest at, but also heights they cannot.

I watched as a flight of marble stairs appeared in front of me. There were two shiny quarters placed on a step. They began to quiver, then raise themselves onto their sides, only to roll down a step.

They can rest on the steps, but not at any heights between the steps. In advanced physics we learn that very small elementary particles exist in such discrete states.

If we think of, say, a little plastic bag with two quarters in them, they can exist in these discrete states, but with different 'head or tail' combinations.

I watched in awe as the flights of stairs separated into two sets. On one lay a plastic bag containing two shiny quarters, once again separating into two translucent pairs of superimposed coins. One consisted of two quarters, one heads, one tails. The other also contained two coins, one on heads and one on tails—only in reverse order, with a red sticker stuck on top. The other set of steps had three different steps occupied with coin bags. On the bottom lay a solid coin bag, with quarters both on their tails. On the top lay yet another solid coin bag, in which were two quarters on their heads. In between lay another pair of translucent plastic bags, both clear and without a sticker, heads and tails, and tails and heads.

I could not quite figure out the pattern. I reached for the translucent bags, which sat overlapping surreally on top of one another. When I touched them one disappeared entirely, and the other solidified, along with the other bags sitting on different steps.

As you can see, some of those states are in fact not one single, determined state, but more than two states overlapped. Let's call this a superposition. Well, at least until you touch them and they collapse.

The initial image reappeared, of the steps with overlapped bags of change. *If you look at these steps, on the first step the bag is solid, but on the second, it's a superposition of two different bags.*

These are all part of a very special physics that attempts to show us how things behave when they're very, very small. They no longer act like the objects we see in everyday life. Things aren't solid anymore, they're just possibilities or something of the like, sitting in a haze until we touch them, and even when we touch them, they refuse to reveal all they are to us.

But some studies were done by scientists of our kind in an attempt to explain where we come from, and they have managed to extend these models to macroscopic objects, in this case humans. This theory involves a new inter-pretation of superposition. We don't look at a superposed state as a haze of possibilities, we look at it as a new geometrical figure, something that has more than one face, and can show one of those faces when observed.

The steps enlarged until a single step reached my chest. On the bottom step appeared a woman, looking around, confused.

On the first step, we have an ordinary human. In a four-dimensional space they exist in a three-dimensional configuration. If we go back to the example of a hypercube, it's like a 'flat' hypercube that's flattened in four-dimensional space until it is three-dimensional; only a cube. If we go back to the example of the cube, it's like a 'flat' cube, say, a square, basically flattened to only one of its faces.

But it all changes when the Wind touches her. In some cases, when the excess energy from the Wind passing through our three-dimensional world is just right, no less but just right for this human, it brings her to the next state. And the next state is a superposition. Geometrically it is no longer a flat surface, but a four-dimensional part of a hypercube. On one of the faces is our initial human form, and on another is a second form. We see this transformation as a spin into the air, after which the person turns into an animal. The form can be anything but usually tends to be mammals and birds.

On the second step now stood a woman, superimposed like a ghost in the movies, with a capybara. The woman took to a twirl in the air, and her human body faded away, leaving only the lethargic-looking rodent lying on the step.

And we Enrici can consciously and at will change our forms. This is done, essentially, by spinning the 'hypercube' around, in a direction that doesn't exist in our three dimensional space. But we know where it is, thankfully, because one of the gifts we possess is the sense of the fourth direction.

The wall, I thought. There was always a thin wall, to the right when human, to the left when a lioness. It was a surface of some sort; I could not feel it solidly with my fingertips, but I knew it was there. If I closed my eyes and thought hard, I could touch it, not quite the way I touched everyday objects, but in a way no less real; a mild tingle would ripple through, and instinctively, I would know I could spin right into it and morph into another shape.

So first and foremost, the voice began, *we must learn how to change, but that comes naturally. Something possibly more important would be to learn how to not change. We have to be able to know when to change and when not to, and act accordingly. This is more crucial than anything, especially since we live undercover from the rest of the humans.*

Undercover. I mouthed the words internally. The world began to fall away, fading into a dark haze and reappearing before me as the savanna I'd seen earlier. Arnold stood in front of me, one foot resting on a cream-colored rock.

"So today we're going to learn selective transformation, or more simply the art of not changing. This is important, as for inexperienced Enrici any motion similar to that of transformation can get them turning when they shouldn't. It's really one of the most important things, to avoid changing at the wrong place at the wrong time."

That was exactly all I did for the rest of the class; jump-spins in the air like those of a skater, but without transforming. It was, unlike what I'd thought, quite a challenge. When I kicked off into the air, a whirlwind would envelope my body, and out of a newly formed, yet persistently adhering habit, I would let it carry me. I'd be taken into a heavy stream of ether like a fish swept in a current, and I'd break through the wall, the sweet ring of chimes sounding in my ears; and on my padded lioness feet I would land, muddled and sheepish. It got easier only around the tenth time. I'd trained myself to ignore the rippling wall. I managed, narrowly, to avoid it— instead I fell back on my human feet. A ripple propagated through the air like a lingering echo, drifting *al niente* long after I landed. As I went again and again the ripples ceased each time, until I could jump, or spin, or jump and spin without disturbing the wall. The class did not end, however; for some time I was stuck there on the savanna, jumping and spinning obnoxiously into the air.

Another half an hour had passed, and I had begun to question my life. It reminded me of this one time I went to this event as a toddler; the girls were learning basic drills with balls while the boys were off in the field playing a game of soccer. I'd thrown a tantrum, and my mom had taken me by the hand and brought me to the soccer coach. That had been the start of the history between me and the ball. But this was different. It didn't seem to be a place where throwing tantrums would help. I kept at it, reluctant—and by the end, I was fairly good. I finished a lengthy sequence of transformations and simple spins on demand, and Arnold congratulated me with a hearty smile.

"Now you're ready to take the test for the A1 Level Transformation certificate. You can take it anytime from a month later. We're going to test your ability to do controlled transformations, just like we did a while ago. It's going to require not just a subtle control like you've demonstrated today, but also a complete focus. You can arrange it with Sophie after this class." Arnold clapped his hands together in a peppy manner. "Well, great job, that's it for today! Class dismissed."

The savanna dissolved, and as suddenly as I'd emerged in the foreign landscape, I found myself back in the sitting room. I stretched my back, and then my arms, and jumped up and down a bit to ease my stiff muscles.

Upstairs, I found Sophie on the phone with someone. I wondered for a moment if I should just leave or stick around a while to say goodbye. I decided on the latter, having had some questions I wanted to ask; I took a few steps back and pretended to be very interested in the patterns on the furniture, worried I would disturb her while she was in an important conversation.

"... the gem. I see," Sophie said. I tried sheepishly to tune my ears back out from the conversation, perhaps remove myself from her—but the word had caught my ears, and I was, even though I probably shouldn't be, invested.

"... so if I understood correctly, prosecution demands gem expulsion."

Sophie's face was serious, and she listened, nodding and agreeing, for what seemed like a minute.

"I see... you want to prove it wasn't Justin."

"... Allegedly the person who did it has a kinetic gem. We'll have to have someone look into it. I can talk to Anne and ask her."

Sophie listened for a while more, and once again, nodded into the phone. "All right. I'll do that. Anytime, honey. All right, see you. Bye."

Sophie hung up and turned to me. "Sorry, Sarah. There was an important issue. My husband's a lawyer at the CE Court. And there's a... troublesome case going on."

"Oh, I'm sorry," I said quickly.

"It's going to be all right. How did the class go?" Sophie asked kindly.

"It was okay," I replied. "I did a lot of..."

"Controlled transformation drills?" Sophie finished the sentence. "That can be really exhausting. Well done, Sarah."

I thanked her. "Oh, by the way, Mrs. Russell,"

"Sophie," she corrected with a warm smile.

"Sophie," I repeated awkwardly. "I wanted to ask you something."

"Sure, go ahead."

"About gems," I began, self-conscious. "When will I find out which gem I have?"

Sophie nodded warmly. "Right. I was just about to tell you."

Sophie led me to the couch and offered me a seat before she continued.

"The Office of Original and Juvenile Enricus is going to issue an order for a gem test within a couple days. Then we'll prepare something called the Lapillocognal Serum, where we have to go through a process called Linking. Linking takes a full day, and links the Serum to the gem we mean to examine. Once it has, your gem will be ready to test, and we'll set a date and time that suits you."

"When do you think that will be?" I asked cautiously.

"I'd say about a week from now."

In a week.

"In the meantime, you can take a look at this," Sophie said, producing a sheet of paper from a pile on one of the tea tables. "It's a leaflet about the gem test. Explains how it's done in detail. You might want to give it a read before your test."

I took it in my hand.

There was a strange silky quality to the paper, and the words seemed to have been printed with an interesting type of ink—it looked as though the ink was still wet, but nothing came off when I pressed my fingers to the letters.

"Written in special ink for security purposes," Sophie said with a smile as she saw me peer at the print. "Your test is most likely going to be in a week or so, possibly a bit earlier. I'll let you know soon enough."

"Thanks," I said.

I stared at the tiny prop-up calendar on my desk. Somewhere around a week from now. It was torture to wait, but there was surely something else I could do in the meanwhile. I decided that I could find out a bit more by asking the others.

I strolled up a floor after lunch, near the seniors' homerooms, in the hope that maybe I could run into Calleigh or Lillian. I did get lucky. I found Calleigh strutting down the hallway, humming a tune that sounded somewhat familiar. I hurried to catch up with her brisk pace.

"Calleigh?"

Calleigh spun around, and upon seeing me, her lips went up in a huge beam. "Hey, sweetie! What's up?"

"Can I ask you something?" I asked.

"Sure, anytime," Calleigh replied sweetly.

"What's your gem?" I asked.

Calleigh's eyes glistened excitedly. "Aww, sweetie, you heard about gems!" she began. "Well, my gem's called the Nonverbal Communication Gem. It's called NVC for short. Some people in the old days called it the Silent Whisperer. So essentially, as you can see from the name, it's a gem that allows you to talk without vocalizing. Quite useful, actually. The communications we can do in our other forms are very limited, because we obviously can't speak the way we normally do—that is, excluding those of us who have some very unique forms, like for example parakeets, which is actually quite fun to watch, I've seen one before, it was one of the coolest things ever and I was honestly a little jealous, because I mean, *I'm* a bird too, but I can't do that! But anyways—sorry I digressed. Anyways, since most of us, like you and me, can't speak the way we do when we've changed, my gem comes in handy..."

Calleigh did talk oodles, and I found I had sort of zoned out, murmuring 'interesting, interesting.' When she finally paused to draw a deep breath, I seized the chance to ask the important questions.

"So how does it work? What does it feel like?"

"Actually, I can show you. But then I need to change if I wanted to, so hmm, let's see, how about the room in the basement you FT-ed in?" Calleigh suggested, her eyes gleaming.

I frowned. "Are we even allowed to go in there?"

Calleigh shrugged. "I don't know, but we have our ways."

The 'way', turned out to be nothing more than tiptoeing and looking around like some thief in an animated movie. But it did work. More like, we got lucky.

The room looked a bit more chaotic than it did before. Apparently, the technicians were trying to figure out what was going on and had ransacked the room; wires and skins were littered all over the floor.

"I don't know if you're going to like the feeling of it. For some people it seems to be a big scare at first, but then when you get used to it, I'm pretty sure there's no other gem that's this convenient. Well, I mean maybe there are some. Some gems are really cool, there's even a gem that works very much like magic. You could be shooting different colored sparks from your fingertips, who knows?" Calleigh's eyes twinkled jubilantly. "Anyways, sweetie, are you ready?"

"Yeah," I replied with a nod. "Let's do it."

Calleigh changed. I let out a little gasp; her transformation was elegant, like a cutscene from a ballet performance. From a frilly gold whirlwind emerged an ash brown eagle. The eagle looked at me intelligently; the round, stern eyes penetrated mine, very much unlike human-Calleigh's snowy half-moon eyes.

Hello, Sarah.

Calleigh's shrill voice penetrated from someplace at the back of my head. I jumped, alarmed. The eagle cocked her head to the side as if to laugh, and a jingling laughter made its way into my head.

It was the most peculiar feeling. It was like something was speaking through the back of my head, except it wasn't—the sound seemed to come from every single point of my head and yet none of them, somehow bounding inside my skull as if it were a vast chamber. It was nothing like I'd experienced in the Phonie. Arnold's voice had then come like a sort of background noise—it did not have a distinct source, but it felt only natural that way. This was different. It was more real, more physical, more tangible. Yet it did not belong in the physical world, neither did it belong within the scopes of physics as I knew it.

So, Sarah, how does it feel? Did it scare you?

"Not really," I replied uneasily. "I don't know, maybe a little bit, but it feels really... strange."

It's only natural, replied Calleigh. I tried to picture the voice coming from the eagle—it eased a little bit of the bewilderment.

The eagle cocked her head to the side again—which seemed to be eagle-Calleigh's trademark gesture that she used in place of a smile—and took to a twirl, landing daintily on the spot the eagle had been, a big grin on her face.

"So, what do you say?"

"That was... that was impressive," I replied, shuddering. "*How* do you do that? Can you talk to *anyone*? Or do you have to make eye contact or something?" I asked, remembering the penetrating gaze of her eagle eyes.

"Every gem is different. It's like an actual gem. You walk into a gem store, or I don't know, just picture some little stand in a Christmas market somewhere in Switzerland where they sell little gemstones, and you see all these little carved stones on the counter. Every stone looks different. Every geode looks different. Has different hues, different folds, different specks of little stardust here and there. Every crystal looks different. The parts where they catch light give different glows. The way the colors blend, the clarity, the depth, how they're positioned on the rock—all different. See, those gems, even when you carve them into a shape you want, they're going to have that uniqueness in them. They're going to be that one gem and not any other. Know what I mean? It's exactly like that." Calleigh went on. "As I said, but can't stress enough, *every gem is different*. They have different modes, different ways they work, different strengths, and different sensations. For instance, if you met another NVC, and *they* changed and spoke to you, it would feel very different from what you felt now. That's what I like about gems. Anyways. For me it's intention. It's really convenient. I can talk to whoever I want to as long as they're close enough, and it will take no less than someone very skilled at gem arts to block me out with a defense gem. And yes, with the help of my brother, you can even say things back to me. I could also learn to make it a two-way channel myself, but that's quite hard. My tutor once said it would be harder than getting a second gem, seeing from the way my gem specifically worked. The lines kind of fade at that point. There's a bit of a hazy area between the Nonverbal Communicator, and the gem they call the Mind Reader. I would kind of be stepping into that realm if I learned to do that. So well, that can't be easily done, but if I actively listened, sometimes I feel like it works a bit, I get a vague idea, maybe a very muffled voice, but then I might have imagined it. Still a long way to go, really." Calleigh shrugged.

"I didn't know you could have second gems," I remarked.

"You can," Calleigh chimed. "It's an advanced level art, and I mean really *really* advanced, but you can get a second gem by practice. My parents both have multiple gems. My mom has two and my dad has three. The record is thirty-nine, set by this Indian man in the 1990s, and it hasn't been broken since. It's really hard. I'm thinking of taking some courses and practicing for a second gem, but I haven't really decided which one I want to do."

"*Thirty-nine*," I remarked, enthralled.

"Well, I could tell you all about this if you want. You know, in the 1860s, there was a..."

My mind began to leave me. Phantom of the Opera. That's what it was. I smiled, not because I'd found Calleigh's story amusing, but because I'd finally remembered the tune Calleigh had been humming earlier. It was the song Christine was singing while she walked past the stone angels.

The next on my list was her brother. As soon as I finished all my classes, I swiftly packed my bag and raced outside.

The football field was on the far east side of the campus. The sun would blaze toward the campus in the morning, and onto the stands in the afternoon. I thought of the usual shouts and laughter coming from the field, and the droplets of water dispersing into the hot air from the fountains, and felt a slight warmth spread through my chest. I loved this time of the year.

There were two ways I could get to the football field from the west wing where my classes finished. The first was through the gym. I could go out the north entrance, take a shortcut through the extension of the gym building, passing by a dozen giant humans, twice my size, sweating intensely. Then I'd be in the north parking lot. Past the band container, where the sound of the blaring brasses seemed well to crack the earth, the path led to the ice rink up north. That was where the hockey team trained. Often the Kingsley Puffins would stride down the parking lot in a pack, in their red varsity jackets with a puffin on the back holding a hockey stick. The usual lot was Nathan Lynch, the team captain, and his crew, Matthew, Cole and Carlos. Carlos was the most beloved of the pack. He would always saunter down from the ice rink with the rest of the squad, a pompous grin on his face, a mint chocolate frappe in his hand. I found it somehow obnoxious, the silly contrast between the bright green sludge and the blaring red of the Puffins jacket. And that face. The grin plastered on his face, soaked in pride and love for attention, was the kind that lingered on one's face as they talked; one you couldn't quite tell if it was genuine or mocking.

The spot was always littered with cigarettes, sometimes even with a group of fangirls. They'd always ask for a sip of Carlos' frappe, and would go nuts—a ridiculous fit of giggles—when he took another sip from the same straw. Each time I saw something stupid like this happen I desperately wanted to whisk myself off to college.

The chaos, however, could be easily avoided; I could take the other route through the library. And that was what I did. I went up two floors, to the junction between the main building and the dome-shaped library. The crossing was a sort of hallway suspended in midair, with glass windows on either side spilling rays of refreshing afternoon sun. Out the windows I could see the east courtyard, where I could see some gruff seniors studying on the picnic tables, and Brian Harold in his usual spot under the tree. Some kids crouched by an artificial pond to the middle—I had figured they were looking at goldfish, but a while later I could see one of the plunge their hand into the pond and pull out a battered, wet cell phone.

I cantered through the hallway, down the stairs, and out the building into a blazing afternoon sun. Birds chirped on the trees, and an occasional swarm of dragonflies came and went before gliding off to the pond. I flitted down the path to the central courtyard, past the cosmoses lining the brick building. A glitter of voices came to my ears. I grimaced. It was the usual chatter, coming from the pack of girls I scorned. They talked of someone's fight at someone else's party, some other girl's relationship and the classes this boy was taking—I shook my head, regretting that the chatter had somehow broken my bubble of happiness and spilled me out onto high school reality. School was a place where you had barely the time to get on with your own life, and yet there was at least one person who had a lot of spare time on their hands they could use to get on your nerves.

I spun around to find the origin of the voices. It was an ensemble of three voices; a high-pitched screech, a very fake, exaggeratedly dynamical falsetto, and a sickly, salty caramel. It was the usual lead trio of baboons by the ice rink. One of them was Dina Christie, who was in a relationship with Carlos. She was a promising female version of him, wearing that contemptuous smile wherever she went. I wrinkled my nose at her fake strawberry curls and salty voice—they seemed to be talking heatedly of some little quarrel that happened a couple days ago, when suddenly, the Christie girl rose with a wave of her hand, and came strutting into my path, colliding with me—and an approaching Carlos.

The girl seemed to be made entirely of bone. I rubbed my sore shoulder, cursing between my teeth. I was met, annoyingly enough, by the girl's scowl. I scoffed. *Well, if* this *is how you apologize!*

"What the hell are you doing?" chuckled Carlos at his girlfriend, a muddled smile on his face. On came a series of cheap drama, namely the girl adorning her salty voice and voicing an unnecessarily lengthened '*Whaaaat,*' and the boy cooing her with, '*Be careful, babe.*'

I scoffed again. I was, as of today, officially done with this ridicule. I turned to leave, and gone a few steps flexing my shoulders, when the boy's voice stopped me.

"Hey."

I spun around.

"I think you dropped this," Carlos said, holding out, to my horror, the leaflet about gems that I'd gotten the day before.

I took the leaflet from his hand, bewildered. I hastily crumpled it in my hands.

"*'Do you want to go see a movie with me?'*"

I squinted. "Excuse me?"

The girl stood chiming in, peering at the leaflet from where she stood.

"It's what the note says," sneered the girl.

I frowned, aghast, thinking she must be challenging me to a fight—until I remembered what Sophie had said earlier about the special ink. The frown then turned to a curious smile.

"What's wrong with you?" I could hear Carlos whisper. So that's what it was. It was as though I were living in a magical world—the leaflet was, in a sense, *bewitched* to show gibberish to the eyes of an outsider. But did it mean Carlos had seen something different? Perhaps the sorcery didn't work consistently, and it showed different things to different people. If they read the same note it as two different things—

Awestruck and shaken, I quickly folded up the paper in my hands so that even if they happened to experience a clash of realities, they could at least blame a trick of the mind. I was by no means prepared, however, for what he said next:

"What's a gem test?"

After a long trip I finally arrived at the football field. The sun blared onto my face, and I squinted as the shrill blue of the sky met my eyes. It was the sunniest a day could be.

"Hey, Sarah! You're finally on time!" called a voice from the side of the football field. I turned. It was Madison. Madison Decoste was, well, my best friend. She was our fullback and reserve goalie, and most importantly my favorite on the team. The bubbly laughs, the straightforward comments, the genuine interest in anything I had to say, her signature orange headband on her frizzy curls—she was a blessing.

"On time?" I asked, confused. "What—oh!"

Oh, right, it was Thursday. On Tuesdays and Thursdays we had soccer practice. I shook my head, in disbelief that I'd completely forgotten. Since last year I was on the girls' soccer team—named, dramatically enough, *FC Athena*. Most of us were playing for fun, and only a handful looked to make it a career, of which I was not a part. Lillian was irreplaceable, and the team had been on the wane since she quit. But I was one of the few strings that held it together. I felt the frontiers of life on my skin when I raced down the field, and the team appreciated my quick, spontaneous choice of timing to leap into action.

"I actually need to, uh, talk to someone," I said quickly. "I'll change and get started in a few."

Madison narrowed her eyes. "Girl, you're never on time. And you didn't even come to practice on Tuesday."

I smiled sheepishly. "Sorry, I'll be back in a second. Love you, Madi."

With that I rushed across the field to the other side. The football team was getting ready for practice, chatting, getting hydrated. Chase saw me first and greeted me with a wave of his arms. Then he jogged over to me, dragging along another boy I soon recognized. His name was Andrew, and he was the other half of the acclaimed defense duo—tall, dark-skinned, buzz-cut, slender in a way that made you wonder where his strength came from. I had not really seen him talk; he didn't seem the talkative type.

"Hey, you haven't met Andrew yet, have you?" Chase asked; the enthusiasm in his voice reminded me of Calleigh.

"No," I replied with a friendly smile. "Hi, I'm Sarah."

The boy gave a timid smile and introduced himself. "Andrew," he said quietly. "I'm on the football team."

"I know," I replied. "You're literally famous."

"So what brings you here?" Chase asked, greatly enjoying this get-together. "On your way to practice?"

"Well, I came to ask you something," I began. "But then I saw something else—"

The boys listened intently like a couple of giant bunnies.

"And uh... now I have two things to ask," I concluded.

"What are they?" Chase asked.

"I can't ask you here," I said, eyeing Andrew. "I need to ask you in private."

Chase didn't quite seem to understand; he merely beamed and said, "Trust me, you can ask me anything in front of him. This dude goes everywhere I go."

"No, it's..." I began, unsure how to put this. "It's an *eagle* sort of issue," I said, putting an emphasis on the word.

The boy, however, broke into a laughter. I looked at him for a while, baffled. "He's one of us, Sarah."

"One of us?" I echoed in confusion. "How do you mean—*oh*."

I looked up at the boy as realization dawned on me. I did not think the two girls and one boy would be the only other Enrici that ever existed—but it was still strange, in a surreal way. How much more was there to find out about the world of these creatures?

"Yeah, I am," Andrew added quietly. "I'm an eagle too, like Chase is. You don't have to worry."

"Is Carlos?" I asked cautiously. *If Andrew was also an Enricus, perhaps...* "Is he... is he also one of us?"

"Carlos from the hockey team?" Chase echoed, confused. "No. We're the only ones here. Calleigh, Lillian, me and Anrew, you. No one else."

"He could read the leaflet."

The boys looked very confused.

"The leaflet?"

"About the gem. It's written in special ink, I've heard. Dina Christie couldn't read it. She thought it was some note to ask someone out."

Chase laughed. "Now that's kind of funny."

"No, I'm serious, Chase. Carlos could read it. He asked me what a gem test is."

The boys fell silent. "What did you say?"

"I said I don't know," I replied with a gulp. "Just that I found the leaflet somewhere."

"I would just forget it happened, if I were you," replied Chase. "I don't think he's going to pay that much attention."

I agreed. The boy seemed far from attentive, and far, at least so I thought, from smart. It wouldn't mean anything to him.

"Now what is it you originally wanted to ask us?" Chase inquired.

I cast a quick look around before I questioned sheepishly:

"Well, now that there's two of you..." I began. The boys eyed me attentively, and I swallowed before I continued: "Can you show me your gems?"

It was a bit more chaotic than I expected. Their eyes widened like pairs of diskettes, and they frantically looked around for a second before they spoke in a hushed whisper.

"You can't just walk up to us and ask us to show you our *gems*," whispered Chase scornfully.

"Uh, sorry," I apologized, confused. "I didn't know it was that personal..."

"No, no, not that," replied Andrew, laughing. "We're in the middle of the football field, Sarah."

"Our team is watching, your team is watching, those freshman fangirls in the far corner are watching..." Chase explained, nodding toward the far corner.

I laughed. "I didn't expect you guys to freak out, I was worried for a second that you two would just change in the middle of the football field—"

Without waiting for me to finish my sentence, the pair grabbed the sleeve of my jacket and began to sprint. I started, thinking I was being kidnapped for a while—but they skidded to a halt behind a fence, a corner facing the side of the band container.

"You were right, we would if you dared us to," said Chase solemnly.

I rolled my eyes.

"But well, you didn't, and I feel like you won't, so we didn't," he continued.

"So can you show me your gems?" I asked curiously.

"Sure," Andrew replied. He cast another quick look around before he continued. "My gem is called the disorientation gem. It confuses you. If I do it properly I can make you worse than wasted, but I'm far from that level. But I'll show you anyway. Here. Try to answer the questions Chase asks."

Then swiftly as a wind, the boy twirled into a dark brown eagle.

Just as earlier with Calleigh, a strange sensation enveloped me. Andrew's eagle eyes seemed to take an intensified glow, and suddenly I was hit with a whoosh of wind; one that wasn't tangible, but nevertheless there.

It was as though something lifted me up by the feet into a haze. I stood, deeply befuddled; what was I doing behind fences and trash cans to the side of the football field? Confounded, I tried to move toward the football field, I believed I originally had some business there, maybe I was going to practice—but my steps got somehow tangled and I was stuck with my left foot crossed over to my right.

"Hey, Sarah," Chase said. "How are you feeling?"

"Great," I found myself saying, although I'd believed the contrary—until a moment ago. I realized I was indeed feeling quite good. The haze wrapped like velvet around me, and it was as though I was sinking into a heap of cushions.

"Are you doing this to me, Andrew?" I managed to ask.

Andrew looked at me with an innocent expression. "No, it's what it feels like."

"It's what *what* feels like?" I repeated, trying to make sense of what he was saying. It seemed I'd forgotten something, except that I had no clue what it was.

Chase chuckled. "What is your name?" he asked again.

Of course I knew what my name was. "S—" I'd opened my mouth to reply, only I couldn't continue. What *was* my name?

"S—S—" I continued hissing stupidly like an old snake. The boys were doubled up in laughter, and I would normally have scowled at them or something, but the haze was enveloping me from all sides now, and I was in delightful bliss—

A shudder passed through me as though some cold wind slapped me back into reality. Andrew had transformed back into his usual figure, and the effect was instantly gone—but for a faint jingle in the air. I uncrossed my ridiculously crossed legs, then burst out into laughter. The boys also doubled over in laughter, punching each other in the arms and gasping for air.

"That was impressive," I whispered in awe. "And hey, stop laughing."

Finally managing to draw a deep breath, Andrew spoke up. "I mean, it's a pretty impressive gem, not gonna lie. It makes people forget what they know. Think what's normal isn't normal and what's not is."

"Do you ever use that in games?" I asked with a deep frown.

"No, hell no," replied the both of them, looking incredulous. "We would never use our gems in a game. Even if we could."

"Wait, it isn't possible?" I asked, confused.

"You'll learn in time, but we can only use our gems in our other forms, unless *some other gem* makes it possible for us to do it in our human forms," Chase answered.

"We never swore an oath but we consider it a golden rule that we play fair," he added. "You know how even when we're in our human forms, we have a little bit of an enhanced, well, capacity, depending on what your gem is, or what your form is. If your form was a fish for instance, you'd be better at swimming. If your gem is strength, you'd become a little stronger. It's like that. It's part of you. Now that's already an advantage."

No, I did not know—but now I did.

"Look," Andrew added quietly, as though somewhat offended. "I enjoy football. I like it the way it is, where I test my limits, try to see what I can do with skills and practice. I'm not ruining it like that."

I felt bad. "Sorry, sorry, Andrew. I really didn't think—you know. I didn't mean to offend you boys."

"I know," Andrew said with a smile. "And it's fair you think that."

"Do you want to see my gem or not? It's really cool," Chase said impatiently.

"Oh, please," I said. "Show me. I'm dying to see as many gems as possible."

"It's called the Augmentation gem, a.k.a. the Fighter's Beacon. It's one of the—"

Just then the piercing sound of a whistle penetrated the air, and we all jumped.

"JACUS, RUSSELL! GET BACK HERE! WHAT DO YOU THINK YOU'RE DOING?" Barked the football team coach, waving his hand furiously in the air.

"Oh, crap," cursed Chase under his breath.

"FIVE LAPS FOR BOTH OF YOU!" hollered the reddened man. The boys grimaced.

"Shoot, we got to get going. Meet you at Vanna Daya sometime, I'll be there to take classes as well," said Andrew before he sprinted off.

"Damn it, Sarah. I'll make sure to show you my gem soon. Really, I promise," Chase whispered.

I winced. "I feel responsible for those laps."

"Don't be," Chase said before—"RUSSELL!"—running off after him.

"I'll buy you both ice cream sometime!" I shouted after them, to which they responded with an OK sign raised above their heads.

"Sarah!" I heard a call in the distance, and reality came back to me as quickly as it had gone out. It was Madison again, looking as confused as I'd done when Andrew had his gem on me. I held up my hand at her, then rushed to the stands to change into my soccer shoes.

When I was back, Madison galloped toward me in a blink. She nudged me hard in the ribs.

"You were talking to *Chase and Andrew*?" she whispered.

"Yeah," I answered uneasily.

"Do you even *know* them?" Madison demanded.

She had a point. A few days ago I knew close to nothing about them.

"Uh... met them at a, uh, party," I lied.

"*You go to parties?*" Madison's eyes widened.

Oh, darn, I should have chosen something else to say.

"Listen, Madi, I'll tell you all about it later. Just not today."

"Sarah, I don't like this. It's like you don't love me anymore," Madison pouted.

I rolled my eyes. "I know I'm acting weird, but trust me, there's a good reason. I'll tell you when the time comes."

"*And* introduce me to Andrew."

I rolled my eyes again. "And introduce you to Andrew."

The practice began with a bunch of basic drills. I was in a good shape today. Although I was still preoccupied with what new Enricus things I would be learning tonight—not to mention the subject of gems—I was functioning. My dribbles were nimble, my shots were precise.

Coach's whistle blew, and the mini match began. It was my team against Madison's. Her team had Angela May, the team captain, on defense. She was one of the most driven people I had seen, and was truly a wonder; she was possibly the only one who could match the ex-captain Lillian in skill. The team also had Nakato Powell on fullback, and she was insane.

In a few moments my team's wingback passed the ball to me. I trapped it with my foot and began to dribble it toward the goal post. Madison came at me, flinging her feet dramatically under my joints in an attempt to take the ball; but I gave it a subtle outwards nudge with my foot, and Madison tumbled onto her side before me. Another girl in defense lunged at me after Madison, but she also fell away to my side, sliding on her rear end. *Ouch,* I thought to myself as I passed the ball to our ready striker. Scattered cheers came from the boys, who were sitting around and watching as we took the full court. I grinned ear to ear, panting heavily, as our striker made a beautiful goal.

The first ten-minute half ended and we were victorious. I caught my breath, drumming my legs so they would not cramp. I downed the contents of my water bottle in one big gulp; it was hot, and I was sweating like an otter straight out of the water.

The second half began, and an opportunity came yet again. I took the ball and began once again to dribble it down along the right hand side of the pitch. A midfielder and wingback rushed to Angela's aid. One of them lunged aggressively against me, but I nimbly dodged, sending the ball rolling past her right foot. I then sprinted through the opening between Angela and the midfielder, rushing, with the three well behind me, to reclaim the ball—adrenaline began to pump through my veins, and I could feel the air dig sharp into my lungs like menthol. I raced for the goal post, exhilarated, as the wind flew into my face. I was then met with Nakato, who lunged for me in her usual predator-like manner, but I swiftly sidestepped her and landed a hefty left foot shot straight into the rear of the goal post.

The mini match ended, and we'd beaten Madison's team three to one. I'd scored two goals and one assist. Coach was smiling ear to ear like a Cheshire cat, offering me a high five with a hollered "Fantastic, Sarah!"

I was, on the other hand, still in disbelief. What had I just done? I'd never played this good before, nor felt this surreal sense of power. *Was this a gem? Was this what a gem felt like?* My head filled with endless wonder as we trudged to the benches, elated but bushed; as soon as I seated myself on the bench Madison rushed toward me with a face of disbelief.

"Damn, girl! What's gotten into you?" Madison said between heavy breaths, gulping down water from her bottle.

"Did they give you drugs?" She asked in a hushed whisper after she pulled me to the side. "Like whatever drugs *they're* on."

I laughed. "No, it's nothing like that. And they don't do drugs, Madi."

"Sarah."

I turned to find Angela approach me with an approving look.

"Great play, girl, looking forward to your play in the match against Milford," she said, patting me on the back. "If anyone can beat Milford to pulp it's you. Kingsley's counting on you."

"Thanks," I said breathlessly, gulping my bottle of water.

Angela acclaimed me with a lopsided smile and walked off. Madison flashed me a look while we walked over to Coach for a post-match briefing. Angela was a typical sporty girl, something close to six feet tall with a sleeked back platinum ponytail, all about team spirit and heated pep talks. She'd been vice captain around the time Lillian was team captain. They'd gotten into a fight, quite an intense one. I had no idea what it was about, but I remember Lillian storming out of the locker room one day never to come back.

Speaking of which, I needed to find Lillian. The only remaining member of the squad that I didn't get to talk to was her. But the problem was that she couldn't be seen anywhere; truth is, the only time I'd seen her at school since she quit was the day I'd changed.

"I really don't think so, Sarah," I found a doubtful Calleigh saying a few days later in the living room of Vanna Daya. "I don't think your gem is being good at soccer…"

"You have no idea," I whispered. "I normally can't take on Angela and Nakato. And two other midfielders. This got to be a gem."

"Sarah, you know we have slight advantages that comes with our forms. You're a lion form Enricus, you're naturally stronger and faster. Chase and Andrew practice a lot, but *this* is a really big contributing factor," Calleigh explained.

"That and the fact that the quarterback's purple. Bright purple," Chase pitched in from the couch. "Chips, Sarah?"

"He has synesthesia," Calleigh muttered. "It's kind of a thing that runs in the family, I guess. Mom has it, he does, I don't. Come on, I'm the artist."

I looked at Chase, then back at Calleigh. "That's really cool."

"It is, but Calleigh hates it. She's just jealous," Chase said with a shrug.

"Of making it on the front page of the Lincoln Tribune with the title *Impenetrable Jacus-Russell Defense Line*? No thank you," Calleigh retorted. "But it should have been me. I could have found more uses for that talent than sacking the quarterback."

Chase rolled his eyes. "Calleigh, I deserve it. We both know I'm doing awesome stuff with it. And about the gem, I mean I did see you at the mini match. It was really impressive. We were all just kind of gawking at that." Chase said excitedly, shoving some chips into his mouth.

I excitedly seated myself on the couch beside him. "Do you think it's a gem?"

Chase shook his head. "If you play like that in the cup *you're* a gem, but no, I don't think so. Calleigh's right."

"How do you know?" I asked with a frown.

"Gems are a lot more powerful—distinguishable. And... I told you before, gems only work when you've changed. Unless you're mastered a very, very advanced art. And that's almost no one. It never happens to newly changed Enrici."

"Oh." I nodded absently. "Right."

"But your gem is obviously going to be incredible. You'll find out when you do the test. No rush," Chase comforted.

I pouted. "I seem to be the only one dying to know what my gem is."

"I uh," Chase began thoughtfully. "All of this happened to me when I was too young to even know anything, so I can't really help you there, but I did hear that it's a big thing for Original Enrici."

I nodded. "I don't know why, but I just can't stop thinking about it."

Chase pinched his chin, and squinted dramatically as if lost in thought. "Well... we could go somewhere deserted, I could show you my gem, and then maybe you could buy me ice cream like you said..."

I studied the boy's mischievous eyes. For a moment I wondered if he was flirting with me; it was only natural—I had not known him for long, and I had yet to learn that it was just the way he talked.

"Oh, right." I clapped myself in the forehead. "I do owe you that. But there's no way I'm doing that without Andrew."

"Aww, you figured out my plan," Chase pouted.

Calleigh frowned. "Why would you owe my brother ice cream? You sure it's not the other way round?"

"I sort of got him in trouble," I said sheepishly.

Calleigh narrowed her eyes.

"Come on, Sarah, you're getting me in trouble right now," Chase protested. "Look Calleigh, I swear I'm not the one who changed at school..."

"What?" Calleigh gasped. "Chasey, you can't—*oh my god*, I just can't stress *enough* the *importance* of *not* violating the Code and getting your whole entire life thrown down the gutter, you don't *ever* listen, *do you?*"

"I swear I didn't—" Chase said indignantly.

"It doesn't even matter at this point if it was you or Andrew, oh, god, you guys just—you guys are *un*salvageable. Do you hear me? *Unsalvageable.* Look. I'm not saving your butts if you two ever get yourselves in trouble with the Committee. I can't, I won't. Come on, Chase, you're in high school. You're old enough to know what you do and don't... really? On school grounds?" Calleigh went on.

"Calleigh, it was me," I said, apologetic. "I asked them if they could show me their gems..."

"I know," Calleigh whispered with a smile. "You asked me the same thing."

I looked back at her glinting eyes, confounded. "And you..."

"And I changed on school grounds, too." Calleigh declared proudly.

Chase threw his arms into the air. "Wait, what? And you're giving me hell for this?"

"I went to the basement," Calleigh strutted. "Where Sarah FT-ed. This isn't *remotely* the same thing as changing wherever you were, probably the football field or somewhere nearby, in *broad daylight*—come on. Just please, *please*, I ask you, just keep yourself alive. Both of you. All right? I need to have this conversation with Andrew. When's he dropping by?"

Chase sighed. "Never, if you're planning on telling him off."

I chuckled. This, it became clear, was no more of a serious matter than playful bickering. At that point I decided to let the siblings quarrel.

I rose quietly. I crept to the little door behind the waterwall. The door to the basement lay open, and I decided to take the invitation. I walked on down the flights of stairs like I'd done each time I had a class. Sophie, sometimes with an excited Calleigh trotting along, had been the one to lead me through this door, but for some reason I decided to test if I could open it. I studied the keypad, and found a small crystal hemisphere at the bottom of it.

"I am Code Name Seven," I declared without hesitation.

My heart leapt in excitement as a short hum sounded, followed by a movement in the copper door, opening a slit at my eye level. A golden light flickered, and I moved toward it—and as Sophie had done, stared into it with my eyes wide open. The light flickered green.

Yes, I thought, as I remembered what Sophie had done, and proceeded to change. It was swift; I was getting better and better. A quick twirl, no bumps into the wall, and I was on the ground in front of the metal door—morphed into a majestic lioness.

Another slit appeared in front of my eyes. I gazed into the light. It seemed brighter than the first one, except that it may have just been my lioness sight. I waited patiently as the light scanned my eyes. Nothing. I waited some more, and still nothing happened—I was just about to turn and leave when the light flickered yellow.

Restricted access.

I jumped. The voice had just come from somewhere inside my head, ubiquitously, like it had been with Calleigh's communication gem.

"What are you doing?" came a shrill cry. I turned, startled, to find Calleigh and Chase running down the stairs. I changed back in haste.

"I just," I began, abashed. "I wanted to take a look at the library."

To my relief, Calleigh's eyes twinkled. "Aww, you could have just told me!"

"Sorry," I apologize quickly. "I thought you guys were, uh... busy."

Calleigh came to stand in front of the door. "Nah, it wasn't even serious. I know Chasey's not gonna go around putting all of us in grave danger, right, Chasey?"

Chase groaned. Calleigh twirled deftly into an eagle, and the light scanned her eyes once more. Soon after, the door opened.

It wasn't the first time that my eyes landed on the aureate walls, baroque chandelier, marble pillars; but I was sure I'd gape each and every time. We marched through the arched doorway into the library, our footsteps echoing behind us. It looked like one of those places where worlds were dreamt, and classics were written; along with, possibly, a couple of letters between the pages, preserved for years for venturers of the future to find—professing undying love or deep concerns for humanity.

"When was this built?" I asked.

"Not as ancient as it seems," Calleigh replied. "It was originally built in 1905, the headquarters, and it actually didn't take that long to build it. But they expanded the hall in 1915 when the Lincoln headquarters hosted one of the biggest CE conventions. Ever since, they've been regularly remodeling the place. But the house, it was completely taken down and rebuilt about thirty years ago."

I ogled.

"So here you are," Calleigh presented. "This is the library. You can take any book you want, as long as you write your name in that"—Calleigh pointed to a roll of classic-looking parchment at the far corner—"roll. I know, right. Looks a bit old-fashioned for a library you need to do a gem-enhanced retina scan to come into. But if you think that those features were actually introduced a bit later when we built the Phonie along with several special archives, it makes a bit more sense. You know the Phonie hasn't been around for too long, if you think about that it's not too weird."

My thoughts had once again begun to drift from the contents of her talk. Absently I reached out at a mahogany bookshelf. The tip of my fingernails tapped the wood, and the sound echoed dryly through the breadth.

"I'll leave you two here, Chase needs to find a book, too," Calleigh said after a while.

Chase groaned. "It's not... *fine.*"

Calleigh smiled charmingly. "By Atkinson. *Rosmerta* Atkinson." With that, she turned around and trotted away.

Chase and I exchanged glances. "In case you're wondering, *that's* what it's like to have a sister," he said with a shrug. "Don't recommend it all that much."

I chuckled.

I scanned the area. There were a *lot* of books. Fiction. Nonfiction. Some novels about Enrici, apparently, some of which I believed I might have seen in regular bookstores. Nowhere in the titles was the word *Enricus;* instead, the books told of werewolves, witches and foxes in hats. I continued on, past a few tall shelves—ones that could only be reached standing on a little ladder that sat in the corner—and came across a dusty corner, home to much older books. I peered at the top shelf and saw volumes that could have belonged to another era; the books were hardback, with spines made from fine vellum, titles printed in gold leaf across the faded covers. I studied them in awe, wrapped in the thrill of holding history between my hands. The contents, however, did not amuse me much. Most were academic texts from long ago, written in voices too terse and pedantic to be of interest. I carried myself to a more brightly lit area, where the books looked more like the books I was used to seeing.

Chase had found his book and left not so long ago, but I continued my exploration. I wandered through the sections labeled Science and Technology, then to the Fundamentals of Enrici. Down the middle of that row, something caught my eyes:

The Complete Catalogue of Gems

I peered at the book in curiosity. My heart began to thump steadily as I reached for it. The book was thick and heavy, so much that I could not hold it in one hand. I tucked the book affectionately under my arms, scribbled my name on the parchment, and left. Chase saw me out, and Calleigh ran out to say goodbye, trotting down from her room upstairs with a blob of paint on her face.

Back home I sat in front of my desk, my physics homework spread in front of me. I slid the book out from beneath the exercise sheets, running my hand on the cover. Discreetly, as if opening a *Librorum Prohibitorum*, I opened it.

The prints were small and scholastic, delicately listing gems after gems. I flipped to the very beginning.

Introduction
Multidimensional Spectra of Direction, Modes, and Strength

Each and every gem is unique. Even within the same classification and name, there is a broad spectrum of what's called direction, mode and strength.

The direction differentiates the effect of the gem. For instance, a telekinesis gem would come in various directions, including ones that allowed the holder to move solid objects, and ones that are more effective on fluids such as water. An interesting variant of the telekinesis gem is also present, known more popularly by the name 'weather changer.'

The mode is how the gem operates. Being the very abstract powers they are, a certain physical path is required to exert its powers on the physical world. The modes allow the Enrici to do this. Common modes for gems that influence the object's psychology are eye contact and physical contact, although some gems with less restrictive modes work when the object is within line of sight, or within view.

The strength also differs with every gem and every individual, and is very fluid for each individual. It is subject to change depending on their stamina, and can be improved through practice.

I drew a sharp breath. I flipped the page to where lists began. The gems were classified into five classes, Kinetic, Physical, Psychological, Communication and Uncategorized. I grabbed a thick bunch of pages between my fingers and flipped to a page in Kinetic.

Climatokinetic Gem

The Climatokinetic Gem, also known as the 'storm', is a gem that exerts control over the kinetics of a large body of water and air, normally in a way that adheres with fluid dynamics.

The exact function is still being researched. Being among the hardest gems to master, an effective and significant control of the weather is very seldom witnessed. The nickname was first given to the gem after a renowned gem holder, a Florida man with a whale form in the early 1910s, stirred up a powerful storm that destroyed quite a portion of the west coast of Florida, the most notable account being of a giant pillar of water ascending into the sky.

I skimmed through the ongoing sections, through Flight, Heat, and Invisibility. I came to a stop at a familiar name.

Augmentation Gem

The Augmentation Gem, more familiarly known as the Fighter's Beacon, is a gem that enhances, augments or makes accessible the gems of other Enrici, usually within close proximity.

This was the gem Chase told me he'd show me.

Although it cannot do much on its own, the Beacon is one of the most powerful and influential gem of our kind. The powers of the Beacon are exerted in four directions: the first being enhancement of gems within the range. Within this direction there is yet an endless spectra of functions, based on which aspect of the target gem it enhances. The holder must familiarize with controlling the gem in such ways to master the art. Beaconing in the second direction changes the accessibility of the target gems. The Beacon can, in this case, enable holders of target gems to employ their gems in their human forms as well as their Enricus forms. Beaconing in the third direction enables other Enrici within proximity to access another Enricus' gem. This can be especially convenient with communication gems. The fourth direction is a very advanced and abstract art in itself, that *combines* gems to synthesize a new function. It could be very useful for...

The book went on for an entire chapter about the beacon. The beacon, to my astonishments, could do an endless list of things. Two beacons together could produce something close to a miracle. It was called *double-beaconing*, or Enhanced Gem Augmentation; with double-beaconing, the Navy had transported an entire ship full of hundreds of soldiers hundreds of miles. Usually, on severe impact or any such trauma Enrici were morphed back to their human forms—which was another thing I'd learned in the footnotes of the book. It was apparently a phenomenon scientists could not completely elaborate. But seldom, on abrupt impact, they could die in their alternate forms and never switch back. Some families preferred to have them changed back before they buried them, and in this case double-beaconing was needed to morph them back. The list went on about different gems that could be double-beaconed, and the things they could do.

The cackle of the car in the driveway shook me back into the human world. Remembering I had to defrost a chicken before Mom came home, I set off to the kitchen, thrusting the book under the bed along with a bunch of papers and notebooks.

A couple days later Sophie stopped me after my training to hand me a little silver slip. I took it in my hands, my heart beating hard.

"The date for your gem test," she said. "The paper's gem enhanced, designed to crumble to ashes within a couple days. You might want to avoid keeping it near anything highly flammable."

"Thanks." I managed to say.

I peered at the paper, and saw etched in the center a date.

MONDAY, SEPTEMBER 27TH

As I walked down the street in my neighborhood, the world became a castle of mist, the ground a thin pad of pearly clouds. I walked as if carried by the wind, lost in elated reverie—*a gem*! I mouthed the word once again, unable to explain why it gave me so much joy.

I looked down. I could feel the wind on my bare forearms, tickling my very veins with a soft early fall caress. I felt invisible power build within my body, sending a ripple of tingles to my fingertips. I could do things I believed to be impossible. I just needed to find out what.

What would it be? I tried to imagine, conjuring a list of gems in my head. Nonverbal communication. I remembered Calleigh's voice penetrating into my head. Interspecies communication. The communication gems came in manifolds, and one of them gifted you with the ability to talk to animals. Oh, to hear an ensemble of birdsongs and know what went on in their feathery little minds. Disorientation. There was a special kind of disorientation gem, I'd found, that disoriented the sense of direction. In a battle earlier in the civil war of our kind, it was used on an enemy fleet by one of the troops. Up was down, and down was up—direction disappeared, and hundreds of birds crashed into the walls of a tower. It was a horror, but the gem could be used for something else entirely. Perhaps design a stage. Perhaps take the spectators on a strange journey. Or perhaps my gem would be something more basic, like strength enhancer or speed enhancer, the latter what Lillian was said to have. It sounded basic, but it was a classic; I tried to imagine how it would feel to bend a bridge, to race in a blur across endless corn fields.

I closed my eyes. It's the middle of a busy street downtown, and I'm standing on four feet, a lioness in the heart of the city. I raise my head and let the wind find me, because I know I can catch it, let its currents take me in its glorious arms—and I jump. A tremendous roar, my hind legs kicking dust onto the crowd of gawking passersby, and I'm in the air. I take flight and speed builds. The wind tickles my face, blows my hair back like a stream of stardust. I soar past giggling leaves and shimmering treetops, and I stretch my paws to touch the soft leaves as they pass by. Dewdrops scatter and bounce on my skin like hundreds of crystal beads. I gasp in exhilaration, seeing every pattern, every fold of the leaves as they whizz past.

Or what if—

I'm now on the edge of land. I claw my feet into the sand, and feel the warmth seep in deep, seconds before the soft lips of the ocean lap at them, a pleasant coolness trickling in between my toes and claws. I don't know how to I do it, but I gently nudge at the air and the waters recede, rising in glamorous and terrifying walls to either side. The starfish hang in the blue background like stars, and a school of fish swim like the milky way. I've split the ocean.

Just then a rude thump against my body woke me from my reverie. I zoned back into the world in front of me to find a balding man walking briskly away, turning briefly to shoot me a scowl.

"Sorry," I apologized. "I mean excuse y—"

But the irritation did not last long; they melted away and disappeared as I thought of what I had down the road. The sky glinted blue, and the blaring orb cast a warm, mellow haze onto my face—and I was hopeful.

And the day finally came.

I'd been on the edge of my seat the whole day. When the bell rang I looked down to see my notebook filled with little doodles of gems. I bolted out the campus and to Vanna Daya.

I had to wait a while, as Sophie made some preparations. Sophie led me to a room down on the side of the hall, a meeting room for about twelve people. I seated myself on one of the chairs. On the walls were several paintings framed in deep walnut wood. I wondered if they were also Calleigh's. The style was quite different from what I'd seen up in the living room; these were more baroque. The somber background, the resplendent figures and sheer drama in their faces—it could have been Calleigh, but I doubted it; perhaps the artistry ran in the family. I peered curiously at one of the paintings. A young woman was standing in the middle under a surreal spotlight, her fair hands grasping a bow, her lips drawn back in aggression. It seemed I could hear the warcry.

Footsteps sounded outside, and my heart leaped. It was happening. I was about to find out what my gem was.

Soon Sophie walked into the room carrying a mahogany box with gold linings on the edges. A soft clump sounded as she put it on the table, and with a mixture of excitement and bewilderment I wondered what I'd find inside it. Sophie undid the latch with her frail hands, and with a heavy click the lid sprang open; revealing, buried in soft cushions of red velvet, two glass vials, each filled with clear liquid.

"This is the Lapillocognal Serum, or the Gem Reader Serum," Sophie explained, placing her index finger lightly on the crystal stopper.

Sophie continued. "It uses something called Entanglement to read your gem. The subject drinks the Serum in one vial, and in a few seconds the examiner will be able to read from the Serum in the other vial. It's linked to the examiner, which is me, and will show the result in a form that is most natural to me. In my case it's going to be colors that I link to each gem. Have you heard of synesthesia?"

"Yes, I've been told you and Chase are synesthetic," I replied.

"Yes. I associate colors to each gem and its function. As much as I would love to show you examples, the Serum is very expensive and difficult to make. So I'll try to illustrate as close as possible. In the case of a Kinetic Gem, it would turn blue. When a Physical Gem drinks it, it will turn a shade of green. Communication Gems would turn the Serum red, and Psychological Gems orange. Chase's gem, the Beacon, would turn the Serum a deep chestnut brown," Sophie explained.

"But aren't there many varieties of gems in each class? Can you tell exactly which one it is?" I asked.

"Yes. I will know what it does from reading the subtle shade," replied Sophie confidently. "Remember, the Serum is linked to the examiner. It was prepared in a very sophisticated way, in such a way that it gives me all the information I need to identify the gem. And it's very accurate. There has never been a single error in gem identification using this Serum."

It was curious—I wondered if I would ever understand these complex mechanisms, if there was a way to see this new world under as sensible an understanding as I did my old world. But what mattered now was not the *how*; it was the very question of what my power will be. I drew a deep, shaky breath. "Okay. I think I'm ready."

Sophie smiled warmly. "Great. Let's get to it."

Sophie picked up one of the vials, and gently pulled on the little sphere on top of the stopper. It fell away with a little jangle. She held the vial out in front of me, and carefully I took it from her hand. It was icy cold, with, so faint I thought I'd imagined it, a minty scent coming from it.

"Now I want you to identify yourself the way you do in the Phonogral," Sophie instructed.

I nodded. I grasped the vial tight, and looked into it. I knew what to say; there had, according to Calleigh, been an error in the system, because of which the Phonie could not recognize me by my name. I'd had to tell them the *code name* I had heard Sophie use, one that, come to think of it, I had heard whispered in the hallway the day I changed. It turned out that those were code names assigned by the Secrecy Committee; it a way to make it harder for humans to identify whom the message was concerning, should it by any chance be intercepted. With the invention of the Phonogral it was no longer necessary; but it remained as a sort of common practice. Calleigh was Buttercup, and many of the others did not even remember theirs.

I drew another deep breath. The bug was likely fixed by now, but I stuck to the old version anyway; for no reason in particular, I liked the ring of it.

"I am Code Name Seven," I declared.

Then something happened. The liquid turned from transparent to an icy blue, but it grew hot in my palms. I flinched. The heat was beginning to sear into my palm, but I held on—something told me this wasn't real heat I was feeling, that it wasn't physically damaging, and something else told me that if I dropped and broke the vial now, I would have to wait who knows how long to find out what my gem was.

The heat died down in a few seconds, and the jingles of the windchimes were audible again. The sound came from all directions, and along with it a cool breeze that tickled my face. I inhaled sharply in awe as the Serum then turned a pearly, swirling purple. The Serum in the second vial turned the same shade; then the jingles died down, and they turned clear once again, as if nothing had happened. I wondered if I'd imagined it all.

"Now it's ready," Sophie said.

Nervously I brought the vial to my lips.

It smelled sweet, with a tinge of something like grapes somewhere in the bottom note. I parted my lips and let the liquid enter. It was ice cold, unlike it had been to the touch. I emptied the vial and shuddered from the chill. A fruity note floated in the air.

"Very good," Sophie said. "How do you feel?"

The tips of my hands and feet began to tingle, and my head began to flush. A glacial sensation spread to my chest and enveloped my body. I shivered as I felt the frost crawl down my arms and legs, then into the depths of my stomach. A soft jingle began to sound again, but this time it was coming from inside me; I felt it grow until it was an ensemble, and soon a symphony. I closed my eyes, dazed.

"I'm... not sure," I whispered, trying to steady my breath.

"The effects of the Serum can be a bit strong. Just try to breathe deeply."

I did. The sensation seemed to calm a bit, and in a few minutes all I felt was a pleasant coolness throughout my body. I nodded at Sophie. "I feel better now."

"Now I want you to change," Sophie instructed.

I rose from the chair and walked over to the middle of the room. It was spacious; changing here would not be a problem.

"Good," Sophie said, turning to the second vial.

She frowned, squinting at the vial. Then she walked over to it, her shoes making click-clack sounds that echoed through the room. She picked up the vile and squinted at it some more.

"What... it can't be," she whispered to herself.

My heart pounded in bewilderment. My head went wild, and I wondered what it was that she was seeing—if my gem was, perhaps, something dangerous.

"Sarah, could you change back, and then change back again?" Sophie asked with a shaking voice.

I did as she said. But nothing changed—there was silence as Sophie glared at the clear liquid in the vial.

"Sarah, you can... change back," she said.

I did.

I walked over to the table, my hands cold with dread.

"What is it?" I whispered.

"You... don't have a gem."

I staggered, the breath knocked out of my chest. Sophie rushed forward to hold me up by my shoulders.

"Are you all right?" Sophie asked, concerned.

"Does this... does this happen?" I asked shakily. "Are you sure it's not a mistake?"

Sophie's face darkened. "It does, but very rarely. We're going to schedule a retest in the following week."

I found a scintilla of hope. "Do you think I'll have one by then?"

Sophie's face was still bleak. "In most cases it takes about a couple days to a week for your gem to form, a week and a half at the latest. In fact, in cases like this... I can't say it's likely."

My heart sank.

"But we'll see," Sophie added quickly. I could see from her face that she didn't believe I had hope.

As I got off the bus and walked down the street a couple blocks from home, the world seemed to haze out, leaving me alone with my thoughts. I gazed silently as the concrete blocks receded beneath my feet, one, two, one, and another, steadily and mockingly as if they knew.

Why? Why me?

Time flew by, and time flew by diligently. It didn't really seem to care that I was a living defect, so I too, tried my best not to. I paid attention in my classes, I studied, I wrote essays. And in my free time I read. I'd learned about the Enrici and how they built their society, on how they built their capital on the Highlands of Alpha Enrica. I'd learned that Miranda, the third ruler of the Kingdom, had brought her men on an expedition further north, and discovered an entrance that led to an opening on the star's surface. They'd built there a city, and at its heart a palace. It had since been the monarchs' residence before the republic.

It was another one of those days. I was walking home on Friday. I'd dropped off my books at school, since it was one of those rare days I didn't have much to study, and I'd done all my homework even before the due date. My backpack was light, and only a tin tumbler rattled inside with each step I took. My footsteps, however, were heavy. I headed up the porch, humming a tune in an attempt to lighten my mood; but out came a meager, cracking note which made me feel worse than I'd started out. With a sigh I threw open the door—and found, to my surprise, a pair of large leather shoes.

"...Dad?"

Footsteps sounded, and I found him strolling into the living room, already comfortable in a shirt and sweatpants.

"Hey, Sarahbell."

I grinned and threw myself into his arms. He laughed and set me down.

"Look who's taller," he said, peering at the top of my head.

"Dad, it's only been three weeks," I objected.

"I still say you're taller."

I chortled. "You always say that."

"Well, ever since I transferred to Detroit I don't get to see you often, every time I do it looks like you've grown a mile," Dad insisted.

I smiled. "How's work?" I asked.

"The usual," he replied. "You don't want to hear the details."

"I *do* want to hear the details," I objected. "Well, unless I'm not *allowed* to ask about it, you didn't tell me you worked in homicide for ten years."

"You were too young then, honey," Dad said with a sigh. "How's school?"

"Okay, I guess," I replied.

"Nothing fun going on? No dates? No cute boys?"

I wrinkled my nose. "I don't have time for that."

Dad laughed. "Why?"

I shrugged. "I'm busy doing physics. And... soccer."

And leading a human-lioness double life. And *discovering that I'm missing my substance.*

"You got to tell me about those," Dad said, pointing a finger into the air.

"Sure," I replied. "But I have some homework to do. We can talk about it at dinner."

"Sure. Your mom's working late tonight, I'm gonna be defrosting the lasagna. Thank goodness you mentioned it."

I headed to my room. Part of me was wishing I could talk about all this with my mom, and my dad, the two people I loved most in the world; gems, no gems, whatever haunted reason this nagged me each and every moment. But I couldn't. It was simple as that.

Instead I pulled a rugged paperback book from underneath the bed. It was my subconscious that chose this book; I'd found myself scribbling my name on the parchment and walking out of the library with the book in my hand. Although I'd regretted it instantly, I could not bring myself to put it back. I stared mindlessly at the cover of the book, wondering why it called out to me. Carefully I ran my hands through the title, which read:

On Gems.

I skimmed through the catalog. Some familiar names were visible, those I could recall from the book—but some I had never head before. I halted at a gem with a peculiar name.

The Diamond

The Diamond was discovered and classified in 1823 at the Marseille Convention, and is known to have belonged only to two individuals: Queen Enrica and Queen Serena, respectively the first and last monarchs of the Kingdom. The exact function of the gem is not very well known, due to the scarcity of data. In written language, the Diamond is conventionally capitalized regardless of its usage as the gem itself or the holder.

Interesting. I thought. *But how can you identify a gem without knowing much about what it does?*

The rest of the passage did not tell much, however, and I soon lost interest. I flipped through a few more pages, past the catalog and to a chapter titled '*history of gems.*' There I came across something that made my heart sink:

The Slag Hunt

The Slag Hunt is a practice that was widely popular during the medieval era. Gemless Enrici, called Slags at the time, were caught and tried, most of which ended in their death. They were accused of being frauds; some claimed they were witches, and others claimed they were aliens posing as Enrici. When a suspected Enricus was unable to perform an act to show their gems, they were brutally murdered, even publicly executed.

The following painting is a description of

I sighed and shoved the book into my backpack. I closed my eyes and leaned far back on my chair until it felt dizzy. *I shouldn't have done this*, I thought. It didn't make things any better to know what could have happened if I'd been born centuries ago.

Just then a knock sounded on the door. It was Dad.

"Done with homework?" he asked.

"Yeah, I was just reading," I replied.

"You looked a little upset," he said.

"Through the wall?"

"No, when you came home. And your mom's been telling me that. That I might want to talk to you," he replied.

I smiled wearily.

"Do you want to talk about it?" Dad asked carefully.

I pressed my lips together, considering. "Okay," I said finally.

We sat on the wooden picnic chairs in the backyard. Mom had gotten these from one of her patients. She'd said he beat depression, and something that helped him all the while was carpentry. It was a cozy little chair, and beautiful, too. It was simple, nothing much ornate about it, but somehow it was comforting.

"So what's bothering you?" Dad asked.

I sighed. "I feel like... I'm missing something."

"Missing something?" he repeated.

I nodded. "Like I don't have something I'm supposed to have. Like I don't have something I want."

His eyes glinted.

"Hold on. I'll bring some tea. I know exactly the one to make you feel better."

A while later he reappeared holding a teapot and two tiny teacups.

"What's that?" I asked.

"Evening primrose," Dad replied. "It calms the nerves."

I took the cup from his hands. It was a sunny yellow tea, steaming hot, with a couple yellow petals soaked in it. The scent was comforting. I sipped some, and the mellow flavor spread through my body, relieving the tension and warming my chest.

"How's the tea?" Dad asked.

"Good. Thanks, Dad," I replied.

He smiled. "So, about your problem."

"Sorry, I'm doing a bad job explaining it, I guess," I muttered.

"No, no. Sarah, honey, I think I understand exactly how you feel."

"Really? You're really talented. You're one of the best in your area."

Dad smiled.

"When I met your mother, Sarah," he began, "and learned more about her, the deeper things, more of the things she could do, I wished I could be more like her."

I looked up at him. He smiled warmly, crinkles appearing around his eyes. His eyes did look a lot like mine; the color, even. But those wrinkles—I don't think I recalled seeing those wrinkles.

"It made me feel weak, when I found out all the things she could do that I couldn't. I'd only gotten to know that world but it had been taken away from me. Stolen from me."

I felt a teardrop form and roll down my cheek. I rested my head on his shoulder.

"That's exactly what I feel," I murmured.

"Sarahbell, it's going to take some time for you to learn, but it's not the end of the world. The world is out there, there's everything you need to make something out of it."

Chapter 3
Pierced

It had been three weeks since the blackout.

My life had taken an abrupt turn, and yet another; but my daily routines remained unchanged. I took classes. I did homework. I could focus again. I didn't have to contemplate what little truth remained and what would tumble away. No longer did I feel like a mythical creature, and I daydreamed only a little. Things were going back to normal, except that every other afternoon, I was in the Phonogral, racing through endless savannas on all fours.

It was another Tuesday afternoon. The bell rang, and I strode to my locker with a pile of books and notebooks balanced on my arm. It was like any other day; limits of functions, more work and energy. I longed for the hours to be over. I couldn't wait to be home, have a snack, perhaps make myself a milkshake. Perhaps I could take a stroll, find a little secluded area in the neighborhood, where I could transform—I had never changed outside, felt the sun and breeze on my golden coat. I wondered how it would feel, whether it would feel any different than the basement or the Phonie plains.

Buried in this swarm of unimportant thoughts, I absently fumbled with my locker combination—anticipating the rest of the day to go as peacefully and ordinarily as it had so far. But this anticipation was shattered the next moment, when, with alarming force, something slammed right into me.

A loud bang sounded as my locker flew open, and I was thrown onto the floor. My ribs and shoulder throbbed with pain. I cursed as I sat up, looking at the mess of books and papers scattered all around. The culprit, I'd found, was Carlos Pierce. My eyes landed on the hem of the red jacket disappearing across the hall, a gush of wind sweeping behind. I froze in place.

I listened again, holding my breath. My heartbeat gradually accelerated as it got clear that I had not imagined the sound.

On any other day I would curse under my breath and forget it all in a matter of a minute or to, or perhaps wish to myself that he would trip over a twig and rocket down a sinkhole. But this time it was different. I halted in alarm, my head running wild; in the air, now so clear that I had no doubt, was a jingle of windchimes.

I thought back to the butterfly in the library, the golden beetle outside the courtyard, and finally to the moment when Carlos had picked up the leaflet and read it correctly. The pieces of the puzzle finally fit together, and I knew now with dawning certainty: he was about to change.

Without further thought, I tore off after him. The boy was fast on ice, and naturally he was fast on the ground as well. And to make matters worse, he was desperate. I raced down the stairs after the sprinting skater, flinging myself around the corners like a slingshot. I was no bad runner; I was Kingsley's best attacking midfielder. But I was no match for someone who was desperate; someone who, without knowing what was happening to him, knew where to go.

I spilled onto the parking lot after him, heaving past groups of staring kids. I stopped short to take a breath, spitting out fumes like a dragon breathing flames. Then feeling like a plaster board had just knocked into my head, I saw him get into his car. *Damn it*. I should have thought about this. I had to stare, barely catching my breath—as his red Subaru squealed off in haste.

I lived close to school, and didn't drive—in fact, I didn't even have a driver's license. He was going to get away and change in plain view of everyone. I was at a loss of hope; I'd done all I could, but it was over.

So I was about to turn away, when gruff and beautiful as always, Lillian walked across the parking lot toward her convertible. I had a sudden idea.

"Lillian, Lillian," I called. Lillian stopped and turned. "I need a ride."

"Where?" Lillian asked brusquely, chawing on a piece of gum as the convertible accelerated into a ferocious speed. The smell of menthol dissipated into the air as the background blurred away behind us.

"Um," I craned to look over the other cars in the passenger seat. Just then I spotted the red Subaru Impreza speed through the gaps in the traffic. "Just—follow that car."

"Who's that?"

I sighed. "Carlos Pierce," I replied.

"Pierce?" Lillian repeated, pulling on her sunglasses from her head. "You didn't seem the type to tail Pierce."

"What else do I do then, let him change in the middle of the road?"

Lillian snapped her head toward me. "Let him *what?*"

I sighed. "Lillian, he's going to change. He's about to FT."

Lillian didn't respond, but I heard the car roar as if in protest as she pressed down hard on the gas pedal.

"How did you know this?" She asked after a while.

I shrugged. "I ran into him in the hallway and... I heard him."

"Interesting," Lillian said simply.

We followed him out onto the road. The red Subaru raced like lightning, but Lillian, sitting back, chewing on a piece of gum, was closing in on him. She had the gas pedal pinned down under her foot; I watched in awe and terror as she shot nimbly through openings between the traffic. Carlos may have been desperate, but Lillian was skilled; and she was skilled enough to match that desperation. It went on until the light turned red—and we managed to halt, inches from a black Porsche.

"Oh, crap," I muttered.

"Didn't you just see me save like ten grand?"

I sighed. "We lost him."

Lillian did not reply. In my head I could picture an animal—who knows what, a buck, a bull, perhaps a giraffe—standing in the middle of the traffic, confused and dazed in front of passersby stopping to stare; some would perhaps run off in a frenzy, and horns would honk... Disaster was the only word that I could formulate. I groaned.

"I know where he's going," Lillian said, almost as if she'd heard my chain of thoughts. I turned to look at her.

"How?" I asked. "No, it doesn't matter. Where?"

"Halliday."

"The semiconductor company?"

"They have labs here in the fresh air. Their property is basically a large area with a lake and woods and stuff."

"We can go in there?"

"Long story, but yes we can. It's not just an ordinary semiconductor company."

"What—I'm confused. Forget the company—how would he know what's happening to him?"

Lillian shrugged. "Oh, he has no idea," she said simply. "But he knows what he wants. After all, he can read street signs."

I thought back to the day I first changed, and the strange desire that overtook me, the strange instinct that guided me to a place I'd never been. I did not object.

Carlos Pierce was one of the boys in my year, and surely not my favorite. I'd often see him parade the campus in his favorite red varsity jacket, sipping—of course—his favorite mushy green drink; and the little cloud of fluttering little giggles would envelop him like a kaleidoscope of butterflies, and freshly each time I would wish I were somewhere else.

He was one of the Puffins. He would almost always be playing forward, the way I almost always played attacking midfielder. He was known for his aggressive playstyle—he would dive for an opportunity that wasn't there, with no reflection whatsoever on their consequences. Most of the times it wasn't fruitful, but by what I thought was sheer luck, sometimes he would end up scoring—and girls would go crazy. It seemed the boy was well liked by a lot of people, be it his teammates or a certain little crowd of girls; they would bombard him with snowballs and paper airplanes like they straight up hated him, which was, I was convinced, some new, yucky way of fangirling over someone.

I could not possibly think of a reason for this, well, *fangirling*. I didn't have much time to actively follow school sporting events, but I'd watched a couple of his games. He was ridiculous. He was a good skater and he was fast, but that wasn't what sports games were about; he was by no means a good *player*.

But then again, it might not have been related to skill at all. I'd often heard kids say that he was good looking; once I had been shoving some textbooks into my locker when the usual group of girls walked by whispering: 'Oh my god, did you see him with his hair pushed back? He looks like a page ripped out of a Chanel magazine.' I'd rolled my eyes in contempt, despite the fact that I'd never even seen a Chanel magazine my entire life. He wasn't *bad* looking, if something like that even existed. He looked, well, like himself; ruffled chocolate brown hair, faint crooked smile always on his lips, nose dabbed with light freckles—and a snooty look always in his eyes.

And it by no means helped that I despised the rest of the hockey squad for similar reasons. They were practically a bunch of apes set loose on this ground of learning. They would sometimes be seen hollering something between insult and worship at each other from separate ends of the hall; and sometimes nonsensically showing off their agilities or whatnot twirling and tossing books over peoples' heads. Other times they'd be seen basically entangled with their girlfriends, with whom they seldom lasted over a month. Carlos had been, surprisingly, with his girlfriend for a couple months' time—probably because she was practically a copy of him, her head full of feathers and frappé. I'd had biology with her the year before, and if I had a dime for every time she would giggle obnoxiously in a presentation, I would have saved up enough for college. The lot of them seemed to think school was for the drama—*seriously, that one time Carlos burst into the classroom proudly announcing he'd skipped chemistry, I swear. What made him think he's not going to need chemistry later in his li—*

A jolt of acceleration shot me back into reality. I groped the seat to find something to hold, horrified, as I watched the light just turn green.

"Lillian!" I hissed.

"I have good reflexes," she said dismissively.

"No, you—" I was about to object, but something silenced me. I decided, instead, to ask:

"You know the directions?"

"I've been there a lot. When I get stressed, I hunt."

Leaving an unwanted image in my head, of Lillian ripping an elk's throat, she accelerated even more.

A moment later I was walking through the woods alone. Lillian had motioned for me to go ahead while she picked up her phone.

The forest was thickly packed and concerningly vast. I stopped in my tracks, out of ideas and hope as to how I should track down this monster, when an obvious thought hit me—At times like this, I didn't need ideas and hope; I needed senses.

Immediately I changed. I was enveloped in a tingle of new senses, and for a brief moment I wondered if I would ever grow used to it.

I tuned my ears to my surroundings. I could hear like I never have done; especially in a forest full of rich sounds that nature voiced. Every bat of wings in the distance, every draft of wind rustling against leaves in the treetops, was naked to my ears. And overhanging the harmony was the sound of wind chimes, growing more and more violent each second. I sniffed the air. Among a plethora of odors my nose caught a human scent, different from the one I'd left before I changed—and much farther away. I followed its trail immediately.

And soon, about five minutes into the walk, his scent became stronger— and it changed. I knew instantly that *he* had changed.

My first thought was to run after him, to the opening in the trees where I knew he would be. My second thought, strangely enough, was to change back.

And I did. I could not exactly say why, perhaps I'd thought back to the moment in the basement that I tackled Lillian like an angry wildcat, or perhaps I just wanted to be able to speak to him, use words I could not in my feline form. Either way I knew it wasn't a good idea to fight the beast; I'd picked up from his scent exactly what he was.

The woods were strangely silent, as though the animals had picked up news of the newest intruder. Carefully I stepped into the opening; there he was. The sunlight spilled onto the grassy meadow, and in front of me stood a majestic animal like none other I'd seen.

Quite unlike his human self, the creature was a splendor. He was a dark brown panther, his sleek coat the color of his hair; his eyes were a daunting emerald, intense and eccentric. The panther was humongous—never had I seen a panther this big, be it in the zoo or on a screen. A part of me tensed. It was only natural, the most instinctive of fears; but a part of me, albeit small, knew he was no normal panther, and that I had to go and help him. I breathed, gathered my resolve, and approached the animal.

The panther waited, still as an intricately carved sculpture. The wind brushed my face, carrying with it a soft trace of the boy's scent, both of his human form and of his feline form. The mix was foreign, no longer human nor animal—something in between, something of both, and something that was neither. The two scents contrasted one another and yet shared a little base note, a pivot point; an undertone that gave away that the panther and human were one.

The animal tensed as I neared him. It seemed the world had fallen silent. I thought back to the moment I'd changed in the basement—there was sudden silence, a sudden stillness as if a draft of wind had blown and died, a tense serenity as if I'd traveled into the eye of a storm; and with my lion eyes I could see the flakes of glistening dust in the air flutter and settle into the murky background. I tried to imagine what the world would look like to those emerald eyes, how the stillness would feel on his skin, if he could catch a hint of my feline scent through smell of my hair. I took another step forward. It might have been my wandering thoughts, or the fact that I got close enough to see him properly—but I was, all of a sudden, no longer afraid. The eyes I met were human, and from up close I could see that his hair, around his neck and on his head, bore a ruffled texture much like his human hair.

So instead I found myself letting out a little chuckle as I got down to my knees, leveling my eyes with the panther's.

"Makes sense now," I said, "How you could read the leaflet when your girlfriend couldn't. Can't believe it took me this long to figure you were going to change."

The animal looked back at me tensely, as if trying to figure out what was happening. The sun glared into my eyes but I refused to blink—I had read somewhere that cats needed to see your eyes to know you meant no harm.

"Carlos, I know it's you. I'm not here to hurt you. I'm here to help you change back."

The panther's whiskers twitched, and he seemed to relax a little.

"You're going to have to be imaginative," I said. "You're going to have to feel something that isn't there. Well, it *is* there, but it's not tangible like everyday objects—"

I stopped. I was fumbling, and it seemed he was getting more and more confused. I decided to stick to more straightforward means. I stuck out my hand right next to his face.

"Can you feel my hand with your whiskers?"

The panther twitched his whiskers and ran them over my palm. The panther gave me a long look before he nodded.

"Feel my hand again," I directed. "One more time. You're going to have to remember this feeling."

The panther's whiskers grazed my palm, and I stifled a laugh as it tickled. The panther felt around on my hand a couple more times before he looked at me with quizzical eyes. I pulled my hand away.

"Now, Carlos, you're going to have to try and feel that wall. It's there, right where my hand was. Feel it."

The panther did as I said. His whiskers twitched as though trying to find something in the air—but his expression was filled with blank confusion. He shook his head.

"It's not going to be easy," I said with a sigh. *Especially for you*, I thought, *since you aren't the most imaginative type.*

Carlos tried again, all the while staring at me with a muddled face.

"You know, it helps if you close your eyes."

He did. He may be gigantic, but he was just a cat. When his eyes became little slits, the panther looked a lot like a purring cat.

"Do you feel it?"

The panther twitched his whiskers, his brows and nose wrinkling softly in concentration. In a while the cat nodded.

"Good. Now listen carefully. What you're going to have to do now is jump through that wall. It's not going to hurt. It's going to feel kind of like breaking through the surface of the water. And you're going to change back. Can you do that?"

The panther nodded.

"Good," I said as I rose, backing away from the animal. "You're going to need a little space."

The panther nodded. He seemed to brace himself, his eyes turning to slits again—then with one swift motion he sprang into the air; only to fall onto the grass in a heap of fur.

The panther groaned.

"It's not going to be easy," I said. "I didn't get it the first time either. Be patient."

The panther nodded, braced himself again, and jumped.

No good. I sighed. *We're going to be stuck here a while*, I thought.

And we were. I had lost count in the early twenties—and that seemed a while ago. I'd almost given up hope when the panther spun into a hazy halo of gold, emerging, on the ground and panting, as a six-foot human.

The boy looked around, letting out a little, befuddled laugh—eyeing the world as though he were seeing it for the first time. He raked back his ruffled hair, shook his head in disbelief, then turned to face me, his eyes full of wonder.

"Did I just turn into a panther, Sarah?"

"Well, yes," I replied.

Carlos looked back at me with a muddled smile. He extended a hand, an incredulous frown in his brows.

"Give me a hand up?"

I took his hand and pulled him up. He had a steel grip, which loosened when I winced. From up close I could see that he was taller than I'd thought, probably by an inch or two. His eyes had a smile in it—his nose was softly freckled, and they wrinkled lightly as he smiled; a smile that had something of a refreshing quality to it. And yet—in less than a second, the spell was broken; he was the usual Carlos I knew—the cheesy, stuck-up sideways smile, his hand stuck obnoxiously in the pocket of his favorite red varsity jacket. He no longer felt familiar, reachable, or understandable; once again he belonged in a different world, one that I snubbed. Suddenly I was hit by a wave of fatigue, and my head began to swim just like it had done when I first turned.

"*What the hell,*" Carlos let out an exhilarated breath. "What *was* that?"

"Long story," I replied. "If you want the short version, you're an Enricus, you can change into animals, in your case a panther."

Carlos looked at me like he'd been hit on the head by a sizeable trash can.

"Well..." He seemed unable to decide what to say. "Well, you're a lion, aren't you?" he asked. It seemed he was surprised by what he'd just said, as though the thought had never really formulated into words inside his head until the moment he voiced it.

"Well yeah," I replied. "You... noticed."

"I could smell you coming."

So, he was level-headed, I thought to myself. *Impressive.* I was prepared to fight, like Lillian had had to with me.

"Of course you did. I changed right up close. I thought you might attack me if I went as a lion."

"I..." Carlos began, ruffling his hair in disbelief. "Wow. This is incredible."

"Should be," I said simply.

"This is the most, you know, *realistic* dream I've ever had," Carlos marveled. "So I just turned into a *panther*. And you're a *lion*. Can you turn? Right now? We can, I don't know, *fight*, or something. I've always wanted to try..."

That explained the level-headedness. I laughed. "You think you're dreaming?"

"Obviously."

Maybe it was because this was something I wanted to do every time I saw him, or because I was sick of saying long and abstract things after the last hour's struggle. For whatever reason, I flicked him hard on the head with my fingers. Carlos, obviously taken off guard, stood with his mouth stuck open.

"You're not dreaming," I said softly.

Carlos stood frozen, processing the situation, his eyes darting between my hand and his own hands and feet. I watched gleefully as realization dawned on him.

"Well," I said after a while, a contented smile on my face as the Carlos' contorted in bewilderment. "Lillian should be here by now."

"Lillian's here," said a voice from behind. Lillian was leaning casually against a tree trunk, sipping—what was that, a can of Red Bull?

"What the—how long have you been here?"

"A while. It was interesting to watch."

Carlos eyed Lillian with a curious stare.

"*Lillian Shaffer*. One of us."

"One of *you*?" Lillian repeated, looking disgusted. "Whatever that means, I don't exactly want to be one, Pierce."

Carlos shrugged. "Well, if you change your mind, you're welcome to sit with us. Especially now that I know you've got superpowers."

Lillian scoffed. "Cute stuff to hear from a day-old baby, but no thanks, bugger. I might be inclined to break Matthew Brand's ribs again," Lillian replied smoothly.

I frowned. I faintly recalled a story I might have heard at lunch sometime, of Matthew hitting on Lillian and her kicking him in the ribs.

"If you say so," Carlos responded with a shrug. "Matthew's gonna be sad."

Lillian rolled her eyes. "You mean he should be *glad*. He just got his ass saved."

"Guys," I called. Much as I loved to see Lillian knock Carlos out like that, this had to end. My head was beginning to swim in fatigue, and all I wanted was to be at home, in my own bed, basking in solitude. "He just had his FT, Lillian. You got to take her to Vanna Daya."

Lillian shrugged. "Well, she's right. Let's get you going, Pierce."

"Get me going where?" Carlos asked, puzzled.

"The Headquarters," Lillian replied with a sigh.

Soon after dropping me off at the school gates, Lillian's convertible drove off with an excited Carlos behind the dash. I was embraced by the sight of the welcoming backdrop; the clear blue September sky, blocks of brick houses bathed in golden sunlight, and flittering bugs in the downy wind.

I hadn't noticed how good the weather was. Kingsley High was an awkward twenty minutes' walk from home. I headed down the street, thinking it had been a long day, and that I needed a moment in peace. *It's strange, though,* I thought to myself as I passed Ms. Picker's front yard with a swift greeting. *How did we know where to go when the change was imminent? No one had told us. We were Original Enrici. We were alone. Was it written, somehow, in our genes, which had only been changed moments before the transformation?*

I rummaged my mind for memories of my biology classes, where we learned about Charles Darwin and Gregor Mendel, and looking at plants planted in little plastic pots, we drew family trees of peas with all these different traits. It made sense for Inherited Enrici to have evolved to prefer solitude when changing; although I wasn't sure if it was long enough in the eyes of nature, humans and Enrici had been in conflict for a quite a long while. It would have surely benefited them to seek to change where they could not be seen.

But Original Enrici? Why did they also share the same instinct? My mind wandered off to the various possibilities. Did the source of power that brought us to transform—namely the star—have a way of saving and documenting the evolution of the species?

The train of thoughts, however, was not fruitful. I found I had wandered to the same spot I'd been weeks ago, the little shortcut through the park where I'd seen butterfly Sophie. I tried to picture the majestic creature in the air again, fluttering past blossoms as though it could sprinkle its colors into a trail behind it. My mind wandered off the dead end of science, and to simpler matters—then I found myself thinking of Carlos. Carlos Pierce, of all people, an Enricus?

My thoughts flashed back to the image of the panther, his human eyes, the puzzled expression and ruffled coat. There was an odd, unexplainable comfort in seeing Carlos in that form. I wondered why—perhaps we showed most humanity when we were animals, and perhaps to a girl nearing adulthood, human connection was more intimidating than a gigantic predatory cat.

I walked on, thinking about Enricus social life. How interconnected was this society, and how much did that society mean to the Enrici? It seemed Lillian didn't care for anyone's company, be it Calleigh, myself or the boys. Calleigh seemed to *love* people, on the other hand—I could already picture her trotting excited toward me like a little puppy. But I couldn't quite see her with anyone else in the squad. She was more like a spring breeze, a draft of wind picking up subtle scent of lilac; she shone in your view a short while—correction, a *long* while, all the while talking a *lot*—before she scampered away and disappeared into the flowerbeds. Chase and Andrew were different. They'd greet you with the most wholesome hugs, but then merge you into the backdrop as they quarreled, wrestled, joked and laughed. Although I knew they were always trying to make me feel welcome, I couldn't help but feel like a third wheel around them, sitting wedged somewhere between the bond of friendship—*bestfriendhood*—that had been there since the beginning of time.

Then there was Carlos. I simply could not imagine myself in any social gathering that Carlos was in, neither did I want to be. It seemed he was everything I wasn't, and I was everything he wasn't. I thought of his large figure cantering across the hallway with his friends, greeting each other with crooked smiles and aggressive bumps. I thought of the flock of girls he'd joke around with. I thought of his smile, blithe, somehow looking like he was mocking you. *No*, I thought. By no means did we belong anywhere near each other. And yet, now, we shared a secret. He was a panther and I was a lion. I remembered the time I'd dropped the gem flyer at school, and the confusion in Carlos' eyes as he read the contents aloud. It felt strange—I was connected by an unknown force of nature with people so much different from myself. *So incredibly different*, I thought with a foreign sense of novelty, *like Carlos and I. Would we ever cross paths again?*

I stumbled, almost toppling over a stone step. I realized I'd stepped into my front yard lost in my train of thoughts; suddenly reminded of how much I wanted to fix myself a cup of tea and take a long nap on my bed, I walked inside.

I'd hastily washed, run into my room, changed into my pajamas, and come back downstairs when I found a small plate of watercress sandwiches with a note from Mom.

Sarahbell,

I'm going to be a little late tonight. There's chili in the pot.

Love, Mom

My mom was a psychiatrist, and she'd come home a bit later than I did, sometimes a lot later. She'd often leave snacks or sandwiches on the dining table with little notes in her perfect handwriting.

I smiled, poured myself a glass of milk, took the note and plate up to my room, and plunged down on my bed happily and lazily nibbling the sandwiches. My fingers absently played with the edges of the note from Mom, when an uneasy thought popped into my mind.

Will I ever be able to tell her what I am?

I let out a long sigh. It seemed a lot of secrets came with this life, and the weight of it would be mine to bear. What would it mean to tell someone what I was? What would it mean for them? Would it put them in danger? Somehow my thoughts flashed back to the cloaked figures I'd seen on the day I first changed, those Calleigh called the *Secrecy Committee*. But then, I asked myself, what did it mean to hide this from someone? How would it feel keeping such a fundamental secret from people you loved?

My head pulsed. *I swear this is giving me a migraine*, I muttered to myself. Today had been an awfully long day. I could think about this later. I finished my sandwich, pushed the plate away onto the bedside table, and sank down onto the bed.

It would otherwise have been an incredibly sweet moment, where I'm wrapped in blankets and three plush pillows, rubbing my legs against the cool the bedsheets. I'd drift softly to sleep as the blue of the sky gleamed brilliantly outside; I'd forget about math homework, think sweetly to myself that I'd do it the next morning. I would probably trade in a fulfilling breakfast of boiled vegetables, scrambled eggs and bacon for an hour of busy scribbling, but on some days it would be worth it. The breeze would brush my neck, birds would chirp in the distance, and, in the clarity of daylight, I'd be able to observe as sleep came to me, feel my mind and body sink sweetly into bliss.

But I was, unfortunately, buried under a mound of feelings, if not thoughts. My head throbbed at every pulse, and every so often I had to remind myself to breathe. I stared at the ceiling, trying to shake off all the questions. It seemed I'd have a hard time sleeping, day or night.

Calleigh was—as usual—overly excited about what happened the day before. She chanted on and on and on about how she had gotten a message from the CE that Carlos was going to change.

"See, they found out only hours before he FT-ed. Can you believe it? *Hours!* When Andrew turned, I think it was when I was thirteen, my dad got informed three days in advance, and when you did, we got the message the day before. And for Carlos it was like three hours or something! Obviously they thought they'd let us know right away, but something must have gotten in the way, because the message was sent with a Phonie *three hours ago.* Sarah, if it weren't for you, seriously—we'd all have been in great trouble. Carlos would've been, for sure, I know it's not his fault, but there are policies, we can't risk having everyone see him... I can't even imagine what would have happened! Sarah, you really deserve an award."

I pretended to listen, getting carried away in the middle and ending up with an unbidden image of the hooded figures in Carlos' doorway. I shook the thought off.

"By the way, did I ever tell you about this new project? I'm working on a series of paintings of animal silhouettes. This is going to be awesome—I'm going to fill the silhouette with abstract shapes that sort of symbolizes their *character,* you know, the *human* character. So with the shape of the animal and the symbols and all it kind of resembles an Enricus, and I'm going to feature eight Enrici in history in a sequence that has to do with how they influenced one another... you *have* to see this one finished. It's going to be great. Oh, there goes Carlos."

I looked, and found Carlos walking down the hall, his obviously empty backpack slung casually over one of his shoulders. He caught my eyes and began to walk over.

This was my chance. Talking to Carlos wasn't the best thing in the world, but at least with him I had a better chance of having a finite conversation.

"Actually I have something to check with him," I said quickly. "I'll catch you later, Calleigh,"

I raced over to Carlos, unable to shake off the feeling that Calleigh was watching me with a weird smile.

"Hey," I greeted.

"Hey," Carlos greeted back. He looked somewhat different from the day before. There seemed to be a bit more color in his face than the bony pallor of the other day—he probably got a full night's sleep. Great for him.

"You all right?" I asked.

Carlos smiled. "Yeah, perfect."

"Impressive," I commented. "How's this not keeping you awake at night?"

"Was too tired, I guess," he replied. "I went home and then it was morning."

I chuckled. A part of me envied him for how peaceful his life seemed—no swarm of thoughts to torment you, just a still little silence in his head. I wished I could do that at times; simply turn off my thoughts until morning came.

Carlos snapped me out, however, from such thoughts. "So... Sarah, are you free tonight?"

"Not tonight, I have a quiz next Monday," I replied. "But maybe next week. Why?"

"I wanted to buy you dinner or something. You kind of saved my life yesterday," Carlos said. "I might have gotten shot by the wildlife sheriff people if it weren't for you."

For a second I contemplated whether he was worth my evening. I studied his face. It was full of life and colors. He seemed quite unlike myself when I'd first transformed—*no question marks floating around his head*, I thought, *only a puddle of exclamation marks. That energy might be just the thing I need.* And food, food was definitely worth my evening.

"Sure," I said. "Is Thursday okay?"

"Yeah, sure," he replied. "Practice ends at six, when's yours end?"

"Five thirty," I answered. "I'll be near the gate. Come meet me there."

"Gotcha." Carlos said before jogging off.

At ten past six the next Thursday, a damp Carlos led me through the parking lot, his backpack flung carelessly over his shoulder. He smelled like grocery store shampoo.

"What do you want to eat?" Carlos as we walked toward his car.

"Well, I wanted to try this pizza place..."

I told him about this new pizzeria Calleigh had mentioned. They apparently had some of the most controversial pizza ever to be made. I didn't mind—I wasn't the most canonical pizza eater, and I loved experimenting.

"You're going to have to give me the directions," Carlos said as I hopped into his Subaru.

"I'm terrible at navigating, but I'll try my best," I assured.

Carlos chuckled. He turned the key and the engine whirred to life. I couldn't help but notice his right hand, set comfortably on the stick.

"I didn't know you drove manual transmission," I commented.

"Old school, but I like it. I think it's cool," Carlos replied.

"Isn't it hard?"

"Not really," Carlos replied, contemplating. "You wanna try?"

"Right now?" I asked, astounded.

Carlos shrugged. "Why not? Everybody else has left, you can't hit anything if you want to," Carlos said coolly.

"Okay," I said dumbly. "I did grow up watching my mom do it."

We switched seats. I nervously adjusted the seats—Carlos seemed to have legs twice as long as mine, and the seat was pushed way back—and buckled up.

"You just have to press down on the clutch, put the stick into first gear, and slowly let go of the clutch," Carlos explained calmly.

"I did take the permit test," I said indignantly as I did as he said. The engine skipped and purred before falling silent.

Carlos chuckled. "You have to let go *slowly*."

I started the engine again. The engine purred back to life. I did as he said—I let go ever so slowly, sliding the gear into first, and the car rolled a palm's width forward before the engine died again.

"Are you sure we can get dinner tonight?" Carlos teased.

"I got this!" I retorted.

"It helps if you start pressing on the gas pedal, and kind of switch from the clutch to the gas pedal," Carlos explained. The situation felt strangely familiar; only then I was teaching a panther to change back.

On the third try—at long last—I managed to get the car rolling. We slid out of the parking lot and rolled toward the gate.

"Now shift into second," Carlos instructed. "And... third."

It turned out to be fun. It was about thirty minutes' ride from school, only it would have been ten if anyone else but me was behind the wheel. With *'No, no, Sarah, you're literally scratching the sidewalk,' 'Try not to climb onto the gr-rrass pitch, I said try not—'* and *'Don't you think we're going a bit too far to the left?,'* some *'Sarah, we have to go in* now *or we're staying here forever.'* and many a *'Slowly. No, it's fine, don't panic. Just...* slowly.' I managed to pull into the parking lane. When I got out my legs were shaky, and my stomach was growling in angry hunger.

"How do you do this? My legs are going to be sore tomorrow," I complained. "And I'm hungry."

Carlos laughed. "You did pretty good for a first timer. You have potential."

"Hope so, I killed the engine eleven times today. Can't afford to do *that* again," I breathed. "Let's go inside, I'm starving."

The restaurant was a pretty hut-like diner. It was, in fact, what I'd always imagined a holiday hut somewhere off in the Italian end of the Mont Blanc would look like. Carlos and I sat on the modest terrace, beyond which a warm skyline of the park was visible. I had to admit, Calleigh knew great spots. She had been talking nonstop about this restaurant for about a week now, and I had begun to fantasize about it. My fantasies came true when the waiter brought out a giant disk of pure artistry; I stared for a long while, my eyes twinkling, at the sight in front of me. Carlos chuckled.

"I wanted to thank you, Sarah. I really don't know what would have happened if you didn't follow me," said Carlos, placing a slice of gorgonzola steak pizza on my plate. I stared, half-listening, at the majestic sight in front of me.

"I did what I had to," I said simply, taking a pickle from the dish. "How was Vanna Daya?"

"It was hot, I liked the house. And the tutorial video thing was cool," Carlos replied.

"Did you get to see what your gem is?" I asked. It had been only a week, and for me it had taken much longer. But perhaps he'd had it sooner—his FT happened within hours after all. My chest throbbed a little.

"Yeah, that part was hot too. Mine is called the Memory Gem. I can mess with peoples' memories..."

I raised an eyebrow. "You're not really going to, are you?"

"Are they going to shoot me if I do?" Carlos asked, his eyes childish and curious as if he had nothing but fluff behind them.

"No, I heard the Enricus Violation Investigation removes your gem permanently, but all the while you shouldn't go around *messing* with people," I said sternly.

Carlos laughed awkwardly. "I'm not really that serious."

I flushed, a bit embarrassed. "Good."

For a while we sat slicing pizza in silence. The waitress came by to ask if there was anything we needed; I asked for another glass of water.

"So um, when was it for you?" Carlos asked after a long silence.

"My FT?" I asked, picking up another slice of pizza. The sirloin slices glinted tantalizingly, bathed in barbecue sauce. "I had it only a month ago," I replied.

Carlos looked amazed. *"A month?"*

I nodded. "Remember the blackout?"

Carlos' mouth dropped open. "That was you?"

"Lillian. She helped me change back."

Carlos took another slice of pizza onto his plate. "So does the Cabinet keep tabs on humans too? And find out when they're going to change?"

"I heard they, like, detect pre-FT signs. Lillian's been on my tail for a whole day."

"And you too?"

"Me what?"

Carlos popped a sirloin slice into his mouth. "So... they sent you to be my angel."

I choked on my pizza.

"I don't get sent to be peoples' angels," I replied. "I heard you."

"You mean those jingle jingle sounds?" Carlos asked, amused.

"Yeah," I replied.

"Cool. So I wasn't the only one who heard it," Carlos said with an amazed grin.

"You and I were the only ones," I explained. "None of the other Enrici heard it."

"What about the others? Like... everyone else. The normal... guys."

"They can't hear it. Not unless they're about to FT. At least, that's what I heard."

"This shit is awesome. It's like a secret society or something," Carlos whispered before he placed the last slice of pizza on my plate. "Here."

"Thanks."

There was a short silence as we ate.

"Oh, yeah, right. There's something I wanted to know," Carlos said suddenly.

I looked up from my plate. "Mm-hmm?"

"What is your gem?"

Lying carefree on top of my blankets, staring blankly up at the ceiling, I replayed that stupid question in my head. Over and over.

Gems. What about it was so enticing, beckoning and fundamental, that I was so empty and lost without it?

Back in the medieval times in the old world of Europe, an Enricus without a gem was considered a fraud, a fake—not a complete, whole being as they were. Many of them were tracked down and captured, and met sickening fates. They were tortured until they cried out that they were imposters, that they were insidious shapeshifters in the guise of an Enricus. Then they were killed by predator Enrici, and sometimes burned on stakes, as crowds of Enrici called out names—*slags, witches*—with eyes burning with hatred, with mouths curled in the somber sweetness of what they called justice. 'It is only right that they are torn down,' was what they said, and what was recorded. The practice soon ended, and was banned by law; but mildly it continued, a history of hatred, a history of crowds, a history of what they used to call virtue.

This, however, was not at all the reason for the hollow in my chest. It was there since way back, way before I'd read anything about the slag hunts of the Middle Ages.

I rolled onto my stomach and buried my face in the pillow, only to get a light whiff of the stench and think perhaps I'd better wash it. I threw the pillow into the laundry basket in the corner, only to see it bounce off the rim and fall onto the floor. I sighed, feeling somewhat sorry for the lump of cotton sitting skimpily in the corner.

It wasn't about history, nor was it about anyone else. I knew somehow that without the gem I was never complete—for some unexplainable reason I was locked away from my own essence, always missing something but never finding it. They were right. I was a slag. I was incomplete.

When I get stressed, I hunt.

In my mind I heard Lillian's voice again, uttering these words mindlessly as we spilled onto the road, the gas pedal pinned under her foot, her hands effortlessly turning the wheel and sending the both of us jolting to the side. A light seemed to flicker on in my head as I considered it—maybe I could try it. I could go hunting.

Chapter 4
The Starstruck Hunter

I did not stop to think. I slipped into the first sweatpants and shirt I laid my hands on and I crept out of the house.

The neighborhood looked strangely unfamiliar, the silhouette of houses black against the murky sky, like ridges on the back of a slumbering dragon. Soft shadows fell like a duvet, lulling the homes and silent streets to reverie. I rubbed my fingers together as if I could, in some way, grasp the thin fabric of the night—the cool air found home in my chest, and the soft glow of streetlamps played a game of tag with my shadows as my footsteps found its way through the streets.

The park behind the semiconductor company was closed, but I knew a way in. I ventured to the spot Lillian had parked the other day. To the side there was a steep hill leading to the woods, where the electric fence outlined the area. It was put there 'to keep the wild animals in', according to Halliday policies, but no, I knew very well that it was in fact there to keep the humans out. I remembered Calleigh going on about it forever, that this fence was gem powered, and it only worked on ordinary humans, and would not sting even a bit when an Enricus touched it. I crept toward the fence, checking left and right. Not a single figure was visible. I squeezed through the gap and into the park.

I pulled through a thin lining of trees, barely thick enough to keep the park hidden from passersby. I raced uphill, for something like a minute or two until the rugged canopy thinned at last; I rose from the bushes and pressed my back against the wayward vines, looking silent and daunted at the sight before me.

I had never seen this place at night. A plain the size of a couple baseball fields stretched before my eyes, with a lake glistening in the middle like a black pearl. Beyond its edge was a tall, thick forest of trees, pitch black and unrevealing against the horizon like the gaping throat of a tsunami, the blade of a tide forever suspended in the heights as if time itself had halted. I shuddered.

Dark had never scared me the way it did now. It was in essence nothing but an absence of light. I'd reasoned, whenever my hair would stand on end in the plummeting shadows of night, that it was only an illusionary fear that came with a lack of something we'd known. I had come to find fascination in the blankets of black, to love the feeling of uncertainty, to fathom a search of the unknown when the lights left us. But this moment, it was different— the darkness was grand, something far greater than I would ever hope to be. It had the majesty of a lofty cave, the beauty of a Renaissance artwork, and the dread of an unyielding monster.

I can't do this, I thought. *I'm not doing this. How on earth do animals live here and sleep here?*

Wait. I came to a halt as I mouthed the words I'd just said in my head. *How did animals...?*

I turned back to the daunting nightscape. This *was* the home of so many animals. This was the only home they'd known. Perhaps, well, *perhaps*—

I threw myself up into the air, into a powerful spin through the surface.

It had been quite a while. The last time I changed was a week ago, at Vanna Daya, in a class on Transformation. A tingle rushed through my feline body.

The night vision of a lion was impressive. With the shining eyes of a lioness, lined below the waterline with creamy white fur, I could see the brightness of night. I stared calmly at the gray foliage, then at the horizon brimming with blue. A sudden swirl of peace wrapped around me.

I ventured a step forward. The shadow fell away behind me, and I brought myself into the night's pinlight. The moon was hardly visible, but the sky was a shade of pale blue, descending onto the lake like a veil of silk. The soles of my four cushioned feet dug into the cool ground, and it was almost as if I could feel the subtle hum of the rich earth. The air smelled like scattered pinecones, and distant chirping of creatures and scurrying of rodents filled my ears with vigorous music.

I had not had it for long, but I found my lioness body to be quite admirable. I had sharp senses, and I was powerful. I did not need to test it to know.

But I did anyway. I began to race around the lake as fast as I could. My robust feet pushed the ground to oblivion far behind me, the rhythmical *pat pats* dissipating into the distance. I passed blurring trees and protruding boulders, then leapt through an opening into the woods.

The light was even fainter under the thick canopy, but my eyes soon adjusted to the darkness. I nimbly dodged trees, propelling myself in swift turns as I navigated through openings in the thickly packed forest. The sprint could not last long, however—after running several hundred yards my muscles began to burn, and my stomach began to feel uneasy. I toppled back into the clearing.

Panting, I looked around the area in search for a good place to hunt. The lake was shaped like a bean, one of the round edges sitting alluringly close to the periphery of the woods. A deer could pop just out from the trees and it would be merely yards from the lake. This would be where grazers would come out to quench their thirst, should they wake from their nightly slumber.

I crept a little closer. The stark, cold air of night seemed to punch my lungs into life. Rustling leaves twinkled like millions of rich black gemstones, and soft ripples on the face of the lake sent starlight into a tender waltz. Silently and in awe, I inhaled. So many smells. So many smells at once. As I tuned my ears to the silence, the surroundings slowly came alive with rustles of bugs and distant hooting of owls and nightjars. The tap, tap, taps of padded little feet were audible, occasionally accompanied by a delicious crunch of fallen leaves, withered grass and twigs. Fluttering wings beat through the dark, and then sounded a soft tap of clawed feet finding home on a branch suspended in the air. In its own, reticent way, like hushed whispers of mellow secrets against the inky fabric of the sky, the night lived.

Just then a shiver caught my senses, and I held my breath. It was a young deer emerging from the far side of the woods, small antlers poised above the unknowing head. I watched quietly as it strode toward the lake, stopped at the edge, and arched its neck until its muzzle touched the water. I could hear the soft lapping of water through the quiet. Crouched low and still, I kept my eyes on the deer. Suddenly a waft of wind carried the animal's delicious scent to my nostrils, and I started—my nostrils flared, my chest tensed, and I took in every molecule of the smell I possibly could. Blood rushed through my veins, and my heart began steadily to gain speed. Everything that had been swimming in my head receded to blackness, and I had only one thought: hunger. I dug my hind legs into the ground and reared for the attack.

I timed my attack to the moment the deer turned to leave for the woods. With alarmed cries birds flew off ahead of me. The deer sensed me on its trail and began to run for its life. I followed. I was fast; as I pounded across the field I steadily gained on the deer, until I felt I could make the leap—then just as it reached the edge of the field where the woods began, it disappeared into a tall bush, as suddenly as an animal possibly could. I slammed headfirst into a tree and got flung off the ground, landing in a whimpering heap.

I stood up, mesmerized, looking at the bushes where the deer had disappeared. Where had it gone? I searched the area in an attempt to find it, perhaps hiding behind some bushes or cowering behind a tree—but it was nowhere to be seen.

I sauntered back to the lake to get a drink of water. My throat was patched like sand, and my legs were sore from the chase. I brought my lips to the water. It was pleasantly cold. I knew exactly what to do, although I'd never drunk water this way—I began to lap up the water into my mouth, slapping the surface with my tongue just like a cat. I filled up on the little water-pillars until I was contented; and then I glanced at the rippling surface below. The midnight blue, bedecked with stars, held a wobbling reflection of a feline face. I stood there, staring at the water, until the rippling steadied and the surface calmed into a subtly rocking looking-glass.

Staring back at me, with hungry, lonely eyes, was a beautiful creature. I observed the face of the starstruck hunter. A pair of hazel eyes stared back into mine, buried majestically under the fold of skin that formed her brows and forehead. Delicate patterns filled bits of her face. There were dark spots over her brows, a white lining below her eyes—and dotted curves where whiskers grew. My gaze landed on every corner of the animal's face with wonder, then returned once more to her eyes. They'd been crafted in the way of a lion, devoid of expression but hunger and satiation. But through them I could see a human flicker, something I had not seen in photographs and videos of lions, nor in the creatures at the zoo.

Before I could stop myself, I cried out loud. My torso rumbled. My ribcages vibrated like an engine coming to life. A dry, hollow thunder resounded from between my teeth; echoes came bounding from the forest, the residual rumble prying into the marrows of night. Nothing moved, not a single animal made its way down to the lake—I was alone. I felt that weight on my shoulders, on my gleaming coat, on my cold paws.

While I stood basking in the music of the night, time passed and stars slid from the roof of the sky. The hooting of owls slowly died down, and the sky was beginning to take on a brighter hue. *Oh, no*, I thought. I perked up my ears. *I need to get home.* I began to race the way I'd come, no profit, no prize won—toward home.

Oh, *wow*. I intensely regretted last night's decision.

The morning was quite precisely hell. I ripped open a granola bar as I left the porch, and with my forehead wrinkled in sheer irritation, stared at the pea-sized hole I'd just made in the corner. I cursed under my breath. I hurled the entire thing into a trash can and strutted angrily down the merrily lit street, pissed at the disgustingly torn wrapper, sight of people, and the very fact that the sun was up. I hadn't *slept*; whatever the shiny orb was doing up there, it was making a huge mistake.

Ugh. Another day at school. Homicidal was the only word I could find to describe my mood as I walked through the gates of Kingsley High. The cheery chirping of birds and comforting shape of the library dome I'd loved so much did nothing to cheer me up.

I dozed through all of the classes in the morning. I could barely keep my head up, let alone keep my eyes open. I'd wake up shuddering every five seconds as my head sunk and startled me. Then I'd battle my eyelids once more, but to no avail; it wasn't long before my sight slowly blurred and my eyeballs seemed to spin in separate directions, slowly pushing the world out of focus. There were some blessed thirty minutes in between where I somehow found myself alert without yet another bang of the head, but even in those minutes I merely stared blankly at the blackboard without a single word entering my head.

Lunchtime came, although all I remembered from the morning was the way my desk would oscillate softly, back and forth, coming closer and drifting farther as my head nodded away. I absently grabbed a panini and an avocado smoothie—someone shot me a strange look as I lifted it off the ice—

and found Madison waving her hand at me in the distance. I waved back and shuffled over to her table.

"You look like hell, Sarah," Madison exclaimed as she scanned my face. "Like one of those dead fish in the grocery store. With the dead fish eyes."

"Thanks," I replied drily.

Madison gave me a strange look. "Studying for midterms already?" she asked.

"Something of the sort," I replied.

Madison narrowed her eyes. "Hey."

I lethargically followed her eyes and turned my gaze on her. For a fraction of a second the world shifted in and out of focus like a camera trying to focus in the dark. Madison raised a hand right over my eyes and snapped her fingers.

"Hey. What's wrong with you?"

I started. "What?"

"I feel like there's something going on."

My throat grew hot. I gulped.

"There's nothing *going on*, Madi," I insisted.

"Is it Chase and Andrew?" she asked, persistent.

I frowned uneasily. "What do you mean, *is it Chase and Andrew?*"

Madison shrugged. "I don't know, you weren't close with them, now you talk to them every day."

"No. I just um, got to know them. At a friend's house." Well, it wasn't entirely untrue.

Madison pointed a finger directly at my face, and I jumped, startled. "You're gonna have to tell me all about it, girl."

I blinked uneasily. "I will." I stared for a while, trying to find out if she was satisfied with my answer. "I really will," I added tiredly.

Madison dismissed the subject with an unconvinced stare.

"So tell me what I missed," I said, trying to sound as cheerful as I could.

"You're not supposed to *miss* these things, you're *vice-captain*. I still can't believe you saw them fight and still left because you had a *what? A date with Carlos Pierce?*"

"It wasn't a *date*," I protested. "And I had to shower. And put on some fresh clothes. And hey, how did you know I was with Carlos?"

Madison shrugged. "It's a small neighborhood, kids talk a lot, word gets around quick. But seriously, Chase and Andrew last week, now Carlos? What *is* going on, Sarah?"

"I promised I'll tell you about it later, Madi," I said with a sigh. "Tell me about what happened. I'll see what I can do to help them mend things."

"Well, I think Nakato provoked Angela a bit when she said she thinks it's best to go a bit defensive against Milford. They had a bit of an argument. It's not getting better, but it's not getting worse either," she explained, still eyeing me strangely.

"You think any of them are going to quit? Like last year?" I asked.

"I think Lillian was just being Lillian last year. Angela and Nakato— probably not. If someone leaves it's most likely Nakato, but even that I think is—well, really not gonna happen."

"Good," I said drily. "We need Nakato on fullback. Things are going to be very different without her."

Madison eyed me silently.

"We need *you*. Whatever you're doing, don't do anything ridiculous, Sarah," Madison said sternly.

I gulped. I wondered if hunting deer at night counted as 'anything ridiculous.'

"I won't," I replied.

Throughout the rest of the day I was ridiculously cranky. English really didn't make sense, Susan Grebler was terrible as usual, and in physics we did conservation of energy, which was basically a whole bunch of disgusting equations. To make matters worse, Mr. Sussex neglected to erase that one blob at the edge of the board until the end of class. When the bell rang I shoved all my books into my bag, scoffing at, well, just about *everything*, because obviously the whole world was trying really hard to be stupid today.

The ridicule was unending. As I passed homeroom I saw Carlos and Dina intertwined by the locker practically gobbling each other up. I merely shuffled my way out of there with an eye roll, mentally puking into a large garbage sack. All I could think was, that maybe when I get home I could make myself some strawberry milkshake in the blender, throw open all the windows and sit in the crossbreeze, but then I'd have to do physics home-work and I just... I just *hated* equations. This day sucked, this month sucked, hell, maybe *life* sucked—but the thought soon vaporized again as soon as it had come. I didn't seem to be able to keep thoughts in my head for long.

I didn't exactly remember how I'd gotten from one place to another, but in some moments I found myself zoned out in front of my locker, and in some moments on my bed with an exercise sheet spread open before me. That afternoon I was in front of my desk, sitting in a soft crossbreeze made by opening my bedroom and door and window. I looked down absently at the sheet of paper on my desk. It was a physics exercise sheet. It was blank except for a couple drawings of swim shorts, which I seemed to have colored in with different colored highlighters. My mind had been wandering to this class some weeks ago when Mr. Sussex talked about how his dad would wear swim shorts all year long, and I'd been trying to remember what had brought him to the subject in the first place.

I stood up, shaking all the miscellany from my clouded head. I needed to grab myself a glass of water. I shuffled to the kitchen, took a cooled pitcher of water out the refrigerator, and poured it into a glass. The water climbed up the glass like a skateboarder on a half-pipe and splattered everywhere. I smeared the puddles of water with the bottom of the glass so it would dry up sooner. Then I shuffled back to my room, taking a big gulp from the glass. It sent a shiver down my back, and I snapped into momentary consciousness. I picked up a dull pencil from the floor and began to work through the pro-blems.

It wasn't long, however, until my attention wavered again. I absently scoot-ed over to the side where my desktop was sitting, and punched the power button with my big toe. The screen lit up with a harmonious hum. With my eyes fixed aimlessly on the screen, I opened a search engine and typed: *lion hunting videos.* Then I hit enter and scrolled through the results. Most of them were videos with crappy resolution, but there was a high-resolution clip from a documentary. I clicked on it.

I pulled out my headphones from the drawer, plugged them in, and put them over my ears. Then I hit start.

It started with a few long shots of the rich savanna in the summer, and the barren wasteland it soon became. Then a lioness sauntered into the frame, her eyes stale and hollow. I cringed. Her wispy coat had no trace of opulent glamor. Her ribcages were showing against her chest, protruding tersely against the thinned-out skin. She turned her fagged face to the camera.

Those eyes, I thought. That was the stare of a predator. I realized what the problem was. I wasn't a real predator. I could never be as good as those majestic beasts driven by agonizing hunger. Not unless I trained myself like them. *Exactly* like them.

So I cut my diet to breakfast and some snacks. The match against Milford was drawing closer and we had practice every day after school, which was a good thing. I told my mom that coach got us pizza after practice, or that Madison and I grabbed dinner already. It was a painful lie to tell, with my stomach hollow and searing.

I did realize it was easier to focus. Well, on hunting, nothing else. Every time I went to the park and the wood's night air entered my lungs, instinct would seize me. The backdrop instantly faded away; it was just me and terrible hunger. My muscles would tense, my hollow stomach would broil against my ribcage, and everything would go blank. It wasn't the fresh tingle I'd felt the first night I changed and stood in the woods. It was an irresistible urge, an elementary desperation.

But instinct was not enough to make me a good hunter overnight. Success did not come that easily; I still scared away my prey before I got close enough to pounce. I lost them in all sorts of places, the edge of the woods, the middle of the plain. I still fell a little short in all my chases, no leap was enough, and every little crunch beneath my feet gave me away.

It was terrible. I went to bed about an hour before sunrise each day. I felt faint all the time. It was like my sanity was slipping away, and with that my humanity. One night—probably the seventh or eighth—I'd been roaming the edge of the woods searching for prey when I caught the scent of a human. Probably an employee at Halliday, working late night hours. Upon feeling my stomach churn and my mouth water, I changed back hastily, shook and terrified, and rummaged the area for a bush of berries. I shoved the lot in my mouth, not even caring if they were poisonous. From then I added another little chunk of bread to my diet. Fortunately I had never again been appetized by human scent.

It was a normal Monday morning, and I was walking down the hallway half dead. My back ached like mad. From my shoulders to my thighs, it was as though my muscles had melted and somehow been strung together the wrong way. My legs seemed to move on their own, bending and popping weirdly, stupidly scratching the ground as I walked carelessly down the hall.

"...Sarah?"

I found myself face to face with Madison. She looked worried.

"I think I called you like three times and you didn't hear me."

Obviously there was also something wrong with my attention.

"Sarah, you look... sick," she said.

"Um... yeah, I just didn't get enough sleep," I told her.

For three weeks, I said mentally. It's been three weeks since I first started hunting. It was doing its job of relieving the stress I got from... honestly, with my head swimming like this I couldn't even remember what stressed me out. I mean, I could barely remember who I was. I felt faint.

I found Madison had handed me some effervescent vitamin C tablets, thanked her, and tried to walk on, but I staggered, and found Madison clasping my arm.

"Sarah, what the hell is wrong with you?"

"I just don't get a lot of sleep these days, Madi," I said wearily.

Her eyes narrowed. "Studying?" she asked.

"Uh, yes," I lied.

"You're still not going to tell me what's going on, are you?" She asked, looking me in the eye.

I stayed silent.

"I didn't think so. Ever since that Thursday you've been acting funny. You talk to people you've never talked to before. You're awesome on the field one day and then you're absolutely terrible. It's been over a month and you still don't tell me what's going on, in fact you *avoid* me," Madison hissed.

"Madi, I—"

"At this point I don't even know what you're up to, but if this is the way you act, honestly I don't care anymore. Do whatever you want. Just don't talk to me again."

Madison shot me one last toxic glare before she turned and walked away.

I stood there dumbfounded.

After about five minutes that I needed to process what even happened, I continued shuffling down the hallway.

I'd been hunting three weeks straight, weekends off. I'd limited my diet to two small meals a day so I'd have the motive when I hunted. But I wasn't successful that often—well, to be precise, I'd never been successful even once—and I was always hungry, to the point that I no longer felt the hunger. It was at that point a hollow in my stomach, stubborn and persistent, one that felt like it would never go away.

But the bigger problem was sleep. On the nights I hunted, which was pretty much most of the times except weekends—and the days my body cramped and ached from my monthly battles with nature—I got about two hours of sleep daily. One of the ironical things about being utterly sleep deprived, was that you couldn't get as good of a sleep as you normally could. Every morning around sunrise I'd creep back into the house and into my room and lie on my bed. Then no later would come flashes of random shapes and colors, strange noises—and then my body would freeze over. I panicked at first, but ever since it became some kind of wicked daily routine, I let it be. After several seconds my consciousness would follow my body down into the depths, and I would be asleep.

Weekends were different. A good sort of different. In fact, they were the best. I slept pretty much all weekend. Mom was mortified, but I could not fix myself. For quite a while I woke up some time in the afternoon on Saturday, had something I could call breakfast, and sat up a few hours reading or getting some rejuvenating sunlight—and I'd go back to sleep. Those hours were blissful, and I'd lol on the bed or sofa, paying out my sleep debt until my neck ached.

But the fatigue still wouldn't go away. Monday mornings were terrible, even though I'd gotten more than enough sleep the night before. Every Monday I'd pull myself from the bed like a fisherman pulling aboard a mandarin[1] bigger than his little boat.

And here I was, dead and shuffling down the hall of Kingsley High School on a Monday morning. I could barely remember how I was feeling before Madison had come raining on my parade, making things worse than I'd thought possible—but I vaguely remembered, that I thought, that I needed to remember that I thought, that I needed to celebrate.

It dates back to the Friday night a week before. I had been on the edge of the woods, just as I had the very first day I went hunting. I was standing, trying to keep still, watching, looking out for movements in the distant trees, when I saw a shiver at the bottom of the bush. I tensed. My eyes fixed on the trembling leaves, and my ears pricked forward to pick up the sound. I twitched my whiskers, breathing in the air, trying to make out a trace of scent. It was a rabbit.

Rabbits weren't normally at the top of my priority list, but I was hungry. All I'd had throughout the whole day was a bowl of cereal for breakfast, and a banana I'd gotten at the cafeteria. I could feel my stomach roil and my mouth fill with saliva.

I coiled and waited patiently until it got nearer. Soon the small creature emerged from the bushes, its eyes innocuous and unknowing. Without wasting so much as a second, I leapt at it, sinking my teeth into its throat. After a loud squeal, it fell limp.

It was my first successful hunt.

---

[1] I think Sarah means marlin. She's sleep deprived. – Suinne

I'd had a couple extra hours of sleep that day. Over the weekend I celebrated, by making myself a very poorly done crepe with Nutella. But Monday night found me with the worst feeling ever. It was a dirty feeling, like I'd stepped in dung and couldn't clean it off—I was turbulently and disgustingly, tired and alone. I discarded the idea of going out for a hunt that night, and instead made myself a messier version of the crepe I'd had in the weekend. Then I thought of Madison and cried.

Did that really happen? Did she just... end *things with me?* I looked at the vitamin tablet still lying on my desk. I hadn't touched it since she'd given it to me. For some unknown reason I tore it open and poured a tablet into my palm, then popped it in my mouth like I'd do with a candy. The thing bubbled up on my tongue with a pungent sting. I chewed it down angrily.

But what could I do? The ability to give a shit, I found, also required some good sleep the night before. I was certainly not in the shape to think about things like that. I finished the crepe and gulped down a glass of milk, and dropped dead on my pillow.

Things hadn't gotten that much better for another couple days or so. I'd caught my second rabbit something like three days later, but in between I'd been unsuccessful.

And then I caught my first deer. It was exactly a week since I got my first rabbit. The struggle was real. The final, decisive leap was a gamble, a reckless venture—my feet kicked off the ground a bit earlier than usual, my back and paws outstretched to bridge the gap. The tips of my claws punctured the animal's skin, and I instantly crunched and curled onto its back; there I shot once more for the bared throat, into which my teeth sank without resistance.

Instantly a bleat escaped the deer's throat, switching to a breathy howl as I punctured the windpipe. It was a sound that would have horrified me, were I in my human form; but to a lioness who had just landed on her game it made no difference.

The animal thrashed in a fervent attempt to throw me off its back. It was stronger than I'd anticipated, its kicks hefty and muscles hale. I gripped it with my paws as I hung on—I could not afford to lose it this time. Little by little I sunk my teeth deeper into the animal's neck. I could taste the blood trickle in my mouth, and instantly a passage seemed to open into my stomach, to the hollow that needed to be filled—I grasped the flesh with my watering mouth, battling its desperation with mine.

And soon the deer went limp. I could feel its life falter and go out, and the grazer fell onto its knees, then onto its side. A wispy breath escaped for the last time—and as I let go, carmine blood trickled from its gaping wound and soaked the earth below. I stood for a while in disbelief, staring at the life I'd taken. What grasped me was not a human grief; it was the euphoria of a hunter, pumping into my bloodstreams from the cores of my genetic instructions.

The euphoria, however, did not last long; it wore off with the satiation. I was still in the worst shape, still fragile and sleep deprived. And worse, I was hungry again, only worse than before.

It was terrible. It was as if I was holding on by a thin string every second I breathed. I lost weight, dozed in every class, and one day, to top it off, got back AP physics midterm results that said:

Forty five percent. Sarah, see me after class.

I stared blankly at the paper. My writing scrawled to some unintelligible set of lines halfway through each problem. And the answers were all wrong. I squinted. I thought this was just boring equations.

Some moments later I was sitting on a stool in the teachers' office, studying a Stitch and a cute stuffed dog perched on the desk.

"Sarah, is everything all right?" asked Mr. Sussex, bringing some papers and seating himself in his seat beside me.

I nodded. "I just... didn't have much time to study," I blabbered.

"This isn't something *you* have to *study* for, this is *elementary mechanics*."

"Sorry?" I said stupidly.

"I'm certain you'd have done quite well if you weren't dozing off during the exam. You seemed completely unable to focus. I have no intention to pressure you but I was expecting a lot more from you. Your placement test result was excellent."

I tried to find something to say, maybe an excuse. I noticed that Mr. Sussex was wearing sandals over mismatching socks, one bright purple and pink, the other cobalt blue and turquoise.

"Mr. Sussex, your socks," I began.

"Sarah, I'm not joking around. This is important. Linda was very worried about you. She said you've been sleeping through homeroom. And Calculus," he continued, letting my comment slide.

"I..." Well, I guess then Calculus wasn't a plausible excuse either. "I've had a lot on my mind, and I was studying at night, mostly. I think I've been really sleep deprived these couple of months," I said.

"How are your parents okay with that?"

"Um, I um, normally study a bit after my mom's gone to bed," I lied.

"Is anything happening? At home or with your friends?" Mr. Sussex inquired.

"No, everything's fine," I replied. "It's just... we've got to prepare for the season semifinal, we're going to be playing Milford and they're a strong team. And I'm also um, looking at colleges, so. I was a bit busy."

That seemed to do it. Mr. Sussex touched his beard. "Well, it does seem you have a lot on your hands."

I nodded convincingly.

"You have to take care of yourself, Sarah. It's not just about grades. It's important to stay healthy to do any *one* of the things you want to do."

I nodded convincingly, and Mr. Sussex let me go. As I walked out the door and into the hall, the floor began to spin. My head felt light, and my heart beat weirdly. I placed a hand on the wall, pressing hard into it until the tips of my fingernails went white.

A couple of minutes later the spinning steadied. I turned to leave, only to bump into Lillian. *Since when had she been standing right behind me?*

"*What the hell,* Lillian."

Lillian said nothing. She grabbed me by the arm and began to march me off.

"What the—" I cried.

She stopped at a nook in the exterior of the building. I found myself trapped in the nook, a narrow-eyed Lillian in front of me, inquisitive.

"What—what—what is this?"

"How often do you go to the park?" she demanded.

I stood there, tongue-tied. "What—how—what?"

"Every day? Every week?" Lillian persisted.

I regained myself. "Uh—every night," I replied. "How did you know I went to the park?"

"Because you made quite a mess. Your smell is all over the place," Lillian replied.

"Oh. Sorry," I apologized quickly.

Lillian flicked her eyebrow. "Why are you apologizing? I didn't mind."

"Uh," I babbled. "I thought I messed with your hunting."

"Oh no. You don't smell like food, not even remotely," Lillian said with a shrug. "You can't confuse me."

"Then why are you acting like this? It's not like I'm supposed to stay off your grounds."

Lillian shrugged. "I was just... curious. Why did you start hunting?"

"I just thought..." I hesitated. "If I'm going to be gemless, I'll at least be a good hunter."

Lillian nodded slowly.

"Judging from the trail you left I'm guessing you dive straight into the chase without waiting. And seeing from the prints you leave you make rough turns. Your steps aren't quiet enough. Hunt that way, and you're not getting yourself anything to eat."

I was offended.

"That's really none of your business, Lillian," I snapped.

Lillian stared, an eyebrow arched up for seconds before she burst into laughter.

"*What* now—" I began angrily.

"*Ace,*" Lillian exclaimed.

"What?"

"I like your attitude. You know what? I'll train you."

I stood there, opening and closing my mouth. Lillian flicked her eyebrow as if she'd already gotten her answer.

"Midnight, Halliday," Lillian said before she seemingly twirled into thin air.

Later that night, I was at the park, demonstrating the way I hunted. As usual, I failed. I trotted awkwardly back behind the trees where Lillian stood leaning against a birch trunk, arms crossed.

I was sure Lillian would find it least—

"Impressive."

I cocked my head to the side, since I couldn't speak.

"I guess this is where we're different. I've never seen cats hunt." Lillian straightened herself from the tree and uncrossed her arms. Of course. It wasn't my hunting skills that impressed her.

"I found out about you coming here the very first day you hunted, but I didn't ask you right away. I just thought I'd lay back and watch and see if you get any better, but from the first day up to now you're the same." Lillian frowned. "That night you got your kill. I'd say it's a miracle."

Ouch.

"You need more of everything," Lillian said, beginning to circle an invisible area in front of me. "Speed. Agility. Strength. Strategy. *Perseverance*. I'll show you how it's done."

Without another word Lillian changed.

It was the first time I ever saw her change. There was the swiftest possible twirl, and I was face to face with a black and white wolf, sleek and strong, staring back at me with electric blue eyes. Lillian as a wolf was ravishing. The stark black and icy white of her coat contrasted like an iceberg against a wintry night, blending narrowly at the edges into a misty silver. Her posture was an elegance I had never seen—her stance was a rebellion against the night, and her walk was a dance that conquered the earth.

But Lillian did not leave me to marvel for long. She began to cover the grounds in utter silence, in search of the antelope I'd just lost. I remained a good distance away, keeping the wolf the size of a pea.

When she did finally find the one I missed, her footsteps slowed to a stop. She did not have to hide in the bushes the way I usually did; despite the vivid contrast of the shades of her coat, the motionless wolf disappeared into the backdrop of the night. The wolf, I could see, was silently calculating her course—and soon when she was done, she leapt into pursuit of the animal. Each of her steps were meticulously chosen; she navigated around me, keeping herself and the animal in sight, as she wore out the animal in a chase around the woods. I raced some distance after her, watching closely as she deftly led the antelope into a narrow shaft behind a rock.

Then she tackled it down before my eyes.

"What do you think you're doing, Sarah?" a voice shouted into my ringing head. I found I'd fainted upon seeing Lillian take the antelope down, and I'd been morphed back into my human body.

"They call you the queen of the jungle, and you *faint* when you see me hunt."

"I..." I croaked. "I don't know. Guess I'm just tired."

"I told you before, but you need more of everything. Tonight I'm going to teach you to stay still and wait."

"You need to *teach* me to stay still?"

Lillian shrugged. "Well, apparently you can't do it yourself."

I could not object.

"Get up," Lillian ordered.

I did.

"Change."

I did.

"Now follow me," she said, before she changed.

Once again feline, I followed the wolf deep through the trees.

Lillian was no ordinary human, nor an ordinary wolf. Even with padded feet, a perfect silencer the entire cat family had, I could not be quieter than this wolf in front of me. She slipped through soil and rocks alike as though nothing were beneath her feet but air.

We had paced through the woods in silence for about fifteen minutes when without a warning, she changed. She motioned for me to do as she did. I did.

"If we walk one or two minutes this direction, there's a place where wood rats dig burrows."

"Rats?" I repeated in disbelief.

"What, you think you're out of their league?" Lillian sneered.

"Well, obviously," I replied, offended.

"We're not hunting them," she explained to my relief. "There's a very small valley down there where the wind gets a bit strong. If you stand facing the wind you can get a lot closer to your prey than you normally can without them noticing you. Even those with very keen noses."

Lillian pointed toward some random direction with her chin.

"Now these boys have shit eyesight, but they can detect movement like ghosthunters. What I want you to do is get as close to their watchdogs as you and I are right now."

Lillian wasn't standing all that close from me, but for predator and prey, it was an excruciatingly close distance.

"Remember to move slow, make no sound, and stay completely still between steps. Let's go."

I did.

It was impossible. Lillian would watch leaning against a tree, and each time I turned back after setting rats into a panic run, she shook her head in discontent. This repeated for what seemed like forever. I'd give my all, but the rats would dart away the moment I approached them, and Lillian would let out an irritated sigh. But days after days passed, and I got closer and closer. Once or twice Lillian would raise an eyebrow, but she still didn't say anything. Then one time she nodded, finally, and moved on without a further word.

It was in a way a humbling experience, being taught to hunt by a wolf while being the so-called queen of the jungle. Experience and dedication, I discovered, could mold one beyond what's given at birth. Lillian was good. There was no doubt. She was exceptional. She was better fit for a title like the queen of the jungle than I was.

Lillian taught me a catalog of things. She taught me stealth, she taught me strength. It reminded me of the first few months in the soccer team. Lillian had been a notorious captain before she quit, who believed everyone else but her needed an impossible lot of practice. She was right. Her nightly lessons proved that much. I followed through with whatever amount of practice she thought I needed; I stayed still for hours, I raced up and down hills countless times a night. I chased countless prey at her directions. And with that I slowly improved. It wasn't long before I could be proud.

"By the way," Lillian began. I came to a halt.

"Did you sneak in here every night?" she asked.

"Yes, why?"

"I know it's faster, but if you want to sneak in do a better job. There's been a report that a lion form Enricus has been sneaking into grounds every night. I saw it before Robert did and deleted it," Lillian explained.

"Oh."

"You know you don't have to do that. Here," Lillian said, handing me a plastic card.

It was an employee ID card, with my name and picture on it. I twirled it in my fingers with a frown. "What is this?"

"Calleigh forgot to give it to you. You're doing an internship in Halliday."

I made a funny face in confusion. "I am?"

"Only on documents. Should be useful. You can walk in through the front gate, if you show this to the security. And this also means you can legally drive here on your own at night. Because you're driving to work."

"Oh. But I don't have a driver's license," I said.

"Aren't you sixteen?" Lillian asked with a frown.

"I've been putting it off for a bit," I replied, feeling somewhat stupid.

Lillian shrugged. "Not in your case, then, I guess. But it should come in handy anyway."

"Uh... so I don't have to give it back?" I questioned, confused.

Lillian looked at me as if I were stupid. "You can keep it. Why would I want an ID with your name written on it?"

I chuckled and pocketed the card. We walked up the edge of the woods in silence, until the trees thinned behind us and disappeared.

It was a cloudless night. The broad-shouldered girl led me through the clearing, her figure ethereal against the deep blue sky. She was elegantly built, and her footsteps, even her human ones, were light and minimal. The girl seemed to know no fear. It seemed the dark was her home, and night her nest; I could only wonder if it had always been that way.

There was nothing about her that was inviting, and I knew she didn't like people much—but for some reason that day, she had seemed a little more approachable than any other. Before I could stop myself, I had opened my mouth to ask her something I'd been wondering for long.

"Lillian, how does it feel to have a gem?"

Lillian remained silent for a while, looking inscrutably back at me.

"Well, not much different," she replied after a while.

"But I'm sure you don't feel the way I do. There's... there's something *empty*. I can't say what it is exactly. A gem is nothing but just a special little power, but I feel so hollow. Lost. It's like I'm nothing."

"I know," Lillian answered.

"You know?" I repeated.

"Well, we're made that way," she answered simply. "Nobody still knows why."

"I heard some people don't have gems for years, but then they get theirs all of a sudden. Do you think that could happen to me?" I asked.

Lillian looked at me, silent.

"I think you should focus on hunting," she said after a while.

I shrugged. "I guess I should."

I whisked through the woods. Lillian trotted behind me, watching me closely as I set down the slope, tracking a trail of scent left behind by an elk at its heat. After a while of tracking I glimpsed it on the edge of the woods. I began to approach it in silence, concealing myself in the shadows. Once I got close enough, I put everything I'd learned into practice. I observed, calibrated, and sprang. The elk began to sprint, but I was faster; I tackled it down and took it out.

I released the elk's throat when it went limp between my teeth. The smell of the fresh meat was tantalizing, and my stomach churned. Not bothering to resist the urge, I fed on the animal then and there. When I looked up, licking the blood on my lips, I saw that Lillian had changed, and was patiently watching me feast on the meat. I backed a few steps and changed, then with a huge grin asked her:

"How'd I do?"

Lillian looked back at me, not voicing a single word, her expression somewhat unimpressed.

"Well...?" I voiced sheepishly.

Lillian opened her mouth. "Not bad," she commented matter-of-factly.

Well, I'd at the same time expected more and not expected more. At least she said *not* bad. It was progress, after three months of soccer practice and a month of hunting, where she constantly told me I was bad in every way possible.

We walked down the slope in silence. The rest of the night went by silently. I was tempted to ask more about gems, but I stopped, remembering the way she'd dismissed the topic. I instead thought of my scrumptious kill, until Lillian nodded me goodbye at the parking lot.

Lillian's training was paying off. For the fifth day in a row, I scored. In fact

I'd gotten so good that I hardly ate while I was human. This new scheme involved worrisome parents and truckloads of lies, but I managed. I grew a weird habit of getting my weekly share of sleep in one day, and instead eating a tremendous amount at night. And yet—because of the bizarre mechanisms that governed the bridging of forms, I was in a better shape than before.

That night, like the previous nights, I demonstrated my stunt and changed back before an evaluating Lillian. She stood against the same birch tree as she did every night, and looked at me with silent eyes.

"Well?" I said.

Lillian finally opened her mouth to speak. "I don't think I have anything else to teach you. You have good physique. You're fast, you leap like forty feet. And you learned well."

A huge grin crept onto my face. "Really?"

"Mm-hmm," Lillian replied. "I am resigning."

"*What?*"

"I think you're forgetting that I need my sleep, Sarah," Lillian said.

"But you skip a lot of school," I retorted. "I figured you normally hunted at night."

Lillian looked me dead in the eye before she said, "That's none of your business."

I shrugged, somewhat offended. "Well then," I said. "I guess I'll just hunt by myself."

"You can bring Pierce, you know," Lillian suggested casually.

I narrowed my eyes and halted. The girl looked at me, her face indifferent as usual.

"*You can bring Pierce, you know,*" I echoed. "Really? I could *learn* from you. You want me to start teaching a newbie to hunt?"

The girl gave a little shrug. "He might be good."

"I know you don't mean it."

"Look." Lillian wheeled around to face me, her hair flying violently and landing in a glorious mess around her face. With a slight, elegant and feverish flick of her hand she got the loose strands out of her head and behind her ears.

"I said I don't want to do this anymore. Humans don't normally hunt at night. If you want to do it you're going to have to find someone else."

I gaped for a second, unable to retort. Everything she said was right—and it occurred to me only then that she had been, for the past weeks, pulling herself out of her bed and into the trouble of coming here each night. I gulped.

"All right," I said.

Without a further word, Lillian turned around and led the way down. I merely watched her dirty blonde locks swinging behind her, in a dance as fierce and fervent as the girl herself.

Chapter 5
The Emerald-Eyed Panther

Oh, praise thee, sweet bliss of sleep.

The first day was a precise definition of heaven. My bed felt like a nest of puffy, warm clouds, and to my own disbelief, I stayed in it all night. *Two. Nights. In a row.*

I woke up the following Monday, refreshed for the first time in eternity. I fleeted out of the house, greeting the freshly rustling trees with shimmering emerald leaves, wholeheartedly ready to go flying into the air among the tweeting birds. I even found myself grinning hard and waving as Carlos and Dina passed by at school. Carlos turned his head to give me a funny look as I disappeared around the corner.

Ah, the classes. I'd paid attention in all my classes—at least before I started a double life as an apex predator—but I had never found them genuinely entertaining until this moment. I sat through all of them, even Grebler's English, beaming like a madwoman, feeling the rumble of life as the thingamabobs turned and whirred in my head. *All these voices,* I sighed. *It's been quite a while since they'd made sense.*

For a whole week I lived my life in bliss, drenched in the beauty of everyday life. Sleep was a delirious gift. Each day I woke with an elated smile on my lips, humming tunes in a cracked and froggy voice. I listened intently in the front rows as the teachers explained algebra and science. I worked through the contents of the lecture in my head until the entire framework presented itself as a simple little picture. I was happy. Things were good, and I was awake enough to appreciate them. It was not long, however, until I found myself thinking about the fresh chill of the night air, the soft trail of delicious scent peeking from between the dense canopies. I longed to tread the trails in the sleeping woods, to race through the hills after prey. I was a lioness. It was a fact I could no longer ignore.

Some days later I finally gave in. I sneaked out again at night, my body light and supple—and I took the night bus once again to the park.

It was not the most pleasant excursion. I had to separate with my bed, which at the moment I had vowed my life to. As soon as the chill burrowed through my jacket and into my bones, I began terribly to miss the warmth of a cotton blanket wrapped around me, the serenity of my own home, the sleep I could get—but there was no going back; tonight I was hunting.

I was soon back at the park. The warm skyline, the fresh smell of trees and grass welcomed me home. I pranced into the air in a nimble spin, landing softly on the crusty earth without a sound. I set off into a run, the air cool and crisp on my coat. I cornered a deer in less than an hour. Having returned to my human diet, I didn't bother to kill it; instead, I called it a day and started back for my blessed bed.

It was a good night out. But something was missing. The idea of having company did not sound bad; they did call humans social animals, and I had to admit, I missed the looks Lillian and I used to exchange when we met at our rendezvous point.

So at lunchtime a few days later, I was again contemplating whether to bring company to my hunting trips—when I was interrupted by Carlos.

"Hey," Carlos greeted, setting his tray down beside mine.

"Hey," I responded, putting down the tuna sandwich I'd been happily nuzzling. "Why are you by yourself?"

"Cole's gone to the gym, Nate's gone to get his blades sharpened," he replied simply. I looked at his tray—he had two sandwiches in a pile, and his usual mushy green drink in a cup. "And Matthew's with his girlfriend."

"What about you?" I asked. "Where's your girlfriend?"

"She's with the girls today," Carlos replied.

The girls. He probably meant the flock of girls who constantly fangirled over the hockey squad. I mentally wrinkled my nose. Such a bad example for the future generation of women.

"That sounds fun," I said dryly.

Carlos chuckled. "Not really."

I pushed my books away—one of them a hunting log written by an award-winning mountain lion form Enricus—to make some space for him.

"So what's up with you? You were in a good mood for the whole week. Did you get into college?"

I laughed. "We're in the same year, Carlos."

Carlos shrugged. "I mean, you're smart. They might have begged you to come."

"Way better, actually," I replied. "I got *sleep*."

"What?"

"I haven't been sleeping for like two months," I said matter-of-factly.

Carlos seemed astonished. "Are you even human?" he exclaimed.

I explained to him what I'd been doing every night these two months. I left out the part concerning why, or the part where Lillian taught me. Carlos listened with his chin on his hand, his eyes shimmering intently.

"Can I come with you?" he asked after a while, concluding my contemplation on company. I thought for no longer than a second before I replied with:

"Sure."

Midnight came. Carlos' red Subaru was waiting for me outside, softly whirring beside the porch. I snuck in and we took off toward the park.

Carlos was pure comedy when he hunted. He might have fared well on the ice with his aggressive play, but lack of patience wasn't the virtue of a hunter. The panther, I learned, couldn't keep himself still behind a bush. Neither could he wait for the perfect moment to strike. He went off after every little trail of scent, and leapt at every moving thing he saw—frankly, he was terrible. I spent the night, and some nights that followed, unable to do any hunting of my own; I had to run around making sure not to lose the eager, unpredictable cat in the forest.

When a few days passed, however, he began to show some improvement; though he still chased away all his prey, he gave himself away with a faint rustle beneath his feet instead of outrageous snaps of dry branches. We soon came up with a nice hunting plan. I'd take the lead and chase the game close to Carlos, and he would finish the job. It was a brilliant plan, and it never worked. So we turned it around. We took instead to having Carlos dive into the chase immediately, leading the game to me, where I would finish it off. Only then did it feel right; Carlos was a fast runner, and he had fine reflexes.

The strategy soon became standard code. We'd carry out our teamwork. He'd let out a paralyzing roar, and the chase would begin. I'd be standing at the meetpoint, braced and ready. Then I'd leap onto the animal. Each time we succeeded we would let out a little cackle that sounded a lot like a wobbly laugh. We succeeded multiple times, until Carlos said he wanted to try doing the entirety of the job by himself. Then things went back downhill, and we stuck to not catching anything. Each time he'd look a little disappointed, and I would tell him it's okay.

I fell into a routine of sneaking out every Monday, Wednesday and Friday, hopping onto Carlos' Subaru, and heading to our hunting grounds. Every day it took me less than an hour to corner prey, and Carlos forever to deal with the exact same one. Since he refused to share my kill until he had his own, neither of us preyed on the animals at the park. Instead we took turns making sandwiches—both of us made terrible ones—which we ate hungrily after three hours of intense chasing. And we talked. We talked about hunting, game, and animals. We talked about movies, school, practice, and Brian

Harold—

"The guy you dated?" Carlos had responded.

I made a funny face. "How do you know that?"

Carlos shrugged. "Our school isn't huge," he said simply.

"I wouldn't go so far as dated," I objected. "Smoothie, movie, ice skating. That was it."

Carlos beamed. "You skate?"

I laughed. "Oh, you should see me on skates. I'm your nightmare."

"I can teach you sometime," Carlos suggested. "Nothing on the ice can scare me."

"Oh, I *will*," I said. "I *will* scare you. I'm sure."

"Was he good?" he asked.

"Brian? No. We were both terrible. We held onto those giant plastic penguins like our lives depended on it. That was the last date." I said with a chuckle. Carlos chuckled, and gazed long into the sky with brows furrowed as if imagining me on the ice.

"Hey, I'm curious," he spoke up after a while. "What about him made you, you know, get really into him?"

"I heard him talk about relativity, at lunchtime," I reminisced. "I can't forget that look. That—intense look. Everything he said was basically punching the air."

"What's relativity?" he asked with a frown.

"It's Einstein's famous theory that space and time aren't absolute. Instead it's a kind of giant bulk called spacetime that squish differently depending on who looks at it. You have your time, I have mine," I explained.

"But aren't we having the same, well, *time*, right now?" Carlos objected. "I'm in yours, you're in mine."

I pondered. "I mean, we're at rest relative to each other... so... yes," I replied softly.

Carlos chuckled. "Sounds beautiful."

"Really? You're surprising me today," I said.

"I was kind of curious. You know, wanted to, um, know some of the stuff you do. You seem to have a lot more fun than I do," Carlos remarked.

I narrowed my eyes. "Are you kidding?"

Carlos looked at me, earnest. "No," he said. "I mean it. I wanna try seeing what you see."

I think I spent the rest of the night trying to convince him that what I saw was just the world as it was. It was the same peaks against the fabric of the cosmos that made its way into my eyes, the same faint glow of nightfall that traveled through the hollows in my chest: the little, grand, peaceful dark that made me ask what I was missing, if it was my gem or something else.

One day Carlos miraculously had his first kill—a clumsy raccoon—which I had lured into an opening and left to him. The aftermath was a bit overdone for such a small kill—we'd changed so hurriedly in elation that we almost staggered and fell. Then we leaped into each other's arms, Carlos laughing, and me squealing, both of us so loud it startled night owls. We then made a plan to celebrate the following hunting day. And we did.

We brought a picnic blanket and spread it by the lake, and feasted on a basketful of cupcakes I brought and wine coolers Carlos snuck from somewhere.

We cheered to our kill, sipped the wine cooler from plastic cups, stared off at the dark horizon and repeated the process. I had never brought so much as a wine cooler to my lips before, and to my surprise the liquid didn't burn my throat. There was only a faint hint of weird flavor, which left behind a soft warmth, a lingering aroma. I drank the thing like it was soda until a soft weight grasped my chest and my body seemed to melt. The breeze was nice and cool, and the peaks in the distance glided from side to side before my eyes. This, damn it, this was probably what they called tipsy.

"Sarah?" Carlos said after a while.

"Mm?"

I looked away from the beautifully swerving horizon into his eyes. His eyes were a very bright green, sort of like the color you see when you're sitting on the driveway daydreaming, and a light breeze displaces the shuddering early-summer leaves and shots of sunlight glimmer through thin emerald leaves. I could only imagine, for I've never really sat daydreaming on the driveway. When I daydreamed I was mostly walking down the street—or in bed, or in class, or... just anything but on my bums on the driveway.

Carlos threw a startled laugh after observing my face.

"You're not drunk already, Sarah, are you?" he said with a kind-of-like-a-frown kind of smile.

"Probably not?" I replied with a giggle. "Maybe. I don't know."

Carlos made a horrified face. He looked like he'd been struck between the eyes with a pickle.

"Please, Sarah, don't tell me you're already drunk."

I giggled. "I. Am. Already. Drunk."

Yes, I was; it was getting clearer now that the words came out all funny and slurred. Carlos clapped his hand to his forehead.

But we'd planned to see the sun rise from under the seas anyway. I lay sprawled on the grass, staring up at the slowly rotating sky. The night sky was beautiful. Once when I was young I was so mesmerized by its beauty that I wanted to paint it. So bad. So, *so* bad. I gave it a try. I drenched a brush in warm water and painted a piece of paper blue and black. Only all I could see was black. I tried again, and again, but somehow I couldn't make a difference.

I reached a hand up as if I could touch the velvety sky. What about—what about that blue was so elusive that its hues couldn't be recreated on paper? Perhaps it wasn't the only thing that disappeared when you try to chase it with your eyes. For some reason I thought of *gems, game,* and *Madison.* Then those faded, and I saw Lillian's irritated eyebrows, then Sophie's bewildered face as she peered at the blank vial—

I shook my head. This, I thought to myself, was one of those moments that called for a good run around the lake. I pulled myself up onto my feet. Carlos was fairly tipsy himself—he stared at me goofily as I changed and nodded for him to follow. It took him several tries to change successfully, but he did eventually, and we raced into the night.

The world spun, but I could run like a comet. We were both extremely fast;

the world melted into a glittering blur as we raced past it. I don't quite know how, but I was laughing a cropped-dry lioness laugh. We ran in a full circle around the lake and made back for the picnic blanket, on which we plopped down again, panting. Panting, come to think of it, was a funny word—I let out a lazy little laughter, which Carlos copied without quite knowing why. Why did they call it panting anyway, I thought. It had nothing to do with pants.

"You know what Sarah," Carlos mumbled under a heavy breath.

"Hmm?"

"I like your name," Carlos said lethargically. "It rhymes."

I normally correct people on their nonsense. But not when I'm drunk, apparently. So I simply replied:

"Yours too."

And then we stayed silent for what seemed like forever, until, well, Carlos broke that silence. I liked the way it broke, kind of like little shards of fake candy glass under your fingers.

"I like hunting with you," Carlos said.

Did his eyes glow in the dark? His eyes were a very bright green, sort of like the color you see when you're sitting on the driveway daydreaming and all of a sudden—I don't know, come to think of it it also kind of looked like potion, you know, the typical stew in a witch's cauldron kind of potion.

"Some things... disappear when I'm here," Carlos added after thought.

"What do you mean?" I asked lazily.

Carlos looked back up into the glistening dome. Whoa, I breathed silently to myself. It was amazing. His eyes were a very bright green, sort of like the color you see when you...

"Nothing," Carlos replied a while later, around when I'd forgotten I'd even asked a question—but with his answer I remembered, and I turned to look at him. Carlos opened his mouth to say something.

"You know, like," Carlos started carefully, as if he were opening a box that lay unopened for the longest of time. He gulped. "Like what I dream about at night."

I turned and looked at him. His eyes glimmered once, and no more.

"What do you dream about at night?" I whispered.

"I'm not going to tell you tonight," Carlos replied.

I considered. Maybe they were weird. We had been hunting partners for some time, but not for years. It was understandable; hell, I wouldn't unleash all my weird on him.

"Well then." I pulled myself up. A little more running around wouldn't hurt. It never did. "Then you can race me instead."

And he willingly did.

Things can be quite liberating when you're good at them. The stars and trees were obviously chasing me as well, but I was still a good runner and so I didn't bump into any of them. Once or twice I did see the moon approach me but for all I knew, it could have been me jumping.

We raced over streams, over boulders. I ran in front, my paws glinting silver beneath me, and Carlos followed, his rhythmic steps echoing like music behind me. We didn't stop until we reached the peak. There I looked up at the scape of the land spread before us, and gasped.

The moon was full. I'd never known that a full moon could be so bright. It flooded the peaks, plains, and pearly waters until everything was hazy silver. Like a monochrome sort of twilight. All these mesmerizing colors—but monochrome.

Without a word exchanged, we both changed. We stood there on top of the world, panting like a pair of beagles after a long run.

"Have we been here before?" I whispered between my breath.

"No," Carlos answered.

"Have *I* been here before?" I asked again, confused. I was pretty sure I'd never seen this. If I'd seen it, I'd have remembered.

"That I don't know," Carlos replied, looking up from over the cliff with a smile.

"It's my favorite place," I slurred on. "I love it. I need to come back here. Do you remember how to come back here?"

"Yes," Carlos replied.

"Can you bring me? But like, the *real* question is," I giggled sloppily, and went on: "if you can *find* this place again. Because you can't seem to be able to find your prey…"

Carlos comically grabbed his chest. "Ow. That hurt."

I rolled my eyes. "But I mean, you're doing okay for a *kitten*," I went on. "You don't have to feel bad 'cause I'm a better hunter. I'm the queen of the jungle. It's a jungle thing. Savanna thing. Whatever. Kind of like you're supposed to be stronger as a human," I ranted on, staggering. Carlos reached out and grabbed my arm. He *was* strong.

"You might want to be careful, we're… kind of standing on a cliff," Carlos warned in a low voice.

"*Wiiill dooo*," I drawled. "Can I have another wine cooler?"

Carlos sighed. "I don't think so. Come on, let's go to the lake. I know exactly what you need."

With that Carlos led me back down, occasionally reminding me to watch my footing with little whining noises.

"Water," Carlos said, changing back. I blinked at the giant body of water that had suddenly materialized in front of me. We had somehow arrived back at the lake. "It's going to help you. I didn't know you were so…"

Lightweight. I thought, as I teetered forward to lap up some water.

When I was done—and my nose wet from, well, me dipping my face in the water a couple times, Carlos reaching out to stop me but failing—we set off toward home.

"Let's call it a day," he had said. "You're drunk, we need to get you home."

We trotted down the slope and walked—me mostly staggering, Carlos mostly holding me up—to the bus stop. Carlos got on with me, and we sat at the back, my mind wandering through many things. For a moment I thought about Lillian. I toyed with the idea of her bringing a pack of wolves to the park. Briefly I worried about the chances that our grounds overlapped and we got into war. We would have to fight a wolf, or worse, a pack of wolves, at some point; but it wouldn't be much of a threat, would it? We were about twice their size…

I realized I'd drifted off on the bus when he woke me with a soft nudge on my shoulder. I looked around, dazed.

"Remember who you are?" Carlos asked with a chuckle. "We're home, you need to go to bed."

I stretched. It had been a long day, I mean night, and the alcohol was fading from my head, leaving me limp and tired. I refused to let him help me sneak in, as I couldn't even *fathom* what would happen if we got caught. Instead I gave him a lazy smile and carried myself up to my room, and plopped down face first into oblivion.

A couple weeks passed since then, without either of us running into a pack of wolves, or worse, getting hammered.

Both of us were radically improving in terms of hunting skills. I could do basically whatever I wished to; I could lead my prey wherever I wanted. I could kill whenever and whatever I wanted. I was lethal. My teeth were precise, my claws were keen, my paws were silent, and my body was strong. I was the apex predator. Carlos wasn't half as good as I was, but he was now a better version of himself. He could lead his prey to me, or deliver a final blow on my count. And better yet, we made a team like none other.

One Friday we were at the park again, for the last hunt of the week. Carlos was sullen, unlike his usual self; he drove in silence, and didn't speak much as we walked up the hill and through the opening in the canopy. I eyed him closely.

"You okay?" I asked.

Carlos dropped his head and sighed. "Yeah, I guess," he replied. "It's just, uh... Dina and I broke up."

"Oh," I said. I haven't had an experience that I could properly call a breakup. Even though I think I did cry a single teardrop, an awkward period of silence after the date with Brian probably was not much to compare. I decided to tuck away any other consolation I could think of. I simply said:

"I'm sorry."

Carlos looked, well, less devastated than I thought people suffering breakups would look. All I had as reference were girls crying mascara or breaking mirrors on TV shows, and Madison locking herself in the locker room and wailing. Come to think of it, I might have seen the more dramatic cases.

"No, don't be," replied Carlos with a sigh.

I stared awkwardly at the ground, pretending to show interest in the way the grass was growing. I could tell Carlos was looking away; I decided to break the silence.

"Hey, um... I have an idea," I said. "Something that might make you feel better. I used to do this a lot when I was little. On the porch or on the roof."

"Do what?" Carlos asked quietly.

"Just... lie and look at the stars," I replied. "We don't have to hunt tonight if you don't want to. We can just spend the night stargazing. You don't have to say anything."

Carlos looked at me, seemed to study my eyes for a bit, and smiled a weary smile. "Sounds good."

I didn't even understand why he said that, or if he'd done so much as look up at the sky before he agreed. I had begun to regret the suggestion myself, the moment I looked up to the sky. The sky was clouded over, a pearly haze casting an otherworldly glow of across the grassy meadow. It was hardly dark, almost as bright as twilight, but in a disappointing way—it was an unbearable sort of lightness that made you miss the dark of a clear night sky.

We didn't say a word about it, however. We found a cozy spot by the lake, lay side by side, and looked up into the pearly gray.

"Can you tell me what you dream about at night?"

Silence. It took me about a minute to gather the courage to turn my head and look at him. Carlos was staring off into the dim celestial, his lips firmly closed.

"Or not. As I said, you don't have to say anything," I said softly.

"The stars are pretty tonight," Carlos said.

I flushed, but somehow I was sure he wasn't being sarcastic. I may have imagined it, but his eyes softened and glistened.

"I had an aunt," Carlos spoke after what felt like forever. "Her name was Leyla, she was my dad's sister.

"She... was a single mom. Well, until her baby caught the flu and died. Ever since, she never stopped drinking. She'd get drunk, and then her eyes go, like, deep red, and she's just crying and looking at you like she hates you. Always.

"And then she got into all sorts of drugs as well. My mom couldn't put up with it. She left. She never came back."

Silence. I tried to find something to say.

He looked to me, faintly smiled, and said as if he read my mind;

"Don't say anything. You don't have to."

Carlos looked ahead at the sky once more. A trace of pain traveled into his eyes, and for a moment he stayed silence as if he couldn't bring himself to speak.

"I really don't know what's worse, between losing my mother like that what I had to see afterwards," he continued. "I have, like, faint memories of my dad yelling at Aunt Leyla. And one day, when I was young, like seven or eight or so, I was alone in the house with her, and I opened the door to the second-floor bathroom, and she got up from the bathtub screamed at me. I don't even remember what those words are. I just remember that they were disgusting. And she had a knife. She threatened me with the knife, so I backed off. I got so scared, I cried. But she didn't care, she just went and locked the door.

"And later that night, my dad broke down the door to the bathroom, and I don't know if I was meant to see it or not, but I saw her there. She was lying there dead, in a pool of blood."

I didn't know what to say.

"I dream about people. And doors. They're hiding something behind the doors, screaming at me to back off. And I do. I don't want to approach them. I don't want to look behind the doors. Because I think I know what I'd see."

The pearly clouds had grown only thicker. I turned to look at the boy. His eyes met mine, and for a moment it felt like I was seeing them for the first time. Something went through my chest that resembled a muffled sort of pain. The world rippled a bit, and the color in his eyes wavered. Before I knew what was happening, Carlos' hand swept under my eye, and it was then that I realized I'd been crying.

"Hey," Carlos said, his voice barely above a whisper, his words slow. "I stopped having those dreams at night. Ever since I started hunting with you."

"It's because you don't sleep at night," I said through a stuffy nose.

Carlos burst into laughter. "I do," he retorted after a while, his voice still breaking into little pieces of that laugh. "In the mornings. And When I doze off in the afternoon. And I do have dreams, but it's something else now. Never those nightmares. Not again."

"What is it now?" I asked.

"I'll tell you another day. But I'll tell you this, it's not bad."

"I hope, I mean you, I—" I started. I couldn't put into words what was in my head. There was a strange feeling in my chest, something I could not explain—it was a lonely, yet warm sort of feeling I had yet to learn the name of. It felt like Christmas. A sad sort. I touched the boy's face with my eyes, hoping, from somewhere deep within my heart, that all his dreams would be good.

None of us said anything. I soon turned my eyes from him, and we quietly watched the pearly haze flow toward an end of the sky, like a river made of dreams. Dark spots formed here and there where they thinned, and soon little patches of clarity had appeared between the veils. Our eyes adjusted soon to the dark—amongst the clouds we could see a beautiful midnight blue; and in them myriads of stars.

I spent the following weekend waiting for our next rendezvous. But come the following hunting day, I was greeted by something unexpected. Carlos' Subaru did not stop by my street to pick me up; I waited, puzzled, for a couple more minutes, but there was still no news of him. It was only much later that my phone dinged. I flipped it open to see a single text:

can't come tonight. sorry.

I was beaten.

>   You can't just do that! What's up?

I wrote back.

A minute passed, and another, and another, and I sat staring at the dead screen. But no reply came.

That night I hopped onto the night bus alone. I couldn't help but glimpse every couple minutes at the darkened screen. I was hoping for a good reason, or maybe a change of mind—but it didn't happen. I walked in through the gate that day, instead of sneaking through the parking lot. The thick iron gate opened when I brought my ID card to the pad. To my right, beside the array of buildings and labs, was the entrance to the park.

The entire night was sickeningly silent. No message, no ring on my phone, no good game, only utter silence. I ended up catching nothing. Tired and distracted, I carried myself to the night bus around four and headed home.

As soon as I woke up the following morning I reached for my phone, only to find that there still wasn't a reply from Carlos. I stared blankly at the screen for a minute or two, then headed over to the bathroom to splash some cold water on my face. *What was he doing?* I stormed to school grumpy, promising myself that I'd find Carlos and demand for an explanation. But he was nowhere to be seen. Did he really not come to school today?

It was the day after that I'd finally caught a glimpse of Carlos. He was walking down the hall with his boys, his backpack slung carelessly over his shoulder.

"Carlos!" I called.

Carlos stopped. He told his cohorts, Nathan and Cole, that he'll catch them later, and turned to face me.

"Why are you avoiding me?" I hissed as soon as he got close enough.

"I'm not," he argued.

"You are. Is it Christie? Did you get back together? Does she want you to quit? You could at least tell me—"

"I'm *never* getting back together with her," Carlos said indignantly.

"Then why? If you regret telling me that that night, just *say it*," I hissed. "I don't understand why you're treating me like this."

Carlos sighed. "Listen, Sarah. It's nothing like that. I'm sick."

I narrowed my eyes. "You don't look sick."

"I am. It's uh, kind of something I wouldn't talk about here," Carlos whispered, looking around at the passing crowds.

I thought about it for a moment. "We can talk in private."

"I uh," Carlos began uneasily. "I'll... I'll write you when I'm better. Until then we should... we shouldn't do this."

I stood there, confused.

"I'll write you, Sarah, really," Carlos assured before running off to catch his friends.

Exasperated, I watched his jacket flutter behind him.

Chapter 6
Princess Rena

Days went by. I didn't get to see a lot of Carlos after that; I'd seen him in the hallways a couple times, but he would not even cast a glance my way, and instead disappeared into the crowd in seconds.

I spent most of my afternoons doing homework. Or worse yet, sprawled on the couch trying not to think about the recent happenings. It never worked. Soon I took to exploring the library in Vanna Daya a bit further. I had a talent in distracting myself, and I could do it while being productive.

One afternoon, though, things took an interesting turn—when my lingering eyes hovered over a book with a childish pink cover. It was wedged between some scholarly archives on nineteenth century Enricus history, as though someone had hurriedly shoved it between random books. I ran my fingers over the backbone—it was made of buttery leather, quite well preserved despite the trace of age. I picked it off the shelf and turned it over in my hands.

Faint and almost faded, I found the title:

Princess Rena

I was never a big fan of fairy tales. The ridiculous curses, princesses sitting like a flower on a lily pad waiting to be saved by a man—I grimaced in distaste. I remembered walking up to my dad one day and asking who he liked better, between a crown princess and one who had married into princesshood. I'd told him I preferred the heiress, like Ariadne and Andromeda, and he had looked thoughtful a while before he disagreed. *It's a way you could be princess even if you weren't born one*, he'd said. *That is, if you wanted.* The conversation had ended in giggles, and for a decade or so I had not thought of princesses again—that is, until this moment.

I ran my fingers along the edges of the book. The cover was a milky pink leather jacket on wood, in the middle stamped a sleek figure of a crowned girl; hair flying, sword resting by her ankle. I felt the gilded figure of the girl as if I'd known her. Something about the book felt like home.

The book kept me company for the next couple days. It was exactly what I needed to wipe out the mess in my head.

It was about a princess Rena, who was born heiress to the throne in a kingdom where evil lurked. Rena had a friend, Harvey the Hardy, who was one of the king's knights—the most loyal and brave. They'd grown up playing in the creeks and mountains as children, and their friendship lived on even when they'd both grown up.

All the while, however, a clan of evil sorcerers continued to haunt the kingdom. One day the king sent out troops in search for them, and when his men came back, it wasn't what Rena expected to see. A ragged, bloodied and terrified knight delivered the news in a quivering voice, and brought before the king his knights' remains. The princess saw Harvey there, dead and unmoving, and knew he would never return.

Rena decided from that day on that she would train to kill them. She trained every day, with swords and with bows. She did not stop until she got good enough to beat the king's best knights.

And one night while she was training she was met by an old man, crouched in the side of the clearing, watching her intently.

"Who are you? What do you want?" asked Rena.

"You can't beat them," the old man said quietly.

"What do you mean?" Rena demanded.

"You can't beat them. Not with a sword or bow," the old man said again.

Rena thought it strange, and sought to see the man again, but he never appeared.

The princess then went to the king. She went to his throne and bowed gracefully before him.

"Father," said the princess. "I want to travel the world. I want to find a way to defeat them."

The king tried to stop her at first, but knew she was resolute. He packed bread and gold and sent them along with her on the best horses.

The princess walked for days, weeks, and months. After a long journey she came to the edge of a forest. The forest was dark and mystic, swirls of enchanted colors damp in a pearly mist. Rena navigated herself through the thicket for days on end. There was not a sound but the rustle of leaves under her feet. It was one of those days that she heard music. It sounded like the song of nereids, crystalline and celestial. She couldn't make out the words, nor did she know where it was coming from. She began to follow the sound.

It was a long journey of unending doubt. She walked for days on end before she got any closer. The sound was nothing but a distant note, so far away that she at times thought she'd imagined it. It seemed to want no more to lead her than to mislead her, but she would not let herself be misled. On the forty seventh day she finally arrived where the music sounded. She stood at the heart of the forest, where the thick groves of fern turned to an arcane purple. There in the middle was a stone pillar, on it placed a glowing orb—it glowed blue, like the stars she'd seen in the evening sky in late winters and early spring. The song, she found, was a riddle, hidden in mystic and profound tunes:

> *What's mirrored and by arrows bound*
> *that's felt but never grasped,*
> *That runs to what shan't but be found*
> *Yet seen from outside, lasts?*

Rena thought. She wandered into the forest to roam its depths, searching for the answer to the riddle. She thought for three nights straight, before she returned to the stone pillar where the orb lay. She had found the answer.

"Time." Rena smiled. "It's mirrored. A stone rolling on the ground could be rolling one way or another. If you look back in time, you wouldn't know which. But an arrow breaks this delicacy, for it cannot fly backwards."

Rena continued: "It's felt every moment we live, but never seen or held. Unforeseen moments quickly turn to what's past—the present is so thin that it's never in our hands. It leads us to our ends, which can only be met and not escaped, but if you could somehow stand outside its mighty dimensions," Rena took a cautious step back. "If you look from a world where past, present and future all lie before you, it's... still."

Upon her answer the orb seemed to expel a brighter glow, and melted into a stream of water that shone like a luminescent opal. A parchment lay where the orb used to be, milky white on the stone pillar. She took it in her hands and gently rolled it open.

> *If thou must go to where it ends*
> *And thine youth where nothing's past*
> *And shine, the light that makes amends*
> *Wouldst thou then raise thy mast?*

"Whatever it costs," Rena whispered in reply.

The words charred like embers and disappeared, and new words appeared in its place:

Follow me.

Millions of glittering lights rose like dust from the ground, and arranged themselves into a softly glowing stream, trickling onwards and onwards into unknown distances. Rena followed without hesitation. The trail led her for days and nights away from the heart of the forest, to where trees thinned and curtains of mountains unfolded. The stream trickled onwards, leading her up the trails and down, peak after peak.

On one of those evenings she wandered into a cave to rest. Night fell, draping the mountains in soft darkness, and she fell asleep. It was the middle of the night when she woke; she found a pair of eyes looking back at her.

"Show yourself!" she ordered as she backed to a wall, reaching for her sword. With a low rumble, the walls chipped away, and a scaled dragon stood before her. Rena raised her sword and held her ground.

After a perilous fight, the dragon fell. Rena stood on the edge of a cliff, her hair flying in the wind, her sword at the hem of her dress, the blood dripping onto a trail on the rock—just as in the engraving on the cover of the book. To her alarm and awe, an old woman climbed out of the dragon's limp skin.

"Who are you?" Rena demanded.

"I am a prophet," answered the woman. She approached Rena and whispered her a prophecy.

The content of the prophecy, however, could not be found—a page had been torn out from the book, just where the woman's prophecy would have been. I ran my hands along the jagged edge of the paper, wondering if it was coincidental or if it had been ripped out on purpose.

My reading sessions often got interrupted by school and life—but I continued when I could. The story went on as Rena traveled on a vessel to a distant isle, where she knew she would be facing her enemy. She arrived at a highland laid with rubble, and in the heart of the ruins was a fallen castle. The princess drew her sword and approached it. In the distance she saw a shadow, and the shadow approached her, quiet and cautious. When it emerged from the light she saw, and lowered her sword.

"It seems you've come a long way," said a man, his feet on the rubble.

"You're not him," Rena whispered.

"I'm not who?"

"The one who killed my friend."

The man approached her, his bare hands raised.

"No," said he, "I'm not the man you're looking for."

Rena looked at him warily. No, he wasn't the man she was looking for.

"Do you live here?" the man asked.

"No," Rena answered. "I come from far away."

"For what?"

"To fight."

The man looked at her a long time before he said; "You're in no shape to fight."

"I'm ready," the princess said, but the man would not fold.

"You need rest. You need food. Come, let me get you what you need."

The man led her across the sea to land, and to a tavern in the mountains, where she filled her hungry stomach. She spent weeks there, letting her body heal, and all the while trying to find trace of her enemy. The man would tell her stories of wondrous things he'd seen from his distant home, and something else happened—she fell in love with the man.

They spent a long time together. They told stories and shared their worries until one could tell what the other was thinking without a word said. The princess healed, and she was stronger.

One day she was looking over the mountains when a stampede of horses came to her, on them mounted a score of knights. They descended from the horses and saluted the princess.

"What is this?" asked Rena.

The knight fell on his knees. "Your highness."

"What is it?"

"The king has passed away. Your highness is to return to the palace."

Escorted by her knights, Rena rode to the palace where she was born and raised. The palace loomed bright and empty. All the maids and chamberlains left the palace to let Rena mourn. In the empty palace the princess, now the new queen, knelt by her father's bed and wept.

Rena was crowned queen of the kingdom. The book showed a fine illustration of the girl, looking somewhere around my age. Although the illustrator had not cared to draw in a pair of eyes, and her face was blank against her rippling dark hair, I could see them, staring resolute into the air.

After the death of her father she ruled her kingdom. She was a fine ruler; she was praised by her people. But she never forgot what she'd always meant to do. She could not forget; it was there forever ingrained in her mind. And so the queen prepared herself further. She honed her swordsmanship and prepared her weapons, just as the prophecy had told.

I soon arrived at the final chapter. Rena the queen once again went to her enemy; she knew exactly where they'd appear, for it was where she'd lured them. She traveled far, far from where she'd been born and raised. Her travels led her to a seashore where a basalt cliff loomed. The war of her life was coming to an end.

"At long last," said a voice. She turned to see a woman, sleek, cold-eyed, her moonlight hair running down to her waist. It had been she, all along—she was the one who killed her friend, and she was the one who killed her subjects.

"I know you've been after me," said the woman.

"And I knew you'd come to find me," Rena replied.

Rena reared her sword and took on her. They fought for days on end, and fumes of steam crawled from pools of broken glass. The woman gave a brilliant smile before she sunk a shard of glass into Rena's heart.

The queen fell.

I blinked.

This is the end of the book?

I flipped back to the cover, and the title written once again inside in curly print. It was most obviously a fairy tale for children. Never once have I seen a children's book like this, where the heroine dies off abruptly in the end, her life's mission left unaccomplished. I pinched the last page between my fingers. This was where the entire storyline was crushed into extinction.

I leaned back until my head hit the headboard, and slid down onto the bed practically folded in half. Was everything in vain? Harvey's death, the princess's odyssey, the ingenious answers to the riddles? Had the queen wept for nothing, fought the dragon for nothing, and walked in solitude for countless days to no avail—had she devoted her life only to die at the hands of the evil that had so viciously killed her friend? I sighed. This was by no means a children's book. It could only have been a device of some sort. Maybe they had intended to write a sequel. Maybe the entire book was some kind of code that had to survive some kind of censorship.

I spent the next couple of days ransacking the library, trying to find a sequel for the book. I was sure I'd looked at pretty much every available corner, but couldn't find anything remotely like this volume. I put the book back where it belonged, and decided my search for the weird truth had come to a dead end. I dismissed my curiosities about the princess in the pink book, and for some days it did not pop back up.

School was, well, school. I strolled down the halls holding my books in my arms after physics. I glimpsed Carlos across the hall, and for a brief second I thought our eyes had met, but he turned away before I could even be sure. *If that's the game you're playing.* I sighed, throwing my locker open to dump my books. It had been a tiresome day, for some reason, and it hadn't helped that I'd seen Madison in the cafeteria at lunchtime, pulling that same little stunt where she ignored me completely. Suddenly a teardrop tickled me, and I quickly wiped it off before anyone could see. I sniffed loudly and obnoxiously, trying to shake everything from my mind.

"Hey, sweetie, how's it going?" asked a merry voice.

I turned to find Calleigh, dressed in some ridiculous green shirtwaist dress that made her look like the kid in a Christmas choir that had to dress up as an elf.

"I was just about to go to English," I replied quickly.

"You had Grebler, right?"

I nodded.

"Know that I feel your pain."

"It's fine," I said. "I can just think about... homework."

Calleigh opened her mouth as though to say something, and then pursed it again. Seemingly she decided to move onto a different subject. She looked around dramatically before she spoke again.

"A little bird told me you and Carlos aren't in the best of odor."

Ouch.

I scoffed. "So you follow high school gossip now?"

"No," Calleigh chimed. "It was my own observation. I like to metaphorize her as a little bird."

I sighed. "Some days you make friends, some days you lose them," I remarked simply. I probably sounded way more indifferent that I was, but there was no need to go on about it. I instead found a subject I'd had buried in my head, one that Calleigh could perhaps help with. I seized the moment.

"By the way, I have something to ask you," I began.

Calleigh looked at me, her eyes twinkling.

"There's something that's been bugging me a little, and come to think of it now, I think you might know something about it."

Being the Calleigh *you are*, I added mentally.

As though she'd heard what I'd said in my head, Calleigh instantly brightened up. A smile found its way up my lips as well.

"Shoot. You can ask me *anything, anytime*," Calleigh went on like a set of chime bells.

"Have you ever read a book called... Princess Rena?"

Calleigh's eyes rounded abruptly. "Princess Rena? Where did you find that book?"

"Library downstairs," I replied. "Why?"

"They don't make copies of that book anymore," Calleigh replied. "I didn't know we had a copy. It must be a really old one."

"Why don't they make them anymore?" I asked.

Calleigh shrugged. "Not the hottest read nowadays, also not much of a valued classic."

I frowned. Something was off.

"I see," I said slowly. "Well, I wanted to ask you if you knew about it. About the story—It was a really strange ending for a children's book."

"Oh, it's more a historical fiction than a children's book," Calleigh answered. "It's based on Queen Serena."

"Queen Serena?" I repeated. "The last queen of the monarchy?"

"Yes."

"The one with the Diamond," I breathed.

"Sarah, how do you know about this?"

I frowned. "What, the Diamond? I read about gems."

Calleigh eyed me cautiously. "You're not still upset about the gem test, are you?"

"No," I replied. I wasn't sure if I was being truthful. "I was just curious."

Calleigh's face lit up again. "I'm glad to hear that, sweetie. I'll have to get going 'cause I have an assignment to turn in, but yeah. Keep up the spirit, Sarah. I'll talk to you soon. Tell me about the book. Princess Rena."

With that, Calleigh bounced away.

That was odd, I thought. I had never seen Calleigh that distracted. I could not shake off the strange feeling that she was hiding something as I continued down the hallway into Susan Grebler's boring classroom.

I paid another visit to the library the following day, this time to rummage through the history section. I found what I was looking for. I tucked the book under my arms and hurried home.

The History of the Monarchs

I recognized quite a number of details from the fairy tale. Queen Serena did have an endeared childhood friend, whose name was indeed Harvey. She did travel the world in an attempt to avenge his death. She also had a rumored lover, Thomas the Traveler. Nothing was known about him, except that he was dressed peculiarly.

It turned out, however, that the story wasn't entirely historically accurate. *Of course*, I thought. *I didn't think she would have fought a dragon.* The details of her travels were also not known, making most of the events written in the book fictitious. Tales of her battles with villainous creatures were told from time to time, but as far as we knew they had been spun from peoples' imaginations. There were artworks depicting the queen face to face with a scrawny old woman, though, which seemed to have been inspired by stories told verbally around the time of her death. Nothing more was known about these artworks or the stories that bore these inspirations.

It was true, however, that she'd heard the news of her father's death during her campaign. She returned to the palace to rule for another fifteen years. Her father, King Elieser, had been heavily influenced by modern politics; he had written a constitution, and laid a foundation for a systematic leadership. Serena, inspired by this, gathered her subjects and organized something called the Cabinet pro tem, which would take effect in her absence. Serena then nominated her true friend and subject Alfred Kirkland to lead the Cabinet pro tem on the event of her death. Then she went off on her journey, leaving the Cabinet in leadership. It could, by the decree declared upon establishment, be overridden at any time by the queen herself, but it never was, as Serena died shortly after. The Cabinet pro tem then evolved into the Cabinet of Enrici.

Not much was known about her death, just as not much was known about her truest friend's death. Some said she was deranged, and some said evil did lurk in the corners of the world that had so cruelly taken her friend. I could not shake off the feeling that her campaign was more than personal, but there was nothing that supported or denied my theories, nor anything that told of whom she was battling. The news of her death had come as a message from one of the knights that had served her. The contents had been lost from the archive, but it was rumored that the cause of her death had been a stab wound to the chest.

I looked down and realized I'd been rolling the corner of the page between my fingers, and hastily straightened it out. Powdery paper dust came off on my fingers. *It was almost as if she was anticipating her own death.* I rubbed my fingers on my chin. But surely her objective wouldn't have been to die in vain. She had set off to avenge her friend, and meant to succeed. If they were that powerful and she knew it well, shouldn't she have done more to prepare? Shouldn't she have at least organized a party of some sort, ensured that the work would go on well after her death? Or did she? Did someone carry on the legacy and honor Harvey? Was her own death, by chance, part of the plan?

I looked down and realized I'd been rolling the corner of the page between my fingers again, and closed the book. Something kept nagging me at the back of the head, and I couldn't ignore the thought that this book was hiding something. It seemed it had ended curtly for some unknown reason, and its author never had the chance to articulate the whole story—

After all, who was it that killed the vengeful queen so swiftly and easily?

The subject of the unknown killer stayed in my head all the while during the following days, but I couldn't find much more on the monarch or her schemes. I'd gone through eight books, but little was written about the queen's death. School slowly crept into the center of my life, becoming the main focus once again; I spent my days taking care of homework after homework that was dumped in my hands, resenting that at some point in the middle of the school year, teachers seemed to forget you took multiple classes. All the work kept me occupied, and for quite a while I didn't get another chance to go back to the library in Vanna Daya.

It came as a fresh surprise, therefore, when Calleigh stopped me in the middle of the hall one day.

"Hey, what's up?" I asked casually, hoping there wouldn't be an eternal discourse about something she took interest in lately. The response that came out of her, however, was something I'd least expected:

"Sarah, I found something. About Princess Rena."

I caught my breath. "What about it?"

Calleigh took a step toward me and looked swiftly around, which with her petite build and vigorous manner turned into an exaggerated gag.

"See me after school. I have a book you might want to take a look at."

I met her later at Vanna Daya, where she handed me a single volume.

"Not a lot of things are known about Queen Serena," Calleigh began. "Even though she was the last to rule. You'd naturally expect more information on her than any of her precursors. But there isn't."

"There isn't a detailed record of her death," I said matter-of-factly.

"No." Calleigh gulped. "But there's this."

I looked down at the book Calleigh pointed to. The volume had been well tended to. It looked almost untouched, as if it had been unpopular all its life. I carefully wrapped my hands around it, and flipped open the front page.

Petite Histoire
On the Kingdom of Enrici

Compiled by Ben Rushmore

"Look into the chapter about Serena," Calleigh suggested. "It might not be all the information you wanted, but it's the only thing I could find that gives more information on Serena's death."

My heart leapt. I reached for the book with what must have been sparkling eyes, but Calleigh pulled back.

"There's one thing I'd like you to know, though, Sarah."

I looked at her. "Hmm?"

"If this information is being kept secret, there's probably a reason. I think you should stay away from this subject, Sarah."

I frowned. It was very unlike Calleigh to dismiss a topic, and further to do it with a solemn face. Something inside me screamed that her knowledge on this subject didn't end here, but at the same time I was sure that this was all I could get out of her.

That night I sat wrapped in blankets, peering into the volume Calleigh had lent me. The book was written in a witty voice, covering little rumors about Enrica's heirs, stories and anecdotes from all the corners of the discreet kingdom of shapeshifters. I sat reading through the chapters, until my eyes caught something of interest:

> The death of Queen Serena had come a sudden blow. Close to no account remains of what had happened, or what had killed her. It was rumored, however, that the late queen had been killed by pirates, on an island near the coasts of Iceland.
>
> A brigantine known as the *Ranger*, which had been the flagship of the notorious pirate Charles Vane in the 1700s, was known to have met a tragic fate in the coasts of Columbia. However, it has been rumored that a vessel identical to the wrecked brigantine had been found on the shores where the queen had died. The brigantine was discovered displaying two battered flags flown by Vane—a black pirate flag and the English flag, and a third flag with the image of an upside-down dagger.

Pirates? I questioned. Nowhere in the text was word of a mysterious woman, only talk of Vane's ship which went on for another half a page. It was something else, however, that made me sure that this was somehow relevant to the truth. With thick charcoal pencil, the parts following the description of the three flags had been crossed out. It wasn't all—I squinted to find a jagged handwritten note between the lines; under the word *pirates*, someone had written with shaky hands:

THE DEVIL'S LADY

I had chance to talk to Calleigh only a couple days later. I found her sitting in front of the easel in the living room, focused on a swirl of colors. I returned the volume into her hand, thanking her for lending it to me. Calleigh seemed cheerful, and oddly comfortable, unlike the last time I'd seen her. When she went back to painting, her eyebrows almost a line on her forehead, I seized the chance to ask a question.

"By the way, has anyone borrowed the book before me?" I asked.

Calleigh looked at me. "No, I don't think so," she replied. "Probably not for a couple decades, at least. We don't have any record of it, this book's not even listed in the library. It's been sitting in the corner with some damaged volumes."

Interesting, I thought to myself. "That's funny."

Later that evening I typed the alias into the search bar for the hundredth time, but nothing turned up. The mystery of the unexplained death of the queen had hit a dead end with only a childish nickname. With a sigh, I pushed the idea into a corner of my mind along with the idea of gems.

That night, for the first time in a week, I went hunting. It was like the old days, before Carlos, before Lillian. *Maybe I* was *back in the old days,* I thought suddenly with a pang in my chest. Maybe it had all gone back to before Carlos. Before Lillian. I closed my eyes and thought back to all those little friendships that had ended as abruptly as they'd begun, to Madison's hurt eyes as she walked away. The woods were grand and silent, and I was alone. Excruciatingly alone.

Almost habitually I began to scan the area. I started at the little glade where Lillian would transform every night, and the clearing I'd helped Carlos change back. And the lake. The lakeside was sorely empty without him. The scent was clear, no wolf, no panther, but in the distance I caught a whiff of prey in the air. It was an elk. My lioness instincts clicked in, and any thought of hunting partners melted swiftly away. I set out in search of the elk.

It wasn't long till I glimpsed its sleek body in the distance. My ears twitched, and whiskers shuddered. I crouched low in the bushes. The moon glided a short arc, and finally the grazer was distracted. I calculated one last time before I dove into the chase. The elk took off, and began to sprint to-ward the woods—but I would not let it disappear behind those curtains. I took off after, slowly closing the gap. My thighs began to burn and my lungs felt like they would burst. When I got close enough, I lunged, firmly placing my paws on its back as I readied to deliver the coup de grace. But things did not go as well as I'd planned. The elk's hooves slid on the ground, sending clouds of dirt everywhere, and it hopped onto its front legs, hunching up to mule-kick me hard in the flank. I fell back, doubled over in pain.

I'd lost deers, I'd lost rabbits. Many animals had escaped my grasp but never once have I been kicked by an elk. I grumbled, my ribs searing terribly, as I watched the elk dart into the trees and out of sight. *Damn*, I cursed. I rolled onto my feet and changed. A glaring pain shot from my ribs as I landed from the spin. I dragged myself laboriously to the edge of the woods, plunked down underneath a tree, and rested my head on the bark. My eyes watered. I rolled up my shirt to find that my side was beginning to turn a nasty shade of blue, and tried to press my hand on it to stop the bruising. I was met by a sharp, blinding pain. I winced.

"*Owww*," I whimpered.

I buried my face in my hands. Heat rushed to my eyes, and my face wrinkled in anguish. I began to sniffle. I think it was some minutes, perhaps an hour, until an image of Lillian popped into my head. In my mind's eye I could see the girl standing with her arms crossed, dressed up in her usual black leather jacket and boots. *What the hell are you doing, Sarah? Are you going to curl up here and die?*—I could hear her say. I stopped crying and smiled pathetically as the husky voice echoed in my head. I sniffed and pulled myself up to go home.

I didn't hunt for a few days following that day. It hurt even to walk, and I couldn't sleep on my side. It was a bad bruise—hopefully I hadn't broken anything—and I winced every time I saw the screaming purple spot in the mirror.

I went again in a few days as the pain got bearable. But I didn't end up catching anything, and the more I spent time in those woods alone, the more

I began to think about Carlos. I had never liked not knowing things, and it drove me insane to have my hunting partner ignore me without knowing why. I stomped home, and the following morning stomped directly to the ice rink. I'd heard the hockey team had morning practice occasionally. I was hoping it would be today.

And yes, I was lucky.

I seated myself, arms crossed, in the front row of the spectators' seats.

The team was doing some sort of exercise, dribbling pucks through lines drawn on the ice with a marker. The coach was shouting some remarks from the benches: *Newman! Lynch! Faster! Brand! Your aim is shit! Pierce! Do you think AT ALL?* I saw Carlos shooting through the ice in the middle. He was certainly fast. He seemed quite often to make the wrong calculations, however; I sat watching as Carlos sent the puck flying out to the wall, and the coach let out an irritated holler.

Somewhen in the middle, Carlos glimpsed me. He did a double-take, only to turn away and ignore me. I kept myself from walking onto the ice, for I knew that would end bad in many ways; instead, I waited until the coach called for a five. Carlos didn't come toward me, as I thought he would—instead he skated off to the far corner where he stood talking to his teammates, chugging a bottle of water.

"*Ha,*" I scoffed.

I pulled myself up. I was losing my mind. I began to head over to the gate when I saw a boy—I recognized him, his name was Nathan Lynch—talk to Carlos, shooting a glance my way. The boy soon began to skate over to where I was. I waited with the last bit of patience I had until he got to my end and braked loudly, spewing ground ice everywhere.

"Hello," he greeted, flashing a big, mocking grin. "How can I help you?"

Nathan Lynch was the hockey team captain, a senior; he was this flamboyant jackass, a cheesy flirt, the kind of obnoxious teenager to fly around the hall and bump into everyone half the time, slide into a corner to make out with girls the other half. Although I most obviously despised him, at this moment I could not be more grateful.

"I need to talk to Carlos," I said calmly.

Lynch shot me a look, as if to say something along the lines of, '*Interesting.*' I ignored him.

"I'll bring him over, but you owe me a kiss," Lynch whispered, a playful smirk in his face.

A wire snapped in my head, and without thought I pulled off one of my shoes and raised it to my head. "Shut up or *this* is what's going to be kissing you," I snarled.

"Whoa, whoa, whoa, easy," rapped an astonished Lynch.

"Now bring me Carlos," I commanded.

The boy zipped his mouth with an awkward smile and at last strode off to the other side of the rink. I waited, arms crossed, breathing heat from my flared nostrils. There was a short conversation before the two, and a quick glance from Carlos, before a reluctant Carlos headed over, his helmet off and his hair drenched in sweat.

"You wanted to talk to me," said Carlos uneagerly.

"I can't take this anymore. You're telling me, or we're never doing that again. *Ever,*" I snapped.

Carlos sighed and closed his eyes. He bit his lip until a part of it went white. He stood frozen awhile, contemplating, before he spoke up.

"Fine," Carlos said finally. "Meet me in front of your house tonight."

Night came, and I snuck out the front door. I found Carlos sitting on the hood of his Subaru. He welcomed me with a stiff smile, opening the passenger door for me. I had an endless lot of questions, but I decided to save them for another moment. I hopped on.

Without a word, Carlos softly pressed down on the clutch and turned the key. The engine hummed to life in the silence of the night.

"You got to promise me something, Sarah," he said, keeping his eye on the stick, pushing it into first gear.

"*What's going on, Carlos?*" I demanded finally. My voice had come out a lot less harsh than I'd wanted it to be. I cleared my throat.

Carlos pushed the gear back to neutral and turned to face me.

"Just promise me. Whatever happens, don't be surprised."

I looked back at him, bewildered. "I can't promise that. I don't even know what it's going to be."

Carlos sighed and ruffled his hair with his hand. "Just... just try. Or pretend. And don't ask me why. Don't say anything."

I wrinkled my brows. "I'll try."

"Thanks."

We drove in awkward silence to the park, and headed in awkward silence to the lake. There, Carlos stood before me, looking somewhat nervous.

"Now what is this?" I demanded.

Carlos brought a finger to his lips. "Shh. You promised me you won't say anything."

I crossed my arms in front of me. "Fine," I said. "I won't say anything else."

A nightjar churred in the distance. Carlos looked around nervously, unlike the many times he'd stood at this very spot and changed—a parading jump, a boisterous twirl high up in the air—and took a deep breath that seemed never to end. Then he closed his eyes, took off from the ground, and changed.

I frowned, trying to make sense of what he was even thinking. A chocolate-brown panther stood before me with a quizzical look on his face. The panther paced around in a circle, staring at his feet; I raised an eyebrow as the cat did a full circle and stood in front of me again, his eyes darting between me and his own paws.

He then changed back. It seemed I wasn't the only one confused; the expression on his face was a mixture of puzzlement and relief.

"I thought something was going to happen," he muttered.

I looked at him, baffled. "Is this some kind of joke?" I snapped.

"No, no," Carlos replied quickly. "I really thought... I had this weird, *feeling*, that something would go wrong when I change."

"And it didn't," I said.

"No."

"So you avoided me for nothing."

Carlos sighed. "It wasn't for nothing," he said. "I was sure something was going to go wrong. And um... I wanted to avoid changing altogether."

"This makes no sense," I breathed.

Carlos sighed and rubbed his eyes with both his hands. "I know. I'll tell you more about it sometime. When I know for sure that... well, you know."

I frowned. "No, I don't."

"You promised me you won't ask. I'll tell you in time."

I opened my mouth to retort, but thought of Madison. Something throbbed in my chest. Well, she could have trusted me. I had a reason. Maybe he did as well. It could take weeks, months, perhaps even years—but someday I would find out. He would tell me when he could.

"Okay," I managed to say.

Carlos peered at me. "Do you believe me?"

"I'll... try to," I replied.

Carlos didn't say anything else. Instead, he put his arms up into the air.

"What?" I said again, looking quizzically at Carlos, who was standing there like a scarecrow with his arms open.

"Come here. Give me a hug."

I can't say why, but it nudged me into a sudden realization that I'd been very, very tired. I wanted nothing but to be in my own room, lying in my own bed, staring at the ceiling with not a thought in my head. I retreated from him and folded my arms.

"You ignored me for *days*," I pointed out with a sigh.

"So you won't?" Carlos asked softly.

I looked at him a while, trying to decide what to say. Nothing made sense these days. Come to think of it, nothing had made sense since the day I changed in the basement. I let out a weary laugh, thinking back to when I thought Lillian was trying to kill me. Maybe I just needed a break. From hunting, from being gemless, from being what I am. From everything.

"Let's call it a day," I said at last.

"Carlos, I think I'll take the bus home tonight." I said as we headed down the hills.

"It's late. I'll drive you," Carlos said.

"No I really don't... it's fine," I replied.

"I'll at least walk you to the bus stop," Carlos insisted.

I sighed. "All right."

We walked in silence. The night was quiet. There wasn't any traffic on the road. It had rained in the afternoon, and the road was glistening softly. Only the streetlamps gave off an aureate glow, growing sparser as we turned away from the bigger streets.

"Sarah," Carlos called softly. I turned to look at him.

"I did avoid you." His eyes were earnest. "Truth is..." he trailed off, his voice cracking drily. He swallowed before he continued: "Truth is, I was scared of losing you. I thought that when I changed... something would happen that you wouldn't want to see."

"This... still doesn't make any sense, you know," I said with a sigh. "But I promised you I won't ask about this."

Carlos gazed at me without another word.

"What?" I demanded, unable to bear the silence between us.

"I... want to know you believe me," Carlos said softly.

I was tempted to say I already told him, but stopped. Carlos was a tall, broad-shouldered figure, who could probably take me in one arm with effortless ease. But at this moment he seemed, well, not small, but *breakable*. I thought of Madi's cold stare, and of the solitude of carrying a truth I couldn't tell. I didn't know what it was he was keeping from me, but he was my hunting partner. If he needed someone to believe him, I could be that someone.

I took a small step toward the boy. There was hardly a lamplight in sight, but behind him spread a curtain of millions of stars. Curtained softly by the shadows his brows cast, his eyes looked afraid, and his lips were pursed nervously—it was as though he were shaking alone behind a wall. Before I could stop myself, I reached for his face and rested my hand on his cheek. He was warm.

"I do," I replied.

A long sigh escaped Carlos' lips, followed by a mellow smile.

"Am I still not getting the hug?"

A wearily smile made its way onto my face. I stepped forward to give him a hug. Carlos wrapped his arms close around my neck, burying his face in my hair.

"So annoying," I muttered under my breath.

"What?" Carlos chuckled, letting go to look into my face.

"Nothing, jackass," I whispered, a weak smile forming at my lips. *It's just that... I realize now, that I kind of missed you.*

The bus rolled in. I waved to Carlos and hopped on, exhausted, and rested my head on a damp, cold window. I dozed off until the bus stopped a couple blocks from home, and walked wearily until I got to my doorsteps.

Oh no.

I froze in place, for standing in the doorway with her arms crossed was my mother, Dr. Holly Verona.

I opened my mouth to speak. Nothing came out. I cleared my throat and tried again.

"Mom, I'm really sorry, I didn't..."

"*What do you think you're doing?*" Mom demanded harshly.

"I..." I desperately rummaged my head, trying to find something to say.

"I want to know everything. Why you sneaked out at night, what you were doing out at four in the morning."

"I was..." I began, trying desperately to think of something that would divert her attention from what I was actually doing. "I was at my friend's house, doing drugs and watching porn," I lied.

Mom raised an eyebrow.

Obviously that wasn't believable. I tried again.

"Angela and Nakato had a fight, and we needed to talk about it."

"At four in the morning?"

I began to study the patterns on the floor as if they could somehow save me.

"We couldn't risk the team falling apart," I began, wondering if she would buy the story. "We can't lose either of them."

"And this was whose idea?"

My head began to spin. "Mine," I said.

Mom sighed. She seemed to take it; not that it was something she'd be happy with.

"I'm not having this. You're grounded. No 'talks', no friends, no practice."

"*What?*" I retorted. "But we're playing Milford in two weeks."

Her eyes were stone cold. I fell silent.

"And I'm going to make sure you don't sneak out at night," Mom said sternly.

I felt my heart sink. "Mom, it's the semifinal. They can't do it without me."
"No, and that's final. Now go to your room. Go to bed," She ordered.

I sat staring at the ceiling up in my room, my face burning, my limbs aching, my mind still in disbelief. The silence pierced my ears, and I closed my eyes and swallowed to chase it away.

My phone dinged a while later, and I raised it reluctantly to my face.

`did u get home?`

It was Carlos.

`Yeah`, I replied.

`I got busted. Can't make it from tomorrow`, I typed.

Crap, I cursed, burying my face in my pillow.

It was needless to go on about the ways my life was terrible. I couldn't look straight at my mom's stern face without a swirl of mixed feelings, probably something along the lines of guilt and irritation. I had tried to explain to Angela that I had been grounded, which she didn't seem to comprehend. She gave me until the final practice match to show up, which of course I couldn't make. I spent the afternoon crying the day I lost my place on the team. Nothing seemed to be working out.

I loved being on the team. I stared wistfully at my uniform hanging on the doorknob. It was colored a light, toned down teal, with 10, VERONA written over the back in white. I was proud of it, everything from my number to the crest on the chest depicting the goddess of war, underneath which in bold print was labeled ATHENA. I guess I really had to say goodbye to all that, just like this. This was stupid.

And as for what Mom said, she did make sure I could not sneak out. She made sure to come home early to sit at her study. Every night, she dragged her mattress down by the front door—and slept there. I felt terrible.

I came to terms with it soon. I told Carlos to go hunting by himself. He was reluctant, but after a few days he seemed to miss it—and when I told him he could perhaps send updates to me over text, he decided to go. I snuggled in bed that night, my phone beside me. I could stay up reading while he hunted.

I had, in a box kept under the bed, a set of books I'd borrowed from the library at Vanna Daya. I spilled them onto my bed. *Gems.* No, I wasn't going to dwell on gems. *The Physics of Enrici.* I would be interested, but tonight I was hoping, somehow, to get lucky and find out more about the queen's mysterious killer.

History of Enrici

I reached for the book. It was one of those heavy, leather-bound books you'd find at the back of the library. It didn't look like a lot of people went looking for it. Between the pages there was a checkout card; the orange slip had faded to apricot in the edges, but the list of names was short, the last entry being from eight years ago. I flipped carefully through, pausing briefly at a black and white image of a cave painting.

Magura Cave painting, Northwest Bulgaria. I'd seen it often in history textbooks, but never really paid close attention. The painting was of a crowd of dancing men and ducks, drawn in thick paint on what looked like a crumbling rock wall. Somewhere to the middle was a whirlwind, to the left of a man with a tail protruding from his rear. There was another dust devil on his right, along with a group of dancing men, ducks, and some creatures I could not quite name.

The caption read:

> The Magura Cave paintings, very well known to the general public as depictions of ceremonial and religious events from the Paleolithic and Neolithic era, are in fact among the very first representations of prehistoric Enricus existence.

I took a closer look. The top section had two swirling lines on either side of a person. It seemed the bottom half of the painting was describing an Enricus' human form and animal form—with funny figures in the middle that seemed not quite human, nor distinctly a type of animal. It all made sense. I gasped as I traced a finger along the line of the drawings, the intricately painted figures, the stretched neck of the creature on the far right.

A buzz from my phone snapped my attention from the book into reality. I looked, to find a text from Carlos.

hey i just got here. will tell u when i catch something

I smiled.

Remember not to strike too fast, I replied.

The phone buzzed again. My hands were on the keypad, already preparing to type something.

will do :)

I smiled again. Finding nothing good to say, however, I let go of the phone and turned back to the book.

I turned to the page about the Enrican Civil War. In the fifteenth century, there had been a war between Enrica's forces and those who wanted to take over the monarchy. The latter had, in an attempt to overthrow Enrica, took to extreme means, and allied with dangerous forces.

Were these the pirates? Would one of them be the Devil's Lady? I scribbled a note on the edge of my physics notebook, along with a bunch of question marks. It seemed the book was written unnecessarily vaguely, like everything had been about Serena's death. I thought back to what Calleigh had said earlier. What was this about pirates, and why did it need to be written in the vaguest way possible?

Whatever they were, I'd found further down that page, the dark forces had different motives than that of the Enrici. They had no more than used the Enrici, and as their plans failed, slaughtered many—almost half—of their allies. Enrica did not take this. She formed a powerful army; she wiped out the enemies, along with the Enrici who had allied with them. She and her son Percival, who was later crowned the second monarch, continued to hunt down the remaining enemies, reducing their figures until they were vastly outnumbered. The kingdom of Enrici then entered a peaceful phase.

I pondered. *If it really was the case, why aren't they telling us? Why isn't there a clear answer on who they were, or if they were indeed the same people who killed Serena?*

The phone buzzed again, breaking me out from my chain of thoughts. It was another text from Carlos.

`had a rabbit for dinner ;)`

I smiled.

`I knew it.` I replied.

I stared at the screen. It was three in the morning. I closed the book and stacked up the rest to put them back in their place under the bed. My eyes were hot and dry from all the reading; I closed them and lay flat on my back.

Minutes passed, and the phone didn't buzz—I wondered what he was doing. By now he would probably be content with his meal, would perhaps be on his way down to the edge of the woods. We'd both had those fake employee cards, but we preferred sneaking in through the side. It wasn't just faster. It was exciting. It reminded me of childhood, of all the sneaky little things I used to do. I wondered if it was the same for Carlos, if he, amidst the nightmares, had a memory he cherished. With a little pang in my heart I hoped he did; a smile crept up my lips when I thought of a toddler Carlos slipping through a hole in the fence to someplace he shouldn't be.

The phone buzzed again. I jumped. I flipped it over at once, to find a message from Carlos:

`going down now.`

Well, true. He would have to change each time he wanted to text me updates. It's not that I expected him to write me the whole time or something—

`wish u were here.`

I paused. Something fluttered in my stomach, and I grabbed the glass of water from my bedside table to chug it down.

`I wish I wa`
`I wish I`
`I wish`

```
I wi
I
```

My fingers hovered over the keyboard for a while, before replying with a colon and parenthesis.

Several days passed. I stayed home each night, getting text updates from Carlos. He'd caught a couple bunnies, and once even a deer. I, on the other hand, had been doing a lot of reading in bed.

It was another one of those days. I'd been reading about Miranda, the third monarch of the Kingdom. I recalled what I'd read about her: she was the one to discover 'Alpha Enrica', which was later renamed the 'Alpha Enrican Highlands'. There she'd built a small settlement, which she later expanded and declared the capital. The book told tales of her escapades, and slipped in little details about her here and there. It was said she was a skilled horse rider—and that she'd often worn green dresses. The book chronicled her journey up north with hundreds of cavalry, painting their route on archaic maps.

I looked up from the book. The image of my room now felt like the strange reality, and the worlds in the book the ordinary one. Images of palaces, folds in stars of higher dimension, and a force of armed men in iron armor danced around as I closed my eyes—and among them emerged a pirate ship, great and old and mysterious, bearing a flag of an upside-down dagger. And yet it wasn't the last image to swim in my sea of thoughts. I had brought into the frame, for some reason, images of me and Carlos hunting together. Those images pushed all the other things away and out of the frame, first Miranda, then the pirate ship—and filled my head, with sounds of padded footsteps, cackling laughter, and flashes of eyes. A sensation of longing swept past me. I missed hunting with him.

Right then the phone buzzed, and I hastily picked it up from my lap. It was Carlos.

```
look out the window.
```

The window? I tiptoed to the window, pulled back the blinds and cracked it open.

Carlos had his car parked outside the yard—and was sitting on the hood, looking up at me with a smile.

"*What are you doing here?*" I whispered.

Carlos took out his phone from his pocket and typed something into it. My phone buzzed again. I flipped it open to check the message.

sneaking you out.

"What? *How?*" I whispered at him, back at the window.

Carlos cast a quick look around before he whispered: "Jump. I'll catch you."

"You can't catch me from *there*, you'd need to get inside—" I began to whisper, but to my horror, Carlos glanced around once more at the empty road and changed. The panther then leapt over the fence and into the yard, and spun, once again, into his familiar figure.

Carlos stood there, right under the windowsill. The moon touched the tips of his tousled hair, giving it silvery highlights. He beamed up at me.

"I got you," he whispered.

"*Are you insane?*" I whispered back. "If anyone sees you you're dead."

"And they didn't," Carlos retorted with a grin. "Come on, jump."

I rolled my eyes. This was insanity at its finest. My mind was invited once again to the delicious idea of running through those woods again, of dipping my feet in the lake, tasting the bubbling spirit of night against my skin—

I carefully opened the window wide, and pulled myself up onto the windowsill. Carlos held his arms out and nodded. *Oh, no, I'm not doing that,* I thought. *Instead I'm doing* this.

I jumped.

"Or that," whispered a confused Carlos with a shrug, as he watched me fall on all four of my feet.

I curled up my lips into a feline smile. I had to say, that was for sure an impressive transformation.

"I can see that you don't trust my reflexes," Carlos added in a disgruntled voice.

I quickly changed back and stood smugly in front of him.

"I do. It's just not every day that I feel brave enough to do this," I said indignantly.

A big smile crept up his face, and then mine. Carlos pulled me in into a tight hug, until my feet dangled inches above the ground. I squeezed him, burying my face in his hood.

He finally set me back down on my feet, and gazed into my eyes with a huge grin. It was with a sweet little ball of warmth in my chest that I realized how much I'd missed this, that little smile we exchanged before we stormed off into the night like partners in crime. I'd missed the way his softly freckled nose would crinkle as his smile widened—it usually meant we were heading for an adventure.

"It's so good to do this again," Carlos said.

"Shh," I whispered. "We have time for this in the park. We're not done sneaking out."

"Oh, right," Carlos whispered. "Wanna jump over that fence?"

I smiled. "Sure."

And we did.

It was wonderful. We drove to the edge of the park. We snuck in like we always did; then sprinted up the woods, dodging trees and leaping over deadfalls as we raced. We drank by the lake, splashing water at each other with our paws. Then we lay on the grass, looking up at the clear night sky, the fresh grass pleasant and cool underneath our bodies.

"I missed this," I whispered.

"Well, I made it happen," Carlos said smugly.

I turned to look at him. The rays from the moon were soft and gentle on his cheeks, lighting up his contours in a pleasant way. I had to admit, he was good looking. His lashes were longer and thicker than mine, and for a moment I was jealous.

"You know, Sarah," Carlos began, turning to look at me. I turned and stared once more at the stars.

"Hmm," I answered.

"Have I ever told you this," Carlos asked softly.

"Tell me what," I asked.

"You are... really, you are..."

"A great hunter?"

Carlos chuckled. "That, too, but..."

"Annoying?"

"No, god no. I can't find the right word."

"I'm out of ideas," I said. The world had gone silent, and only our voices streaked the void.

"Bright," Carlos said, his eyebrows furrowed as if he weren't quite satisfied with the choice of word.

"I just wanted you to know..." he said, his voice barely above a whisper. "I don't care that you don't have a gem. And if anyone cares, they should go in the gutter. Sarah, *you* are the gem."

A fuzz of warmth spread through my chest. I turned to look at him, and for a moment our eyes met—it was a little exchange of so many unspoken words, words we had managed to package into the quickest of glances in the many nights we'd hunted together.

Chapter 7
The Fair

"What in the world is the fair?" I asked finally.

It was something I'd heard about a million times starting the previous week. All they seemed to talk about was the fair. Chase and Andrew opened their mouths and closed it again, then threw Calleigh a quick glance. I realized what I'd done, but there was no force quit button to the Calleigh machine.

"Thought you'd never ask, Sarah," Calleigh began. Out the corner of my eyes I could see Chase do a facepalm.

"So the fair is one of the biggest events of the year. They gather up young Enrici, from around the whole state, and there's gonna be exhibitions, shows, contests, booths, games... all kinds of stuff. We used to participate in one of those booths but not this year, 'cause I was busy prepping for art school. But of course I'm going to pay a visit, and *you, have, to, come.* They also have a banquet with the best dessert. Last year they had this huge cake, the icing was this hard buttercream in all these unicorn colors. I will never forget that cake. In fact I tried to replicate the cake the day after—"

I cleared my throat. "Uh... Calleigh?"

"Yes?" Calleigh paused, and looked innocently at me, batting her eyelashes. I groaned internally.

"So what are the exhibitions about?" I asked, feeling bad I'd interrupted her.

"Usually skills and tactics, and new discoveries," Calleigh looked at me a while before adding quietly: "This year the main theme is gems."

An unpleasant swirl passed through my stomach. Calleigh seemed to notice, and quickly changed the subject.

"Meanwhile you can help me choose a dress. See, I have this purple one with ribbons... come on, I'll show you."

"Calleigh," I stopped her. "It's okay."

Calleigh looked at me with puppy eyes. "It's... okay?"

"I meant I'm okay," I replied quickly, realizing I had worded things weirdly. "I could give it a look, sure..." I added reluctantly.

Calleigh's eyes gleamed again.

School went on. I wasn't grounded for long, and soon I could go back to Vanna Daya—it also meant I could go to the fair, perhaps see what all the excitement was about—but it had not been without cost. It had, for the biggest part, lost me my place in the soccer team for missing practice. One day I saw Angela stride down the hall, her mile-long legs covering twice the distance of a regular person with each step—and I thought for a second that we had locked eyes, only for her to turn away coldly. I felt a knot form in my throat.

The world, however, kept on turning. The hallways were filled with what seemed like meaningless chatter; food, homework, gossip, plans for the night, impressively chaotic and utterly useless quotes—"*Do you think the reason butt cracks are vertical and not horizontal is so they wouldn't clap like castanets every time we run?*"—and I quietly carried myself through all that nonsense, functioning not quite well but passably, getting things done even if at the last minute.

One lunchtime I passed by the football field, where I spotted Madison by herself stretching in the corner. She stopped in the middle and plunked down on the grass, nudging the ball sullenly with her feet. I couldn't see her face from where I was standing, but could well picture what expression her face would bear—and a pang went through my chest. I felt a sudden urge to run to her and tell her everything, that I could turn into a lioness, that the reason I'd not been myself was because I'd been staying up every night hunting. I tried to imagine her face when I blurted out those words to her. I could see her doe eyes wide in shock, staring back at me without a word. No, now was not the time. I could not say if the time would ever come.

A sudden veil of solitude seemed to wrap itself around me as I thought of all the people I could not tell this to. I pictured the faces of my own mother and father, their smiles, the warmest smiles I've known. My stomach knotted. I felt a cold, dank embrace on my shoulders, the whisper of a vast loneliness I'd never yet known. Here I stood, estranged from the world of humans, and yet also incomplete as an Enricus. One day I felt all right, but another day not quite—and on those days it seemed evident that I was on my own.

Soon I burst out from my little bubble as I saw Madison kick her ball into the floodlight, where it jammed hopelessly between the lamps. Madison let out a curse, swinging her fist in the air. I stared helplessly as she plunked down on the grass, presumably in tears. My chest throbbed. I knew exactly how much she cherished that ball. It was a replica from the '08 World Cup; I remembered when she brought it to school, a proud smile on her face, and flicked it into the air in a graceful arc. For a moment she could have been in a world cup promo video.

Not long ago we were the best of friends. We talked about everything, giggled about, well, more than everything. But things had changed. We simply could not help each other.

But in a way we could, I said to myself, as I ran to the field much later that day. The place was empty. With a racing heart I did something risky. I took off into the air, twirling into a magnificent swirl of dust—and knocked, with a blow from my heavy paws, Madison's cherished ball off the notch.

The last couple months had changed my life, and it had made irreversible tears in it. But as I tiptoed to Madison's locker a while later and placed her ball down in front of it, I felt a tiny little part of it heal.

It was the day of the fair. I followed an excited Calleigh through the gates of a giant marble building. It was called the Regent's Convention Center, owned by Halliday Corp. I drew a breath as a giant hall opened before me. The hall was decorated with ribbons of all colors; on the sides were statues of tigers, bears, buffaloes, whales and countless more animals, sculpted impressionistically with bronze strips. Calleigh pranced inside ahead of me, her footsteps almost a dance. She had chosen the purple dress with ribbons; the other option had been a calmer brown dress with black collars, but Calleigh seemed in love with the wilder one. I had disagreed at first—but seeing Calleigh twirl with amethyst ribbons flailing behind her, I realized that she looked better with a smile.

Lillian had not been interested in coming in the first place, and Chase and Andrew had a match to prepare for. The only ones to come with me were Calleigh and Carlos. Calleigh led the two of us through a heavy door to an auditorium, full and bubbling with chatter. It seemed that this hall was more than full with boys and girls around my age.

Calleigh smiled and waved a number of times while we ploughed through the swarm. I took a middle-row seat, and Calleigh and Carlos took seats next to mine. Soon the hall darkened, and the chatter died down.

A pinlight clicked on, and I gasped as an elephant emerged from behind the curtains and onto the stage. An applause erupted, and the elephant ambled to the center of the stage, letting out a boisterous toot, then twirled in a flutter of gold beams into a brawny young man. A loud applause erupted from the hall.

"Hello, my favorite people," the man cried. The crowd seemed to love him.

"Loren Mayer here. Welcome back to the Fair 2010, it's going to be the best there's ever been, I can promise you. You see—Jim and I," he nodded toward an elderly man sitting on the front row, who nodded and smiled, "wanted to make today the best day of your life so far, so we put a lot of thought into it, day and night. One morning Jim calls me, and he goes, hey, Loren, I have an idea. And I go, yeah, what's that? And this man straight up goes, 'a chocolate fondue.'"

A light laughter came from the crowd.

"And I'm all, what do you mean, Jim, we do chocolate fondues every year. And Jim goes, no, buddy, you're gonna want to see this. And I walk into the hall and see—" he pointed ahead, and the crowd turned to face— "—that."

Only then did I notice the giant marble fountain in the center of the room. It looked brand new, gleaming elegantly like a Renaissance sculpture, embellished with hundreds of tiny animals around the edges. But it was empty. Nothing was coming out of it. I peered curiously at it, as did hundreds of eyes. The crowd let out a little burst of laughter in seeing the empty fountain.

Loren began to wave his arms, and the crowd laughed again. He continued to move his arms about, comically, as if he were practicing telekinesis. The laughter got louder and soon turned to cheers as the fountain hummed to life and chocolate began to run down in glossy arcs.

"Anyways, yes, that thing was freshly built exclusively for that purpose. We've never, you know, used it as an *actual* fountain, so you don't have to worry. It's a chocolate fondue. That's all it is. Now when do we get to try it? At the banquet, which is going to be in—" he looked at his watch, "—about an hour."

"So back to the subject of the fair. As you all know this year's theme is gems. We have a hundred and twenty teams participating today in the gem exhibition, and there's going to be an evening of games, and a set of performances which," the host paused dramatically, "I can assure you *none of you* has ever seen before."

The introduction went on for quite a while. I paid more attention to the whispers from the boys in front, about a game that was going to take place tonight at the courtyard. It was, to borrow their words, legendary.

Loren soon wrapped up, but no one rose from their seats. In a lollopy jog the man disappeared offstage—and soon returned with a clipboard in hand. I found they were about to do a roll call, which I thought was a terrible idea, as there seemed to be hundreds sitting in the auditorium—but it went by quicker than I thought, and halfway through he called out my name, after

Calleigh's and Carlos'.

"Sarah Verona?"

I raised my hand.

"You didn't list a gem."

I felt a thousand eyes turn to me. The gaze seemed to burn, and I opened my mouth to speak, but nothing came out. I cleared my throat.

"It's because I don't have one," I said, my voice shaking.

The effect was immediate. Whispers and murmurs filled the hall, and I could see alarm pass through the host's eyes. I felt a lump rise in my throat as more faces turned for a glimpse of me.

"Uh, I see," Loren said uneasily. "Okay. Uh—no problem. We'll um, move on to the next, um, person—Emma Rice?"

The murmurs slowly died out as the roll call continued, but I could still feel occasional glances from here and there. When, at long last, the roll call was over, Calleigh quickly pulled me out into the exhibition hall. Carlos was studying me, but I pretended not to notice; at this moment I did not want another gaze on me.

We poured out into the hallway, then into the grand hall—the exhibitions filled the hall and extended into the courtyard. Hundreds—had he said a hundred and twenty?—of booths were lined up against the walls and down the middle, like a complex network of streets and avenues, each of them vaunting sights that made you blink and look again. At one of the booths to the side, a buttercup cat was poised on the table, floating a book in front of her. At another roamed a tiny antelope the size of an apple. I stared with my mouth hanging open as the antelope grew back to its usual size.

We passed a booth that said 'The Four Pillars of a Memory Gem' and another where a fish was floating in a bubble of water. Several booths down I realized Calleigh and Carlos had disappeared, probably pulled somewhere by the enthusiastic kids beckoning them to their booths.

I took a quick look around and wandered to the Memory Gem booth, and a boy in a gray hoodie welcomed me with a big grin.

"Hey," I greeted.

"Hey." The boy greeted me, picking up a deck of cards. I waited nervously to see if he would mention the roll call incident. He didn't.

"Wanna see a magic trick?" the boy asked cheerfully, to my relief; perhaps he had been sitting too far and hadn't seen my face. Whatever the reason was, it seemed not to matter much to him that I was gemless.

"Sure," I replied.

The boy shuffled the deck of cards, and they fell into his palms in graceful arcs. He fanned them out evenly and held them out to me.

"Pick a card."

I did.

"All right, now look at the card. And don't tell me what it is."

I did. The boy took the card back, and placed it on the top of the deck.

"Now we're going to shake hands," said the boy.

"And I'm going to forget the card," I said.

"Exactly," the boy replied.

"Sure, let's go." I extended my hand.

"And before I change, there's something I have to tell you. You have to be thinking of your card when we shake hands. *Or things could go wrong.*"

I gulped.

The boy changed, and in front of me stood a silver gorilla. I giggled and extended a hand, and the gorilla took it. It gazed intelligently into my eyes, and I felt something light and soft engulf me like a veil in the air. The sensation disappeared as quickly as it had come, and the gorilla changed back to the boy. I looked curiously at him.

"That's it?" I asked.

"That's it," The boy said with a shrug. "Do you remember your card?"

Of course I—

I frowned. I did recall looking at the card the boy had handed me, but:

"No, I don't," I breathed.

The boy smirked. "No, you don't. But I know what your card is."

"What is it?" I asked.

"Can't tell you just yet," the boy answered. "Now, allow me to return the memory back to you. Oh, you might get a little headache sometime before or after."

The boy changed once more and turned back into the silver gorilla. He comically pounded on his chest, then extended his hand. Some of the passersby giggled.

I took his hand. The same sensation found me. A thin veil seemed to envelope me, but this time accompanied by something else; a gush of wind, or a set of slithering ribbons, seemed to make way into my head. I felt a brief coolness on my temples—and then the sensation was gone. The boy changed back and stood there, arms triumphantly crossed in front of him.

"Now do you remember your card?"

I gasped. "I do," I replied.

"It was eight of spades, wasn't it?" he said.

I nodded.

The boy looked pleased. He opened the first card on the deck to show the eight of spades lying face up.

"Now what I did first is called wiping, and what I did afterwards is called planting. I didn't exactly *return* the memory back to you, I just planted my own memory of your memory. You're going to forget it soon, because memories that aren't your own won't really stick to you," the boy explained. "If I wanted to *return* your memories to you, though, it would be very complicated. With trivial memories, the bond between the memory and its owner, or *pillars* in more precise terms, don't have the chance to form."

I wrinkled my brows in curiosity. "What are pillars?" I asked.

"Something that lives in each memory," he replied simply, brows intensely furrowed. Behind his irises was a strange glow.

"The more complex gems are sophisticatedly intertwined with something called pillars," he went on. "It's like a basis that the gem is built on, and works kind of like a set of conditions for the gem to carry out its complex functions."

I frowned. "That sounds really complicated," I remarked.

"Well, yes. Pillars are something special that come only with the more sophisticated gems," he said, a hint of pride in his eyes.

"Now about the four pillars of the Memory Gem—"

But he didn't get a chance to finish. At a nearby booth, a prairie dog stood balancing five spoons on its nose—well, until a little bee buzzed into its face. With a loud set of clashes, the spoons toppled over, knocking down a set of aluminum cups and a house of cards—and then the prairie dog itself, which swirled in the air and turned into a very young girl barely out of fifth grade.

I seized my chance, however, when the chaos was subdued.

"So... what about the pillars?" I asked.

"Well," the boy grimaced. "It's hard to explain with words, so let me show you another magic trick. Here. You're going to have to focus a little harder than before on your senses—on your Enricus senses."

"That I can do," I replied.

"Now pick another card."

The boy extended the shuffled deck again, and I took a card. The boy changed once more, and I felt the familiar sensation again, then he changed back—

The boy's eyebrows curled, and suddenly his eyes weren't at all like before. They glared at me with a ferocity that didn't seem to match his skinny exterior.

"Do you remember your card?" he asked slowly.

I did. It was the Queen of Diamonds.

"Unfortunately I do."

"Because you were thinking of something else," said the boy. I nodded.

The boy gazed silently at me a while before he spoke. The next thing that came out of his mouth was like a blow to my head.

"The Devil's Lady."

I staggered. "How do you know the Devil's Lady?"

The boy's eyes gleamed darkly, and seemed to take a different shape altogether—he was no longer the thin, awkward looking teenager. His eyes were intense, his mouth curled into a strange smile.

"I just took interest in them," he replied.

"Them?"

"Well, she isn't the only one there is, although she is the most loyal..."

"Most loyal?" I repeated.

"To the devil, of course. Well, it's only a nickname. He's also known as the First Original."

"What is this we're talking about? Who are these people?"

"They aren't as much of *people* as they are undead," the boy said, his voice quiet and dramatic.

I scoffed. "Undead, like zombies? And—and vampires?"

This time the boy let out a low chuckle. "No, they aren't rotting corpses or bloodsucking humanoids that can't go out in the sun," he replied. "They're complex, sophisticated things. With them the symmetry of time is realized, the myth is broken—static, no change in entropy."

My head swam. "Lifeless," I breathed. The boy's use of present tense was somewhat unsettling, and I had to take a step back before I could speak again.

"Who's the Devil's Lady?" I asked at last.

"Victorina Archer."

My heart skipped. *Victorina Archer*. I said the name in my head, thinking back to the story of I'd read of the fallen queen. I'd gotten closer than I ever was; I could finally learn who the killer was.

But I was interrupted when a voice sounded out of nowhere, along with a hand placed gently my shoulder.

"Hey, Sarah, the banquet's ready."

It was Carlos. Before I could say anything, I found myself swept up in the crowd, Carlos' hand guiding me the way we'd come—and the blaring dark eyes of the boy in the gray hoodie disappeared into the distance.

"What are you doing?" I demanded.

"I thought you wouldn't want to miss the banquet," Carlos replied. He picked up two paper plates from the side and handed one to me.

"Where *were* you?" I asked. "I couldn't find you anywhere."

"I was two booths away," Carlos replied casually without even looking up from his smoothie. "Looked like you were having fun, so I minded my own business."

"Until you barged in in the middle of something," I retorted.

"Because the banquet's ready," Carlos said indignantly.

I looked around. It was a spectacle. The chairs had been removed, and replaced with tables on which lay treats of all kinds. On one of the tables were classic miniature sandwiches. Filling another table were miniature eggplant panini, grilled tomatoes and mozzarella... On one corner were desserts of all sorts, the cupcakes Calleigh had mentioned, iced with swirls of colors I'd never even seen. Another corner had macarons and nougats, and a table was dedicated to ice cream. But the most marvelous sight was in the center, where a circle of tables surrounded the giant chocolate fondue, with baskets of fruits lying on top, waiting to be coated in chocolate.

Carlos walked over toward me with his smoothie, a mountainous green pile he'd gotten from a machine nearby. He had a proud smile on his face.

"Did I still barge in in the middle of something or was it worth it?"

I gave him a smile. "Worth it," I replied. It was a lie; alluring as the banquet was, there was nothing else I could keep in my head than the single name I had heard earlier.

But that changed when several girls approached us with sweet smiles. Trying my best to push the thoughts out of my head, I smiled warmly and greeted them.

"Hello, I'm Brittany," said the blonde girl in the middle.

"Carlos," said Carlos, extending his hand. "This is Sarah. My friend and hunting partner," he said, putting his hand on my back. The girl eyed me in a strange way, and I couldn't help but flinch, remembering the whispers that had filled the hall earlier when they'd called out my name.

"Ooh, so you live in Lincoln, right?" asked the girl to Carlos. I narrowed my eyes. *Really?*

"Yes, we do," Carlos replied.

"That is *so* cool. I might have to come to the Lincoln headquarters for a test sometime. We should hang out. Maybe go for a coffee," tinkled the girl.

Carlos smiled stiffly. "I don't really like coffee, to be honest."

"Then what do you like?" asked the girl, smiling sweetly. Her dimples were adorable. Annoyingly adorable.

"Mint chocolate chip frappé," Carlos answered. "I'm obsessed with it."

"Ooh," exclaimed the girls.

"We can do that," suggested the Brittany girl, lightly touching Carlos' arm with her hand. "Frappé boys are the best. Coffee boys, *ugh*," she added, shaking her head and wincing at the last syllable.

I rolled my eyes in complete disbelief. Whatever the hell Frappé boys were, I didn't even care; but *really?* Is this why they came over here to talk in the first place, treating me like a floor lamp the whole time?

The conversation, however, was soon interrupted; a buoyant voice had sounded from the distance, calling out Carlos' name.

"Carlos!" It was Loren. Carlos responded with a nod; it seemed they had already become friends. "You have to meet Michael. He's a Memory Gem like you!"

"Ooh, *Memory Gem!*" exclaimed Brittany. The girls giggled. "Tell me about it. What's your Mode?"

Instead of answering the question, Carlos shot a glance at Loren. "Sorry.

I'm kind of needed."

"Seems everybody needs you," said Brittany, glancing at me. I was still speechless, barely able to believe what was happening. "Well, talk to you in a bit," she flounced.

Carlos smiled. "Sarah, I'll catch you later," he said before jogging off toward Loren.

"Uh," I voiced—unlike what I'd intended, my voice cracked awkwardly. "I think I'll grab something to eat, too."

I turned to leave—but what came out of the girl's mouth froze me in place.

"You're the Slag, aren't you?"

I halted. I felt like my breath got knocked out of me.

"Excuse me?"

"The Slag," repeated the girl—Brittany. "Means you don't have a gem."

I stood there with my mouth open, appalled.

"Well then, technically you're not really one of us," said the girl to her right.

"*Slags* at the fair, ugh," Brittany muttered, flapping her hand like a dinosaur head. "I hope I don't have to see you at the test."

With that, the girls left before I could say anything. I stood there, glued to the floor, with my soul whacked out of my head. I felt a lump rise in my throat.

I cannot say how I ended up there, but a few minutes later I was in a bathroom stall, leaning against the wall. Tears welled up my eyes, and I tried to swallow them with no avail; for long I stayed, hearing the word *slag* in my head over and over again, watching ugly teardrops spatter on the polished tiles.

It was much later that I rubbed the tears off my face, took a long hard look in the mirror at my reddened eyes, and walked back outside. Everything was just as it was, vibrant and festive. The crowd had extended to the yard outside, and groups after groups of boys and girls were chattering and laughing as they passed by. I spotted two familiar faces, and against my hopes, so did they.

"Hey!" Calleigh came running, followed by Carlos.

Crap, not now, I thought. "Hey," I replied, trying to sound casual.

"How's it going? Have you made some friends?" Calleigh asked merrily. She apparently had not picked up on anything.

"Yeah, um, yeah," I replied, trying to sound as cheerful as I could. Carlos' eyes met mine, his eyes observant. He opened his mouth to speak, but stopped. I felt something sink softly.

"Um, I got to go," I said, trying to break the silence. "My mom's cooked dinner."

I could still feel Carlos eyeing me, but he didn't say anything.

"You sure?" Calleigh asked. "There's going to be a standup comedy tonight, and then this insane game of Capture the Flag down at the park. It's not the kids' game you're thinking. That one's the real thing. A lot of... *hunting* involved."

I shook my head. The lump was in my throat again. "Sounds fun, really, but I got to go," I added quickly.

I ran for the bus, which I barely caught. I rested my head on the shuddering windowpane and mindlessly let my head rattle. The sky was an awkward gray, like a deep frown before the downpour of heavy rain. I tasted the salt on my dry lips as the streets passed by.

Later that night I was standing in a field, with cornstalks tickling my shoulders. I was running, swinging my arms frantically around to beat the thick, stubborn stems from my face. I didn't know what I was running from, but I knew I had to run.

I don't know how long I'd run, and my knuckles stung from the cuts from the fierce cornstalks. I halted. I realized there was a sound coming from all around me, almost ambient. It took me a moment to find out what it was.

Whispers. I could make out some words, maybe a couple more. *Gem. Gemless.* Maybe even a couple sentences. *She's a slag?* Brittany's laugh came from somewhere to my left. I turned. There was nothing to be seen but endless gold.

I began to run. My feet got caught in the stems, and I batted corn cobs from my face as I struggled through the stalks. But it was to no avail—the whispers did not cease a bit. They followed me. I turned again and ran in a different direction, then again, and again—but no matter which way I turned, the whispered made way to my ears, distinct as though coming from right next to them. The more steps I took, the louder the whispers grew—until they rang like sirens, threatening to pierce through my eardrums and all the way to the core of my soul.

And out of the open something swooped in at my face, screeching horribly like metal on china. I ducked. It was a flock of gigantic black birds. Their claws were about three inches long and sharp like steel, glinting menacingly as they shredded strips of air into my face. Terror seized my guts, and I slowly backed away.

If only I had a gem, I found myself thinking. *They're attacking me because I'm not one of them.* I batted furiously at the birds, trying get them out of my face. Once I had some room I began once more to run frantically; all the while muttering between my breaths, I need a gem, I need a gem, I need a gem.

And something came. A white crane cawed gracefully in the distance. Startled birds fluttered out of its way—I stared in awe as the crane glided toward me, its wings spread sleekly like a blade of platinum. Just then I saw something glisten at its feet. The bird cawed again, and I realized it had dropped something—I extended my hand, and readily something heavy sank into my hands. I peered down and uncurled my fingers to find a brilliant-cut gemstone.

I stared. *What?* I thought. *What am I supposed to do with it?*

It did not take long until the birds saw—and they knew, that I was no less helpless than before. One moment they seemed to peer at me, then another, they rose—

I screamed as the birds attacked again. They seemed to laugh and scoff in a series of sickening cries, hovering over my head, mocking me. They swooped in again for me, this time even fiercer.

I pulled myself up from bed, drenched in sweat. I shook my head, trying to shake off the images and sounds from my head.

For a moment I sat unmoving. The house was utterly quiet, and not a sound came from Mom's bedroom or anywhere else. The silence had turned so loud it felt almost tangible; I drummed on my bedsheets to break it.

I crept out of bed to get myself a cup of water. The hum of the refrigerator was the only sound in the slumbering house. As I carefully opened the cupboard and poured water into the cup, my thoughts flashed back to the whispers in my dream, to the contemptuous eyes of the girls at the fair—then to Carlos. With a strange little pang I remembered his eyes as he turned away. What did I want? For him to comfort me? For him to walk up to the girls and tell them they shouldn't have said that? I scoffed. He wasn't the one without a gem. I was.

Silence fizzled and burned into my ears, and again I heard the word in my head:

Slag.

Maybe I was wrong. Maybe it wasn't okay, as someone had said. And maybe I *was* alone.

Some days passed, and although I hadn't forgotten the incident at the fair, it had receded to a dark little corner in my head instead of filling it. I brought myself once more to the investigation of the queen's murder. With a strange chill I recalled the name the boy had voiced, and the rhapsodic way he had went on about the undead creatures. It was strange—it seemed he knew more about them than he should.

The search, however, was not very fruitful. I'd typed the name in the search bar many a time, but nothing turned up—except for some social media accounts for someone named Victoria Archer. I even tried the catalog at the library, but it had yielded nothing. I was stuck at a dead end once more.

So instead I returned to my everyday life. I went to school, I paid attention and took notes, and I even walked by the football field again. On several occasions I saw Madison. She looked like her usual self, an orange headband on her head, her curls dancing merrily as she ran. I missed her.

After school I headed to Vanna Daya for my classes. Calleigh wasn't in the house, nor was Sophie. Chase and Andrew, however, were home, both of them fresh out of the shower with soaked hair. They welcomed me in with warm bear hugs, dripping cold water onto my back.

After the class—consisting mostly of long talks on the history of the species, all the while revealing nothing about the pirates—I wandered to the library to pick out some more books. This time I decided to check out the far east corner. I found rows of academic volumes—On the Microbiology of Enrici, Fundamental Studies of Alpha Enrica—all of which, from the moment I opened them, I decided not even to try. I walked on until I found some delicately decorated books—*what the hell Latin*—and further on, until I found the first column of readable text.

History Section:
Simplest Possible Version of Enrican History
Enrican History of War

I snuggled in bed later that evening to read. The book was full of mysterious scripts and runes, puzzles and diagrams I could not quite decipher. I opened a page to a long passage written in a slightly familiar alphabet.

I thought briefly of a certain friend of my mother's. *Reagan,* I mouthed with a pleasant familiarity. She had once shown me this alphabet when I was young. A curious system it was—it was a phonetic writing system, crafted singlehandedly by a king and his scholars.

I looked back at the archaic writing. Apparently it was a poem, found written on a piece of paper and preserved in a delicate wooden box. It had been discovered, according to the book, alongside a carved image on porcelain; on one side was an old woman transforming deftly into a large turtle,

西方사를밧바上帝ㅣ나시니
冠아래玉顔비치건좋대노려업다
손이슈石函여러重重히淡粧호고
氣槪는히를롤떠싸해나라이오시니
바믈롯자山行호매怪獸ㄷ리시의여디고
나믄짜해쓰들나려하로開闢호노라
戰塲사흥몬직에將助ㅣ나노라니
실갈놀바미빼므러어롬그티솟노라
上帝人命받즈바뫼나마나가니
喜聲이바회룰쌔아온싸히히搖動호니
溪谷이그두ㅈ믄구로미거텨시니
半ㅣ스러딘싸해太平聖代오노라
연하눈구비치매冒險家ㅣ나노라니
弱水룰내리건너내룰이룬바믈걷너
人影아니머므러간흔서믈초자시니
비룰티와사로물노내새싸흘이럿눈대
살미티다로거가매春秋之秘신드라니
새로연먼洞窟에브리켜디어세라
섯두리나마가매木匠이나노라니
荒野애싸흘드뎌며지블지어올이노라
붙그샌그골서기둥을세오

밤煙氣프어둛제둛흘다마시니
하눌시쟝마룬의뎌宮殿을지여시니
기리곰보는사루미니줄줄모르리
별빗얼흰섬바미策士ㅣ나노라니
빗길홀솔펴녀고바롧길흘여러녀고
秘策을쎄드라니金剛으쎄빌거
畵幅매그림그러더슬크게지슨듸
秋風이더나가고쿤오라湧動호니
四季ㅅ긋니룬나래올로스러디여라
서룰여희며새싸우회룰女人이니로느니
이따우희흫취나린새쌧어며니
아쳘슝여逃亡야성올여희여갈져긔
자괴아니기틴그덜구론아니뵈니
겨슬바물神出고녀룹바믈鬼沒호나
오로쎄린히몬그츌츌모로노라
먼西方ㅅ큰沙漠애아히나노라니
올해드레프곳그리비스니
누늘쁜觀氣메는흰비치심드송아
빗손써쁘룹나져믄일호노라니
갈자븐소니라와눌카빔나러안자
온쳣거믄바룹믈눕긔져치와미로다

and the other was the same turtle sitting peacefully on a rock facing the sea.

I flipped the page to find a photograph of the carving. It was intricately done, lines of different colors—a swirling earth, a milky celadon, a softened brick red—filling deftly carved grooves on the surface. I gazed for a while at the face of the turtle, wondering how long it had taken to make this.

But as I gave it a longer look, it seemed to change the way I saw it. The turtle on the sun-kissed rock no longer looked tranquil; it was as though it were gazing at the horizons of fate.

Peaceful? I thought to myself.

The turtle looked out onto the seas with its large, knowing eyes, and in their depths was an unmistakable hint of disquiet. A storm was coming.

Chapter 8
Vanna Daya

Days and weeks passed. Mornings seeped shrilly through your skin, slithering insidiously through the warmest of blankets. Familiar landscapes grew alien. The cold, hard earth was wild and barren. It belonged to no one, and everyone who stood on it were only outlanders. Every morning people would stride down the street, their backs hunched and their arms grasping the hems of their coats, in hurried, guilty footsteps of a trespasser.

The chill was refreshing, but it drove away game. The park was still but for a soft blanket of light snow that would come and go. Mom stopped sleeping by the door, but we put a break to our hunting routine anyway. I slept eight hours a day, woke up feeling blessed, and gobbled up human food with glorious appetite. Life was good.

As the sunlit hours grew shorter, I turned to research. It seemed I'd read close to every history book centered around the Enrican warlore and the stories of the monarchs. But I'd gotten no warmer. The single name was the only information I could lay my hands on. In a couple weeks I'd gone through everything that could be of help, only to come to a dead end; I decided unwillingly that I'd take my mind off of it for a while.

Still I did not stop reading. I spent days indulged in the book *Six Not So Easy Pieces on the Biology of Enrici*. It discussed complex matters, like the transfer of nutrition and physical stimulus between forms. It covered—in very sophisticated prose—how Enrici could think in a human way in their alternate forms. Many were still mere speculations, and along with those a number of risky ideas were raised on the extension of human consciousness. I sat for hours after school wrapped in my blanket with a jar of Nutella, entertained by the magical science.

While I feasted on knowledge, trees shed leaves on the streets, and the metasequoia dropped fuzzy needles onto the brown gold carpets. The branches cleared, and the pumpkins on Ms. Miller's yard disappeared; and coincidentally, she appeared on our doorstep one day with a pumpkin pie. A modest plateful of turkey made its way onto our table, still with the best stuffing—our family all got together, which was a rare occurrence.

I spent most of my days alone and lost in aimless thought. I did not have much company to share discussions on Enricus science. Calleigh, as much as she seemed to take a childlike interest in science, wasn't the sort of person to listen as you talked. Carlos wasn't the best option when you wanted to talk theory in depth, at least so I thought—and Lillian; somehow, I got the feeling that she was avoiding me. The last time I'd seen her was from the other side of the hall, where she cast me the swiftest glance and disappeared into a classroom. Company wasn't something I had in abundance. My thoughts somehow flashed back to a certain tall, bouncy girl that I'd spent most of my Tuesday and Thursday afternoons with before all this happened. I pictured her soft frizzy curls, and the headbands she would always wear on her head; mostly orange, but some days a bright neon pink, some days spring green, some days dotted yellow. With a sigh I shook off the images. Well, it wasn't my fault. It was she who had decided she didn't need my company anymore.

And so, in cozy solitude, I continued down the road in search for knowledge. I read about how our memory worked and much else, until winter finally undressed the last of its frock.

It was December twentieth. It had just started snowing for the first time in ages. Fuzzy flakes of snow flitted and flounced as I stood alone in the courtyard. The sky was pink and fluffy, and the longer you gazed, the more it felt like the wind was carrying you up, floating toward the top of the cloud's canopy where the snowfall first started. I let my head lol back as I stared up at the sky, captivated, convinced that I could do this for hours on end without getting bored.

"Hey, Sarah," said a familiar voice.

I turned. Carlos stood dressed in a red varsity jacket he seemed to really like, his cheeks a light pink from the chill.

"Carlos," I greeted.

Carlos strode over and lifted his head to look at the sky.

"What are you looking at?"

"Snow," I replied. "It's pretty."

Carlos squinted. A snowflake landed on his nose and he grimaced. I giggled.

"You're right. Never really took a good long look," Carlos commented.

I looked to find him craning up at the sky like I'd been doing a while ago, squinting into the falling snow. A smile crept up my lips.

"So, um," Carlos began, taking his eyes off the sky. "What have you been up to? I haven't seen you after the, after the, you know."

Right, the fair. Carlos looked at me uneasily as though he weren't sure if bringing up the subject was a good idea. I looked down at my feet. I wasn't sure either; I couldn't decide if I wanted him to talk about it.

"Reading," I replied finally. "Enricus science."

And a legend about a certain monarch, I added mentally, *who was murdered by some sophisticated zombie pirate.*

"You'll never not impress me, Sarah," he added, "Seems you got a lot of time on you now that we don't hunt."

"I do, actually," I replied. "I mean, I still have schoolwork. But it's better than before, and I'm not constantly sleep deprived. What have *you* been up to?"

"Practice," Carlos replied simply. "And a lot of off-ice training. I get knocked out cold every night."

I nodded. "Right. I keep forgetting you're on the hockey team. Prepping for the next season?"

"Yeah, we got to play to win." Carlos grinned proudly.

I smiled a bittersweetly. "Sounds fun," I remarked.

"Yes, and I'm constantly in pain." Carlos chuckled, pointing at his bruised knee underneath his shorts. "And I kind of miss hunting with you."

I swallowed. "Yeah, true. I mean, same."

I'd forgotten much of what's been occupying my mind lately. Carlos' nose and ears had turned to a shade of pink that reminded me of strawberry gelato. A couple snowflakes landed on his lashes, and then another on the tip of his nose. The one on his nose melted into a droplet of water, but the ones on his lashes stayed, like coarse bits of sugar crystal.

"Oh, by the way," Carlos said, breaking the silence. "Did you get the… invitation from Calleigh?"

"The *what?*"

"The invitation. This," Carlos replied, producing a crumpled slip from his varsity jacket. It was an ornate golden slip, the edges cut into frill-like patterns.

"A Winter Meeting in Vanna Daya," I read. "*For a whole week?*"

"I'm pretty sure you got one of those as well."

I heaved my backpack up front, zipped it open and began to rummage through it. I could see no reason Calleigh would give Carlos an invitation and not me—

"There you go."

I found the slip folded in half and jabbed between the pages of my Calculus book. It seemed I absently shoved it in there, thinking it was some scrap of paper and never caring to look. I felt kind of bad as I studied the slip closely; it was written by hand and with much care, in lithe, courtly handwriting of an artist.

A Winter Meeting in Vanna Daya

Chat & games, picnics outside at Halliday, hunting, gem training sessions, and more!

Sunday, February 6th – Saturday, February 12th

I looked up. Carlos' eyes sparkled. "So, are you going?"

"I'll have to ask my mom," I replied. "But Calleigh didn't make it too clear if we have a choice or not. Did she?"

"That and it sounds fun," Carlos said. "The Mock Carnival starts on the twelfth, though, I kind of wanted to go."

"I completely forgot about the Mock Carnival," I said. "I've only been there once with my mom when I was little, but I heard the fun stuff's after midnight. Shame they don't let you in. I guess I can take a look when I'm eighteen," I said.

"Well I've been," Carlos confessed sheepishly. "Snuck in every year since seventh grade. Nothing special, just a lot of drunk people."

"Ouch, there goes my fantasies."

"And fun music."

"A little better, but not as good as I expected."

"And... the show," Carlos flushed.

I nodded slowly. "The... show."

"You know, like a, strip..."

"I mean, I kind of already knew from the way you said... never mind," I said awkwardly. Carlos looked at me with a smile creeping up his face.

"Yeah. Just, uh, that and nothing else. It's not much of a big deal."

"I figured. The names of the shows were interesting, but back then I was too young to understand anything, so. I remember seeing this play at the history booth, but I didn't really understand what was going on."

"The history booth," Carlos repeated.

"Yeah."

We got silent, and I wanted to say something, only didn't know what.

"There's actually a sad history with the Mock Carnival," I ended up saying. For some reason I thought of this guy who, on his first date with Madison, went ahead and spilled two hours' worth of trivia. I regretted opening my mouth; but it was too late.

"Really? What's that?" Carlos asked.

"A lot of people died. It was during war, the carnival was actually some sort of ploy to drive out the raiders," I said quickly.

A crease formed on Carlos' forehead. "Dang, I didn't know that."

There was silence again, and I wondered if Carlos was thinking about the war or about how bad I was at conversing.

"Well, um, I've been to enough Mock Carnivals, so I think I can skip it this year," Carlos said after a while. "I'll probably be there, you know. Calleigh's thing, So, um, let me know."

"All right." I swung my backpack back onto my shoulders. "I'll... text you. About this."

"Sure." Carlos smiled brightly. "See you around."

With a wave, Carlos disappeared around the corner.

Bold of Calleigh to host a meeting on the day of the Mock Carnival, I thought.

The Mock Carnival took place in Lincoln every February, in triumphant memory of the one winter in 1778 when a little girl's brilliant ideas saved the town from a raid.

Legend has it that when the British forces traveled deeper into the west, a group of raiders had joined them, and come raging into the inlands of America. It had been passed down by word of mouth that a small boat had come rowing up rivers, with a dark mast bearing a pair of eyes foreign to all— and a sinister chant sounding from the deck:

Into the brand-new world we climb
Take all the gold and rum and wine
Pay with dark, and pay with vice;
Make good, it's good; embrace, entwine!

Come see the darkest glory shine,
And ships arise from sea of brine
To wake the nights, the morn' entice;
Make good, true good, vile truth enshrine!

And the townspeople were sent into a frenzy. Men and women died, houses were burnt. The neighborhood was enveloped thickly in despair; all until one of them, a young girl, devised a genius idea. They began to lay a trap. They spread word of a carnival. They prepared food, wine and music. Come carnival night, all the farmers, craftsmen, maidens, and urchins gathered, decked in their best garments, some in delirious costumes—and began to dance. As they heard the clatter of boots in the distance they led the women and children further back; the ring of dancers were now the strongest of men, some in tuxes, some in costumes, some in dresses the maidens wore, but the raiders did not look closely; they were already soaked in verve. So when they got wasted on the barrels of wine, tore down stands and screamed for more food, the town's best men, together with soldiers, ambushed the raiders and saved the town.

Ever since then, at every end of winter, they celebrated. When thin coats of snow slowly melted into gooey slush and the first tinge of buds came splitting the bark, the town was busy with talk of the carnival. Much later the name *Mock Carnival* was coined. It became the biggest event in town, and most of the schools around the area had a week-long break around the time.

I had, like anyone in town, had my fair share of the Mock Carnival. Without even so much as a date to the dance, I could skip a year of the fun for whatever Calleigh had in mind. But fate twists in magical ways you cannot fathom—little did I know then, that the carnival was exactly where I would wind up.

Mom approved. She had a long conversation with Sophie over the phone, and told me I could go, but that I had to be careful at all times, especially when doing 'outdoor stuff.' I agreed.

The day came. I packed my suitcase and dressed in my usual outfit: a shirt and jeans with a beaver-colored hooded jacket on top. Mom volunteered to drive me. I hopped onto her Honda and curled up comfortably in the front seat to doze off for the little ride. In short periods between my heavily shut eyelids and the mild, sparkling sun, I could taste the delicious sweetness of afternoon bliss.

We arrived at Vanna Daya, and to my surprise Mom didn't say much before she dropped me off.

A honk sounded behind me, however, when I headed for the porch—and I saw Mom roll down the window. I sighed and went back for her.

"What, Mom?"

Mom smiled. Even though my lips resembled my dad's more than hers, our smiles looked quite alike—her lips stretched into a thin curve, and between them twinkled two slightly large front teeth. She produced a wrinkled paper bag from her purse and held it out. "Take some scones."

I took it. The scones were squished, like they'd been wedged between some books all along the ride.

"All right," I said with a chuckle. "See you."

"Have fun, Sarahbell. I love you."

I felt a bubbling warmth on my chest and grinned. "Love you too."

I rang the familiar doorbell, and a cheerful Calleigh sprang out to give me a bear hug. She smelled of some exotic herb; she had probably tried on a new perfume.

"Hey, how've you been, sweetie?" Calleigh chimed. It occurred to me that she sounded a lot like a generic mom.

"Good, how've you been?" I asked. Calleigh's eyes gleamed the way it did before she started talking a bunch, and I wish I had somehow avoided asking her whatever sort of question.

"Well, I've been working on some interesting projects... which I'm going to tell you all about, of course. But we have to get you all set up and comfortable, 'cause we have a bunch to do..." she squealed on, and I was only grateful that her talk was cut short. "Really, Sarah, can't believe you're finally here. *Ohhhh* my god, I've been waiting for this. It's gonna be so much fun. I've got so many plans—and we can totally have pajama parties!" And then it occur-red to me that at the same time she also sounded like a generic toddler.

"Are you going to let me in or not?" I asked with a grin.

"Oops," Calleigh squealed. Her voice had risen an octave at least; another octave and I wouldn't be able to hear it. "I com*pletely* forgot that we're standing in the doorway. Sorry. Here, let me take your suitcase."

"It's al—" It was too late. Calleigh had taken the suitcase by the handle, and wavered and swung as the weight of the suitcase flung her around.

"It's fine, Calleigh, really. I'll take it. It's not even that heavy," I said, taking the suitcase back.

The house was empty, unlike what I'd expected. It seemed I was the first one to get here.

"Where are the others?" I asked.

"Lillie, I don't know where she is. The boys are out in the yard—and Carlos isn't here yet," Calleigh replied. "You're the first one here. I'll show you around your room, and you can unpack and make yourself comfortable. I just got back from a quick errand a minute ago, so I'm gonna get a shower, but after that I'll, be free so—yeah, just hit me up and I don't know. I can show you my newest works. Or some of these turquoise bird figures I made? I've been teaching myself to sculpt these days. I made this wooden reindeer too, I think it's like the fifth thing I've ever made. I can show you, if you'd care to look. It's in the basement. We kind of set up another studio in the basement, oh, not the headquarters part, but the floor right below—I'd totally love to show you all around."

As much as I found her craft intriguing, I'd begun to zone out again. My arms were getting very tired from carrying the suitcase around as Calleigh flailed around the room.

"Oh, sorry," Calleigh apologized again, only noticing. "I'll show you to your room."

"Thanks," I said with a warm smile. *Calleigh. So Calleigh,* I thought with a bubble of affection forming in my chest.

I followed Calleigh up the stairs. The stairs led to a small hallway with two doors facing one another. With bird-like steps she led me to the room on the right.

"This is Lillie's room, but for the moment Lillie's going to be sleeping in my room. This is all yours," Calleigh said.

"Lillian lives here?" I confirmed.

Calleigh nodded. "She's been living with us for some years now. I think it's been around eight years. No, nine—yeah, nine."

I nodded slowly. I sensed it was a bit of a sensitive subject, and as I expected, Calleigh said no more.

"You might want to unpack and see if your bed's the right height and everything. I'm going to take a shower."

See if your bed's the right height. It was the first time I'd heard anyone say that. I brushed off the whole subject of Lillian and heaved my suitcase into the room.

"Will do. Thanks, Calleigh."

I found myself in a small room, very simple and minimalist—a twin sized bed, a large window with a clear view to the sky. Her room didn't have anything to call a proper desk, only a small bedside table. Instead, occupying the corner where a desk would have been, was a weight set. *That explains a lot*, I thought, *but leaves room for a lot of questions.* I ran my fingers along the faded and scarred portions of the bar that her fingers had worn away, picturing the girl lifting a gigantic barbell.

That was it, it seemed—there wasn't a dressing table, nor a bookshelf. I wondered where she did her schoolwork, or if she did any at all. A couple textbooks were stacked in the corner, almost untouched. That was about the only proof that she was in fact a real, solid high school student. I plunged onto the bed, and with a sore behind and a lot of regret, discarded the last sliver of hope that Lillian was perhaps only human.

She sleeps on a rock-hard bed, I thought. *Like a psychopath.*

I looked around the rest of the room with a melody in the background, flowing through the walls from Calleigh's shower booth. Her soft voice and delicate runs melted into my ears, and it seemed to bring a little life into this lifeless room. An idea suddenly struck me, and I made a mental note that I would pick some flowers and put it in the corner. That would brighten up the room.

A while later I headed downstairs. I ran into Calleigh, continuously humming the tune she had been singing in the shower. A carefree toss of her hair sent little drops of water flying into the air. The girl's face lit up when she saw me.

"Are you done unpacking and everything?"

"Yeah, I was just going to head downstairs..."

"Oh! Great. Carlos is here."

"He is?" I asked coolly.

Calleigh smiled, a hint of mischief in her eyes. "Go say hi."

I did run into him the moment I went down the stairs. Carlos strolled into the living room in his red varsity jacket, his hands stuck in his pockets. He grinned when he found me.

"Hi," I greeted.

"Hi."

"Hi. I mean um, did you get to see your room?" I asked awkwardly.

"Yeah, Calleigh showed me. It's, it's nice. Calleigh said it was a guest room, originally."

"Um..." I still couldn't find anything to say. "Can I see it?"

Why would you even want to see his room? I shrieked mentally. *Why do you keep saying stupid things around people?*

But to my relief, Carlos didn't seem to think much of it. He simply smiled and said: "Sure."

I followed Carlos into the guest room. It was a cozy little room, the walls creamy white and minimalistic. The window faced the afternoon sun, and a soft, hazy glow seeped through.

"Suits you," I commented. I don't know why I said that. I was thinking that his room at home would have more colors, something like red. I'd often seen him in red.

"It's a little simple, but it's a nice room," Carlos remarked. An awkward silence followed, and I pretend to be very interested in the one nail stuck in a wall.

"Oh, um, do you want to go downstairs?" asked Carlos.

"Sure, sounds great," I replied.

We headed out the room, comically bouncing off each other as we try to fit through the doorway at once. Calleigh was nowhere to be seen, but we were met by a sweaty Chase and Andrew. Chase was holding a bag full of water bottles and Andrew had a football under his arm.

"Ah, Jacus-Russell," Carlos greeted.

"Look who's here. *Carlos Pierce.*"

After a comically dramatic exchange, the three boys charged at each other, ending up in a group hug that looked more like heated attempts to fling one another off their feet. *Oh*, I said to myself, banging my hand on my forehead as I realized what this was.

Kingsley had two main sports events each year: the football cup and the hockey cup. There was always some sort of heated rivalry going on between the football team and the hockey team. The halls would be a warzone each time one of the games were on, with one gang booing the other. It was fun to watch, until the chants earworm their way into your head in a physics quiz.

"Really?" I snickered, watching the boys topple over onto the floor in one big heap.

"We were just pleased to see him," Chase said, brushing dust from his hands.

"Very pleased," Carlos agreed with a nod.

I rolled my eyes, stifling a bubbling laugh.

Evening came, and Sophie came back home, then Robert. I could not quite determine who the siblings took after; in their father I could also see them both, in his bronze complexion, in the way his eyes crinkled when he smiled courteously. He, like Sophie, insisted that we call him by his first name.

The table was set at seven o'clock sharp, and it was a scrumptious sight. Dishes filled the table like a gala. Salad bathed in sour cream and blue cheese, barbecued vegetables, a potful of soup that gave off an herby aroma… and lamb chops topped with minced garlic. A delicious aroma flitted up my nose, and I could feel my mouth water.

"There's no way you cooked all this," Carlos breathed, stumbling into the dining room. The boys had stopped trying to hurl one another off their feet and sauntered toward the table rubbing their bellies.

Calleigh came from the kitchen carrying yet another plate full of food, and with her frail arms set it down at an empty spot in the middle. It was fillets of bluish fish bathed in mustard and sauce, topped with sauteed apples.

"Bluefish, baked with mustard and apples," Calleigh chimed excitedly.

"It was a gift from our friends in DC," Sophie explained. "Caught at dawn, shipped this morning. A fresh catch."

We happily seated ourselves around the table, eyes gleaming intently.

"Help yourself. We have more in the kitchen if you like."

I took a fillet of the fish and placed it on my plate, slicing a thin sliver to try. The fresh meat dissolved instantly on my tongue, leaving behind a faint watery aroma. The sauce had a buttery note to it, with a distinct, fragrant pull of wine.

"This is delicious, Sophie," I commented.

Sophie looked extremely pleased. "Thank you."

Everyone had lost their words as they started working on the dishes. I banqueted in pleasant silence, while my eyes feasted on the delicious interior of the dining room.

The dining room was exquisite. It was, just like the living room, a glorious mix of the past and present, a patchwork of years, perhaps decades and even centuries. A soft orange light shone from a decanter chandelier suspended from the ceiling, and in the middle lay a long walnut table, off which I could almost smell the blaring sun scathing the bark. It was carved intricately in a way that reminded me of the baroque era, where I wouldn't be surprised if the lights went out and were suddenly replaced with a brilliant crystal pinlight—the beam, stark against the dark background, landing dramatically on a shrieking face. A closer look showed that the edges were embellished with fine curves glinting moon white—probably molded pearl—adding milky highlights to the dark of the wood. My eyes then landed on two curious looking ceramic bottles sitting atop it. They seemed to be salt and pepper shakers. One was white, and one was black—and they had oval balls of different colors painted all over, much like scattered M&M's.

"Sarah, could you pass me the salt?"

"Sure." I picked up both the salt and pepper shakers, as I'd been taught, and then—

"Sarah—what—?"

I froze. It dawned on me that I had tipped over the bottle and been pouring the salt into Carlos' extended hand. Like M&M's.

"Oh, god, sorry," I said quickly, flushed, and handed him a napkin.

Carlos chuckled and wiped his hand on the napkin. Grains of salt dribbled onto the table and on the floor. We both reached down to clean up the mess.

"Oh, don't worry about it, I'll vacuum it later," said Robert. "It's not the first time that happened. I do that all the time."

"You d—?" Chase began, but Calleigh twitched and he stopped mid-sentence. "Yeah, we do that all the time."

My face grew hot. I sat up awkwardly and returned a courteous smile. I glanced at Carlos, and saw that he was wearing a huge smile, pursing his lips as though holding in laughter. He probably had no idea how much I wished to just crawl under the table and hide underneath the salt pile.

The meal then felt like forever. The Russells tried very hard to fill the silence with various topics, but none of it really made way into my head. After we were done, Calleigh brought out a tray of hot brownies straight out of the oven, and Chase came back with a giant bowl of milky ice cream. They disappeared as well, and my mood lightened a little.

"Thanks for the amazing food," Andrew said heartily.

"Thank you all for coming," Robert said, making a pyramid with his hands. "We're very happy to have you here, really. All of us were very excited."

I hadn't heard him talk much, but he had the aura of a lawyer; and I got the feeling that he could talk an entire spinoff book series if he wanted—that he was merely choosing not to. After all, Calleigh had to get her charms from somewhere.

"We're going to be doing quite a lot of things during the week you'll be staying here. I've put up a board in the living room where you can see the schedule, but it's very flexible. If the weather's good you kids could go for a hunt at the park. After all, the whole point of this little get-together is that you guys get to know each other and learn the ways of an Enricus.

"But yes, we do have things better done while we're gathered, like gem drills, and something called adaptive drills—although I've heard a lot of you hunt," he looked at me and Carlos, "which means you're already off to a good start."

It got quite late after dinner, and we prepared for bed. There were a number of things to do the following day. I filled my tumbler with water and headed up to my—Lillian's—room.

I let out a sigh as I finally closed the door and plunked down on the bed. The empty room smelled like early morning in the city just after a drizzle. The quietness of the pale blue-gray walls soothed me, and I wrapped Lillian's blanket around my shoulders.

I had a long week ahead, it seemed, and hopefully it would bring me some profit. I could forget about gems and get to know the squad better. Talking to Robert and Sophie could, perhaps, yield some answers about the mystery of the Queen's death. At this moment, however, I was just glad that I could finally be alone instead of with a pack of people who had just witnessed me pour salt into someone else's palm.

I switched the light off. Darkness fell like a blanket onto my shoulders; the swirl from the evening's little happenings slowly died down, and I drifted in anticipation for tomorrow as I floated off to sleep.

Morning dawned, and the week began.

In the morning we had gem training. More like, *everyone else* had gem training. I wandered around the living room alone—before I set off to a little walk along the boulevard. I wrapped myself in a fleece jacket and draped a scarf around my neck, but the getup was a little overdone; I shook my scarf loose, slightly unzipped my jacket and went flouncing about, feeling the frosty stir of wind on my skin.

It was a good decision. It felt better to be out in the sun than to be in the house, waiting as everyone else worked on their gems in the Phonie. I wandered down the block humming a tune, trying to keep my thoughts away from gems. Down the middle of the street I saw that witch hazel had bloomed. Smiling to myself, I snapped off a branch, and carried it back to the house; then I put it in a little glass jar and placed it by Lillian's window. I was right. It brightened up the room.

In the afternoon we drove to the park. It was a so-called *adaptive drill*, but a picnic was a more fitting term. Sophie had made sandwiches for us to bring, and Calleigh had merrily filled a picnic basket with sandwiches and fruits.

We picked a spot by the flat area near the lake. Calleigh produced a red checkered blanket from her basket and spread it across the bank. She then pulled an iPod out of her bag and placed it carefully on a small portable speaker. We sat laughing and talking about a bunch of little things. Music filled the background, making it feel as though I were in a music video. A minute in I was the girl with thick side-swept bangs, in some oversized shirt and hoodie, blowing bubbles on a skateboard and laughing in slow motion. Kesha's voice blared through the speaker, and Calleigh smiled slyly after I muttered 'Who even is Jack?' Between Calleigh's story about how she'd met someone at the fair and might be going to see a movie with him, or perhaps to a rollerblading rink—and the 'Ooooh's from the rest of the squad—it seemed all my problems and sorrows had somehow dissipated.

As we continued to talk it got colder and colder, and Calleigh began to pass around paper cups she'd brought. She poured hot tea into the cups, and the sound of drizzling tea tapped pleasantly on my ears. It was early February, but the chill was still in the air and the lake had frozen all over, making quite a majestic sight.

And it was probably the first bad idea of the day, that I'd decided to point that out vocally.

"The lake's frozen," I breathed.

Calleigh's lips slowly spread into a grin, a dramatic sort of grin, like one of a cartoon character plotting a heist. Calleigh looked around at the others, as if contemplating the greatness of whatever had just popped up in her head, before she whispered: "I have the best idea."

Calleigh pointed toward her pickup truck. It was a 1955 Chevy Cameo Carrier, which I had no idea how she laid her hands on. To top it all, it was painted; the bumpers were a bright lavender, with sunflowers blooming around the sides. On the bed of the truck, surrounded by tens of blossoming sunflowers, were a couple wooden crates, tied securely to one side with a thick rope.

"I'm always prepared when winter comes. Do you want to know what I keep in those crates?"

⁂

"It's a *terrible* idea," I hissed as I flung my arms in the air, trying not to take a painful fall on my bum. I plunked down onto the ice, massaging my arms which were sore from flailing through the air in desperate attempts to keep myself up.

"Wow, Sarah, I didn't expect this when you said you couldn't skate," commented Chase.

"I thought it was some advanced mockery," Andrew chimed in.

"Do I look that evil to you, Andrew?" I muttered.

Andrew chuckled. "Sometimes, just a little," he replied.

Skates in all sizes, all kinds, in a variety of boot-blade combinations. That's what it was. That's what Calleigh kept in those crates. The problem was that I could hardly appreciate the fact that the blades were neatly sharpened—Carlos had run his fingers on the blades and said, "This is, this is actually really good"—which made them, according to Calleigh, 'easier to skate on.' because no matter how good the blades were, they didn't stop me from wobbling like a paper doll fearing for its life.

While I second-guessed every life choice that led to this, Chase helped me lace my boots and Calleigh chattered in the distance about how she'd learned skating from a distant relative. Apparently figure skaters did suffer from dangers of unexpectedly changing. Calleigh chirped on about how 'toe jumps' were easier to do without changing than 'edge jumps,' and about some girl named Amelia who had to give up her dreams to be an Olympian because she was a 'rare clockwise jumper,' and she kept on landing her axels as a chimpanzee. 'You know how you get swept up in a swirl when you change? Physically it does give you angular momentum. The upside is that you can land a quintuple axel if you use it right, the downside is when you land, you're probably not human,' Calleigh had gone on forever, her eyes, as usual, glimmering excitedly. The story did nothing to make this worthwhile, however, and I was still regretting having opened my mouth to say anything as I rubbed my sore butt cheeks. *Déjà vu*, I thought with a snort. My behind was suffering a lot, ever since I'd gone out on an ice-skating date what seemed like decades ago.

Chase and Andrew had managed to get me back up onto my feet, and were holding me up from both sides. I felt like a paper doll now being craned by a set of dockside cranes, letting out little gasps of genuine fear as the pair pulled me through the ice at a speed that felt like a racecar's. The pair had it so natural, gliding across the ice like a pair of swans—a pair of swans *towing* me forward.

"Sucks that you can't skate," Chase complained. "We'd have loved to play a game of... I don't know, something like hockey."

"We still can," Andrew objected. "We just have to put her on Carlos' team."

"Please," I pleaded. "This is already enough of a nightmare without you guys charging at me with sticks. All I want to do is get off the ice. I'll watch."

"No, I don't think so," Chase said with a grin.

The pair then continued to push and pull me across the frozen lake. The wind gushed past, tickling my cheekbones with a crisp wintry chill.

"You have to push the ice hard with the middle of your feet, Sarah. Kind of like that action and reaction thing. You want to be pushing the ice the whole time, nice and strong, like when you're deadlifting," Chase directed. "You have to have a strong hold on your ankles so—"

My feet wobbled terribly as though I were skating on a rake.

"...so your feet don't do that," he finished with a sigh. "Seriously, Sarah, how are you this bad at skating?"

"*Ouch*," I winced. "*How are you guys so good?*"

"Told you, we came here every year, the two of us and Cal. Pretty much every day when the lake freezes over. Toward the end of February the ice starts to get soft, and if you come around then enough times you learn to change before you fall into the water. Really useful for us birds, I'm not sure how much help it's gonna do you cats and dogs but at least you can keep your clothes from getting wet," Chase chattered excitedly.

"*The ice cracks?*" I demanded, my voice almost a scream.

"Relax, Sarah," Chase nodded toward Calleigh, who was tiptoeing around the ice on the weird rakes on the front of her skates. "It's nice and hard. Not gonna happen today."

"*Damn*," I cursed in panic. "Just... just let me get off the ice. This is my worst nightmare."

The boys chuckled. "Promise we will, just one more lap."

Thankfully they kept their promise.

The surface of the lake had turned to a solid, glossy floor, soft white bubbles frozen in between a deep azure, creating a texture of exotic marble. Calleigh was soaring down the middle of it, turning every so often, spiraling and gliding like a little fairy. Lillian was a blur, racing around the edge of the frozen water, her hair flying behind her as if she were on a highway. But a truly astonishing sight was...

"Damn, he's so at home," Andrew exclaimed, his arms folded over his chest.

Carlos was coasting backwards, laughing, his whole face lit up in delight as his hair flew into his face, tickling his temples—he was turning, braking, stirring up a cascade of snow; another turn, a set of steps, loops... etching the ice with every stroke, a rejuvenating sound of blades scratching ice resonating through the chill of the air.

As I watched him a sudden realization flared up in me, with a thud against my chest—

—that he was beautiful.

Carlos Pierce. *Carlos Pierce*, who, only months ago, was the 'condescending jackass' I used to wrinkle my nose at in disdain. *Beautiful.*

Crap.

Calleigh must have thought I needed to be cheered up even more, because for the past few hours, she had been trying to get me to model for her. I couldn't see how that was supposed to cheer me up, but after a few blinks of her puppy eyes, I folded. I sat in the garden, with Calleigh in front of me at her easel—she had told me she wanted to skip her gem training session that day—peering at me with a brush in hand.

"You don't have to get upset," Calleigh said as clipped a piece of paper onto her drawing board.

"I'm not upset," I replied awkwardly. "I didn't mind watching..." I trailed off, my face flushing as I suddenly remembered what I'd been thinking on the bank earlier.

"No, I'm not talking about the skating. I'm talking about... well, *everything*."

Calleigh's hand moved deftly across the paper. From where I was seated it was hard to see what she was doing. I squirmed in my white rocking chair, trying to position myself so I could peek over the easel.

"Nuh-uh," Calleigh voiced. "You have to sit still, Sarah."

I groaned.

The sunlight fluttered softly onto my face. It was a nice, cheerful day. The chill of February did not bring out the brightest of colors in Calleigh's garden, but with the sunlight glinting mellowly off the bare birch trees in the corners and the pine needles shuddering excitedly here and there, it looked refreshing. I imagined how good it would look in the spring and summer. With my mind's eye I painted blossoms over the bare bushes and stubs of dead herbs—

and it soon turned a delightful shade of green. Dandelions and wood sorrels glistered everywhere. Around a little pond that served as a bee bath, between the little round pebbles that lined its contour, bloomed lilies of uncountable colors.

Calleigh was intent, her gaze almost a glare burning into the paper. She seemed to think I was still upset about my gem. I was, in a way. I doubted it would ever really go away. But the truth was that I had been thinking about something else. And I was upset about it; so I guess Calleigh was more right than wrong—I was upset that I'd been thinking about it.

The one thing worse that catching feelings, I thought to myself, *is catching thoughts.*

"Lost in thought is okay, but I want to see a smile," Calleigh chimed. "Just for a second. I have photographic memory."

I frowned. "If you have photographic memory, why do you need me to stay still?"

"So you have something to do," Calleigh replied, her hands moving thoughtfully across the board. "So you won't get sad."

As I watched her paint, I couldn't help but marvel at the dexterity with which her hands moved. They were sketching lines, the tips of her fingers resembling a dancer's feet. Her strokes landed like music, and she mixed colors like an ancient alchemist, foreseeing, presumably, what the strange combination of colors would yield. From the tip of her brush I saw the births of countless colors—gray green, naple, olive, droplets of celadon, a swirl of sarcoline—all from the scope of the most basic shades. Her brush strokes soon diminished into something so fine it looked stationary; it occurred to me that she was working on my eyes.

From toddler days I could never fully answer the question of eye colors. My eyes were a blend of colors—starting out in a thin ring of pacific blue merging into a ring of teal green, which then dissolves into a mild olive and ends a brownish orange close to my pupils. *'I don't know, I really don't'* had always been my answer to *'Just what the hell kind of color are your eyes'*; and here she was, laying out countless indescribable colors—*purple!*—just to paint a tiny detail of my iris. And she did it with such ease; I took satisfaction from the way she gently rubbed the paper with the tip of her brush and fingers to blend in the colors.

Soon Calleigh moved on to a different part—I could tell from the wider brush strokes—and somewhere in the middle, she stopped to lay a gaze on me so much like my mom's, that I couldn't help but smile a funny smile.

"Honey blonde," she commented. "Used to be one of my least preferred hair colors, but you changed my mind. It's my new favorite."

I giggled.

"See? You're feeling better. See—I told you this would make you better." Calleigh chimed excitedly. "Wait till you see what I've got here. I'm not a hyper-realist, but with my favorite model here I have to be, if I wanted to do you any kind of justice. Take the uncanny out of the valley, and you get a hyper-realistic portrait from me."

I grimaced. Take the what out of the what and you get what? I shook my head, thinking the past hour of intense painting must have finally caught up with her.

Calleigh sifted through her crate of paint tubes for shades of gray, blue and yellow, and mixed them deftly until they turned faint shades of white, a dim sort of glaucous for the shadows, a faded yellow for sunlit highlights. I peered intently, marveling at the sight of the artist at work, at her fragile fingers holding the brush with firm expertise. On her forefinger I noticed a delicately carved ring made of dark wood, the outline of a bird catching the sunlight and glistening cheerfully.

"It's pretty, isn't it?" Calleigh commented, catching my gaze. "It used to be my grandma's. Been passed down for generations."

"It looks like an ethnic thing, kind of like an old artefact," I commented. "It's beautiful."

Calleigh beamed. "I'll tell you all about it sometime. It's a long story to tell."

But it seemed now wasn't the right time; Calleigh, unlike her usual self, didn't talk much while she was focused. With eyes intent and lips slightly pouted, she picked out a tube of dense brown, and stirred some soft gray and honey-oat yellow into the blob of brown. It seemed she had begun to work on the background. I looked at the mess she'd left behind on her pallet; it looked like an abstract painting.

"You can move now, Sarah," Calleigh said as she blended more colors. With much relief I straightened up. I straightened my legs, rolled my neck and stretched my arms—and I noticed for the first time that Carlos was standing in the doorframe, watching.

"How's she doing?" I whispered.

"She's photographing you," Carlos replied, peering at the drawing board. The way he did that—it suddenly occurred to me that he must have been looking at me and not the painting. Out the corner of my eyes I saw Calleigh smile smugly.

"I'm flattered. She's not the easiest to paint," Calleigh said, without taking her eyes off the board. "I spent ten minutes on her eyes."

"I could never figure out what to say when people asked me exactly what color my eyes are," I said. "I think I have central heterochromia."

"Hazel, Sarah," Calleigh said in a comically stern voice. "Let's just agree to call it hazel."

Carlos chuckled, and I felt myself blushing.

Calleigh worked some more in silence. For a minute I looked around awkwardly, suddenly conscious of the boy staying in the doorway, but soon my eyes found entertainment in watching Calleigh hunched over the drawing board, a blob of olive paint having suddenly appeared on her cheek. After a while the girl raised her smiling eyes from the paper and motioned me over to her side. I crept over.

"Oh, god," I whispered.

On the paper was the girl I knew best. She sat proudly in Calleigh's garden chair—a little amendment, I guessed, on the artist's part, because I knew I'd been sitting most awkwardly for the past hour—wearing a brilliant smile, her usual fiery gaze molten into a mellow satisfaction. I marveled at the elaborate brush strokes, of carefree golden hair fluttering to her chest, of the wrinkle that formed around her eyes when she smiled. All from the pink tip on her nose, to the thin lips I'd always thought was bland, Calleigh's portrait was making me feel a surge of tender love for the girl on the paper.

Calleigh carefully unclipped the paper from the board.

"Early birthday present," she said with a smug beam, putting the portrait into my hands.

"Hey," I started. I suddenly felt embarrassed of the words I'd voice next, because they did not feel like enough. "Thank you."

But the look in Calleigh's half-moon eyes seemed to show she understood.

Calleigh gathered her treasury and put them back in her wooden chest, and I carefully rolled up the portrait into a cylinder. For once she was right; I did feel better.

Chapter 9
The Cocktail Party

It was Wednesday afternoon. The sky softened into a mellow pastel tone, and Robert and Sophie made an announcement. There was a trial in London that they needed to attend. Not much detail was given, but it seemed that a fifteen-year-old Enricus was involved.

"Is that a British court case or a CE court case?" Chase asked, his brows furrowed in serious concentration. But something told me he couldn't care less, and he was hiding a smile.

"British," Robert replied.

"Ah. Sucks for you," Chase said. "Is the Committee coming with you?"

Robert nodded. "There is an agent coming with us. In the worst case there might be some operations."

"Operations by the Secrecy Committee," Chase repeated with a grimace. "That's got to be bad. Good luck, Dad."

"Thanks, son. You and Calleigh stay out of trouble."

Chase winked. "Will do."

The boys helped the couple into a cab that had been parked in the driveway all morning. Robert gave a weary smile; then the cab disappeared around the curb.

The Secrecy Committee's involvement could never be good. I thought back to what I'd read during my hunting break. Enrici had not always been kept in utter secrecy from humans; in the prehistoric times, they had been part of the human world—until a spark of distrust led to the massacre of Enrici. In those days most of the population were killed and the remainder were forced to go into hiding. Ever since, the world of Enrici remained concealed from the rest of the world.

The Secrecy Committee was, in a way, the guardian of that world. It was a workforce of specially trained agents and strategists, braced to take action when our existence had somehow been exposed. The ways they could engage were quite unlimited. Sometimes gems like Carlos' would come in handy. A team of Memory Gems were always prepared to 'wipe' anyone who'd been unfortunate enough to cross the wrong path at the wrong time. But when matters got worse, and when malice was involved—or politics, for that matter—things could take unorthodox turns. I recalled reading about a certain Hannah Rennett—one of the most famous assassins to work in the Secrecy Committee. She'd single-handedly stopped a war between humans and Enrici with nothing but malt whiskey.

"I'm pretty sure it won't go that far," Calleigh was saying. "My parents can be really convincing."

"Hope so," responded Chase. "Last time they saved the Secrecy Committee a job they brought home this magic juice and we kind of stole it. It was the best thing ever."

Calleigh's eyes glittered, and Chase's head snapped toward her. For a moment a spark seemed to pass between their eyes. Everyone looked at the pair in confusion.

"You're thinking what I'm thinking, right, Calleigh?"

Calleigh blossomed into a sly smile. "*Totally.*"

The rest were just as clueless as I was. We stood with our eyes darting between the siblings until Calleigh opened her mouth:

"Who's in for a cocktail party?"

It turned out that football was not the only passion Chase had. The other one was, well, very discreet and in most regions a felony.

The lights were off, except a flashlight under a gleaming gold bottle of whiskey, which cast a dancing glow on the ceiling. Music was blasting from Calleigh's custom-painted speakers, and Chase stood among bottles of unidentifiable liquor, purée, a tray of ice cubes and other bizarre contraptions; deftly mixing drinks like a barkeeper.

"You know guys, I took classes," Chases began to boast as he unscrewed a fresh new bottle.

Calleigh laughed. "Yeah, I know, for Jessica's birthday."

"Shut up, Calleigh."

Andrew laughed like it was hilarious. "For those of you who are confused, she's talking about Jessica Hoffman."

Chase scowled. I had only a faint idea of what they were talking about—it seemed more of an inside joke. I suddenly realized I wanted so badly to be part of it, and at the same time *didn't*; it was a strange balance between the Sarah, proud and sophisticated, and another Sarah, one who wanted only to be seen and loved.

But we weren't outsiders for long; Andrew saw the confusion in our faces and began to explain everything. "His ex-girlfriend," said Andrew, cracking up. "And FYI he faked his ID. He thought not shaving for a week would make him look 21. Guess what he *actually* looked like."

"A fifteen-year-old with a beard?" Carlos guessed with a chuckle.

"No, a fifteen-year-old *without* a beard. He couldn't even grow a decent one."

Calleigh laughed hysterically, and Chase shot a scowl in her direction.

"Andrew, shut your mouth or I'm shutting you up," Chase said, holding up a full bottle he took from the shelf. It was labeled 'Absolut' in big blue print. "Oh, this time, try not to eat your pants."

The group laughed. Andrew groaned, and Chase let out a high-pitched laughter that sounded like an eagle's call. He then worked deftly with the liquor—minutes later he produced a glass of creamy green cocktail.

"For Mr. Jacus, I made a Shamrock Shaker. Basically a smoothie. But he's going to get drunk and eat his pants. Just watch."

"Wasn't this what you were going to make Jessica before she dumped you?" Andrew challenged.

"No, sucker, that was Bellini and I don't do it anymore."

I shook my head. I guess this battle had been going on quite a while.

After a while Chase handed me a glass full of clear spring green liquid. It was in one of those glasses I'd seen in movies. I carefully took hold of the stem, worried I would break it.

"Four Leaf Clover. Basically fruit juice, but my personal favorite fruit juice."

"Thanks." I took the glass.

"Better be a light one. Sarah's kind of terrible," Carlos commented, gazing at me and my glass.

"I kind of saw to that," Chase replied, handing Carlos a ready-made glass of... latte?

Carlos took the glass in his hand. The cocktail was a creamy almond in color—it looked delicious. "What's this called?" he asked.

"Orgasm," Chase replied.

Carlos raised an eyebrow. "I like the name."

"I figured," Chase said with a smug smile. He then took three stout glasses and laid them in front.

"For the three of us, I made the classics...

"Cardinale," Chase handed Calleigh a deep reddish pink cocktail with ice cubes.

"Catharsis." He placed a mystic light gold cocktail in front of Lillian. Lillian nodded in approval.

"And Godfather." Chase finished, picking up a glass of amberish, iced cocktail and holding it in his hand.

"Well then!" Calleigh rose, raising her glass—it almost looked like a trophy side by side with her frail arm. "To the trial."

"To the trial," the group chanted. Glasses collided in lavish harmony, adding to the music from Calleigh's speakers: *Love Song, California Gurls, OMG, Airplanes, Forever*—songs I'd remember perhaps ten or twenty years later as a sweet bridge between childhood and adulthood.

The Four-Leaf Clover was delicious. It was, unlike the burning juice I expected it to be, much like nectar with a citric finish. Chase looked at me with a big grin as he saw me empty the glass. I looked around to see that everyone else had downed theirs in the blink of an eye.

"I mean, I don't always drink, but when I do, it's Godfather," Chase commented.

More cocktails were made and wasted, growing simpler and simpler as Chase lost precision. When this bottle of pure whiskey got involved things got, well, chaotic. My focus shimmered and letters glittered, and when sounds reached my ears it was with a pleasant sense of distance, muffled and ringing, as if from far, far away—I think between these moments I'd seen Chase climb up onto a chair a couple times, popping corks into oblivion.

It was at some point in the middle, when we were sitting around the golden whiskey-lamp as though it were some brightly lit bonfire, that with sleepy, sparkling eyes, Calleigh made a little suggestion.

"I suggest we play a drinking game."

"What game?"

Calleigh grinned like one of those horror movies. "The classic. Truth or…"

"Drink," Chase replied lethargically.

"That works, I was going to say dare but then the last time didn't go that well. We could use some brakes," Calleigh commented, quite unlike herself.

"She changed on top of a traffic light," explained Chase. "I dared her. It was funny."

"It was *not* funny," Andrew muttered with her hand over his face. "You both could have ended up in prison, for god's sake."

And so the idea of dares was discarded, and there came to be three huge cups set in the middle, filled to the rim with death potion.

The game started. None of us were quite in the right mind even from the start—Calleigh had a gigantic grin on her face that I'd never thought possible, kind of like the Cheshire cat, and the younger boys were eyeing each other with flicks of their eyebrows that only the pair seemed to understand.

First one down the fire lane was Calleigh. Chased raised his hand like an eight-year-old excited to answer a teacher's question, and asked with comically somber eyes: "Do you ever plan on moving? Like, far from here?"

Calleigh chuckled. "If I ever do, I'm bringing you with me, sweetie."

Chased buried his head in his hands. "I'm pretty sure we can do without each other."

"Love you too, sweetie."

There didn't seem to be much essence to this game; it was effectively gibberish. Next was Lillian—I pricked up my ears, hoping to catch something interesting. I listened intently as Calleigh stepped forward with her question: "Who do you think..."

Lillian raised an eyebrow.

"...is the best hunter here?"

"Sarah," Lillian replied without so much as hesitating.

Calleigh looked amazed. "Seriously?"

Lillian shrugged. "Oh, I thought you meant besides myself."

"Hold on, hold on," said Carlos. "I need to know. Why are you two so good? You two are kickass hunters. Sarah, well, I've seen her hunt all the time, and Lillian—well, I saw you with that rabbit the other day, in the backyard."

"You mean compared to the real-life predators? Nothing builds intelligence in a species like desperate measures of desolate monkeys," replied Calleigh.

"What?" Carlos frowned.

"Forget her, she's being Calleigh," commented Chase. "I keep a list of ridiculous things she says. That thing just made number fifty-one."

"Shut up, Chasey."

Lillian ignored the chit chat—it probably helped that she had been living with them for who knows how long—and frowned at Carlos. "I think you're the only bad hunter here, Pierce."

"Hey," I said defensively. "He's not bad."

Lillian raised an eyebrow. "Look at you, defending him."

"He's my partner," I said defiantly. "And he's good."

Lillian looked at me like she'd heard the most ridiculous thing ever said. For a moment it occurred to me that the girl resembled me in ways I couldn't quite explain.

The party, however, did not wait for the three of us to settle the debate. Carlos hadn't gotten his answer, but it seemed he had forgotten he'd asked anything at all—instead, his focus, as did mine, turned to Calleigh's merry voice as she spun the bottle a third time.

"Chase," Calleigh chimed as her bottle landed, a mischievous smile on her face. An *unhhhhh* escaped from Andrew's mouth, his hand flying in the air.

"I feel like you already know all there is to know about him," Calleigh said with a frown. "Anyone else?"

"Name three ways you're similar to your sister," I said slowly.

Chase groaned and wrapped his hands around his head. "God, that's impossible."

I laughed. "I can give you a minute."

"Well, I am an extrovert—"

"Do you even know what it means?" Calleigh interrupted. "It doesn't mean you spend a lot of time with other people, contrary to the common interpretation, it means you get *energy*—"

Chase was already signaling for this shot, a grimace on his face. "I'll just swig that." Cheers erupted as Chase gulped down the vicious looking liquid in a single breath.

"All right, we're going again!" Calleigh exclaimed, taking the bottle in her hands. She seemed a bit off her mind—and I was on a raft, floating down an insanely fast current, toward whatever zone she was in.

"Not again," said Lillian, groaning as the cork pointed at her.

I shot my hand up before I knew it—it was only then that I realized that something had been bothering me about her. Lillian looked to me, raised an eyebrow and nodded.

"Why did you quit hunting with me?"

Lillian sighed, somewhat annoyed. "I needed my sleep."

"She's nocturnal, Sarah," Calleigh chimed in. "She's totally nocturnal."

I flicked my eyebrow. "You need a better reason," I slurred.

"I don't have one," she said. We stared into each other's eyes a long time before she hoarsely extended her hand. "Come on, give me that."

I couldn't help but feel that there was something more to it, that I'd asked the right question—it was like in the hall, back when I had my FT, when she'd been standing there, and I knew she had something to do with it. There was something she hadn't told me.

But drunk Sarah did not dwell on it for long. A wind seemed to sweep me off my feet, and I decided to leave all thoughts behind; I closed my hot, dry eyes, and my ears rang rhythmically, the noise fading in and out like fluttering butterflies.

The bottle landed on Lillian again, and Calleigh, with a shrug, spun it once more. This time its mouth rested on Carlos. I did have many things I wish I knew the answer to; I tried to pick one of them.

"So what do you dream about now?" I asked through my heavy tongue.

Carlos looked fairly uneasy. "Um... can't tell you now," Carlos said, his voice an octave lower than usual. It had never really occurred to me that his voice sounded good. "Not here," he added.

The crowd roared. I got a group bear hug from the other boys, who congratulated me for my 'third kill'. It did not satisfy me; I wanted *answers*, which was something no one seemed to give me today.

Quite a lot of questions and answers went by. *You broke my canvas, sweetie, didn't you? Well, yes I did. I swear I will kill you. Which one of you do you think is better? You know, Lillian, we've been tallying since middle school and I have exactly ONE more sack than him. Screw you, Andrew. For the hundredth time, I did all the work on that one.* There were some that brought about nemesis. Chase and Andrew emptied each other's cups with: *How's Jessica doing? I have no idea, sucker. Well, go ahead, drink. You're dead, Jacus.*

And then; one confession, but crazier than the one you said on April seventh last year, which was met with a cursing Andrew, snarling 'You know what? You suck. You suck balls.' Chase, with a big, smug smile, replied with; 'Don't even complain. Your shot is tiny.' And then, the usual Carlos: *Calleigh. It's a weird name. Like I mean, it's not weird, but it's spelled weird. So? What does it mean?*

"Warrior," Calleigh replied proudly. Her face bore utter innocence, like that of a child perched on the highest branch of an apple tree, the glow from the setting sun full in her face. Her sweet half-moon eyes, stubborn dark brows, delicate nose and thin lips, with those countless starry freckles— together they made a girl that had just walked out of an old fable, a friend that belonged in daydreams. I mouthed the word warrior, contemplating the contrast between it and the spring-like mellowness of her face. It was funny; she could well open her mouth and let out a warcry that sounded like bird-song.

"It's an old Irish name. Spelled the Irish way too, which explains the weird spelling you mentioned. I know I don't look the warrior type. But sometimes just thinking a bit more deeply about my name stirs some strange feelings. I feel a bit braver, I feel some kind of nostalgia. It's like I'm in one of those stories I love."

I feasted on details. I learned that Calleigh's childhood dream was to be a time traveler, and the main reasons were so she could see a dinosaur and find out what color they were. Another reason, also quite important as she'd stressed, was because time travelers had cool suitcases. 'The metal ones with a bunch of numbered wheels,' she'd said. I learned that Andrew had FT-ed when he was eleven, and the first thing he did was to call up Andrew and drink rootbeer. I hadn't known that far before he changed for the first time, he had known what Chase was—they had been the closest of friends, and Chase had confided in him his biggest secret. Andrew had signed the secrecy document, passed the interview with the Secrecy Committee—one that, apparently if you fail, a Memory Gem wipes you and sends you back—and had been officially granted the secret.

"So naturally it was the best feeling ever when it happened," Andrew elaborated. "I just couldn't believe it. I'd always known about it, I'd seen him change, and now it's me."

"How did you feel when you first found out what Chase was?" I asked.

"Well, that was crazy. Chase told me when we were nine, and I didn't believe him. He showed me, I thought I was dreaming and jumped off the second-floor balcony."

"Ohhhh," I groaned. Chase laughed as if it was the funniest thing in the universe.

"I broke my arm. I had to wear a cast when I signed the Pledge of Secrecy."

Chase snorted loudly in laughter. "They thought you were joking because you couldn't sign your name properly with your right hand. And they almost wiped you. Best day of my life," Chase cackled.

Everyone was pretty wasted by the time it came round to me. I didn't know what to expect. I had no idea why, but my heart was pounding—I was brimming with a strange, sweet urge, just to say something about myself, preferably something I'd never said before. Spilled secrets sounded sweet, and bad ideas even sweeter—if bad ideas could be the good ideas, now was the time. It was as if I'd unlatched a latch I didn't know existed. I wanted so badly to do something I'd regret.

I looked at Chase in anticipation, and I could feel my own eyes glimmer—I didn't know if I should be relieved or disappointed when Chase asked:

"Is that your actual eye color?"

"Yes," I replied.

Andrew slurred with a frown. "Is that even a question?"

"Well, I like them," Chase commented, his tongue just as slurred, eyelids half drooped.

"That's not a question either."

"Well, I guess we're taking it from someone else." Calleigh said, chuckling.

Lillian tossed her hand in the air. "Who is your favorite hunting partner?"

I frowned. "Between you and Carlos?"

Lillian shrugged. "Between whoever."

I thought for a minute. To be fair, hunting with Lillian was more likely to succeed, but Carlos was simply—

"I can't decide," I replied.

"Well, then," Lillian said, jabbing her chin at the remaining shot.

Cheers erupted again, and Chase hummed in delight as he filled up the empty glasses.

The liquid burnt through my throat. It was possibly one of the grossest things I'd ever had. I grimaced like a gnome as the terrible taste froze my tongue and a fireball made its way down my throat to my chest. I swallowed a powerful urge to vomit.

"God, that's disgusting." I choked. The boys burst out laughing.

"I feel you," Andrew whispered.

The world rocked in and out of focus, and soon we resumed. Something like a tribal chant filled the living room. The noise grew into an ensemble—one that resembled the cries of rowdy baboons. Unlike myself, I joined in, cheering loudly, as the bottle spun to a stop in front of Lillian.

"Yes, Andrew," Calleigh said merrily. She seemed to be the only one that was herself.

Andrew looked Lillian in the eye before he carefully spoke.

"Tell me... a good memory in Canberra."

And for some reason, the entire room grew dead silent. *What was going on?*

Lillian's eyes seemed to penetrate Andrew's—then she looked away into the distance and let out a deep breath. "I remember this one Saturday," she began. Her voice seemed huskier than ever before. "When we drove downtown and grabbed some tacos. It was about fifteen minutes' drive from where we lived. My mum had them with extra chili sauce. Me and my dad tried it, and we were both crying." Lillian let out a dry laugh. "We picked up a giant crepe cake on the way home, with strawberries on top. And in the car we played something he called *number baseball*. He said he learned it from one of his mates at work. I won. His strategy was always the same. Completely random. He was obviously trying to let me win."

The room was strangely silent. Quite a number of things were absurd tonight, but my dazed head would not focus on any of them. I sat there, slowly rocking back and forth—or perhaps it was the room rocking back and forth—while Andrew whispered "Thank you," and Calleigh spun the bottle again in silence. My eyes came to rest, somewhat delayed, on the end of the bottle, which was facing me.

"Well, Sarah," Calleigh said shrilly. "What is your grand aspiration?"

I was honestly too dizzy to think about such grand matters, but I answered what came to mind anyway: "Well, I want to be a detective," I drooled on. It was hard to articulate properly. "Like my dad, you know."

Calleigh didn't seem to approve. "That's more like a dream job. Do some more thinking, girl," she replied.

I squinted. "Does it mean I have to drink?"

"Rule says yes," Chase hollered. "Rules are rules. Calleigh's not satisfied with your answer."

"*Why, thank you, Chase*," said Calleigh somewhat dramatically.

"Damn," I cursed under my breath—which smelled like alcohol swabs—and reached for the shot, when Carlos' hand appeared out of nowhere to grab it.

"I'll take the shot," Carlos announced. I felt a lazy thud in my chest as I watched him, somewhat attractively lethargic, bring the shot to his lips and down it. I couldn't help but notice a last droplet of Jack Daniel's suspended on his lower lip, making it glisten like a gemstone.

A low *ooh* erupted from the small crowd.

At this point the room began to sway in and out of focus. I vaguely remember the bottle spinning again, a smooth tut tut tut of the glass against the floor, and then an *ohhh* from Carlos as he grabbed his face in his hands, and Lillian's eccentric eyes darting toward me as she pointed her chin at me, and her husky voice saying, "Do you like her?"

And then I probably passed out.

Oh, to be young and foolish. *Very foolish.*

When morning came, I was sprawled on the floor on a heap with everyone else. My head was resting on Carlos' stomach, bobbing in sync to his breathing. Chase had his head on my leg, which had already lost all feeling. I couldn't even recall how I fell asleep, and rummaging my fragmented memory did not help much either. No matter how much I burrowed into my broken memory, I could not figure out how I ended up like this; the last thing I remembered was some point in the middle of the godforsaken game.

I pulled myself up, and jostled to free my leg from Chase's limp head. The room spun. My head rang, and I felt terrible nausea spring up from my stomach. I headed for the bathroom, which I found was quite a mess.

After I was done throwing up, I stood for some minutes with my head resting against the bathroom door. It was horrible. My throat was dry as roasted desert sand, and swallowing felt like prying open pieces of sandpaper stuck to one another. Groggily I shuffled to the kitchen to get myself some water. I poured myself a glass. It smelled bad. I chugged the entire glass, and immediately regretted it; I had to race to the bathroom again, sick as a baboon on a rocking ship.

About an hour later everyone was awake, and half dead—Calleigh was the only one close to alive. I shuffled to the couch to curl up in a corner, my face buried lifelessly in the armrest. I didn't even have the capacity to think about whether it was legal or not to drink your posterior off as an almost-seventeen-year-old in Nebraska; only one thing was certain, and it was that if anything should be illegal, it should be hangovers, whether you were sixteen or sixty-five. My head was splitting open, my entire digestive system had run dry, and

I got sick from doing so much as tilting my head.

"Someone save me," I croaked.

"Out of hope here too," Chase muttered in the distance. "If there's one thing I learned last night, it's that I'm never *ever* going to do this again," he added, yawning as he ruffled his messy hair.

"Sarah, you all right?" asked a very disheveled Carlos. It was when I made eye contact with him that I remembered where my memory broke off.

"Uh, yeah," I replied awkwardly. A bunch of questions floated stupidly around in my head: What had he answered? *Had* he answered? Does he remember? Does he think I remember? Does he think I *don't* remember? Did I say anything? Do anything? Did I pass out cold or just black out?

"You were pretty wasted last night," Carlos commented.

My face grew hot. "Did I... do anything?" I asked cautiously.

Carlos smiled. "I'm pretty sure you didn't."

"*Pretty* sure?" I repeated, eyes narrowed.

"I, well, I don't remember everything, to be honest. But I think I remember most of what you did, so I guess," Carlos shrugged.

Wait, so he doesn't remember the question?

We were struck by a sudden silence. I desperately searched for something to say.

"I, um..." we began. Another awkward silence ensued as we stopped, letting each other continue.

"I um," I started again as Carlos insisted. "I think I'll get some water to drink," I said stupidly.

"Good idea," Carlos replied. That was the end of our conversation.

Later that day, we bought some sandwiches at a nearby deli, ice pails of smoothies at a nearby smoothie place, and drove to the park. In the absence of Robert and Sophie—and with the entirety of Vanna Daya reeking of liquor—a getaway to the park, in the guise of training, was more than due.

The boys helped Calleigh spread the blanket beside the lake. It was a spot I knew well; a smile crept up onto my lips as I thought of everything that had happened here. I thought back to how Carlos and I used to sit here tearing at our kill, or lie here sprawled on the bank gazing at the stars. It was here that he'd told me what he dreamt about, and it was here, now that I think of it, that he'd first morphed into a beautiful, clueless creature. I glanced at Carlos. I wondered if he was thinking the same thing. Our eyes met briefly before his darted away into the distance—it was short, but long enough to bring a little thud in my chest.

I waited a while to sneak another glance at his profile. A whirlwind of feelings stirred in my stomach, some-thing along the lines of discomfort, disappointment, and nervousness. I looked as he stared off into the horizon, wondering if he would turn to look at me. He didn't. I was both disap-pointed and relieved—*stupid, really,* I thought to myself. Sarah two months ago would have been mortified at the idea, but it was true: I did like him.

Chase and Andrew set the blankets down, as Calleigh handed out the smoothies. She seemed to be obsessed with the color green lately, and had taken for herself a suspicious looking green smoothie.

"This is called Green Power," Calleigh explained, catching my concerned look. "It's pretty good. Made with avocadoes and limes. Wanna try?"

I refused. As much as I had a fondness for both healthy treats and ad-ventures, a daring combination of ingredients wasn't something I could take at the moment. I instead took a delightful looking pink smoothie from Calleigh's hands. Strawberry, always my favorite. As I took a sip I felt my insides heal. It was scorch-ed and horrible still, but there was hope of salvation; without the smoothie, I was sure I could never eat again.

"Mint. My mom always said the Space Gem was mint in color. How interesting." Calleigh commented as Carlos took his smoothie.

"The what?" Carlos asked.

"Space Gem. Alters spatial orientation. Usually messes with distances, isn't your gem the Space Gem?" Calleigh chattered excitedly.

"No, mine's the Memory Gem," Carlos corrected.

"Oh, sorry. I don't know why I was so sure it was the Space Gem. Im-pressive. Memory Gems are pretty rare. Do you want to hear something interesting about the Memory Gem?" Calleigh continued excitedly.

No one exactly answered, but Calleigh went on anyway.

"Did you know that each Memory Gem holder has different modes of wiping?"

"You mean... not all of them do it by touching?"

"No. There were some famous Memory Gems in the past, one of the most powerful ones, he could wipe your memory through nothing but eye contact."

"That's sick. I wish I could do that. One of the dummies in the Phonie was sweaty as hell."

"Well, get this. There was this bloke in an Enrican mission force whose mode was intercourse."

"Intercourse as in... sex?"

"Yes."

"Did he do a lot of wiping?"

"Well, actually he did. And he kept logs, which was the fun part. Apparently there was one time when he meant to wipe someone's memory, but got carried away in the process and forgot to do it. He ended up planting one of his memories instead. A memory of himself wiping someone else's memory."

"Which is basically a memory of himself having sex."

"Exactly. His subject woke up the following day believing she had sex with this woman he had sex with. No one else bought it, as she didn't know anything else about the woman and there was no context at all—not to mention she was very straight—but that caused a huge problem for the CE. He got into big trouble for that, and had to have his colleagues perform the wiping again on his subject. He got suspended."

Carlos seemed to be fairly entertained by the idea.

"The Memory Gem is a complicated art. It's one of the hardest Gems to, well, *wield eloquently*. For you to wipe someone's memory exactly the way you want, you need to train *years*. Planting false ones are even harder, but you know what's harder than that? Restoring memories. When memories are ripped from a person, a bond severs. Restoring a severed bond is unimaginably harder than simply creating a new one."

Calleigh stopped to take a long sip from her smoothie before she continued:

"There's something called Pillars. If you want to restore a lost memory, you have to learn to build the Pillars. You see, when a memory is wiped, each image, each detail is gone. It's not preserved even somewhere deep inside their subconscious. It's simply gone, severed from them. But of course, like everything else, there is an irreversible difference between something that happened and something that didn't. There's a crack in the symmetry of past and future. Our memory is one sided and we know it. We can only remember what's happened, not what has yet to happen. Everything that happens leaves a trace."

I thought back to the boy at the fair and things he'd said about the Memory Gem. Then to Carlos. He had appeared by my side as Calleigh passed out the drinks, and stayed there since; I glanced at him, and saw that he was listening with his brows furrowed, focused and intent. I don't think I'd ever seen him like this. I bit my lip.

"The lost memory still leaves some sort of trace, whether it's a blur, a flash, or a scent. It's like a key and keyhole, broken pieces of string that can later be matched to know that the memory was theirs, and that bond once existed. The most common, and possibly deepest form of these traces are impressions. They're persistent, they drift back to you with pictures or songs from those times... and they're the most powerful headstones to build the Pillars on."

"So how do these Pillars work?" Carlos inquired.

"I don't know exactly. I briefly considered trying out for a Memory Gem as my second gem, but it's a bit too difficult for me right now. Making use of gems requires a lot of abstract thinking and imagination in the first place, but Memory Gems take it to another level. That's why there's so much research done on the Memory Gem, and there's still so much to do. It's not just picturing a wall to your right and spinning into it, speaking into a keyhole, or setting foot on a glowing blue jet that will thrust you forward. You have to lock in with a person, read something they have. You have to rummage through it, sever, plant... I can't even put all of it into words. Memory Gems are among the hardest ones to get."

Once more, something twinged in my chest. I looked up uneasily to meet Carlos' steady gaze. I realized, with a dash of embarrassment, that I both envied and adored him. I wondered if he'd seen what I felt—I couldn't quite read him like he seemed to read me.

"I'm starving," Carlos spoke up, his eyes still on mine. "We should maybe grab something to eat. Who else wants to grab a deer?"

I smiled in appreciation. Carlos turned away quickly, and a different sort of pang shot through my chest. Was he avoiding me?

"Watch it," said Chase with a scowl. "Our parents are deers. Make it something else."

"Sorry," Carlos apologized quickly. "Rabbits, how's that sound?"

Chase nodded in approval. "Better, bro," he said, clapping him in the back. "Appreciate it."

We changed. It was a majestic feeling. In a cinematic unison, the six of us twirled in golden spirals into an ensemble of animals. Three eagles, one a hazy ash brown, a larger one, a sort of scorched gold, one a sleek dark chestnut; then a black and white wolf, a chocolate brown panther, and finally myself, a lioness with a coat the color of honey.

The eagles took off first. Majestic wings spread like flying carpets, trapping rays of sunlight in their gilded wingtips. With a couple flaps of their wings the birds were far up in the air—I stared a while, awestruck, as the beautiful creatures shrank and shrank until they were the size of lima beans. *Oh, to be a bird*, I thought. *How would it feel to fly like that?*

On the ground the breeze was pleasant, tickling my cheeks in a delirious way. The three of us land predators also began to dart into the woods. I laughed as the afternoon breeze whizzed past my whiskers; the laugh came out more of a weird, hollow, catlike cough, and it made me laugh some more.

Halfway up we found a small creek. Crystalline water trickled down past rocks and pebbles, curling into a small whirlpool where the rivulet was held by yet unmolten ice. Instead of jumping over the pool like a sensible panther, Carlos plunged straight in, spraying ice cold water everywhere. *Boys*, I thought as I shook my head. With a sideways lioness smile, I did the only sensible thing: I followed suit.

The water was icy, sending tingles through my entire body. I shivered. I realized we were alone; we had lost Lillian on the way. There was not much company here—at least not much awake—but the blobs of snow turning the woods into a dreamy landscape, and the early birds taking flight into the chilly February air, scared away, probably, by the two large cats that had just thrown themselves into a whirlpool. Snowflakes fluttered down from branches they'd deserted, and before our eyes were tiny snowfalls here and there—then some more, and yet some more as the drooping branches of willows quivered in the cold. Carlos bucked a handful of water toward me, and I didn't retreat; I slapped the water with my paws, spraying the panther with icy water. The panther let out a startled little snort, then came at me again. It was war.

I pawed at him, plunging the panther under the surface. The panther spewed out a jet of water, shaking his wet head in a wintry shower. Purrs escaped our lips that sounded a lot like laughter.

Carlos pulled himself up and we stood in the pond, the cold water lapping on our flanks. For a second we both froze. We locked eyes, two pairs of daunting predator eyes, hazel to green. Carlos strode forward a couple steps—the tips of our noses nearly touched, and I could feel the twitch of his whiskers on mine. And ever so gently, the panther nuzzled the tip of my nose with his. It was the strangest thing; a mellow aroma wafted toward me, and suddenly I was enveloped by a bizarre desire. I nuzzled him back. My whiskers ran over his profile, and I could, with the strangely keen senses of a lioness, feel the contours of his jawline; the dimples and creases, the hillocks and ridges. Carlos let out something like a low sigh. Suddenly the rest of the world seemed distant. Long birdcalls from the hills had melted into the background, and the shudder of icy snowflakes became mere glitter in the sky. I'd forgotten about gems, or the hunt for rabbits we'd embarked on. Nothing seemed to matter but the panther in front of me.

It was at that moment that a loud caw echoed through the peaks, snapping us back into reality. It was time to head down. I had not realized we had come this far from where we began—it would take a while to get back. We both twirled back to our human forms, startled.

"Uh..." I murmured, taking a step back. Carlos followed suit and took another step back, until the distance between us was reasonable.

"So, um," Carlos began, but stopped. It seemed neither of us really knew what to say.

I tried again. "Uh, didn't you say you were hungry?" I bumbled.

"I, I'm really not," began Carlos. "But I guess I am now. How about you?"

"Um, not enough to eat a whole deer, or a whole rabbit... or a whole anything. And also a little bit cold." I'd skinny dipped pretty deep, but the intricate physics of these worlds had somehow eluded common sense—once I was back in my human form, I was only slightly wet here and there, not drenched completely as I should be. But it still wasn't enough to keep me warm.

Carlos took off his jacket, and stepped over to wrap it around me. "Wear this," he instructed.

"Thank you," I mumbled awkwardly.

"I don't feel hungry enough to eat something whole either. Wanna share a rabbit on the way down?" he suggested as he tucked the sleeves securely around my neck.

I nodded, blushing a little. "Sure, sounds good."

Fortunately we'd been hunting partners for quite some time, and we didn't really need words to communicate. With the slightest nudge of the head, we'd made a swift agreement on our target. We made a marvelous team afterwards; I'd lured the rabbit toward Carlos who cast the final blow.

Half an hour later the six of us were gathered back in our picnic spot beside the lake, lapping up water from the lake and rinsing our bloody mouths.

"I feel like things would have looked a lot less savage if we were mostly herbivores," Chase remarked, wiping his clean mouth with his elbow. "Half a dozen different carnivorous animals washing blood off their mouths in the lake is..."

"Amazing," Andrew finished the sentence. "That's the beauty of nature."

"We don't look as bloody in our human forms," I remarked.

"That, there, is the magnificence of Enricus physics," Calleigh remarked. "No one really understands how it works. Getting covered in blood when you're an eagle doesn't get you covered in blood when you're human. Maybe a little bit, 'cause when we change we kind of spin and then it spatters everywhere, but not much."

"Imagine how it would have looked if we were bloody even when we've changed back." Chase squinted, as though he were picturing it in his head. "It's got to look like we buried a body."

"Which one of us do you think they're going to suspect?" Andrew asked absently, to which everyone answered by turning to Lillian. Lillian rolled her eyes.

"She does look deadly, not gonna lie," Chase whispered.

"Watch it, Russell," Lillian hissed as she caught the folded picnic blanket Calleigh tossed her.

Quarrels continued as we headed down to the fences. The three boys would be tossing water bottles around, chugging down what seemed like a barrel full of water, constantly making obnoxious remarks about each other. I watched with a glowing warmth in my chest as Carlos caught a flying bottle in his hands with a big smile and tucked it under his arms. It was a cold day, and I cast a look of wonder at the boy; he had not only taken off his jacket—which was now wrapped around me—but he also had the sleeves of his sweatshirt rolled up, exposing his forearms. Something flurried in my stomach and I tore my eyes away from him—from his toned arms, his ruffled hair, his brilliant grin—and interested myself somewhat diligently in the trees that passed by.

The sky had just begun to darken as we reached the parking lot, gathered to return to Vanna Daya. Carlos announced that he had some errands to run, and that we should get going without him. The rest of us piled into Calleigh's truck—it seemed she had now completely recovered from the horrors of liquid poison.

Carlos gave a vague nod and strode off to his car—only to turn abruptly and jog back toward me. I looked back at him in alarm, wondering if he'd somehow heard my thoughts a while back.

"I forgot my keys, sorry," he said softly as he reached into the pocket of his jacket. The relief was short lived, and it was replaced by something else entirely; a flutter went through my stomach as he reached down and his breath brushed my neck.

"See you in a bit," Carlos said, jiggling his keys, before he turned to leave.

"Carlos, wait," I called, untying his jacket from around my shoulders. Carlos turned and stopped me, putting his hand lightly on mine.

"You can wear it. You can just give it to me later," he said softly.

I stood there a while, looking at the tall figure of the boy as he jogged away. Something was fluttering in my stomach again, this time even worse than before—I was at the same time elated and scared, much like a young aerialist who had just stepped onto a tightrope.

The lake stretched in front of me, gleaming deep blue in dim twilight. I stood near the sidelines of the crystalline water, near the spot I'd laid with Carlos gazing at the stars. It was foggy. The horizon seemed to stretch out forever, no canopy behind the banks, only a flat expanse of land that melted into pearly white oblivion. I absently took a few steps forward until my feet touched ice. The lake was still frozen, just like it had when we'd gone skating. But the ice beneath my feet did not burn. It was bearable; pleasant even. I did not slip, and nor did I fall—strangely enough, I found that I could walk. As if I were walking on land, I took another step forward, then another, then another.

Slowly the fog began to lift. The park was still, the way I'd known it, but there were little oddities here and there; shadowy figures, I found, were clustered around the middle of the lake. Blankly I took another step forward. As I neared the middle of the lake and the fog cleared a bit more, I came to a sickening realization; the things in the middle of the lake weren't shadows. They were people. And there was something deeply wrong with them.

There were six of them. They stood, like myself, on the surface of the ice, completely still to the point it was eerie. The sky had darkened a bit, and what little light reached the bleak blue surface scattered and swirled into a thicker shade. My feet carried me closer to the center, and as strangely pacified as I was, dread began to fill me.

It wasn't like they had yellowed skin stuck on crumbling bones, slits for nostrils and hollows for eyes. In fact, it was the contrary. They had beautiful features. One of them boasted luscious hair, the other sleek cheekbones, and another a beautifully sculpted body like that of a renaissance sculpture. But there was something in their expressions, something deeply unsettling, that made me reel—and at the same time drew me, inexorably, to the center of the lake.

And I realized what it was. They wanted to kill. It seemed they were riveting toward something, too fast to be stopped, accelerated beyond retrieval. They longed and needed to kill; it was a desire, a need so fundamental and so honest that it could be seen right through their eyes.

That was when my eyes set on a woman in the middle. Her hair was a wispy silver, faded of color as though in the blaring Mediterranean sun, thin and damaged although her face preserved youth. Her lips were drawn up ever so lightly in a sickly smile, and her glare penetrated my soul as if I were naked under her scrutiny. With an ecstatic dread I realized that I knew exactly who she was.

Victorina Archer.

For some unknown reason, I felt as if I were sailing through the inevitable, treading a path I was meant to tread. Perhaps it had started when I mouthed her name to myself at the fair, or when I'd read of the revived Ranger—or perhaps, it had all started when I'd found that pink book in the library. Regardless of the reason, it had started; a time bomb set to detonate, a piece of fate made to uncoil. Everything, up to this moment, was no coincidence; They were here for me.

The woman and I locked eyes for a moment. As though she had seen the recognition passing through my eyes, the woman let out a laughter that sounded like crackling embers. Then with a smile so wide it could swallow me whole, she lunged forward, straight for my heart.

It was dark. I blinked, trying to chase away the afterimage of the woman's face. A dim light from the half-moon slipped ever so lightly through the windows, bearing an unfitting serenity; but my heart thumped loudly as I tried to determine what I had just seen. Slowly the numbness receded, and my mind awoke from slumber—and yet my heartbeat did not slow, neither did the image fade; with every breath it became more and more evident that I had just seen her.

I had seen the Devil's Lady.

Nightmares were frail. They could be chased away, in youth with my mom's soothing arms around my shoulders and a cup of hot chamomile tea in my hands, with stories spilt on my parents' brightly lit bed—and as I grew older, with even the blink of an eye. But this was no nightmare. As much as it took place in my bed and in my head, it was very much real. I shot up from the bed, sure of what to do next.

"Calleigh? Calleigh, *Calleigh*," I called, knocking on her door with shaking hands.

There was a mumble on the other side of the door, as well as a ruffling of blankets. The door creaked open.

"...Sarah?" Calleigh had shuffled to the door with her eyes barely open. She squinted as if the hall's low lights were too bright for her. "Are you crazy? It's like four in the morning," she mumbled.

She then switched on the lamp, squinting in its light. Lillian stirred on her mattress in the corner.

"Yeah, I know. Middle of the night. But this is really important. I had this dream," I said.

Calleigh snorted sleepily. "You can tell me in the morning..."

"No, you have to listen. This is important," I said. "It's not just an ordinary dream."

Calleigh tilted her head so far to the side that I thought her neck would break. She threw the door open with a concerningly clumsy movement and beckoned me inside, mumbling something that sounded like: "Go ahead... but eat your shoes."

I crept into the room. Her room was warm, but the early morning chill seemed to seep in through the doors and windows. I shuddered. Calleigh sleepily led me to her bed, where she handed me a blanket to wrap myself in. I took a deep breath and began:

"I was at the park. The place was fogged up, and then it cleared, and there were people standing in the middle of the frozen lake... I could make out some of the faces and they were people I'd never seen before, but something looked so *wrong* about them... and then one of them—one of them was the Devil's Lady. The woman who killed the queen. She saw me and knew that I knew her and... and she tried to kill me."

The effect was unlike I'd anticipated. The lethargy was immediately gone and alarm took its place—the girl was now wide awake, staring back at me in disbelief.

"Did you say the Devil's Lady?"

"Yes."

"What did she look like?"

"Catlike eyes, silver hair..."

"Silver hair?"

"Yes, silver hair. This pale, grayish silver. And bluish green eyes."

There was silence as Calleigh straightened herself up, now wide awake.

"I know it sounds crazy," I babbled on. "You don't have to believe me."

Calleigh looked at me a while before she hurried over to Lillian's mattress.

"Lillie, Lillie," She whispered, shaking Lillian awake.

Lillian lay still, burying her face in a pillow.

"What," came a muffled voice from the pillow.

"I think *they're* here."

In a moment everyone was gathered in the living room, some wide awake, some still barely able to keep their eyes open. Calleigh hurried into the room after a frantic search downstairs, holding a stack of papers in her arms.

"I hope you're all awake, but fine if you're not, because you're going to be," Calleigh announced. There was, unlike her, an air of severity in her voice.

"I woke you all up because this is an urgent matter," Calleigh stated. She spread her stack of papers on the coffee table before she asked: "Sarah, are these the people in your dream?"

My heart skipped a beat. On the paper were deftly sketched faces. I did not have to study them for long to know what they were. I gulped as terror spread through my body; each and every one was correct—they were the faces I had seen in the dream.

"What's going on?" Chase asked groggily. "You woke us all up to talk about some people in dreams? And show us your painting?"

Calleigh silenced him with a look.

"Are these... are these..." Calleigh stopped to gulp hard, then continued. "Are these the people you saw? Are they the people in your dream?"

It was like I was paralyzed, with a mixture of fear, wonder, and something else I could not name. With my eyes fixed helplessly on the glares from the drawings, I mustered a tiny nod.

Calleigh sighed like eternity. The sky had begun to light up outside the window, the dark marine blue coming off into a veiled azure, revealing streaks of red and pink and purple. Calleigh's small figure was nearly a dark silhouette against the lighting sky. Somehow, her frail figure looked smaller than it ever had.

"What's going on, Calleigh?" I managed to whisper. "How did you do that?"

Calleigh opened her mouth to respond, but we were interrupted, briefly, by an enraged sigh in the corner. I turned to see Lillian glowering with pure hatred, her eyes fixed at an unreal point in the air. Calleigh turned her eyes away from the agitated girl, and replied:

"Partly because I have photographic memory, and partly because they're unforgettable in every way."

"Who are 'they'?" I asked.

Calleigh looked at me, in her eyes a swirl of fatigue, anger, and sadness.

"Xentrios," she said.

Chapter 10
The Beings

Not a sound was made. Everyone looked at Calleigh in lethargic confusion—except Lillian, who glared with vile eyes at the portraits before she rose from her spot and strode out of sight.

"What's wrong with her?" Carlos asked.

"It's kind of like a long story," Calleigh replied with a sigh. "But it's because she knows them personally. I think she'd rather tell you herself, but yes, she's met them in the past."

I sat there, barely composed, as my heart pounded against my ribcage. *Xentrios*, I thought to myself. *The pirates. The monsters. The Devil's Lady.* They were all the same thing. I was unable to shake off the sensation that they had found me, not the other way round—that I would not have had this dream had I not been delving in the subject.

And yet I have. As an unexplainable consequence my search had led me here, through the children's books, history books, to the dream—and then to this living room, this table, this moment. I was about to find out everything.

From Calleigh's portraits glared the cold, empty eyes, weighing me down, paralyzing me. A sickening sensation gnawed into my marrows as her words sank in, and my thoughts ventured to those eyes I'd seen in my dream, to the worn cover of *Princess Rena*, to the fall of the queen herself—then to what it meant that Lillian had met them.

"What's this about, Calleigh?" Carlos had asked, jerking me out of my thoughts. "Who are these people? I still don't understand a thing."

Calleigh sighed. "I never thought I would have to tell you about them. Some years after what happened with Lillian, I learned about the Xentrios. Mom and Dad showed me reports on them. With pictures. The reports were burned later, but I remembered everything about them."

"And you didn't tell me?" Chase asked in disbelief.

"You were too young at the time, Chasie," Calleigh responded. "Mom and dad weren't so sure about telling me either, but they thought it was only right that I know."

I looked at the girl, wearing a rigid face that somehow made her resemble an eagle. The fleeting softness wasn't gone, it was still there—but there was something else as well, a depth, a power I had not seen on this fragile face.

Calleigh began. "When *we* came into existence, so did the Xentrios. Or more like, the primitive soup of matter, or energy, or *being* that later became the Xentrios."

For a moment I pictured the birth of a particle from a trembling fluctuation of nothingness. It was like the tales of matter and antimatter—encasing, in a strange way, the symmetry and asymmetry of this world.

"And ever since, we'd existed like two sides of a coin," Calleigh continued. "Some eras they thrived, some eras they didn't. The earliest ones were primitive. They lacked system. They were easily killed. It was like they were incomplete. But then powerful ones turned up.

"They go by many names, and we believe there's also a name they gave themselves, one we don't know—and some of us believe that coincidentally, it was around the time they gave themselves a name that they became powerful. The name *Xentrio* as we know it, comes from the notes of an Enricus researcher in the late 1800s. I think it was a way he referred to the three Originals, as I'll mention, in his personal notes—X, Enricus, trio—but since it was discovered it was used more and more widely until it became more of a proper name for the beings as a whole."

"Anyways, after they named themselves, they were incomparably powerful. They grew and thrived. They built an army. They started working together, gathering, speaking the same words, thinking the same thing, believing the same thing.

"They've always been our enemy," Calleigh continued, her voice falling into a whisper, a soft, melodic tone of a master storyteller. "We never understood why they were always after us, why their sole goal seemed to be us, why they took so much joy in killing us. But they did.

"They were our greatest danger. Thousands of Enrici were killed every year. Back in the time of the monarchs, there were a lot of attempts to hunt them down or drive them out. In the 18th century when Enrica came to the throne, she managed to kill quite a number of the Xentrios."

Calleigh went on for a little while about the things I already knew. The puzzle pieces connected in my head at long last; the unseen enemies the entire race of Enrici had been battling in history were, I'd just found, named Xentrios, and they were responsible for the death of Serena.

"And after Enrica and Percival's campaigns—it was what we call '*the War*'—most Xentrios had been wiped from the earth. The remaining Xentrios disappeared, and for a long time everything was okay."

The room was quiet. Calleigh's eyes glistened like a pair of lanterns lighting up a cave.

"Why didn't they tell us?" I voiced. All eyes turned to me. "In the books," I added. "Why didn't they tell us about them?"

Calleigh looked uneasy. "They preferred to keep it hidden, I think, because they worried there would be an uncontrollable fear and chaos if people knew they still existed. As a result any incident related to the Xentrios after the war were disguised as fairy tales, and they chose to be as vague as possible about them even when describing the war."

I pondered. I looked at Calleigh's drawing—there was no doubt that these faces would stir up the most primal fear engraved in our genes. But what good did it do to hide it?

"But they have to tell us the truth," I retorted.

Calleigh smiled somewhat sadly, and for a moment I could see her eyes open up to something a little deeper, perhaps the couple more years she's lived.

"The truth isn't told that often, Sarah," Calleigh responded mysteriously. "Anything that is told is told through a mouth. Anything that is seen is seen through eyes. That is to say, people say what they want heard. People see what they want to see, or what they fear to see, doesn't matter—all that matters is that we never really see the whole truth."

I stayed silent. For a moment Calleigh looked distant and foreign, and much older than she was. I was reminded for a moment of something I'd read earlier on—that in quantum mechanics, things are but a hazy possibility; that we could not know something in its entirety. I pictured again the packets of coins I'd seen in the Phonie. It occurred to me that through whatever's spoken or written or drawn, I was only seeing a spectrum of what could be the truth; with or without human error, the world ceased to be deterministic. *But that didn't justify anything,* I thought. *We're still owed an attempt.*

And yet when I looked at Calleigh's deep eyes, and thought again of the weight of the situation, all that seemed to matter a little less. What mattered, like it or not, was the set of things I could do with this information. It seemed more was at stake than I could have ever imagined.

Calleigh seemed to process the silence a while before she continued.

"Some of you must be wondering what it is that makes them so dangerous as they're said to be. Well, the history is complicated, and in a way kind of hazy. But we know this much:

"When they started working with one another and developing physical instruments to hold and strengthen their powers, they became stronger and stronger. We say:"

Her voice shrank to a delicate whisper.

"To time, they're immortal."

She continued: "They could be killed, yes. In the CE, armed forces were formed to fight them. But they were powerful, almost impossible to destroy—and they don't... die of natural causes. You see; to put it in an easier way, they're like—zombies. Smarter, less revolting in a sense. But yes, in a way, undead."

"Why don't you just shoot them?" asked Carlos simply. "You said it's possible to kill them."

"It is. But they don't function like we do—it's a lot harder than you think. Besides, we can't risk this business between the two species being known to humans. We can't have them investigate the death of an Xentrio. You see what I mean—a conflict between us and the human race is the last thing we want. There'll be chaos. We'll be threats to them."

She was right; humans, both to our relief and despair, nipped the buds of threats before they bloomed.

"And they seem to hold that to their advantage. They know very well about humans, and many of them even live amongst them, but they had never once targeted them. They did recruit them, or kill those who wouldn't comply. But they'd never deliberately and systematically worked to destroy them, as they did to us. If you've read Princess Rena, Sarah, you'd know, but the dark forces that killed Harvey and his men, those were Xentrios.

"These Xentrios, they were once humans, yes; but the Originals and the ones before them were turned without anyone else turning them. We don't really know how exactly they changed for the first time.

"We like to think of them as an anti-species of what we are, in analogy with anti-matter that exists for corresponding matter. The Enrici were born, so were they. And in many cases, they mirror us; in a way that's too discomforting to be true. They don't change like we do, but they have powers that we don't. They don't have gems, but their powers condense into something that could be stored in material forms."

Calleigh looked around the room, and was met with a painful silence. No one seemed to know what to respond. Calleigh swallowed and continued:

"Only my parents and Lillie and I knew about them. The CE has kept them hidden, for reasons they don't disclose. Many books that mention them, or hint their existence, were burned, which was why I was surprised Sarah had gotten her hands on this book called Princess Rena—well, because it was a book that would have been burned instantly. As for why I never told any of you, it was for our safety. And for reasons I've mentioned before—that we can't risk a species-wide panic that would set us in line of sight of humans. Chasey, I'm so sorry; we thought you were too young for this. But not now. Sarah's had this dream, and I think it means it's time for all of you to know. We can't afford to go on not knowing. Not anymore," Calleigh said. She turned the drawing so that it faced the couch, where everyone sat, fully awake.

"The exact number is unknown, but there's quite a lot of them out there. They have disguises and identities to fit into the human world. We know the identities of seven Xentrios. They seem to be the most important and powerful ones."

She pointed to three faces on the top of her drawing.

"The Originals first."

She took one of her pencils, and pointed it to the silver haired woman.

"Victorina. She's known to have manipulative, or oftentimes seductive, powers."

I breathed sharply. Victorina. The Devil's Lady, the pirate. *The woman who killed Queen Serena.*

"She is the queen of the mind. Her instrument"—she pointed to the glass pendant on the woman's chest—"is this. The Perfume Pendant. The Perfume is no ordinary perfume, the Pendant is no ordinary pendant. If anyone takes so much as a whiff, believe me, even a molecule of it—their emotions are under her control. She can make you feel anything; fear, pain, ecstasy. Instruments of this kind are called Victorinian Instruments."

"That actually works?" Carlos challenged.

Calleigh nodded subtly. "I told you, it does. It would with no question work on everyone in this room. Wait."

Her eyes turned to me—with charisma that reminded me of Sophie.

"Except you, Sarah."

"*What?*"

"It works through the gem," Calleigh explained. "She won't be able to take control of you."

"Oh," I said stupidly. I wondered if this could possibly be a good thing.

"Let's move on," Calleigh's voice snapped me back into the fable. Calleigh pointed at the man on Victorina's right.

"Cuper. He and Victorina are often seen together, like, *together* together. But these things don't have human emotions, so it's thought to be nothing more than physical."

Calleigh went on: "Cuper's strength is physical. His instrument is called the Lock, the most powerful of the Cuperian family. You won't see it in this picture, 'cause he carries it in his coat pocket. With the Lock he controls your movement. But he has a weakness. His weakness is that it needs his focus. He can only control what he focuses on."

Calleigh paused for a while, grabbing a glass of water from the windowsill.

"Then next—we have Darius. He is the head of the Originals, the First Original, the Devil, the Sire, whatever you choose to call him. He is the most powerful of them all."

"Where is he? Is he in the painting?" I asked.

Calleigh shook her head. "This dream—it's something of their doing, although probably not intentionally. We don't know how it happens, but it often happens that when their power grows, they influence things around them in ways we can't imagine. Commonly, in these types of dreams, there are these six in front and sometimes more at the back, but the ones at the back, if any, usually aren't clearly visible. And they're usually in the place the dreamer favors to change in, in your case the park. But Darius—he never appeared in any of those dreams. In fact, only the people that actually saw him knows what he looks like."

I gasped, for a sudden idea had flashed in my head. "Does Lillian?" I whispered.

"I don't know," Calleigh replied honestly. "She never told me that specifically. She never... told anyone the details."

"If we go back to Darius," Calleigh continued. "He has the most fatal instrument out of the Xentrios. His instrument is the Knife—" she said it as if the *knife* was capitalized, a strong emphasis on the sole syllable. "It's called the king of Darian Instruments. It's extremely sharp, can cut right through your skin... and wounds made by the Knife are extremely hard to heal, even with modern medicine. Without the necessary ingredients, the wound won't close. But that's not the scariest part of it. There's something else the Knife does, the primary reason we fear it so much. There's a saying about it in the Enrican world—"

Calleigh swallowed, then added slowly and in a low whisper:

"*It turns light into darkness.* When you're stabbed by Darius' knife, you become feelingless, empty... that emptiness fills up with anger, hatred, poison—a lust for destruction. One that's impossible to defy," Calleigh whispered.

There was earpiercing silence as the meaning of her words sank in.

"And that, is how the other Xentrios are born."

"Ares. Elor. Keena. Rima," Calleigh listed, pointing in turn at the other figures.

"All victims of the Knife. Stabbed and turned by one of the three Originals. They didn't stop there. They went and created more, built an army. As for the rest... we don't know where or who they are."

"Rima—how old was she when she was... you know?" I asked. I remember thinking she looked awfully young, unlike the others—and Calleigh's drawing confirmed it.

"We can't be sure—but around sixteen or seventeen. She was actually Darius' first victim... and first love."

My eyes went wide.

Calleigh nodded. "But she never gave anything back. Not even a tiny bit of compassion, let alone affection."

"She's free to," I said defiantly.

"But Darius didn't think so. When he turned into an Xentrio, he stabbed her."

I was at a loss of words.

"She had a sister. They say she's the only family Rima had. We don't know what happened to her, and Rima never went looking for her after she became a you-know-what. But something worth paying respect to is that she resisted the Knife for the longest time in history. For most people stabbed by the Knife, transformation was almost instant. But Rima fought all the way from dawn to dusk."

In the silence I wondered if that mattered in any way. It was a fight bound to end in defeat—a war that would be lost, a tragedy that was inescapable. The young girl had fought, like peasants at a stone fortress with rocks in hand, like girls on the street waving flags of a fallen empire. A part of me wanted to say it mattered; in a timeless universe, perhaps, the human thoughts that crossed fallen minds did still exist somewhere, intact; and that fight from dawn to the very perimeters of dusk made all the difference.

"This dream," I began after a while, my voice hoarse. There were still questions to ask, and there were still answers to get. "Calleigh, why am I having this dream?"

"I don't know. I can only guess that... this isn't good." Calleigh breathed. "I've called the CE. They'll have their men investigating what's going on. Meanwhile, I'm supposed to tell you as much as possible about the Xentrios. We might have to be prepared for the worst."

Calleigh picked up the drawing in her hand. "I've got to go back to the Phonie. I need to get in touch with the agents at XTM, I mean Xentrio Threat Management. I want you guys to stay calm, and *not leave the house.* Do you understand me?" Calleigh confirmed.

We nodded.

Calleigh briskly scurried away and disappeared around the waterwall.

And when she returned, her face was paler than ever. We glanced at Calleigh, then at each other, as she spoke with a shaking voice:

"Where's Lillian? We have to get her here," Calleigh said, her voice shaking.

When she did come, guided by Chase, to the living room, Calleigh spoke up: "We're going to do a moonflower search."

"*What?*" hissed Lillian.

My eyes darted between the two of them. What is a moonflower search? Why had it upset Lillian?

It turned out, humans weren't the only forms of life affected by Alpha Enrica's magnetic wind—the *Oenothera* were also mutated. A portion of them, blessed by the radiation of the star, turned into the *Oenothera Enricus*, or the Moonflowers. They were the only and unbelievably effective medication against the physical wounds caused by Darius' Knife, and various other injuries caused by the Xentrios' instruments; but they worked well as a cure only when they were alive—dried or preserved, they did not work as effectively.

It was also learned that day, that when the Xentrios planned an attack, they started with burning the Moonflowers near their targets. They preferred to leave no chance.

"This is a sample," Calleigh said, holding up a glass tube. Inside sat a delicate yellow flower, thin, heart shaped yellow petals wrapped tenderly around frail stamens. The flower had a barely noticeable glow to it, a soft, pale, pearly halo. A closer look told me that its pollen glittered, like a slew of tiny stars.

"Now what we are going to do is turn, sniff the sample, split into groups and find the moonflowers. The smell of a moonflower, once you get to know it, can be sensed from quite far away."

Calleigh produced a big roll of paper.

"This, is the map of moonflower distribution in a ten-mile radius from the headquarters."

She unrolled the map and carefully fixed the edges on her easel.

It was a map of the city, from the neighborhood up to the park beside Halliday Corp, then to the streets downtown. Yellow dots were painted in here and there. There were two big clusters situated throughout the city; one at Halliday, and one in a smaller park nearer to the center of the city.

"We're going to search the denser parts first, because that's going to provide more information. We compare the actual distribution of the moonflowers to the distribution on the map. We can't check all of them, but we're going to drive to Halliday and start from there. It should be enough for comparison. The map is pretty up to date, and it should be reliable.

"Okay, listen closely. You know that Chase's gem is the Beacon, and it can strengthen a gem, makes it usable in human form, or give someone else access to its powers. So we know that without the Beacon, all of you can hear me when you're close enough, but you can't speak to me the same way, which makes the whole conversation one-way—which isn't good, because I need to hear from you to figure out what's going on. So we're going to circle the air, me and Chase, and we are—"

"I'm going to beacon her gem so you guys can all talk to her." Chase finished for her. Calleigh shot him a look, but it soon turned to appreciation. This wasn't a time we could rely on her lengthy talk.

"We'll split into three groups of two. We're going to cover the two main areas first, as shown on the map," Calleigh continued, holding up the map for us to see. "We will be communicating with the beaconed NVC. Chase and I will be circling the area, and you speak into the channel when we come in range. I will remember the places where you found the flowers.

"Sarah, Carlos, you're going to Halliday. There's no other option. We can't have a lion and a panther walking around in the middle of the city," Calleigh directed. "Lillian, Andrew, you're going downtown."

"She's a wolf," Carlos objected. "I don't see how much better that is."

"She could pass for a dog," Calleigh said.

Chase and Andrew looked at each other, and shook their heads. "No, I don't mean to offend you, Lillian, but a hellhound is the only kind of dog you'll pass for," Chase commented.

Lillian scowled.

"Well, we have something that could help," Calleigh suggested.

Lillian's face was cold as stone. "No."

"Yes."

The 'something' turned out to be a fluffy pink collar with a large bone-shaped label that read 'I don't bite.' Wolf-Lillian gave a homicidal look as Calleigh fastened it around her neck.

Soon the wolf and eagle rushed off to their posts. Carlos and I headed to the park. It didn't take long; we broke in again through the shortcut as we always did in our nightly hunts. The woods were silent, as if anticipating what was to come.

I trotted in complete silence. In my head I went over Calleigh's little introductory course on how to talk back to her using her gem.

"This is not going to be easy for you two," Calleigh had said, facing me and Carlos. "This is C1 level gem training. I know you haven't covered even the basics yet, but I still need you two to help as well. When Chase beacons the Nonverbal Communication gem—the NVC—you will feel it. At first it will be a little hard to find the channel, but the NVC is the easiest to use aided by the beacon. It's very much like transforming, you will be able to find a doorway where the channel is linked to the rest of us. You'll know what I mean."

"I'm not so sure," I said uneasily.

"It's fine. I'll explain it to you. I'm going to change and talk to you, like I did back in the basement at school. Remember?" Calleigh began.

I nodded. "Yeah, I do."

"Do you remember how it felt when I talked to you?"

"Like the sound was coming from—somewhere, but I had no idea where. It was like it was coming from inside me, but not quite that either."

Calleigh nodded. "This is going to be very difficult. Especially for you, Sarah, because it's purely abstract, and the lack of experience you have with gems is not going to make it easier."

It hurt a little, but I nodded.

"But you have to try. It's like when you change. I'm sure you'll remember the surface and the chimes. When I'm talking to you, you're going to move around. Not physically, but like you do when you change. There's going to be one angle where the sound sort of fades, but you feel it echo as if it were coming from somewhere within you.

"That's where you can speak to me. When Chase is Beaconing my gem, it's going to feel different. You're going to feel a hole, like a keyhole, that opens up to me when you find this angle. You're going to talk to me through that."

It hadn't worked at first, but I'd begun to see what she meant. It was kind of like moving on the edge of a dream, where you had to focus hard on moving your dream-hands, or dream-eyes, instead of the ones lying in bed with you. With tilts of my head I began to notice a faint change in Calleigh's voice as eagle-Calleigh recited Shakespeare. After a few tries I'd found the 'hole' she had mentioned.

There was a crisp chill in the air. Carlos and I trod the path we knew so well. None of us would have said anything even if we could. The bare trees shivered as a slicing wind rushed past. The ground was coated thinly with brown and gold of dead grass. Out of corners grew little sprouts, poking out of the draft soil in anticipation. But there were no flowers to be seen. I could not picture the blossoms penetrating from ground this cold.

Dry twigs broke softly under Carlos' feet. He nudged his chin toward the air, and I looked to find Calleigh and Chase gliding toward us.

Hey guys, do you copy? Calleigh's voice pierced into my head.

Yes, I read you, I replied. *Nothing just yet. Are you sure there even is any? It's mid-winter.*

They may be less dense and more feeble, but they do bloom all year. Calleigh replied. *You might want to rely on your nose.*

Calleigh flew off again, and we were left alone.

We hiked along the usual path to the hilltop. It was mere moments before I emerged from the trees to the view of the entire sanctuary, that a subtle tint of familiar scent found me.

I slinked up to the spot, and found a small plant, sets of fierce claw-like capsules covering a thick reddish stem. An unmistakable scent of a moon-flower crept up from the capsules. I peered closer at a shrub, and saw a tiny speck, smaller than a grain of salt, budding from inside the capsule. The speck caught the sun and glimmered a soft yellow.

I found one, I said when Calleigh came flying back. *On the top of the east hill. Got it.*

We found some more as we traced down the hills all the way to the lake. We then roamed into the thicker woods, where the midday sun ebbed to tinsels of gold-white here and there. Everything was strangely still, and not a hint of another moonflower was present.

But about halfway through we both stopped in our tracks. From somewhere deeper in the woods came a pungent odor. We glanced each other, and without a word made way to the heart of the woods. The stench got stronger and stronger; we stopped at a small clearing where sunlight shone through like a cone of haze, and were met by a sight we'd been afraid to see.

Dust-like particles danced eerily in the sun's golden halo, in a ghastly waltz of death—amidst a thick cloud of acrid stench and drifting ashes, was a bed of flowers; burnt, mercilessly, to pitch-black cinder.

Chapter 11
The Plan

No one said anything as we sat gathered in the living room, waiting for news from the Cabinet. Calleigh sat quietly as well, unlike her usual self, staring mindlessly at the wind chimes by the closed living room window. She hadn't said a word after the phone call with her parents, except that a lightning had struck the control tower, and that they were still stuck on a layover in Atlanta.

Lillian seemed particularly on edge, her cold gaze on the wall. She had been like this ever since Calleigh had mentioned the beings from my dream. I glanced uneasily at the girl, seemingly frozen into a statue, wondering if she was breathing. She turned her head, and I flinched as though she'd pierced me with her glare.

In something that felt easily like an hour's time, a distinct clambering of the wind chimes startled the lot. Calleigh bolted up onto her feet before I could make sense of anything.

"It's the Cabinet," Calleigh whispered. "We got a message from them."

In a while, Calleigh walked back into the room, her face full of bewilderment. I braced myself for what she would say. Calleigh took a deep breath before she spoke.

"We got a profile on the attack," she said, her brilliant voice trembling like it had never done. "It seems they'll strike tomorrow night."

"WHAT?" There came a couple of startled cries. I stared stupidly at the girl, unable to believe what I heard was real.

"They're not targeting us," Calleigh added quickly. Sighs of relief followed, and for a moment I thought everything was going as it should.

"They burnt about half of the moonflowers, unlike what they normally do before an attack, where they wipe out every single bud. Thing is, this time they didn't. It was done hurriedly. Carelessly. This isn't like any other attack in the past," Calleigh said quietly. "It seems," the girl added, barely above a feeble whisper, "they're targeting humans."

This time the room fell silent. Eyes darted between one another.

"The XTM thinks they're planning to strike the Mock Carnival," Calleigh said. "That's where the pattern points to, and the time is just about right."

"*What?*" Andrew cried. We looked to see him, flustered, blurting out: "My sister's going to the Mock Carnival with her boyfriend."

There was a bewildered silence. My thoughts returned to the conversation I'd had with Carlos weeks back, then rewound even more—to the very day in my childhood that I'd gone to the carnival for the first time. The Mock Carnival was the biggest festival held in this town, embodied by the giant Ferris wheel and colorful lights. The fireworks would begin, and the brilliant colors would spark the night—then a parade in costumes would gallop by, celebrating the triumph of the battle.

I remembered that night very clearly. I was eight. My mom and I—we'd spilled onto the festival grounds laughing like a set of songbirds. We saw a play, of which all I remembered was a girl in a white dress and fancy hat, one decorated with a big flower like a grandmother's church hat. Then we'd gotten us popsicles and strolled around, among the lights and rides, most of which I was too small for. I didn't remember all the details, but I cherished the memory. Distinctly I remember that it was a feeling I'd never felt before, surrounded in those lights, chatters, laughter and music—that something, though I didn't know what, was flitting in the air. I remembered the tingle I'd felt in my chest, like my heart had begun to swell like bubble gum into the heights of the sky. It was the night that, for the first time in my life, I'd known the thrill and elation of a young night's celebration.

Anyone could be there, I thought to myself. *Someone like me, someone like my mother. Someone like Andrew's sister. Anyone.*

"Tanya?" Chase queried, alarmed. "Call her now. She can't go."

Everyone scattered into chaos. Andrew was in the corner, worriedly dialing and redialing. Chase watched him with concern. I grabbed Calleigh by her arm and led her to the hallway.

"Isn't anyone going to stop this?" I whispered. "The army? We have an army, right? I learned about it in class. They can for sure hold off the Xentrios and keep everyone safe."

Calleigh's face turned paler. "Unfortunately, Sarah, they reworked the unit placement last March, and there's no unit close enough to us at the moment. And they can't fly here in this storm. They're actually not sure if they can send one by tomorrow night."

"*What?*" I demanded. "What about Teleporting Gems? There's got to be one. They can come, right? Special agents? I heard there's one for almost every gem."

"There are two agents with Teleporting Gems powerful enough, but one was injured in a mission two days ago. And the other... they're doing a beacon powered gem enhancement. Should take weeks. They can't use their powers at the time," Calleigh explained with a sigh.

"What about beacons?" I asked. "Are there any Teleporting Gems with Beacons nearby?"

Calleigh shook her head. "Not that we know of."

I was speechless as it dawned on me what this meant. I could only muster a thin whisper, like Calleigh had done: "*So they can't stop it.*"

Calleigh shook her head again. "No, they can't."

There was silence.

"*They can't stop it,*" I repeated in disbelief.

Calleigh looked at me, her half-moon eyes weary.

"Then we have to stop it," I said at last. "Calleigh, *we have to stop it.*"

Once the idea was brought up, there was chaos.

"You mean fight them?" Carlos asked.

"Fight them if we have to," I replied solemnly.

The chatter died down, and once again the room grew quiet. For a while the only sound that could be heard was the ensemble of hushed breaths. It seemed like time had stretched out forever, while dizzying numbers of scenarios passed my mind, probably passed everyone's minds; and then at long last, Carlos spoke up.

"She's right. We could say there's a situation and get everyone out, and then go for the assholes ourselves."

"And get us killed?" Calleigh cried. "You have no idea. We weren't able to take them down for centuries. You don't know how dangerous they are."

"I do, you just told us," I objected. "That's why we have to do this, Calleigh. We can't let this happen. The Cabinet can't help us, the military can't help us. It's in our hands now."

Calleigh stared ahead, not saying a word. She let out a thin sigh after a while, and nodded. "You're right."

"Although, if any of you would rather not," I said carefully. "Then it's okay."

"Sarah," Andrew spoke up quietly. "No offense, but you're a complete moron if you think we wouldn't."

"...really?" I asked quietly.

"We're with you," Chase confirmed. I looked around the table, and each one of them nodded, even Lillian, with a slight flick of her head.

A weary smile crept up my face.

We grabbed a large sheet of paper and pencils, and set to work. Calleigh sketched out the map of the venue with a quick search on the internet.

"So our primary goal is to evacuate everyone, preferably without going into war with the Xentrios," Calleigh said.

"We could trigger the fire alarm here—" Chase circled a spot on the map. "—and have everyone leave the area."

"There has to be an actual fire or they aren't going to stay out for long," Lillian commented quietly.

She was right.

"We are *not* committing arson," Calleigh said sternly. She hadn't seemed the rule-abiding type, but when it came to greater matters, it was different.

"I could use my gem to convince them not to return," Andrew suggested. "I know it's advanced work, it's still really hard for me to actually *convince* someone of something, but simply confusing them might do the job good enough. Keep them from going back."

Carlos looked thoughtful, his fingers combing through his hair. "But you'd have to change to use your gem," he commented. "How are you going to do that?"

"Damn," Andrew cursed. "Haven't thought about it." The boy stroked his chin in contemplation. "I could just risk it all and go as an eagle. If I use my gem right, I can get away with it."

"What about the security cameras? It's no use if you get caught on camera. We need Chase to beacon you anyway if you want to be able to do it on such a mass of people. And I hate to say this but you didn't even take C1 Gem Training," spoke Calleigh.

There was silence. Calleigh was right.

"Calleigh's right. We really can't do anything if *this* doesn't work."

"But Robert and Sophie are away. We have to stop them or we'll have Xentrios attacking people," Andrew argued.

"If we have a smoke bomb go off in the center part of the festival we can get all the people to clear. I know how to make one," I said.

The room fell silent and all eyes turned to me.

"And if Lillian does the job with her gem it shouldn't be hard to slip past people. On the day I changed she told me she could get me out of the building without people seeing us properly. Control centers should be accessible somewhere in the staff tent, they have a parking lot there, and in order not to be caught on camera Lillian will have to stay moving all the time. For safety we'll have Chase and Andrew stationed in the parking lot to take care of witnesses. And she can cut the lights out. I've seen her do that, too. She was good."

"I was decent, yes."

"The smoke bomb is a bit trickier. If you want to get all the people out you're gonna need quite a large amount. But from what I know you can carry unlimited amounts with the Traveler's Pocket. With techniques like Half-Transformations you don't have to change back, you have enough time to pick those up from the Pocket and set them off."

Calleigh seemed knocked back. "Sarah, how do you know all this?"

"She's been borrowing books every time she came to our place, Calleigh," replied Chase. "She's the expert here. She probably knows more than me."

"Well, I did some reading," I admitted sheepishly. "What do you think, Calleigh?"

"You don't expect any of us to be able to pull off the Pocket, do you? It's an incredibly advanced tactic. They don't even cover it fully until Dimensional Operation and Special Tactics II, and DOST I and II are both Advanced Elective subjects—"

"I did DOST II, actually," Lillian interrupted.

"*What?* Lillie, why didn't you tell me that?"

"Why would I tell you that?"

Calleigh stared back, dumbfounded.

"It's not like I have to tell youse everything I do. I took AE DOST II and I can do the Traveler's Pocket."

"Lillian, this is unbelievable," Calleigh exclaimed.

"But what I can't do is Half-Transformation. I need a little more time and a place where I can transform and transform back again unseen."

"This is *not* happening, guys." Calleigh interrupted. "It's too much of a risk. We'll end up violating the Code. We've done all we could, we're staying out of this."

"Calleigh, they're someone's *family*," I hissed back. "We have to do all we can to stop this."

"*So are you*," Calleigh cried.

She was right. The room fell silent.

"You're someone's family. You matter too." Calleigh said, her eyes almost teary. "And I want us to be safe. I want every one of you to be safe. *You're* my friends. Not anyone else at the Carnival."

I felt my eyes grow hot.

"But we stand a chance," came a husky voice from the side. All eyes turned to Lillian, leaning against the wall with her arms crossed, her eyes resolute.

"We can get us out safe if we act smart enough. We're trained and we know the enemy. Unlike the rest of the lot. They don't stand a chance."

She was right. There were murmurs of agreement across the room.

"If you can find me a place to change and change back, I can make it work." Lillian declared.

"What if we put the entire site into the Traveler's Pocket?" I murmured.

All eyes landed on me, as if I had just suggested we fly a plane to the desert.

"As far as I know they don't have security cameras. We could just... get rid of the Mock Carnival."

"Sarah, do you hear yourself? No one's ever tried it before. And I think it could be dangerous in and of itself, let alone the risk of violating the Code and exposing ourselves. This is not going to happen," Calleigh argued.

"But what's the alternative?" I demanded.

"That we fight them," Andrew said quietly.

Another heavy silence filled the air.

"Then that's what we do," Carlos spoke up. "If we could go into combat with them we need to know their weaknesses. Calleigh, can you pull up some records from the Xentrios' past attacks, some logs, maybe?" Carlos suggested. "If you can show them to me, I'll help find a plan. I play for the Puffins, remember?"

"We are not fighting them," Calleigh repeated sternly. "You have no idea of the *weight* of this situation. We're not fighting, and that's final. We might need to evacuate people, but that's a different matter. I'm going to keep trying the Phonie. Meanwhile you guys try to get some rest."

"Yeah, you don't look well," Carlos whispered to me.

"You guys haven't had much sleep last night," Calleigh said. "And we aren't going to be able to think clearly if we're tired. Go get some rest. We'll talk again soon."

The frantic planning was fruitless; no conclusion reached, just utter chaos. But Calleigh was right. We needed rest. And that's what we did—or more like, that's what we tried to do.

Back in my room I crawled under the blanket. My body was still shaking a little. The sun was still at its highest, but the sky began to darken. Thick clouds gathered at the zenith and huddled close together as if in fear, and soon enough rain began to shower down the streets.

I curled up in Lillian's thin blankets. The sky rumbled like a thousand drums. It was a terrible, deafening roar, one that burrowed through the pit of your stomach and slithered through your marrows. Lightning simmered through the curtains, and another thunder echoed.

I shivered. It was going to be a long day.

The hellhole ended, or at least seemed to end, a couple hours later in great relief—as Calleigh ran around knocking on doors with good news. We rushed out to find her in the living room. Her face had lit up. "I just got a call from the EA, and a unit is arriving by plane tomorrow afternoon. It's going to be all right."

Relief washed over all of us like a tide. Calleigh let out a long sigh and plunged into a frail hug. In a second we were all tangled up in a giant ball, patting one another on the back as if we'd conquered the world. It seemed no one could hear the thunder rumble behind us.

But amidst it all, there was one person who didn't seem to enjoy it much— I lifted my eyes to find Lillian watching from the back with her arms crossed in front of her.

"We don't know if they're going to be able to hold them off," she said quietly.

The five of us disentangled at once, staring silently as the sullen girl.

"She's right," Andrew said at last. "We do need a plan B. Just in case."

In a while we gathered once more at the dining table, going over the bits and pieces of our previous plan that we were able to salvage. It was with a lighter mood, and with less reservation—the unlikeliness of things coming down to our hands, perhaps, was the reason we could proceed with more nerve.

In about an hour's time we had formulated a plan—it involved a Traveler's Pocket, Andrew's gem, and a makeshift smoke bomb, for which we'd go supply shopping the following day. We went over our course of actions, even over what would happen if we were, for some reason, under attack. The plotting wrapped up only as the sun began to soften, and the rain ceased to a damp drizzle.

Afterwards Calleigh ushered everyone to bed. Everyone was strangely quiet, balanced between relief and worry. For a brief moment I met Lillian's eyes, hardened and brimming with an emotion I could not quite name. At that moment two things struck me: one, that she had a story to tell—and two, that it was not over.

I found her on the back porch a while later.

Lillian sat motionless on the steps. She stared ahead at the waning horizon, her hair fluttering beside her face. With the tip of her nose reflecting a line of rosy sunset, she looked angelic. The furrowed toughness in her face had begun to melt like lemon drops at the touch of the cottony evening sun. She swallowed heavily and tipped her head to the side.

"Why do you think they would do that?" Lillian asked.

I thought for a while. "To make people scared?" I responded uncertainly.

Lillian nodded. "I reckoned so too," she said huskily. "But I really don't know. I asked myself that question so many times. But no reason was good enough. The more I asked, the less I was sure."

The girl remained silent a while. The drizzle had stopped entirely, and a damp aroma of grass floated about in the air. The world seemed to be covered in a dewy blanket, on the edge of which blared the setting sun. The scene was peaceful; in a strange, angelic, undeserved way.

"My... gem was a late one. I was gemless like you," she said after a while.

I was stricken. "Really?" I asked.

Lillian nodded, sighing at the ground.

"I didn't have one for nine years."

I gasped.

"But you were so young. And you felt what I felt?" I asked.

"Everyone feels it, Sarah. Every Gemless. I've also had that feeling for as long as I can remember. Hollow, lonely, misunderstood, helpless... I was too young to put them into words but I felt them. I just learned to live with the feeling. After all, I was loved.

"It was always there, but you learn to forget it. At some point I didn't care anymore. I was okay. And... it would have been okay. It would have been okay even if I was still gemless. I could have lived with it. I could even have been happy about it. It's not the worst thing to not have, Sarah. You could lose more important things." Lillian turned to look at me. I saw a strange gleam in her eyes.

I could not say why I felt so tired. I sat on the edge of the bed, resting my head on the pillow propped up against the headboard, and immediately drifted off.

I was at the park again. I was standing on the frozen lake on my skates. This would have instantly turned any dream into a nightmare, but strangely, I wasn't wobbling like I normally did. I was standing perfectly still, steady and secure.

And so were they.

This time the fog had lifted a bit, and I could see clearer. I could see the same figures, the six of them, gliding across the lake toward me. What did they want? My heart began to race, and every part of my body urged me to turn and leave—but I stayed. I had to find out more about them, more about what they wanted. Would they let me find out? It was unlikely—I glimpsed their eyes and knew they'd already seen me. I had to disappear.

And it happened. I did not understand how it happened, but it did. I *had* disappeared. I held my breath as the figures approached me, close enough for me to see their eyes. Yet their eyes failed to find me. The eerie figures drifted blankly toward me, unseeing, unknowing, until they were close enough that I could extend my arms and touch them—I bit my lips, scared for a moment that a sound would escape my mouth.

And then the fog grew thicker. No, it wasn't the fog that was growing thicker. It was the lake, the woods behind, the peaks—the entire park, fading.

The background slowly faded into a thick, pearly white, then began to materialize again—this time it was someplace else.

The place was decked with unlit lightbulbs. Decorating the streets were sculptures, big and small, all of them still and dark—empty, unfamiliar to the point it was eerie. Some snack stands and popsicle stands were set halfway up, and somewhere to the back was a carousel, frozen in place like a frame stolen from the tesseracts of spacetime. Behind the carousel was the signature Ferris wheel, dark and unlit, grand and ghastly. Instantly I knew where this was.

I gasped.

I regretted it instantly, as all six Xentrios turned their eyes on me. I began to back off slowly—

"Sarah?"

I jerked awake with a jolt, tumbling painfully over the side of the bed. A white hot pain shot through my knees.

"You all right there, Sarah?" sounded Carlos' voice from outside the door.

"I'm fine!" I yelled, as I pulled myself up onto my feet. I realized I was drenched in sweat.

"Calleigh made soup," Carlos said from behind the door. "Didn't want you to miss it."

I straightened my shirt, finger-combed my hair, ran the back of my hand against my mouth just in case I was by any chance drooling, and headed out the door.

"Were you asleep? I heard you fall."

"I um," I gave a flustered smile. "Yeah, dozed off."

"You must have been tired," said Carlos.

I sighed. "I guess I was. The search, the planning, the whole situation…"

"It's going to be okay," Carlos assured. "And the EA unit is going to be here tomorrow. Don't worry about it."

I nodded.

"You got a…" Carlos began, somewhat awkwardly pointing at the corner of his mouth.

I nearly jumped, worried that I might have been drooling after all, and tried to wipe it off before he had a clearer image in his head.

"I'll get it," Carlos said. He took my face in his hand as he reached for the corner of my mouth with the other, then brushing my lips ever so lightly with his fingertips, removed a...

"Feather," murmured Carlos as he let it slip between his fingers.

I gulped, my heart racing like mad—I could not tell if it was because of him or the dream.

"You okay?" Carlos asked, stopping in his tracks. "You don't look well. What's the problem?"

"Nothing," I replied quickly.

"I think you should get some rest," Carlos suggested softly. "I could bring you some soup."

I smiled. "I don't... feel like eating. But thanks. Both of you."

Carlos eyed me a while, then nodded. "All right. Get some rest. I'll, um... I'll be in my room. If you need anything."

I nodded.

A terrible, empty knot was forming inside my stomach; I had realized exactly what I needed.

Chapter 12
Lillian Emmaline Shaffer

The night was soft and silent. I peered at Calleigh's bed from the mattress in the corner. It seemed she had fallen asleep before her head hit the pillow. Oh, how I longed to be able to do that. It had seemed so long ago that I'd slept soundly.

Calleigh had lately gotten into the habit of playing music in the background as she drifted off. They were mostly songs from decades ago. Since I had to share her room while Sarah slept in mine, these couple of days I would wait until she had fallen asleep to march to her CD player and turn it off. But this time the music didn't bother me much, and I left Journey to sing softly in the corner of the room, on about how they were forever mine faithfully.

My nights were continuums of images, ones I so desperately wanted to tear from my head. Years and years got me accustomed to those slides that played themselves in my head every night, a sickening private theatre I was forever locked in. I knew very well it would never stop until the day I died; I had only grown a bit more numb by the day, until eventually I could watch them without feeling a thing.

Those flashbacks would usually begin with the days of my childhood, the undestroyed side of time's labyrinthine symmetry. It was a wonder.

Calleigh would often talk philosophies that would interest her, and one of it was the eerie idea that time was a symmetric concept, mutilated by an emergent rule that destroys its symmetry and turns it to a one-sided arrow. I had always found the idea preposterous. Nothing about it was symmetrical, it was forever marred and intoxicated. Everything had changed, and there was no going back. I could only look at the other side of the cliff, the bridge burnt, only an unending abyss between myself and all that I missed. Given the choice, I would run back to those days, time and time again—but the choice was never given.

It all started this one summer. Back in those blessed days I'd wake up to a warm glow of the sun and plunge into my parents' outspread arms. Laughter would fill our home, and we'd joke and improvise stories after stories as we gobbled down pancakes and feasted on birds.

We lived on the outskirts of Canberra, barely on the edge of the city. There were parks and forests and hills I could play in, and each of them housed rich and brilliant memories.

My parents had been good friends of the Russells since way before I was born. They would occasionally come to visit us, with a very excited Calleigh between their arms. Calleigh would bubble up with laughter when she saw me, and, incredibly enough, so would I. We would go running off into the distance, and the girl would change in midair—ever so lightly and beautifully, into an eagle. I would laugh and chase her until I'd run out of breath, never once being able to catch the bird, who so gracefully glided over the surface just over my head. My daily flashbacks would normally start here: Calleigh's messy hair, which she still wears in the same way, and the way we'd shoot off into the distance cawing and howling at the top of our lungs. We were two entirely different minds, one bursting with artful stories and one that sought to explore and strategise. Together we'd made up the world's most sophisticated games and beat them with billions of brilliant ideas. And while we ran around the forests there, happy as ever, plotting world dominion, my mum and dad, and hers—the four of them would sit watching, smiles on their faces. These were years of my childhood; years of mirth, years of innocence, years of happiness. I rolled the words on the tip of my tongue, tasting their virulent sadness. I laughed. Those were sunlight, but night was my home. They were something that could not be brought back, reversed, or made real—something that was lost forever, ever since the one day that changed everything.

I rolled over until the wall filled my view. Calleigh had painted little blackthorn blossoms here and there. I let out a sigh and gazed emptily at the blossoms. Sarah's dream had brought back every detail, vividly as ever, and I knew I would not be able to sleep today.

It was the 20th of July, the day before my ninth birthday, when everything changed for life.

Growing up, I had been a girl flaring with ideas, a brilliant ball of flame that would never stop sizzling. My parents had raised me with games and adventure stories. Birthday surprises from my parents involved me scampering through woods, hunting birds and climbing roofs. There was nothing I couldn't do in the woods. I was built for it. It was almost as though I had been prepared all my life to hunt, fight and survive—but what for? For some strange reason, I had always believed it was all for the one ultimate game, the one ultimate adventure I must embark on. I went to bed each night with my head going wild, trying to guess when and where it would take place, what the objective would be.

The afternoon before my birthday, I had fallen asleep the couch, full and contented. In a moment of skin-deep consciousness between those naps, my keen ears caught whispers. At once I tuned in on those words.

"Already?"

"...It's sooner than I thought... have to go..."

"...going to rebuild the Lock, aren't they?"

"Yes... all of them... we have to find the Knife before they do that, and we'll have all three..."

"What about Lillian?"

"...Robert... I'll call him. He'll be on his way by the time..."

Robert? Seemingly my surprise was another treasure hunt, one that involved Calleigh. I was wide awake by then, my ears perked up trying to catch more.

"...never had a chance to... Lillian..."

"We have no time... for Lillian,"

"She's only nine, Gerry."

"Robert... when he... then she'll understand,"

"When do we leave?"

"In a few hours...I'll be on the lookout... see if there's any movement with them..."

My heart began to race and my body was ablaze. It was a game. A game like none other I'd played. It was the biggest adventure yet, beckoning me to a long-lost prize. Of course, like before, I'll play out my part beyond anyone's expectations.

I let my eyes open only slightly, keeping my breath slow and steady as if I were still asleep. The voices of my parents continued from the kitchen. I had already begun making my plans.

Twenty minutes passed that felt like decades. I'd counted sheep to keep myself from falling asleep, ironically enough, though I knew that I could not possibly be calmed to sleep. I heard my parents coming towards me, and again I kept my breaths slow and serene, hoping only that they wouldn't hear my racing heartbeat.

For a moment there was silence. No footsteps, no voices. Not even a whisper was audible—until I heard something like a sigh, only an arm's length away. A stir. I caught a whiff of floral aroma, and knew it was Mum. It seemed she had crouched down beside the couch.

"Lillie, darling,"

I pretended to stir. My mum's hand reached through my hair, gently brushing it to the side. She rested her head rested heavily against mine.

"Lillian, I love you. We love you. We love you endlessly."

She kissed me softly on the cheek. "You, my little girl, are the best thing that ever happened to us. Mum and Dad love you forever and ever."

"Cath," whispered Dad. His voice stopped suddenly, like a cassette tape that cut off.

Mum hugged me. She held me so tight it got hard to breathe, and didn't let go for another minute.

"Cath," Dad said again, softly.

"You talk to her, Gerry," Mum said. Her voice sounded weird. "You don't know when we'll…"

"Shhh," Dad said. "Lillian, my little cub."

There was a little pause, and I felt his hand caress my hair.

"Sleep tight, Lillie. We'll be back soon."

I pretended to stir. There was silence for a minute or two. I continued to breathe steadily, up and down, up and down, as if I were fast asleep.

"Cath, love, did you leave the note?" Dad asked after a while.

"Yes. All these years we prepared her for this. She's going to be fine."

Did I imagine a slight wavering in his voice? I was waiting to hear it again, to try and make out what I'd heard. I had known only steel-like serenity in my parents' voices, though at times they were hiding secrets and surprises that would only be uncovered days, sometimes even weeks later. But this was something different. I had not heard anything like that before.

But before I could hear more, there was another sound of shuffling, and out of my barely open eyes I saw Dad usher Mum out the door.

"I love you, little angel," he said, ruffling my hair and then planting a swift kiss on my head. Then he left.

My eyes popped open.

Was this it? Was this the game? Was this the game I'd been preparing for all my life?

Yes, I thought. I was sure. And I was sure I would play it right.

Silently, with the swiftest moves I could possibly make, I slipped off the couch, slid open the windows, and climbed out. I could move in almost complete silence, weaving my inevitable noises into the background so no one would notice. I carried myself to the garage without a sound.

They were in my dad's jeep. The engine always struggled to start, and I knew it would be another minute before it roared to life. But there was no way for me to get in the car.

I crawled backwards, until the entrance of the garage came into view. Then inspired by a sudden idea, I concealed myself behind the lawn mower on the side. The car finally started, a set of chipped roars connecting into a single rough hum. There wasn't much more time. I hurried behind the car in silence, and as the jeep rolled an arm's length down the garage, I heaved the lawn mower at it. The car stopped.

"What's that?" Mum's voice sounded.

"The lawn mower," I could hear Dad say through the window. He climbed out of the car and headed towards the garage.

"Need help, Gerry?"

"I'm good," he said—but I knew my mum would get out of the car anyway, as she'd always done. And I was right.

"Here, I'll help you."

I took my chance. I was swift. After a swift little move, I was in the trunk, crouched in a corner. I grinned to myself.

"Gerry."

My mum's voice sounded, strained, barely above a whisper. Then there was a lot of rustling, brushing and breathing—followed by a whisper:

"Cathy."

I held my breath.

"You know I love you."

"Till the end."

"Till the end."

There were no more words. Instead, the jeep took off with a jolt. I slammed into the tail.

My mum was no calm driver. She would speed like hellfire down the interstate, but never had I seen—or felt—anything like this. I grasped at the walls to avoid bumping into one of the jumping toolboxes and passing out.

This rush of air against the body of the car travelled through the steel and into my skin. The rumble and hum of the engine, this rattle of the jouncing car—all this, I felt, was what it meant to be alive, and alive in the fullest. For the first time I felt life with every patch of my skin.

We drove for hours, and I numbed to the fracas of the wheels on the rough road. I curled up in a snug baby-in-womb posture, lulled by the faithful hum of the engine. What took my consciousness was not impact to my head—it was the oddly comforting rocking of the speeding car.

I was quite sure I had ruined everything when I woke up. The car was still, so still and silent that I thought we were back in the garage, and that I had missed the chance to uncover clues about tomorrow's adventure. Drooping with disappointment, I heaved the trunk open, about an inch, to gaze outside.

No, this wasn't the garage.

It was a farm. Cows grazed in the distance and stacks of hay lay in the sun, bathing in its glinting lights. The sight was placid and pastoral. But something… something was utterly wrong. I pulled on the emergency lever and quickly jumped outside.

My body was rigid from the ride. I stretched. My joints popped like bits of candy, but in a while I was as good as ever. I looked around, trying to determine what it was about the place that felt so wrong. The car had been parked in a rush facing a warehouse. I knew that would be the first place I looked.

That was when I saw its wall rip.

I blinked. I brought myself closer. The warehouse seemed many decades old. Corn-coloured paint was coming off on the facade, and the planks themselves had bent and worn so that you could see through the gaps into the interior. The faded red roofs were soggy, like it had failed to keep the rain out. Something told me it had been abandoned for a long time. It had probably not been getting many visitors other than those seeking a discreet rendezvous.

There was strange silence as I neared the structure. I held my breath as I reached out to touch its walls—I ran my fingers along the planks in disbelief. There was a crack just about my height, torn open as if hacked at with an axe. I peeked inside.

They had changed.

The forms of Enrici were an unsolved mystery. There were some rules that were mostly kept, such as that when a pair were what people called 'soulmates,' one of their forms would change, or both would change, so that the pair ended up with forms of the same species. But other rules hardly held—siblings were more likely to have the same form, but they could change growing up. Inheritance of forms from parent to child was less common. But both my parents, somehow, belonged to a family of wolves—their forms were an heirloom passed down generations on end.

My mum was a jet-black wolf, while my dad was a sleek white one.

We would often go to state parks or empty plains and race around. Sometimes we would hunt, other times we would simply play chase, and every moment I changed and stood between them in the fields, I had felt anew a shimmering tingle of being the dawn between the elegance of Night and Day.

But never had I seen them fight. In the dimness they were thrashing against two people, one a broad-shouldered man in blue-black overalls, the other a silver haired woman in a worn white blouse. Something about their faces wasn't right—they looked human, but in the flicker of their eyes, the distortion of their lips in a sentiment I could not name, I sensed something that sent a chill riveting down my spine.

The man stood, with his lips curled, his eyes intent, whispering words I could not hear as he wrestled the wolves. His hand was long and bony, and you could see the bluish veins protruding from it. His other hand was not visible from the angle, but seemed to be grasping something—I squinted against the wall to make out what it was, but failed. Beside him stood the woman, panting with her lips drawn back in a wild smile—her blouse was torn open, revealing collarbones like those of an ancient Greek sculpture. To a glimpse, it looked as though they were bruised.

Something flashed into my mind.

It was a week ago when I'd heard this coming from behind the door—

"At least... we broke her pendant."

"That wasn't my aim."

"We still have a chance for the Knife."

"We have to get to work before the Perfume's remade."

Was this the woman who lost her pendant? Where was this going? The Knife? The Perfume?

It wasn't a knife. It wasn't a perfume. These were *the Knife* and *the Perfume*. These words had made no sense then. It was to me but a set of codes ready to be discovered, a grand world of games never played before. But when I glimpsed the glinting edge of silver in the hand of the man, I knew this wasn't a game.

I threw myself at the entrance. The panels flung me back out with a loud bang.

There was silence. The world seemed to have frozen forever, and I stood shaking. The walls were keeping me out, and it dawned on me that whoever those people were I'd seen, my dear, beloved parents were, with all they had, keeping them in.

A low growl ripped from inside. A threat. It was a desperate threat. Another growl, swift steps… The sound of something whistling through the air, and then another rip at the wall right between my eyes. I stood trembling as more footsteps sounded, more tears, grunts, whistles and cracks—

A deadening howl.

A terrible howl of agony. I staggered away from the trembling wall. Another sound came from the warehouse. A single note, a high note, echoing agonizingly against the rumbling walls of the dead old shed.

Then a low, desperate growl, the sound of feet.

It was like rushing past a train and glimpsing inside it, where you see for a brief moment everything that's inside. It would resemble a view from another world, and you would be left wondering if you'd really seen it or simply imagined it. It was like that. A glimpse of the scene flashed before my eyes; it was like I could briefly see inside of the warehouse under my eyelids, see the dimness curling around my neck, taste the odour of blood in the air.

I was afraid.

I turned, changed, and ran.

I had no idea what I was running for. As I raced into the freeway, with not much thought, I realized that I was faster than the fastest of cars. Everything was a blur. Cars vanished behind me, and my keen ears caught exclamations of spectators as I sped onto the roads leading west.

The sun set ahead of me in a ferociously darkening crimson. I raced down the road, past the cars and through the woods, pretending not to notice the blurred gasps of passersby. Let them see me, let them be afraid. I could not care less.

A gem. I knew what it was. It was something I never had. Somehow, young as I was, I'd pictured myself with an unexplained incompleteness. Not a single soul had alienated me for it, but it didn't change the way I felt about it.

And here I was. The gift had presented itself when I least needed it, when I least cared. When none of it mattered anymore. The wind rushing past my ears, the ethereal blur of the world as I ran faster than anything I'd known—it was something that could have been joyful; but it no longer was. It couldn't be.

I hadn't the faintest clue where I was going. I raced down the road until they were dark. Then I wandered some more, down the road, into town, down streets and alleyways. Kids screamed when they saw me, and parents pulled them closer into their arms. I had to get out of there.

I ran further down the road, further west. I learned later that I had taken the midwestern highway to Beckhom, and I'd gone further all the way to Hillston. Night fell, everything was pitch dark, and I was alone with not a thing in sight but short, stubby trees here and there. The night deepened and I soon ran out of stamina. I had to camp somewhere. I settled somewhere under a shrub, curtained from the rest of the world by tall grass and little hedges of wildflowers. The night was cold, but I did not care—something else gnawed into my chest, a pain worse than any I'd known. As I lay there curled up, a horrible sound seemed to come from everywhere. My body shook. It took me a while to realize I was the one making the noises. The noises would not stop—I could feel it vibrate through my spines, echo like blaring sirens and rolling drums. I wept, wept, and wept for I don't know how long.

I did not know I had fallen asleep until I woke. The sky was dark, and a smooth skyline of hills outlined my view. In the distance the stars would twinkle and owls would hoot. The moon was nearly full. Flames seemed to gnaw at my stomach, burning, searing, dismantling my insides. As though that would put out the fire, I howled. An agonised cry filled the air, cracked and injured, empty and sore. The howl did nothing to calm me. The chill still burned against my skin. I curled up under the shrub, silent, terrified, broken.

I shook against the rough bark. The world seemed to be continuing, strange, empty—while my pain stretched on to lengths I could not foresee. When silent drops of blood told me I had been biting my lips very hard, I gave in to the endless, uncontrollable sobs.

I would never see them again.

I woke again, and this time the sky was light. I found that my insides were still burning, and realized with a sudden flash of instinct that I was hungry. I trotted from underneath the canopy and searched the area for prey.

There wasn't much to eat. I caught some rats and gobbled them up hungrily. When I did I was less hungry, but the sensation in my guts wasn't gone, and nor was the grip of reality on my shoulders. I staggered and sank again to my hiding between the bushes. At that moment I knew, that whatever I did, there was no chasing away the pain. Each moment of my life, with each drop of flavour seeping into my taste buds, each streak of light that touched my eyes and every rush of air I felt through my nose, I would be living with a ghost of this feeling.

I drifted off and woke again countless times. Had days passed? A week, maybe? Two weeks? Sense of time seemed to have molten into oblivion, and the burning was persistent. I fed on wild rats, dead birds, guts left over from other animals' hunts. I did not have enough to drink. I fed on leaves and drank dew off the bushes. Blood was clotted and caked around my jaws, and bits of them stained my taste every now and then. The sky was lighting up again, with bewitching streaks of morning shades, orange, lavender-purple, colours I could not name. But nothing could touch me now. Nothing could make me feel any-thing. I was glazed over in lead. I felt nothing. I *was* nothing. The only thing I knew was that I terribly missed them, that I so desperately and dreadfully longed to plunge into their arms again.

The next thing that woke me wasn't hunger or moonlight. It was a voice, a deep and familiar voice.

"Lillian? Lillian, thank god. Thank god, Lillian—it's Uncle Robert."

I crawled out from underneath the bush. I felt I had better change back, and I did. I could not even remember how long I'd been a wolf. Robert was crouching in front of the bush, the familiar face with the round spectacles and the soft beard. His eyes were wide, his face was flushed, and his hair seemed to have been pushed back in anguish, and it stayed there, caked with sweat.

"Lillian, it's Uncle Robert. You're—thank god, you're okay, you're safe… it's going to be okay."

I merely stared. I did not know what to say, and in fact there was nothing I wanted to say. I may have had a lot of questions, on where I was, what day it was, or how he had found me, but I simply did not care about the answers. It was only later that Robert had told me, all the way in Lincoln, that they'd had to find me using gems. 'Sophie had to listen for sadness,' he'd said, his eyes sad and sorry.

"How long have you been alone?"

Then and there, Robert's voice sounded, and it was the second closest thing to home. Tears would have welled up in my eyes if it hadn't dried up. But I was dehydrated and devoid of sentiments. I'd forgotten how to cry, or how not to. I remained silent.

"You aren't hurt, are you?" he asked worriedly as he examined my limbs. "Thank god… thank god, Lillian. We were worried about you.

We're gonna get you somewhere safe. You're safe now, I promise…"

Safe, the words echoed through my numb head. Safe was the last thing I felt. I saw again the image of the wolves and the man and woman, and the scene played itself in my head all the way to the part I least wanted to see. My stomach seemed to jolt and I fought down an urge to vomit.

"Aren't you hungry?" Robert asked.

I shook my head.

"I still think you have to eat something. We'll eat something, and we'll get you some clean clothes, and we'll talk about what happened."

I shook my head again.

"Lillian, we're going to go to Vanna Daya. Calleigh will be there. She's waiting for you," he said.

Something thudded in my heart as it dawned on me that we weren't going back home. A better way to put it was that I had no home to return to. It was clear, without so much as an exchange of words, that Robert and I both knew: my parents were dead. They had been killed.

We moved to Vanna Daya, which became my next home. But something was missing, and would always be missing. On the day I stepped out from beneath the bush into the brilliant sunlight, I knew everything had changed. The two people I loved most were gone. We would never be together on this planet ever again. The only thing I had left of them were the impressions, forever seared into my eyelids so I saw them every time my eyes closed; the image of the two brilliant wolves, black and white, rearing desperately against the faces of the horrid faces of the man and woman. Little did I know that the fresh tear in my heart would never really heal, that it would split open time and time again to bleed, then harden again into a numb, leaden mess—but still I knew, very well and without doubt, that there would never come a moment I would forget.

And so as I stepped out onto the porch that day with Robert, under the brilliance of the unknowing azure, I knew—that my life would never be the same.

*　　*　*　*　*　*

The pillow was damp.

I quickly pulled myself up. The mattress bounced lightly up and down. Calleigh was on the bed tossing random butterfly snores, but it made me feel no stronger. I could only shrink and shrink against the dark like a helpless bug.

Time had passed. If anything had changed, it was the great clockwork of time. I still saw the image every night with striking clarity, but my heart had hardened; at times the blow to my heart that the flashback delivered left me reeling, but at times it left me still as a lifeless statue, drifting in a calm pool of nothingness, cold and unfeeling.

I closed my eyes and let out a shaky breath. The sound of Calleigh's serene breathing reached me, like pats on my sleeping chest, like the soft sound of lullaby from my beloved mother. I cleared my mind, letting the sound calm me, lead me away from the memories that haunted me.

But it did not change the fundament.

This battle would never really end, and I knew that with painstaking certainty. I would see through to the end the endless trail of agony. I would see it shattered along with its origins or I would see it destroy me.

Xentrios were coming again.

That night I sat on the pale blue sheets of my bed, or Lillian's bed, wide awake. I could hear the lumbering silence of Vanna Daya in my ears. It was dark and heavy, weighing down my limbs as if they were boulders. I remained still. I breathed slowly and quietly; I could not afford to wake anyone. My mind flashed back to the conversation on the porch.

"My mum and dad were... the best Enrican trackers ever. They were in a mission force that doesn't exist anymore... they met each other there, and they met Sophie there. My mum and Robert had been friends before that, since their trainee years, but this mission force was where they all got to know each other. That was where my mum and dad fall in love. It was called the AXE," Lillian said. "Anti-Xentrio Expedition. It ended when they died."

Something sank in my chest. I turned to see Lillian stare off at the crimson horizon, her eyes damp.

"They were hunting down the Originals. They had gone after Victorina and Cuper and destroyed the Perfume and the Lock... and they were about to destroy the Knife. They thought the Xentrios would be finished off if they destroyed all three Original instruments..."

I sat, barely able to breathe. I could not process what I was hearing.

"It was the day before my birthday, Sarah. I followed them... because I overheard them talking and thought they had planned some sort of game for me. I followed them and I saw them... fighting the Originals. And then they knew I was there... and so they stayed and fought when they could have run to save themselves. To hold them off... just because I followed them there.

"And I got scared. I ran. I ran, and they died..."

For a moment I tried to find something to say. My chest had sunken into an abyss so deep I felt I could barely breathe. Just as it had back by the lake when Carlos told his story, my little world cracked open, pulsating in pain, to engulf yet another tragedy. I opened my mouth to speak, but my voice got caught in my throat. I swallowed.

"They could have run and saved themselves if I weren't there. They could have lived if it weren't for me."

Her voice was barely above a whisper, as though she were speaking a truth that hurt too much to utter. I looked at her, at those beautiful features, drenched in a sorrow too deep and a hatred too old.

"They died because I was there. They died because I ran."

A sob escaped her mouth. It was a heavy sob, a lumbering gush of air, something that had probably been there for years—a persistent, undying agony. I began to think perhaps it may have been a trace of this pain that I'd seen pass her eyes the day she told me she couldn't hunt with me. Perhaps having company reminded her of the old days.

I desperately rummaged through my head, but found nothing else to say. I simply gazed at her, watching as she closed her eyes and the last morsel of pain and hatred disappeared behind those lids. Countless droplets of tears rolled down from those eyes, and her lips and brows convulsed in excruciating sorrow.

Carefully, afraid I would break her, I extended my arms toward and around her. The girl was shaking, and hot like a dog—I pulled her a little closer so her head rested on my shoulder. Sobs trembled through my arms and into my chest. Slowly her tears began to soak my shirt, but I didn't care—I sat holding her, cradling her, as the sobbing grew worse and worse and my torso shook with hers. It took me a long while to muster a single sentence:

"Lillian, none of it's your fault."

She did not respond. A horrible sound escaped her throat, like the screech of a dying animal. It felt as though she would never stop. I held onto the girl, afraid I'd lose her into an unending abyss.

The sun gleamed relentlessly on the horizon.

A sort of pain heaved in my chest as I reminisced. Under her damp lashes lay hidden her eyes, a pair of sad eyes, looking through an unseen window in the air at days long gone. I'd always admired her eyes; the power, the resemblance to the depths of oceans. Under her disinterested glare was an epic untold, and for a long time I wondered what was on the other side of that window.

I thought of the afternoon sun echoing off the delicate ridge of her nose, the warmth nestled between her stubborn lips. I'd seen a teardrop travel down her profile, catching a glint of the sun just before it disappeared between her lips. She'd wiped it off with the back of her hand, and I caught a little tremor in her fingers. Just then the image of the girl I knew seemed to shatter. She was no longer the displeased soccer captain, neither was she the unforgiving trainer in the woods. She was no longer the goddess of war.

At that moment a sort of resolve had begun to form in my chest, and I had not yet known what it was. But as I sat on the edge of the bed the night before the Carnival, it became clear—I knew what to do. It all made sense. My options merged into a single course of action, the one and only.

It first took the form of rage. The image of the girl became the embers that fueled the rage. I thought of her shaking sobs on the porch, then of the queen, of Harvey, of all the people who had lost, bore fire and grief in their hearts, and sought to charge, to shatter them, but only broke and shattered against the vile creatures.

The fire then began to burn around the seemingly irrelevant; the sneering girls, the whispers, the hollow I'd always had at the pit of my stomach. For some reason I also thought of the lake, and of Carlos, his hardened eyes as he told me of his dreams. To me, everything vile was now in their name, every pain associated with them—after all, they would revel in someone's torment, in their resentment, in their despair.

Then finally it merged with a longing, a longing I'd had since the moment I first changed. The quest to fill the hollow in my chest had come full circle— if a gem formed to save the holder, then perhaps where danger was where I needed to be.

There was something I'd told no one. When I had that dream for the second time, I knew their motives had changed. Perhaps it was to visit the place and plan ahead, perhaps it was because there was something else they wanted; but whatever the reason, they were coming tonight. If I ventured to the deserted site of the carnival tonight, I knew I would be met by the Xentrios.

Then why did I say nothing to Calleigh? Because an idea had formed in my head, an impulse I could not resist, and I planned to take it. And I needed to do it alone, so my life would be the only one I'd risk.

Tonight, I was going to the site of the Carnival.

Chapter 13
The Night Before the Opera

The silence screamed.

I crouched by the head of the bed, waiting. My ears tuned to the wails of the electric silence, the ticking and tocking of wall clocks in sequential ensembles. Occasional thumping of feet could be heard outside, and I could hear Calleigh chiming goodnight. I leaned back, closed my eyes, and reviewed my course of action.

I get out of the house and into the car that I plan to steal. I drive to the carnival. I laughed. Put this way, the whole plan sounded insane.

A sudden buzz startled me, and I waited a second until my heart sank slowly back into my ribcage. It was a message. I opened my eyes and picked up my phone.

> Sarah, how are you doing? Dad's coming home for your birthday. Love you.

It was Mom.

I held the phone, staring into its screen for a while.

> All good, I texted. About to go to bed. Love you too.

I stared some more. My stomach tightened into a knot so bad it hurt. There was another buzz, and I lazily flipped it open, to find it's a multimedia message. I peered at the image of a funny cat in a hat, with *I love you* written on a corner in Comic Sans. *Moms*, I thought as I grinned. I bet they had a hub somewhere where they got all these mom pictures.

Stay out of trouble. See you in a few days.

I let out a little laugh. I found my eyes growing hot for some reason, and flipped my phone closed. Staying out of trouble was the last thing I was doing. I chucked my phone under the pillow, trying to keep down the tears that had formed in my eyes for some weird reason.

The time came. The house was silent, and I was sure it had been that way for a good thirty minutes. This was the moment I'd planned for.

With the lightest footsteps I could make, I crept to the door. I wiped my hands dry on my bum before I gripped the doorknob, and painstakingly slowly, turned it all the way to the end. *Yes.* All good, not a sound from the rest of the house.

I wondered if they were really sleeping, or if anyone could really sleep. Things could go wrong if they didn't; especially since the next step in my plan involved someone else. And as for why I'd picked that particular someone, well, I had no idea.

I had, during those hours in the dimmed darkness, made plans concerning the car I was going to steal. Or, put truthfully, I tried to come up with reasonable excuses for the decision I'd already made. One of them was that I'd already driven his car once, from school to the pizzeria. I could go something like ten minutes without killing the engine.

I crept silently to the guest room. Not a sound came from the other side of the door. I pressed my ears to the keyhole—still nothing, only a slow and steady breathing. Ah, yes, the second reasonable excuse. He was the thickhead that was most likely to be sleeping like a log by now.

I carefully turned the doorknob and crept into his room. The moon had begun to sink beneath the skyline, and the only light coming through the west window was a dim scintilla of distant streetlights. I waited silently until my eyes grew adjusted to the darkness.

Carlos was fast asleep, lying carefree on his side with his blanket lolling over his legs. I retreated until I was against the wall, as far from the sleeping figure as possible. I found his jacket hanging on the nail in the wall, the one I'd noticed while looking around his room. I crept toward it and I slipped my hand into the pocket. It was empty.

Crap, I muttered under my breath. Where on earth did he keep his keys?

I looked frantically around the room. There was a closet in the corner. I could open it, but I knew I didn't have enough time to rummage through it all before he woke.

Then I spotted something. It was his favorite red varsity jacket, lying underneath his head. *Oh, crap, please not that,* I thought to myself. He might have pulled it under his head in his sleep, or it might have been the way he normally slept, with that jacket on his pillow—but whatever the reason was, he was making it harder to steal his car.

I took a deep breath and crept nearer. The bed in the guest room was quite large, probably twin or queen-sized. I stood near its edge to reach for the jacket, but it was no use. I had to climb up onto the bed. *No, not this,* I thought.

But soon I realized it had to be done. I placed my knee on the side of the bed and cautiously shifted my weight. Nothing. Carlos was still asleep, unknowing and peaceful. I exhaled quietly and crawled up the remainder until I was staring right at his head.

I felt for the edge and found the pocket. Carefully I stuck my hand in and felt inside—but to my disappointment, it was empty. Cursing mentally, I reached quietly for the other pocket. To my horror, I found that it lay underneath Carlos' head. *Please. Please stay asleep*, I thought as I began cautiously to tug at a free sleeve. One tug, then another. Another tug—good, he was still asleep. Another tug, then another—painfully slowly I freed the jacket from underneath his head. Letting out a sigh of relief, I pried into the pocket. My fingers clasped around cold metal. *Found it*, I thought to myself in glee.

And at that moment Carlos stirred.

I froze in place. Carlos rolled over onto his back, still fast asleep. I could not move; I merely stared, suspended there, heart pounding madly, looking down at Carlos' sleeping face between my arms. The slumbering figure wasn't the six-foot, aggressive forward on the ice. His delicate lashes rested under his eyes like those of a sleeping angel, and the soft freckles on the bridge of his nose seemed to glint softly like spots on a rosy Akoya pearl. And his lips—they were parted ever so slightly, a pair of rosy perfection in the dim golden halo.

Cut it out, Sarah, you can't get distracted, I thought, trying to rip my gaze. *You have to focus on the plan.*

And without hesitation I backed off from his bed with the key in hand, and tore out of his room.

I found the Subaru in the driveway. The door unlocked easily, and I climbed in. I felt for the lever on the underside, and pulled it forward to adjust the seat. A fog had hazed the windshield. I turned the heater on, waiting for it to clear. Little cloud appeared as I breathed, and danced a while in the cold air before clearing away. I drew a deep breath and turned the key.

The engine revved and the car came to life. I waited a bit, my heart racing, to see if anyone had heard. No sound came from the house, and no light turned on. *Good*, I thought. It was all going as planned. I pinned the clutch to the floor, pushed the gear stick into first, and slid out of the driveway.

The streets were empty. I carefully pushed the stick into third, and fourth. I pulled through the path I'd studied and rehearsed so many times. The whirring of the engine resonated through the deserted streets, splitting the untouched night into halves. I kept my cold hands tight on the wheel, my knuckles white and fingertips numb, my eyes fixed on the road—and in my mind I desperately replayed everything Carlos had said the day we got pizza. On my lap sat a map I'd sketched on a notepad. It had turned to pulp, but I'd had the turns memorized. Left at the hardware store, a two o'clock at the roundabout. I followed them one by one, until the carousel flitted into view. I killed the engine and peered out through the windshield.

It was... eerie. The carousel was frozen in place as if time itself were frozen, the horses leaping ominously into midair. Half-assembled swings loomed treacherously over dead time. The Ferris wheel, dark, unlit and gargantuan, gaped back at me like the lone eye of a reaper.

I stepped out of the car. The air was chilly, but somehow I could not seem to feel it. My feet carried me, as they did on the day the school blacked out and my life changed for good, away from the car and through the labyrinth of the Mock Carnival. There was no one here—it seemed the Xentrios had chosen the perfect time.

Then I halted. I listened. There was an unmistakable sound of footfall. Perched on the edge of reality and imagination, the sound was no more than a soft tap against the ground, something too subtle for human ears to hear. But something told me it wasn't in my mind; I focused again, and there came another. My heart began to pound.

I breathed slowly. Blood began to rush through my body, so violently I could almost hear it pulsing. I tensed and perked up my ears. The sound came again, then again—then to a stop. I instinctively knew where it was coming from. Slowly and meticulously, I approached the sound.

And as I turned a corner I was met, just as in my dream, by the six Xentrios.

It felt like someone was squeezing at my guts. It was very dark—but even in the dimness, I could see their faces.

The faces, I realized, looked worse from up close. They were perfect, symmetrical, flawless—but there was something about the flawlessness, as well as the unexplainable expressions in their eyes, that made your hair stand on end. Calleigh was right. The horror wasn't something that could be forgotten.

But strangely enough, all I could feel was the sudden gush of blood and the heat of shame and anger I'd felt when they'd whispered my name at the fair. At that moment I could hear that Brittany girl's voice again as she spoke, wrinkling her face in distaste. I could taste the serum on my tongue and down my throat. I could see the horrible black birds swooping in through the gray sky to tear at my heart. Then I was surrounded by memories of the Mock Carnival. The festive atmosphere, tunes played on horns and bedecked with chimes, the chatter of crowds that sent a buzz through my young heart—I closed my eyes and inhaled slowly. I thought of the children filing in on their own little adventures, little smiles of joy as they see for the first time the glitter of lights on a winter night; the six figures who stood in front of me sought to destroy that, to feast on the blood of the innocent. I could not let that happen. This place was my childhood, and I had no intention of seeing it fall.

I stepped in front of them. I could have pounced the moment I saw them, but I knew it would have done no good. I was outnumbered, and all I had in my head about these creatures were the drawings Calleigh had shown me. But there was a flicker of hope, and it was that the Xentrios were not making a move. These creatures clearly had not expected me, and only gazed at me as though in curiosity. I had some time—and I could use it to figure out more about them.

I began to scan each one of them, recalling the details of my dreams and of Calleigh's descriptions. Then suddenly I had a little idea. I took one more look around the lot of them, swallowed, and spoke:

"We've never met, well, except in my dreams," I said. My voice was barely above a whisper and trembling harshly—but it was not in fear; it was in something else. I continued: "But I know who you are. It's good to see all of you in person."

No, that was a lie. It was revolting.

"Hello, Ares," I spoke, greeting a tall, dark-haired man on the left. "Underwhelming for someone who's named himself after the god of war."

The man looked at me, his eyes full of hatred, his lips drawn back as though they would let out a hiss any moment. But I wasn't scared.

"Rima," I said, moving onto the girl with the bright red hair, who stood staring down at the floor. "You don't look that eager to be here," I observed.

"You know what, I'd almost think..." I added, peering at her face, "you're scared."

The girl did not respond, only laid a careful gaze on my eyes. Her eyes bore the same repulsion, the same cold hatred—but there was something else in it that I could not name.

"Keena," I called, turning to the woman with thick platinum-white hair. She stood ready to pounce, her lips drawn back in a hideous sneer. "You like to play games, I can tell," I added. "How about we play my game?"

Blood pumped through my chest and limbs. I walked around Keena and toward the man to her right, slender and sharp chinned, his brows almost gathered into a line.

"Elor," I named. "Try to smile a little more for your pictures. You look... constipated."

The man let out, quite literally, a hiss. I could see the Xentrios tense pack of wolves ready to pounce. I moved on.

"Cuper," I whispered.

The man stood tall and toned like a statue. His features were crisply defined, his jawline cut like a marble cliff. I would have thought him to be handsome if it weren't for the unexplainable revulsion.

I studied the Xentrio. He was, like the others, dressed in garments you could not quite identify the age of—a suede doublet, or jacket of sorts, which could belong in the history of hedonism, and at the same time at an avant-garde gala of the modern world. His boots were seemingly made of fish leather, dressed in shiny scales, new and untouched.

The Xentrio eyed me curiously. No human emotion could be seen in his eyes, but his gaze was no less penetrating. It was slicing cold, yet scathing hot; and all the while darkly ghoulish. He shifted his feet and for a while the front of his doublet opened a bit, and protruding from his inner pocket I could glimpse a dash of copper.

The Lock, I thought. I tried to recall what Calleigh had said about the Lock. It could control your movement, she had said. I could not fathom how the piece of metal could do such a thing.

The Xentrio observed me as I studied the object. I could feel the gaze penetrate me, but I did not back down. I'd come too far. I raised my eyes to meet the searing gaze.

"The last and least, am I wrong?" I voiced softly. "You're not as powerful as the other Originals."

It was another bluff—I knew nothing about their powers except for the brief introduction that Calleigh had given me. But I knew I'd hit the right spot; I heard him draw a sharp breath, and in the murky dark I saw his fists clench. As I saw veins creep onto his hands and wrists like deadly vines, I wondered if he could feel the same rush of blood I felt, the same broil of rage. My heart was pounding vigorously, but not in fear or anxiety; it was the tensing of the body before a hunt. I was preparing to strike.

Good, I thought to myself. *Get angry. You're falling right into my trap. You're getting me my gem.*

I moved on to the silver haired woman in the center. The woman was cold, revolting and stunning; she stood tall and radiant, her silver locks rippling down to her waist in one fervent bouquet. I approached her without knowing. My eyes were fixed on her maddened ones, captured by the eerie glow, by the ecstatic verve—and for a moment I held my breath; I was afraid I would topple into them, lose myself in the perpetual blackness of her pupils.

I could see better as I neared her. She seemed to retain her youth, but through many eras—faint as a trace left in another life, I could see that her cheeks had been weathered with wind and salt. She stood in a deep purple frock coat, tailored to fit her slim body. The edges of the coat was lined with blackened silver beads, on which I could almost smell the brine of the Atlantic.

"...Victorina." I whispered. I took a step forward. A sickly strong perfume permeated the air. I looked down from her face to find a pendant on her chest; a brilliant-cut glass bottle, decorated with aged and blackened silver, filled to the top with purple-black liquid. The substance seemed unlike any I'd seen.

It seemed to be made of otherworldly liquid; clear but clouded, dark and yet lit with enticing shimmers.

"Victorina Archer," I whispered.

The woman hissed. "Don't you dare."

"What brings you here? Isn't this where you were defeated? By a little girl, even."

I had taken a bold guess, but from the flicker in the woman's eyes, I could see I had gotten in right. This was the spot they had been defeated. They were the raiders.

"Hundreds of years ago," I continued. "You sailed up the river thinking you could cull these villagers like livestock. That you could feast on blood and tears. You brought your men, you piled in here like a pack of rascals. You celebrated, got all wasted way too early;

"Only to be outwitted by a little girl," I whispered. Victorina's eyes pierced me with a toxic glare. *So easy*, I thought to myself.

Ever so slowly, Victorina took a step toward me. Her pendant glinted darkly, as beautifully, menacingly and repulsively as the woman herself. Faint clouds of fumes floated from it to dance darkly in the air. A hint of the perfume soon traveled into my nostrils and down my throat—like a flutter of poison, suffocating me, burning me from the inside. I held my breath.

And she smiled. Her smile was absolute. It was icy and cold, and yet quite like the expression of a predator that found its prey. Only she was wrong; I was not that prey. Without knowing I took another step forward, holding her gaze.

And suddenly, without warning, Victorina's arms shot out and wrapped around me, pressing me to her chest. Instantly the fumes rushed into my lungs. They burned my throat, my lungs, scathed the insides my head and ribcage. Every breath I took was torture; I gasped for fresh air, every inch of my windpipe screaming in protest, but the only thing that filled my lungs was agony.

Her arms constricted me and my ears pressed against her chest. I could faintly hear a rhythmic sound, something that could have been a heartbeat but wasn't quite—it seemed to come from another world, from a far, lost realm of unending cold; it was almost like it were beating underwater, beneath endless depths that no ray of light dared reach. The perfume now seemed to fill every corner of my lungs, and my vision began to contract and swim. I felt a piercing pain at the back of my head. *No, this isn't going to be the way I die,* I thought. I gathered my strength and pushed against her. Unlike what I expected, her grip loosened easily. I toppled backwards.

Victorina narrowed her eyes, peering at me, waiting.

Oh, right, I thought. *The Perfume and my blessed immunity.* The dynamic pianissimo of Calleigh's words echoed in my head: *Except you, Sarah.*

This, was a game.

With equal patience I looked back at her. It was a guessing game. I would read her. I would read her and decide what she would want me to feel. Then, with my terrible acting skills, I would act it out.

I didn't know how the Xentrios worked, how they thought and functioned. Whether they were vessels of pure evil or something with a morsel of humanity left, they were bound to have their blind spots. Maybe it made them easiest to fool.

What would I try first if I were her? I asked myself.

Profoundly simple. This was something only profoundly simple people could comprehend. I stepped back.

I shut my eyes tight and began to stagger. I let out short, ragged breaths, covering my head in my hands, shaking my head as though fighting invisible demons—

When I fluttered my eyes open again, Victorina's cold, questioning eyes were only inches from mine. She broke into shrill laughter, the hideous tune echoing off the walls again and again as if she were laughing her soul out.

"Impressive," she said. Her voice was a metallic screech against the night, dense and briny. "Dauntless, but pathetic," she added.

I backed away from her, giving my best terrified look. I'd taken a few steps back when Victorina's next words froze me in place:

"Why aren't you affected by my Perfume, girl?"

I inhaled sharply.

"Unless *that* pathetic face is your expression of pleasure," Victorina whispered. "What is it that you sick creatures did... that shields you from me?"

"I have no idea what you're talking about," I replied.

"Well, yes, you do," Victorina said, stepping toward me. "Is this some kind of gem?" She voiced, seemingly in genuine curiosity. I let out something close to a laugh.

"I wish," I replied honestly. "Let's say for now it's a little trick. Like the one that took you down the last time you were here."

Victorina eyed me as if she were deeply amused. I watched, a part of my stomach jolting and convulsing, as she formed a curious curve on her lips.

"We've come to make them pay," she whispered, like a child sharing a secret. "Tonight is... how do you put it? Prelude, foreplay. A special night, a moment of reminiscence. To *feel*, you see, the venom, the sweetness of imminent destruction... of revenge..." the woman went on, her lips floating up in a vile little smile. "It makes the actual act so much better."

"It won't happen," I said. "You'll have to get through me first."

Victorina's lips curled up further. She let out a breathy little chuckle. The other five Xentrios closed in on me slowly in a collapsing circle; I quickly scanned the room out the corner of my eyes. Classic ring, no getaway. I had to wager.

"Is the name Serena familiar to you?" whispered Victorina.

"Very. You killed her," I said, barely above a growl.

Two-o'clock. Rima, the girl with the red hair. She was, I sensed, the weakest of the six.

Victorina nodded, appeased. I could smell her perfume again. My breath got caught midway.

"I killed your Queen. I killed the Diamond. Whatever this is, this little gem of yours... it can't hurt me, little girl. I conquer every Gem. I am death... that no Gem can escape."

Well, if *that* pathetic face is *your* expression of pleasure. I had to say, even if I died today, I was lucky to be able to quote my childhood heroine while I was still standing. I only hoped that when I died, it wouldn't be without a gem.

"I am no Gem," I said boldly, a smile creeping up the edge of my mouth. "I'm gemless."

And on the heels of that last word, I spun into the two-o'clock direction, changing, pawing down and jumping over the stunned redhead. She gave way easily, and I led the lot of them to the far corner.

From the beginning I had made no plan to escape. I had no intention to. Instead, I shifted to a different position so I wouldn't have my back to any of them.

In the distance Victorina's pendant appeared to glow. I could see her eyes had begun to take on an eerie glow as well, the color sinking deeper, shining brighter, until it couldn't be named anymore—the fumes from her pendant blew her hair from her face as if in a fierce wind, and in the murkiness her locks gleamed a more vivid silver. The woman herself took on a heinous glow, as if she were finally coming alive. She was changing, I was sure, in a way— her body now funneled something greater than before, something far more ancient than she or I was.

It was like in my dream. The six of them stood waiting, ironically, much like a lioness waiting for her prey. I inhaled and held my breath, watching. It wasn't long—Victorina lunged forward faster than I could ever imagine, in a blur, not allowing time to think.

But I didn't think. I was prepared. When Victorina came into range, I took off, teeth bared, pounding my claws on her chest. I sunk my canines into her outstretched arm.

An awful screech filled the air.

There was a deafening shatter, almost as horrible as her scream. The air instantly filled with the smell of her perfume. It was everywhere. My eyes burned, my throat seemed to contract until I felt like I was being strangled. Pain shot through my head like an arrow had dug into it.

Just then I saw a flash of red-gold from Cuper's hands. A blur of metal, bluish strings reaching into the darkness like reared heads of vipers—and suddenly, I was seized from all directions, as though by thousands of thin constrictors. Captured by unseen strings, I lost my footing and began to topple over. My body spun around dizzyingly fast, morphing back—and everything went black.

When I woke up my head was ringing badly. A sharp pain on the side of my head reminded me of the sickening smell of Victorina's perfume. I closed my eyes, and the world seemed to spin a bit as I leaned my head back. I winced. There was a strong taste of bitter blood in my mouth. With sickening clarity, I recalled Victorina tearing at me, and my teeth sinking into her skin. The deadening shriek still rang in my ears, and I shook my head, trying to get it out.

Was she dead? Was *I* dead?

It was when the worst of the ringing ceased, and my head cleared a bit, that I realized I couldn't move my limbs. I looked down to find that I was held to a pillar by a glowing bluish line. I tugged on the strings, trying to free my hands so I could work on the rest. But it was no use. I pushed hard against the pillar but all I could manage was to strain my back. It was like trying to smash steel with shale.

I sat there scanning my surroundings. I was in a chamber of sorts, dark and murky, with a strong stench of rust and mold in the air. My thoughts flashed quickly to a little structure I'd glimpsed as I headed toward the Xentrios—an opening on the ground, a latched iron trapdoor, one that probably led to some sort of dugout. It was probably where everything was stored when the festival wasn't on—and it was, most probably, where I was.

As I cast another look around, a scant stir of noises sounded near the entrance. It was at first a soft chatter, so casual it could almost have been the chatter of teenagers getting about, or of businessmen heading back from their lunch break. But I knew right away that it was them.

The Xentrios entered. A faint streetlight trailed through as a trapdoor opened, and the six ghastly figures climbed down. Their footsteps echoed like macabre music through the hollow chamber. Victorina came in last, adjusting a bandage around her arm, cursing between her gritted teeth; Cuper strolled in close to her, his brows gathered in a tense frown.

I tugged at the strings again, trying to jerk myself free from the strings that bound me. They only slithered tighter, digging into my skin like thorny vines. I drew a sharp breath between my gritted teeth.

Cuper leaned over to Victorina and whispered something in her ear. On hearing those words, Rima, the timid, flame-red haired girl, turned abruptly to the pair of them—and then to me. It was a sideways glance, so quick that I suspected I might have imagined it. But in the sliver of a second I noticed something in her eyes that I couldn't quite make out. The only thing I knew was that it was not a passing thought, a transient flicker that came and went. In that flash I could see time, a long, long time—whatever thought, whatever sentiment it was, it had been trapped there, thickened and intensified, over decades, perhaps centuries. What could it be? A longing of some sort, a desire? *What was it that she wanted? To be like the others?*

Rima turned and backed away, and I snapped out of my thoughts. The path opened for Victorina and Cuper; they stood looking at me with a blank, appeased look on their faces.

"At least she's, well, amusing," Victorina said softly, the last word turning to a poignant hiss. I clenched my teeth and tried my best not to shudder.

Cuper smirked lightly and leaned in closer to her ear. I could not hear the words whispered, but I could see them bring a light smile to Victorina's lips. *That can't be good*, I thought to myself as I suppressed yet another shudder.

Then Victorina's lips traveled up to Cuper's ears, and the pair exchanged another set of words I could not distinguish. Then I saw their lips slither into each other's, and they were interlocked in a nauseating kiss. It was grotesque; it was as though I had walked in on peculiar art exhibition. I breathed, barely containing the urge to gag.

When they were done, Victorina turned to look at me with a coy smile on her lips. I felt another surge of nausea as I saw her blood-red lips curl like snakes. I was then approached by the two Originals. One crouched down beside me and the other circled me like a hyena that had found a carcass. I shuddered as Cuper's hand touched my face; the Xentrio's skin had an eerie texture, as though it were from another universe, and for a brief moment I thought that I could feel his fingertips dip a little through my skin.

Cuper's hand jerked my head up to face Victorina, and I let out a little gasp. I winced—his hand was relentless, and for a while I was afraid that he would crush me like a nut.

"You can't imagine how charmed we are to run into you," Cuper whispered. "Talk to us," he added softly. "Tell us what's on your mind."

For a while I sat breathing tensely. There *was* something on my mind—there was something that had never left my mind for months.

"Princess Rena," I responded. "I heard about her. It was all connected somehow. I knew I had to find you. Because you're going to find me my gem."

"I wouldn't have high hopes about a gem," Victorina mocked. "But I could tell you about your dead queen if you wanted."

Why not, I thought.

"What happened to her?" I asked. "How did you kill her?"

"Well, she wanted so dearly to find me and fight me, so I did. And she was weaker, so she lost," Victorina said, her tone almost a happy chant. I shuddered.

"Because you killed her friend. You killed Harvey," I snarled.

"Ahh... Harvey." The woman's eyes narrowed, trembling slightly with elation. She breathed like she was taking in the aroma of a luscious meal. "Her most loyal knight, truest friend, they say," she whispered. "But he meddled with something he shouldn't have."

"So did you," I spat. "With your sick little philosophy, thinking you can make judgments like a god."

Victorina's lips coiled into a soft smile. "Me? I don't have a philosophy, whatever that is. I just do what I like, girl. I kill. It's simple as that. No words, no cause... I hate complications. I do it the good old way. Slaughter, throw the bodies off the deck. That's it."

I glared at her, my eyes burning with rage.

Victorina kept on her revolting smile, her mockingly tender gaze brushing my face. "But," she crooned, "now that I think of it... there is someone who has one of those." Victorina's voice shrank to a whisper. "If you want to talk philosophy, you might want to meet the Sire."

I shuddered. Something about her tone frightened me, and for the first time today I was afraid. Victorina seemed to sense it in my eyes, and her eyes narrowed into a vile smile.

"Well, unless you don't last that long..."

Cuper let go, and my head banged into the pillar.

"Enjoy your last breaths while they last," he whispered.

Cuper twitched his eyebrows, and the strings rose from my torso like a snake. It climbed up my shoulders, sending shivers down my spine, and cozied at the crook between my neck and shoulders.

Cuper laughed softly, and raised his hand as if to conduct an orchestra.

The strings slithered around my neck like a child's arms, slowly tightening, digging into my skin like burning vines. My breath thinned to wispy whispers, and the pulse of my blood traveled to my lips—futile heartbeats could be felt on my lips, then on my temples. Cuper laughed, and a low giggle escaped Victorina's mouth, hurdling into a shrill laughter.

I watched as the loose ends of the strings quivered and curled—then, slowly and surely, they began to rise toward Cuper's outstretched hands. Obediently the strings landed on his palm. The Xentrio's bony fingers curled around them—the Xentrio then began to weave a knot with the strings, into a complexity I had never before seen. Once it was finished his hands left the knot; but the knot stayed suspended in space, emitting its eerie blue glow. Then, the Xentrio reached into his inner pocket—and pulled out the Lock.

It was a byzantine creation; the body was made of copper, light and rosy even under the dim light of the basement. On the body was a delicate repoussé—one of a brute man holding a thunderbolt in one hand and a double-headed axe on the other. Gilded lines reached from the edges to a horned crown that sat atop the man's head, adding a sheen of gold to the cold red dimensions. It was the Cuperian Lock, king of the Xentrios' physical instruments. It struck me only then that the strings that held me were part of the Lock, or, in a way, something that aided it; the Xentrio could move it at his will, perhaps even feel it—but it did not control my body. With the Lock, more would be possible.

The Xentrio seemed to stroke the lock with his hand, and it clicked open with a heavy snap. Carefully as if engaged in a work of art, he brought the lock to the edge of the knot, then put the shackle through it. The glowing twines attached to the metal as though merging into one, and the body of the lock began to take on a faint bluish glow. I shivered.

What would happen when it closes?

I tensed as the Xentrio's fingers pressed on the shackle. *This may be the end,* I thought; *and it may be a terrible end. I might have been very wrong… about everything.* My heart began to race, this time in fear; panic seized me, but there was nothing I could do. I merely braced myself, gritted my teeth as the shackle began to close—

The lock clicked, a sound different from what I'd expected, something a lot heavier and thumpier, like a bar of soap hitting metal—and something round and white flashed between his fingertips and the Lock, sending it, strangely not yet closed, flying from his open fingers and sliding across the floor—

"No you don't."

Wait… what?

My eyes found something in the distance, surrounded by a halo of dusty light from the entrance.

I chuckled. So I was hearing things. And now seeing things.

I couldn't love that voice more than I did that minute. I was most probably about to die, and die gemless, but at least I would die while my favorite voice was spoken to my ears. It had been this very voice that stirred up little whirlwinds in my stomach, pumped my blood into a feverish lap around my body. I remembered the little chuckles, the snarky little inside jokes we'd shared as we plotted our heist in the woods. I thought back to what he'd told me the night we looked up to the stars; it dawned on me, all of a sudden, that I never got to hear what he dreamed about that night. I wished I could have known, but perhaps it did not matter; he wasn't having nightmares anymore. That was what mattered. I'd perhaps done a little something. That was enough.

And so it wasn't easy to comprehend when my vision only grew clearer, to reveal five familiar figures piling in through the dimly lit doorway, and among them *Carlos Pierce*.

He's here?

Before I could answer my question, a sweet jingle filled the air and the four young Enrici lunged at the Xentrios. Instantly, as wolf-Lillian and eagle-Chase seized his fragile attention, the pressure from the strings began to lift. I coughed violently as my breath returned—my view cleared, and the pulsing in my head slowly ceased.

Carlos ran straight through the chaos to my direction, and got down to his knees, his eyes level with mine. He reached for the knots and began to untie them.

"You okay, Sarah?" he asked as his fingers moved busily over the knot. I noticed that his hands were trembling. He fumbled over the same knot twice, his fingers slipping off the strings again and again—it took a while until he grasped the knot and began to pull it loose. Soon he was done; the strings fell limply at my sides, with Cuper's focus on the others.

"Yeah, I'm fine," I replied. My voice trembled ridiculously. I cleared my throat to try it again. "I'm fine."

"Damn it, Sarah—you disappeared. I found you here with Xentrios and you know what? I don't know half the things *you* know, but I know this; you're not okay."

I smiled weakly. "I'm fine, really."

His eyes fixed on mine, giving my heart a leap, as he raised his hand to clear away the locks of hair from my face. The mesmerizing depth of his eyes froze me, better than Cuper's lockstrings had, for a few more seconds—before he swiftly leaned in to kiss me.

The kiss was short and intense, and I didn't know what had hit me until he was in my sight again, looking at me with a mixture of airs—in his eyes there was yearning, in his brows anger; on his lips sweetness, on his reddened cheeks overwhelming fear. I froze in place. It seemed like forever; his lips had left mine, but the tingle still lingered.

"You have no idea how scared I was, Sarah," Carlos spoke softly, his voice breaking. "Really, you're the worst."

"Carlos," I breathed. I didn't know what to say.

"Let's get you up," he said. I grabbed his extended hand, which was cold and drenched in sweat. The boy pulled me up onto my shaky legs.

"Sarah, I need to go help them," he said, his voice cracking. "Promise me you'll stay back."

For a while I stared at his widened eyes. Even though a tingle still persisted on my lips, and thunderous rainfall of rocks still pounded in my chest, everything slowly came back to me—from the nights I'd spent reading on my bed, the mysterious tales of the queen's murderer; from the dreams, from Lillian's story, to the decision I'd made earlier this night. This was something entirely my own. My search had led me to them, and led them to me—and yet I'd included my friends in it, needed for them to save me. I'd led them into danger. There was no way I could sit back and watch. I would have to lead them back out of danger. I would have to do all I can to protect them.

"I can't do that," I replied. "It's my fault this happened in the first place."

"Which is why you should stay the hell back," Carlos hissed.

"You need me."

Carlos stared.

"If we were to get out of here alive, you need me. You know how good of a hunter I am."

Carlos sighed. "You're impossible."

I smiled. "I know."

Carlos seemed to ponder for a moment, then let out a sigh. "I'm going to stay close by, keep an eye on you," he said. "Call me if you need me."

I gave him a quick nod before I changed.

The scene was wild. The four Enrici were battling the six Xentrios. It was thanks to Lillian's gem—which the others helped themselves to through Chase's gem—that they were still in one piece.

The three eagles tore around the air in a blur, throwing themselves, veiling the others, at the diverted Xentrios. Calleigh was throwing herself at Keena while blurring Victorina's sight, each time bouncing off with her claws full of white hair. Carlos tore in and to her aid.

The Xentrios fought nothing like I'd ever seen. They were fast, they were strong—and they were relentless. But strangely enough, we were surviving; five kids with no plans or patterns, challenging luck—perhaps even fate itself—with nothing but unforeseen recklessness.

Battling two of them was Lillian, who had melted into a gray blur darting around the room. She was taking on Ares and Elor, somehow managing to escape their hands and yet keeping their attention on her. Ares let out a terrible warcry as he swung his fist around. I could see a rusty bronze gauntlet on his hand—something faint was glowing at its knuckles, surrounding it like a cold halo. The faint blue haze seemed to flicker like flames as his fist ferociously sliced the air. *That could be lethal*, I thought. I gasped as his fist whizzed straight into the gray blur. It seemed he'd brushed her, but Lillian went flying, slamming into the ceiling before plopping down with a painful growl. She rose back onto her feet, her eyes full of rage.

Keena stood at the periphery, slashing angrily at the oncoming eagle. She had something protruding from the back of her hand; a closer look revealed a hand accessory of some sort, extending into long silver claws at the end of her knuckles. A dim blue halo surrounded its tips like the one surrounding Ares's gauntlet. *So probably a Cuperian Instrument*, I thought. *I wonder what it—*

A terrible caw echoed through the chamber as her claw slashed Calleigh's side, and she fell to the ground screaming. Carlos lunged for the Xentrio, throwing her back from the eagle, and she extended her hand at him. Another terrible cry echoed. The panther backed from her, and the three turned instead to a slow, tense orbit around one another, bracing, measuring.

Pain. I tensed, grasped by an impulse to throw myself into their aid. But that would not help us—I needed to be at the right place. That was the only way I could get us out of there.

I looked around further. Andrew, with his acclaimed reflexes, was gaining on a diverted Rima, while Chase battled Cuper at the center of the room. Cuper was creating a scene that was almost majestic. A faint haze filled the air as his lockstrings flew about, forming a transparent sphere of glowing blue. For a moment it seemed to have trapped Chase inside, but in a second I found him tearing out of the glowing shadows and lunging for the Xentrio's chest. The eagle swept in for the Xentrio, barely touching him with his claws. The Xentrio then swung his fist around once, and it hit the eagle square in the chest. Chase let out a cry and went flying back, skidding onto the floor and slamming into a wall before he carried himself back up and into the air.

Toward a corner I could see Victorina hissing wildly as she slashed her bandaged arm in the air. She now had Carlos on him as Calleigh cleverly tore in and out of her sight. Despite the wide grin on her face she was fighting disappointingly—it dawned on me on seeing her bare collarbones that her pendant was gone.

The shatter. The smell. The previous moment flashed through my head; I'd broken the pendant. *But her instrument is the perfume itself,* I thought. I was sure I could still smell her perfume in the air when I woke—and I was pretty sure that it was still in the air, only my nose had gotten too tired to notice. Did that mean the others were under her influence? I peered quickly at the five other Enrici as they fought—they seemed no weaker, neither did they seem to be in distress.

Then I remembered something. *The Perfume is no ordinary perfume, the Pendant is no ordinary pendant,* Calleigh had said. Perhaps the perfume and pendant had to work together to produce the effect; without the pendant it was nothing more than sickly fragrance. I had disarmed her of her instrument. And without the instrument, it seemed, Victorina wasn't the most danger-ous of the lot. She'd apparently been, for decades or perhaps for centuries, used to fighting by manipulating; with her bare neck and one uninjured arm, she was less of a threat.

The odds, nevertheless, weren't on our side. We had miraculously come this far, but the Xentrios were gaining on the lot—they seemed to be learning the patterns, winning back their momentum. All of the Enrici were visibly draining; they would not be able to last for much longer. I had to act fast.

I took a deep breath, propelled myself to a turn, bursting through the chiming surface—morphing into my familiar feline form. *Ares*, I thought. *I need to divert his attention from Lillian.* I charged.

The Xentrio turned to me at once. His eyes fixed on me, his pitch black pupils enlarging—and his face deformed into a horrendous smile. I let out my fiercest growl. I could feel the rumble building up from the pit of my stomach, the tremor of my coat against the murky air. The growl ascended gradually into a roar, a roar more terrible than any I'd voiced. The sound echoed again and again through the chamber, dry and hollow, yet fierce and daunting.

I charged. I'd barely gotten close to him when he swung his fist in the air. A glow of silvery blue left his gauntlet and shimmered through the air in a trajectory toward me. A wave of shock landed on my side, and before I knew it, I was sliding across the floor, my ribs throbbing as though I had been hit by a cannonball.

I rose again. I reared myself once more and charged toward his figure. It came again, another blow, then another. I was fast enough to duck under. I jumped, kicking my hind legs against the wall, propelling myself up into the air. A second wave whizzed past my ears and I swerved a little bit—then lunged myself at the Xentrio once more. Wind stirred as a faint glow rippled past, a swoosh in my ears, dying away just before it hit the wall.

I ran at him again. He had his full attention on me, without Lillian darting in a blur to divert his attention. I wasn't Calleigh, or Chase, or Andrew, who knew how to work Lillian's gem through Chase's beacon—but I was fast. I was easily faster than Lillian without her gem. I was the lioness, the apex predator of the savannas, and I was built to charge for my prey, to follow them, to pounce and kill. I charged again. I barely even scratched his arm, but I did not stop—I reared myself and went again, then again. I would have to keep doing this until I land a bite. Approaching him from the front was not an option—I would be right down the line of fire.

Sarah.

I almost staggered to the side and into Ares's fist as I heard a voice penetrate my head. Carlos?

It's Calleigh's channel. Sarah, are you doing all right?

Oh, the beacon. I did my best to think of what to say while I dodged another blow. The dim blue halo whizzed past, and another gust of cold wind brushed my face. I flinched.

Doing just fine, I replied.

Good. I'm doing good too. Hang in there, The EA will be here. Calleigh's sent for help.

No problem, I replied. Another terrifying blow brushed me, and I went sliding across the floor again.

Focus, focus, I thought to myself. *Carlos, I need to focus.*

Right. Call me if you need me.

Another glowing shadow shot past, and I ducked. It landed on the iron trapdoor with a bang so loud and thunderous I thought it could be heard from miles away. I looked to see that a dent had formed. *It would everyone's attention in a matter of time*, I thought; *we have to get away from here. We have to lead the Xentrios away.*

I'd never thought so fast in my life. I scanned the area; Cuper and the eagles' battle was yards away, somewhere toward the middle of the room. Making no effort to attack, I inched toward the scene while defending myself from Ares. It took several minutes until I was close enough. Ares seemed appeased, thinking he had me on the verge of surrender. *No, no*, I thought as I glanced at Cuper out the corner of my eyes. *You're very wrong.* When I was in proximity, I positioned myself cleverly so that if I took a step or two Cuper would stand between me and Ares.

All was set.

When Ares prepared for another attack, I leapt into the air, directly for Cuper's Lock, and took in in my mouth.

I changed.

I wasn't sure if it would work. If it didn't, well, I guess this would be the end. I stood up, bold on my two human feet, dangling the Lock in my hand, taunting the third Original with a brilliant smile.

"HEY!" I hollered. Cuper's eyes lit up like flares as he saw what I had in my hand.

I smiled radiantly. Stupidity always got attention.

I felt the gaze of twenty two eyes as I dangled the lock in my hands in front of the enraged Original. "Why don't you come get it, Cuper?" I challenged.

With an inhuman growl, his feet left the ground. I turned without delay and darted out toward the door.

I went straight for Carlos' car while Cuper's angry footsteps pounded behind me. *One tumble, and I would be dead*, I thought. With frantic strides the Xentrio was closing on me. I felt my pockets for the key—they were empty.

Shit. I'd locked the key in the car.

Without thinking I hauled the Lock at the window. The window shattered easily. I unlocked the door and brushed off the shards of glass with my bare hands. I climbed into the driver's seat, slammed the key in and started the engine. Cuper was out on the road, tearing down Calleigh's truck.

My plot was to lead them to the park. We had to lead them away from human contact, and I knew that place like the palm of my hand.

—And second, and third, and fourth. And—fifth. The car raced down the road at a terrifying speed. I was in the depth of night, and the road was nearly empty. I passed a couple bewildered drivers, one of them aggressively honking; but I could not afford to slow down—

Shoot. I cursed as a terrible screech told me I'd scratched a thick line on a steel barrier. I swerved to the right. My torso jerked violently. I held onto the handle for dear life so I wouldn't get thrown out of my seat. With my heart racing insanely, I tried my best to regain my composure. The park wasn't too far, if my calibration was right. I just had to hold on for a little longer. But speeding like that was not easy for someone with little experience; the car sheered once again as the tires bumped into the side of a sidewalk.

"Shit," I cursed, steering back into the lane. The hills came into view about a mile ahead. "Shit, shit, shit, shit, shit."

"Hang in there, Sarah, hang in there," I muttered to myself. Best as I could, I pictured the journeys I'd taken here with Carlos. I took a right.

As I squealed to a stop at the usual spot by the parking lot, I discovered, to my utter fascination, Lillian's blue convertible parked right in front.

"How did you—" I started as I got out of the car.

"No time for that. Hold on tight."

Before I could say anything, Lillian grabbed my arm, and did some sort of a painful twist—before I could object, I was in the air spinning, the sound of windchimes blinding my sight.

When I opened my eyes I found myself holding onto the wolf's neck as if it were my lifeline. Lillian shot forward, and when she did I was glad I was holding on tight—the world blurred into almost a monotone, and a gush of wind attacked my face, trapping air inside my lungs until they burned. I could barely keep my eyes open, and through my eyelids I could see little branches whir past and disappear.

Lillian slid to a stop, and I was launched into the air. I landed on the side of the lake and rolled over.

"Lillian—what—" I groaned. My ribs throbbed.

"You know this place," Lillian whispered, morphed back in the blink of an eye. Her voice was almost a ferocious hiss. "They'll be here soon. This is the only place we stand a chance."

I nodded.

"You did well. Remember what I taught you. Don't get killed," Lillian ordered harshly.

I gulped. I don't know if she meant to somehow calm my nerves, but it wasn't working.

Ahead of us the leaves parted, and Cuper stepped out from the trees. He drew closer. His eyes crackled like flames licking coal. Besides me a jingle sounded—I looked to see Lillian a wolf again, a menacing growl detonating from her teeth. I changed as well and stood beside the growling wolf.

The other Xentrios filed in, taking their spots. The lake seemed to have lost its color, drained into a dull gray—the sky itself seemed to have lost its vigor, lulled to nothingness by the lifeless creatures. Among the canopy another soft rustle sounded, and from the bushes emerged the chocolate-brown panther I knew so well. Everything seemed to freeze for a second or two, until three eagles appeared from the treetops with a loud caw. Before I had time to think, I moved.

The battle resumed. One by one, we began to lunge at our pursuers; and I took Ares again. I charged, as I'd done before, dodging the ghastly glow of his gauntlet, leaving a thin hairline cut on his chin, plunging into the ground and rounding myself up, lunging again—and another flash from his gauntlet, a flicker of pale blue in the air, and impact, square on my chest. I went up flying into the air. For a moment only the dark blue of the early morning sky filled my sight, and everything was upside down for a second—and I landed, the world quaking as I planted my feline feet firmly on the ground. I growled. I reared and charged again—when something else took me by my hind leg; it was the familiar, pale blue string.

Oh, no, oh, no, oh, no. The Lock. I should have seen this coming. I had not mastered anything like the Traveler's Pocket. The Lock had fallen out of my hands when I changed, and Cuper had retrieved it; a wolf and an eagle could not possibly be enough to keep him occupied. For a moment I could not act, nor think—I simply stared down at the glowing blueish strings slithering around my ankle. I was jerked off my feet, and the sudden, unforeseen impact morphed me back. To my horror and disbelief I saw the strings grow endlessly, and intertwine in the air to form a complex web, seemingly reaching out into the void—and they shot up like a high tide, to fall on five pairs of bewildered eyes. In an instant everyone was captured and hurled to one side of the clearing, all morphed backed and ensnared by the deadly glowing net.

Brows clustered, eyes burning intensely, Cuper was focused. And when he was, his strength was incredible.

Pinned to the ground as if bound by a giant spider's web, I watched as the glowing strings arranged themselves to complex knots, ones with intricate crossings, strange topologies I had yet to see. For the first time, I felt hopeless.

I squeezed my eyes shut, wishing dearly for diversion that didn't come—Robert, Sophie, Enricus soldiers, *anyone*, but of course, not a footstep sounded. The horizon began to take on a faint glow, and the first caw of a crow rang through the cold air.

And just then, the six Xentrios tensed at once. They turned to face a point on the edge of the woods, a patch of darkness between two trees. Victorina dropped a loose end of her bandage, and red-black blood dripped slowly, in a serpentine way, onto the grass.

Then he came.

It was the same nausea, the same terrible grip at my intestines that I'd felt on seeing the six other Xentrios. Only this time, it was nothing like that. That feeling earlier on was nothing compared to this.

A man in a black overall coat emerged from the trees into the broad space. Rose-red clouds preceding the sun cast strange shadows as he loitered forward. He was brutely built, although not as muscular as Cuper or Ares. His gray-black hair, the color of his coat, was cropped short, exposing the shape of his skull. His eyes scanned the area with a cold, knowing glare, as if he could see every atom, every intention that ever crossed one's thought.

He was one of them. And the most powerful one of them. He had not been in my dreams, that was certain—I hadn't seen this face, not in the first dream, not in the second dream. No face I'd seen was this powerful, this *dreadful*.

His eyes were pitch black, his irises contracted to an invisible ring. His brows shaded the dark of his eyes to something even darker; it was as if they would not let out a drop of light, only drink every drop of it, suck it forever into the abyss. I stared frozen at the figure, studying him, his clothes, his hands, his build. On the waist of his coat, a metal pole glowed with a cold, vile silver-blue. It was the handle of a knife.

I inhaled sharply.

I knew at once what it was. That knife, it was the knife that belong to...

"Darius," whispered Victorina as she stepped forward.

Chapter 14
The Sire

The man's footsteps fell again and again around the rim of the lake. His boots were clad in old leather, worn and weathered as though from a distant era. The bits of leather peeling from those boots resembled the kind of bandages that kept a mummy from falling apart, or its age-old curse from breaking out—I could see a scar in the soles that glinted once in the moonlight, and heard in my heart the cries of the lives he had trampled out.

Not a sound was heard. The woods around us had fallen silent as well—even birdsong had ceased to a stillness I had never known. Not one mouse dared to roam. Not one leaf dared to rustle. The world stood still, waiting to find out what this man was about to do.

Painfully slowly, the man began to stride toward me. His feet fell ruthlessly on the grass, and for a moment I feared the grass he'd trodden would go out like candlelight and die at once.

The man's feet came to a halt in front of me, and I could observe him from closer. I held my breath. His face was beyond pale, somehow fallen into a shade of dim blue-gray. As his eyes fixed on mine I felt a shudder pass through my marrows. The man's mouth opened, and his tongue hissed a curse—the sound that came from his mouth was strange, looming, deep and echoing, as if off the walls of an unknown universe.

"You are such a fool," he echoed. "What do you plan to do with her now?"

Victorina winced as though his voice hurt her physically.

"We have the Knife," Victorina whispered back, her voice low, a soft metallic screech.

Darius seemed to pull his lips up in something that looked like a smile, and strode a step toward her. He grabbed her injured arm in his hand and her face contorted in agony, but not a sound escaped her lips.

"A girl like that—" he jerked his chin sharply toward me, "—will turn out worse than Rima. She'll be of no assistance to me. What good is that?"

His voice was barely audible. Rima's face didn't change—I wasn't sure if she'd heard what he just said.

Victorina let out a jagged breath, and spoke in a pained voice; "Rima used to be strong,"

"Only until she turned into a lost cause," Darius hissed.

"And then her life was torture," Victorina replied, a hint of a smile creeping up her pursed lips. "It's her choice to make, but if she chooses to go down that path... then she won't be happy. Neither will the others..."

I couldn't tell if the answer satisfied him, but he let go of her arm, and Victorina toppled backwards like a rag doll onto her knees.

"Very intriguing."

The man's voice was like thunder, rumbling through the earth—I could feel it coming, not only through my ears, but through my knees, and then through my spine.

"It's not often we're met with a guest like this..." the man rumbled on. "You remind me, of a young couple some years ago. Venturing out to meet me, thinking they can take on me with their frail jaws..."

Twigs snapped under the soles of the man's boots, and I could not help but think of something I'd heard not long ago. Out the corner of my eyes I could see Lillian thrashing angrily.

"As much as I applaud their bravery..." the man went on. "History has proven that they were nothing but foolish...

"They came to meet me, the two of them. Two little dogs, with what little training they had, they thought that was enough... They sought to end me... once and for all.

"But what happened to them?" The question echoed through the trees, and for a moment it was as if he were an actor on stage, captivating the audience with his monologue.

"They perished.

"They fell, crumbled like breadcrumbs and disappeared from the face of the earth. Their names disappeared from this planet, along with their expedition, along with their cause..."

A growl escaped Lillian's lips, and then she gritted her teeth in pain as the lockstrings wound tighter around her.

"And yet," Darius continued, unaffected. Something flowed into his eyes, a stream of something that imitated joy. "That is not the worst that can be suffered..." A knot formed inside my stomach. The man took another step and went on: "Well, I never thought much of it... but your people beg to be spared from *this*."

The man's hands traveled toward his belt, and caressed the edges of his black leather sheath.

"It is not long," he continued, "until those of you with some senses realize you were wrong... until you realize it is the best. It is an end to everything, an end to all the toils of life... an end to a world that will forget you, let you crumble away and not shed a tear. Instead you are reborn. You will learn in time that it is the true good, all meanings rectified, due vengeance carried out, your soul free from the confines of humanity... But until then, it is... your worst fear."

Darius took yet another step toward me.

"Which is why..." he rumbled almost melodically. "...I would like to gift it to you."

He seemed to gaze into my eyes for an eternity. Then, painfully slowly, he began to stride around the rim of the lake. His walk was somehow close to a glide—there was a primal eeriness in his movement, something that could not be put into words. He raised his hand, slowly, as if conducting an invisible army of clouds.

"Cuper," he boomed.

Cuper rose. A faint halo of clouds appeared on the horizon. In his hand the Lock gleamed, the red of the copper emitting a strikingly cold glow that I'd never thought possible.

He approached me, and continued what he had meant to do back in the chamber. He worked away with delicacy unimaginable on such brute hands; the strings were strung through the Lock, tied in sophisticated knots around the ring of metal. Then, the Lock clicked.

Instantly I felt my body obey something other than my own will. It was like back in the chamber when I was bound to the pillar, only unimaginably stronger—as if I were a puppet, every cell attached to an invisible string. I found myself rising to my feet.

Out the corner of my eyes I saw the others doing the same. As if it was a signal, as if it was some sort of ritual they were familiar with, the Xentrios sauntered toward them. Ares was the first to reach Lillian. He stationed himself behind her, gripping her shoulders like steel. I could see Lillian trying to resist, her teeth clenched, her eyes full of hatred, but it was to no avail. Elor took Calleigh. Her frail body looked like a china doll's against his tall figure. Keena and Rima took places behind Chase and Andrew. Victorina was behind Carlos, her usual mad smile on her face. A low crackle of laughter escaped her lips.

My feet began to carry me forward. Cuper's eyes were searing into mine, speaking an inaudible command. Several steps in, I realized where I was headed—I looked to see Darius, his thin lips twisted in the faintest smile, reach into his belt and withdraw his Knife.

My heart sank like a battleship. *No, not the Knife.* I tried desperately to claw into the ground, to stop; but nothing worked. Sounds escaped my mouth that sounded unfamiliar, something between a growl and a sob—but my legs did not stop carrying me toward the man in the middle. The resistance, however, had one merit: it irritated Cuper. The Xentrio's brows were furrowed until they were almost a line. He let out an angry grunt, and I pushed harder. With all my strength I slowed myself down, clawing my toes into the ground and—

I slammed hard onto the ground. White-hot pain shot through my knees.

"It's not going to work, girl," he growled. He raised me back onto my feet. I glimpsed blood on my hands.

Cuper's voice was barely human. It sounded to me more like an animalistic growl: "Now don't try anything foolish with me. Follow me, like a good girl..."

My knees still throbbed, but I did not care. I let out a growl in anguish. This wasn't going to work. My strength was draining, Cuper was too strong—too *complete*. My resistance did nothing to alter my course. I was merely carried, like a rag doll, toward the First Original.

Darius extended his hand, his expression blank and anticipating, and gently flicked the Knife around in his hands so the handle faced me. My heart sank as I realized what that meant.

"Take a look, slag," Darius whispered. "Take a good look."

I found myself obeying. I brought the Knife up to my eyes to study thoroughly. It was a double-bladed dagger, about a foot long. The blades were bluish silver like the eyes of the Xentrio himself.

"Adjust your grip... familiarize yourself..." Darius went on.

I did. My fingers flexed around the leather handle. I could see a hazy blue glow at the tip of the blade. The glow extended as a line of shadowy blue, traveling from the tip to the handle. The blade seemed to breathe and pulse as the light shivered on it; I could feel its hunger, hear its thirsty whisper. It mesmerized me—the whispers made its way through my fingertips, traveled through my limbs like the rumble of the earth's ancient quaking. Its messages delivered itself to my core. There was no resisting—I was attaching myself to the vile instrument. And yet, with burning passion, I hated it.

Victorina was laughing. Her laughter, first a soft drizzle against the wind, rose like a tide, dry like a shriveled rose, scathing like its bloodied thorns; it grew in a dramatic crescendo, reaching heights that I did not think possible, ready to pierce me at the heart. Out the corner of my eyes I could see her face. Her eyes bore a hint of amusement. She watched with a growing smile, childlike wonder in her raised brows, as if the entire scene were a play for her. She seemed to see exactly what I wanted and feared, because with a sweet smile bearing all the bile one could ever have, she went for Carlos. A sudden twang of venom shot through my chest as the woman wrapped her arms around Carlos' neck, and brought her lips to his ear. With her vile eyes on mine, and a low cackle bubbling from her throat, she began to nuzzle his earlobe. I could see Carlos' muscles tense, his eyes full of loathing.

"You're going to be building my army. With my Knife. You'll only know once you've done it what an honor that is..." Darius voiced.

I found myself turning from him, the knife held supply in my hand. I began to walk, when I heard a call in the distance.

"Stop!"

I halted.

The voices had come from an opening in the woods. I looked to see who had uttered the command. A squad of about five men emerged into the woods in military attire, sprinting to their places around the clearing. A pack of five wolves followed suit—sleek, strong, larger than any I'd seen. They bared their teeth in warning, in their eyes a cold calculation, in their teeth a deadly resolve. I could hear Calleigh's shrill voice in my head: *The EA are heading over, I've sent them a message.* I felt a sliver of hope form in my chest. They were here.

"We are the Enrican Army. We're not going to repeat it. Release them," a soldier called at the head. His voice boomed through the woods like a warhorn, as if amplified by some kind of special gem. The rest of the men and wolves closed in, stationing themselves around the edges of the forest.

"You are surrounded. Surrender your weapons. Release the hostages."

Darius let out an obscene chuckle.

"Cuper," he called simply, his voice breaking in a grotesque way.

I inhaled sharply as Cuper nodded, and my hand shoved the Knife to my neck. Sharp yelps escaped my friends' mouths. I stood trembling, wincing as the blade dug in ever so lightly.

"I'm guessing you gentlemen wouldn't want this, the girl's quite good. A valuable addition, I daresay, to our cause..."

The man at the head, probably the commander. I could see his eyes quaver ever so lightly. It felt like forever, the painful silence. I felt the cold blade furrow into my skin, and trembled as I felt drops of blood bubble on its fine edge.

"Stop." The soldiers stopped in their tracks. I felt hope drain as the man at the head ordered: "Do not move."

Darius' lips curled in satisfaction. "I say we shall continue, Cuper," he whispered.

Everyone else stood frozen, eyes on me. I moved again. It was as if this were the only path of movement permitted for me. Nothing could fight it; the air itself had seemingly frozen solid. The future was written out. I only had to follow. My feet walked me onwards—Cuper was taking me to Carlos.

Victorina's snakelike, evil gaze met mine—her dark crimson lips curled in a sadistic smile as she sank her teeth into Carlos' ear. An agonizing groan escaped his teeth. I watched as he shook and thrashed, and dark red blood trickled down the side of his face. Pain dashed through my chest.

Please, no. Damn it.

As if they had heard my pleading, my feet carried me first toward Carlos.

My fingers clasped around the handle. I stood in front of him, in front of his widened red eyes, gritted teeth and trembling lips. He seemed unable to make up his mind between hatred and sadness; in his eyes I could see hints of tears, and veins protruded on his reddened temples. He seemed silently to protest as Cuper raised my arm above his chest, ready to bring it down—

No, I screamed internally. Tears flooded my eyes and blinded me, and I struggled to keep my eyes open and seeing, afraid that an accidental swing of my arm would hurt him. It was ironical. It was not an accident that was going to take his life and soul.

I felt my muscles tense. I could feel my body prepare to plunge the knife down. Something was building up in my muscles—not mine, but something of Cuper's; my muscles were merely moving the way he intended, obeying his command. I held the knife fast and hard—and soon, I would bring it down with all my strength.

And at that moment, Calleigh's shrill, high-toned voice flashed through my head. *His weakness is that it needs his focus. He can only control what he focuses on.*

I could tell that Cuper was focusing all he had. On me, on every one of my limbs. And on paralyzing the five other Enrici.

That meant he had a loophole. *What if?*

I waited. I needed to save a little strength, for every drop I had had been drained from profitless resistance. It was going to be a matter of timing, but I was good at that. Although it was in the past, I was a fantastic attacking midfielder. And now, I was a brilliant hunter.

I waited, tense, for my strength to build up. The knife hovered over Carlos' chest, then began its descent toward his demise. With a quick, intuitive calculation, I reared myself, until the right moment came—

And with the Knife inches from Carlos' chest, I spun into the air.

Lionesses weren't very good at holding things; I knew that much. Without the opposable thumbs and right muscles, their paws weren't made for the task. So a deathly grasp had somehow been translated into a push of sorts; and the knife went flying out of my paw. Yes, that was his loophole; as I drove the blade into the frozen ground, the knife shattered to pieces under my feet.

It was like I'd sent a signal. Cuper, taken aback, had lost his grip on all the others. The blue strings quivered and grew dimmer, and slipped limply onto the ground. The five Enrici changed. One by one they charged toward their previous counterparts. At the same time the rest of the soldiers transformed as well, twirling into sleek canine figures in midair.

This time I tore directly at Darius.

I might as well have been mad. The Knife was shattered to pieces, and I could see it out the corner of my eyes, gleaming softly and menacingly as it caught the receding starlight. But Darius stood, hands held up, gripping an invisible handle—as though in his hand, unseen by human eyes, was a dagger he could take me out with. I could not decide what to expect.

The man flicked his wrist in a motion so swift it was nearly invisible. I stepped aside almost instinctively. I heard a hum of air as it vibrated around the unseen projectile, and a sharp, splitting pain shot from my temples. Pain spread like poison across my entire body, pulsing hotly from my neck, chest and all the way to my limbs. Something warm trickled down my neck. I turned to see another one coming at me. I could see it was like Cuper's lockstrings, Keena's claws—and the glowing halo that surrounded Ares' fist. It was a dim-blue projectile, which looked like the blade of a dagger.

Hey kids, came a voice.

Hey kids, can you hear us?

It was the voice of an older man—a soldier of the EA. I promptly heard Chase reply, then the soldier again:

This is Captain Harrison Moore from the EA special unit. We're going to get you kids out one by one. Once we come and distract your counterparts, you're going to follow Seargent Baker there, the black dog with a white spot; he's going to lead you away to safety. Do you understand?

Good, I thought to myself. *The others will be safe now.* I dodged another glowing blade, taking a sharp turn so I could stay moving.

Brown eagle, do you copy?

Yes, came a struggling voice.

We are going to move closer to you. Just keep at it, you're doing great. We're gonna get you out in a couple minutes.

Much appreciated.

I dodged another blow as it came. The attacks grew more frequent and violent, and now I could almost see streams of bluish projectiles flying at me.

Brown eagle, disengaged.

One by one, my friends were pulled from battle. I felt a wave of relief wash over me as I heard; *Panther, disengaged.*

We got everyone but the girl.

The lioness?

She's fighting the First Original, get to her.

We can't, Sarge. We can't reach her. She's too far down.

A bit of silence took place in my head, followed by;

Miss Verona, we need you to hold on a little longer.

I did not have time to answer. I dodged another blade, then another, then another. I was growing closer to Darius, and soon I would have to act, one way or another. I could feel a tremor in my muscles as my body blazed to life. I threw myself at my attacker again.

It came again. This time, it was much faster. I had to merely predict which way it would come before it left his hands; see his hands, and simply know.

I raced at him again. I aimed to jump onto him and land a bite, as I'd done with Victorina. But this time, he wasn't standing in the way for me to sink my teeth into. Instead, his arms disappeared from within reach and emerged under me, landing a powerful, breath-knocking blow into my chest. I flew into the air before falling with a thump onto the grass.

My breath would not return. I gasped for air as sickening pain shook me from my insides. My sides and back shook and spasmed. I grabbed at my throat, coughing desperately to try and suck in some air. Darius strode toward me through my hazy vision.

"I don't know what kind of pathetic lore you're told by your friends," he began. His voice rumbled through my veins, and I could feel it resonate through my chest. I gasped for air. The pain was real, and I was reminded of Victorina's face when he had spoken to her.

"And I don't know what kind of ludicrous cohorts you keep around you and have tell you that you're more than that, but the rest of your world sees you as a half-piece," he rumbled, a smile spreading through his darkened lips.

"You see, I have a very interesting story to tell you someday, of someone who reminds me very much of you," he began. I clawed at the softening ground, still gasping for air. My chest throbbed, and my vision was growing thin again.

"But shamefully enough, you are not good enough to fight like she did, little girl. You are nothing. You may be a half-piece to your kind and more to your friends, but to me,"

His bony hands grabbed my head and jerked it up so it faced him. I was forced to look into his hideous face, the eyes which knew nothing ever but hatred.

"*You're nothing.*"

He thrust my head back at the ground and stood. He stepped back as if to prepare for a final blow.

No.

I gaped at the air, and clawed once again at the ground. My paws found a rock buried halfway in the surface, and my eyes landed on a little dandelion growing from under the slab.

No, I won't go like this.

I pulled myself up. *You called me nothing, but I broke your Knife*, I snarled mentally, as I grasped all of my strength, all my pain, all my fury—and pulled myself back onto my feet. I roared for air, just as a baby cries for its first breath; burning fumes of air entered my hungry lungs. *And I will break you before you break me.* I bared my teeth and let out the harshest growl I could muster.

To me, I said. It sounded as a growl and not as words, but I continued anyway. You *are nothing, with your instrument in shards.*

I leaped again, this time aiming straight for the faintly glowing blade that I knew was about to leave his hand. I don't know if I was insane or led by some strange instinct, the very same instinct that had kept me alive and fed, and brought me to the verge of death I was on—but I tore, certain, at the massless object; I was wagering on my life.

There was a loud, ghastly screech of metal against enamel as the object skidded to a stop between my teeth. The glow intensified, as if friction set it aflame. I gave myself not a single second to stop and think. I held the piece of foreign material firmly in my jaws, and leaped, ready to drive it into his bared heart.

And right then, something exploded.

I was sure that it was the projectile, and that I was either dead or dying rapidly, when I landed squarely on my back. With rhythmic pain pulsing through my spines and a cold, metallic haze veiling my eyes, I struggled to grasp reality; I tried to figure out if I still had that thing in my teeth, or if I was hurt, or for that matter, if I was dead—I could not get an answer, almost as though I were, and ever only were, a disembodied metallic haze myself. But in moments the ringing of my head slowly ceased, and I felt it fade *al niente*, replaced by a mouthful of metallic flavor. I pulled myself up, and tried vainly to spit it out, only to discover by sight of dark liquid that the flavor was nothing but my very own blood.

The blade was gone. So was Darius.

I looked around awestruck, as realization dawned on me that the other Xentrios were gone as well.

Seconds of confusion did not give me an answer—except for a warm ripple of foreign wave in the air, softly traveling through my body and away. My feline ears caught a distant jingle in response to the current. At that moment I knew:

They had left.

One by one, we changed back. Befuddled looks passed between the six of us, then among the armymen—only after a long exchange of unspoken signals did one of them declare:

"It looks like they're gone."

Peace took long to find us again. The pack of dogs paced around assessing the area, and for a while we stood frozen still, wary and vigilant. Then the soldiers changed back, the severity faded from their faces—and with assuring nods they transformed into healers, trotting briskly back and forth to check if anyone was injured.

Some of us had cuts, bruises, and little sprains—my own cuts were treated by a soldier with a german shepherd form, with moonflower extract just made this morning. To our great relief, no one had suffered a greater injury. I inhaled endlessly. I could hardly remember when I breathed for the last time—a surreal sense of safety finally enveloped me, and my body seemed to melt into jelly.

"You're shaking."

A voice sounded from behind me. I jolted back into reality, and remembered, with a blush that felt endless, the kiss in the chamber. The pain seemed to lift and disappear, and instead left a faint sweetness at the tip of my tongue. I turned to face Carlos.

"I... uh, I am?" I found myself saying.

Carlos smiled and stepped a bit closer, placing his hand on my shaking hand.

If he thought that would calm my nerves, he was wrong. Well, right and wrong. It felt as if I were standing on the edge of a cliff, my bare feet on crumbling rocks, breathing in the gusts of wind knowing I could fly.

"So... good morning," I said stupidly.

Carlos let out a soft laugh. "Good morning, Sarah."

"You saved my life," I said softly.

"I did," said Carlos, no denial, no humbleness whatsoever—but his voice was softer, barely above a whisper, teetering over that edge where it would break softly like a wave hitting the shore. A smile blossomed. The sun was in his face, making his eyes glow a strange shade of olive, and his skin a mellow shade of morning's east sky. His hair fluttered melodically from his face, and I was suddenly overtaken by a similar fluttering in my stomach.

And in a moment we were on each other's lips, fierce as lions, mellow as moonflowers. My heart began to race in a glorious drumroll, and cold wintry air fluttered by to caress our hot cheeks as cold fingers tasted them, mine traveling, knowingly albeit the lack of experience, up around his temple, his slipping onto my head and gently enveloping my neck. A pleasant surprise bubbled up my lips and I let out a breezy breath, something between a giggle and a sigh. The sun spilled onto us like the sound of an orchestra playing a late romantic tune, and everything felt right—the nightly hunts, the talks under the stars, the jumps over fences. I was, no, correction, we were, quite gloriously and inevitably, in love.

The kiss had to end, however, as we realized we were still surrounded by a bunch of gawking eyes, a pair of which, were staring in pure disgust from not far a distance.

"Really? Now? Youse look like roo chunder," Lillian voiced as she caught my eye, her mouth wrinkled in distaste.

"Still beautiful," Carlos remarked. I blushed.

I giggled. "Sorry, Lillie."

"After I'm done puking, you can get in my car but only if you keep your hands off each other," Lillian said. "His thing has a broken window and Calleigh's needs to be towed."

"Nope, none of you kids are driving, not after this," said a voice, however. It was the beefy seargent who had, in his black dog form, led everyone off the battlefield. He pointed with his head to a truck sitting in the back. "We are taking you home."

Back at Vanna Daya, more calls were made; Calleigh seemed to have a lot of talking to do with the army officials, and more talking to do down in the Phonie. I was kept busy for a little longer. Three different soldiers came to ask for my account of the battle. They listened intently, taking note of everything I said. When I was finally let off the hook I traipsed to the living room, where everyone had practically melted onto the couch in a heap of exhausted humans.

This changed a little, however, when I walked in. With eyes glowing like embers, Calleigh rose—then strode toward me so violently that I thought for a second she would punch me in the face.

But what came was not a punch, only a shrill cry.

"You know you could have got us all killed, right?"

Chase and Andrew rose as well, then Carlos—my face flushed, and I felt more helpless than before. Calleigh was right. I had messed up.

"I know," I said sincerely. "And I wanted to... I wanted to tell you guys I'm sorry. I put us all at risk. And—and, you saved my life."

"Well, you saved us too," Carlos commented. The boys nodded.

"It was you who changed and broke the Knife, it was you who drove Darius away," Chase remarked.

"And wasn't it you who broke Victorina's pendant and injured her? Without that, this would have been an impossible fight. She's powerful."

My face flushed again. I tried to think of something to say, but there was none—no matter what compliments they came up with, I was at fault; and they were my heroes.

"Sarah, forget the apology," Chase said finally. I looked around at the group. Whatever blame they might have had was gone, and big grins had formed on their—well, most of their—faces. Chase continued, his eyes smiling like half moons: "I know you'd have done the same if one of us went off doing something stupid. That's what friends are for. For supporting each other's stupid shit."

A smile crept up all the way from my heart. It was the moment I realized I had a second family here in Vanna Daya.

In a few moments Calleigh left the room and returned with an EA officer. We got up to greet him. He was a broad figure, quite intimidating with those deep-set brows—and as we shortly found out, a deep voice with a strong southern accent.

"Hello, I am Captain Harrison Moore of the Enrican Army. I've come to thank you all for taking such a profound care of the situation. I'd like to confirm that they have indeed Ported, that is, employed their abilities to move away. We believe it unlikely for them to come back in the near future.

"We have notified the Xentrio Threat Management, and together with the XTM the military will carry on from where you left off. We appreciate what you have done today, but we ask you explicitly not to engage in high risk activities concerning the Xentrios," the captain stated firmly.

"Mr. and Mrs. Russell will be on their way soon, and you will stay notified should anything happen. We will be patroling the area, keeping close watch on the headquarters and the lot of you. We'll make sure no harm comes your way." He looked around and gave a hefty smile of a soldier. "All right. Thank you for your time."

"Captain Moore," I called, to which all eyes turned to me. "Thank you for all you've done," I said earnestly. The captain nodded with a firm smile. "But I have, well, we all have, a lot of questions about what happened," I added. "And I think we have a right to answers."

The captain turned to face me, with a curious expression on his face.

"You're Miss Sarah Verona, right?"

I gulped. "Yes," I replied. "I am."

"Well," he said, hesitant. "The military isn't something you turn to every day for answers, Miss Verona, but we do share your opinion that you are entitled to the answers as anyone else."

"Thank you," I said politely.

"But here's the thing. Our troop was dispatched only because we were at close proximity to the carnival, where the attack was foreseen. We are not the XTM, and we don't have more information on this than you do. I'm sorry, Miss Verona. But I suggest you talk to Dr. Russell. I believe if they are things that can be shared with you, he will share them."

"All right, I will," I replied. "Thank you, Captain Moore."

The captain nodded his head and walked away toward the headquarters, and we were left with Calleigh in the middle of the living room, bringing her hands together on her chest as if to make a dramatic speech.

"Well... do you guys want to go home?" Calleigh asked cautiously. "I'm sure we're all still shook from everything that happened, so if you want to leave early that can be done..." Calleigh trailed on, "...but we can prepare lunch and, well, I do think that we could clear the air with a bit of a celebration, if you guys don't mind."

It was clear she wanted us to stay for lunch. That didn't seem altogether a bad idea. There were unanswered questions, and... things I would miss.

"Sure," I said. "We deserve a little celebration."

Calleigh's eyes lit up. "Well then, see you in an hour," she chimed excitedly before scampering off behind the waterwall.

Chase and Andrew got up from the couch to stretch, and sauntered off. My heart skipped a beat as I looked at Carlos, wondering if we would get another little moment alone—

"I want a word with you," Lillian hissed, raising herself to stand right in front of me. I jumped.

"Uh... sure?" I replied uneasily. Out the corner of my eyes I saw Carlos' eyes darting between me and Lillian, as though trying to determine if she was going to kill me or not.

A moment later I was in my room, or Lillian's room, whatever, for some reason held up against the wall by the girl's fiery glare. Yup, this was definitely her room. Those blue gray walls didn't go well with me, but they went well with her.

"Brings out the blue in her eyes," I ended up saying aloud.

"What?" Lillian demanded sharply.

"Nothing, sorry. I didn't mean to say that out loud. Just that the color of the walls goes well with you," I replied sheepishly.

Lillian ignored me like I was talking gibberish. She instead went on to ask her own question: "Did you go because of what I told you?"

"Was that why you wanted to talk to me?" I asked with a grimace.

"Answer my question," Lillian ordered, crossing her arms in front of her. Her pupils were dilated, and the eccentric blue was some sort of a thick ring around them. The walls no longer brought out the blue in her eyes.

"*No*," I said defiantly. "It's *not* because of what you told me. I went because I wanted to."

Lillian raised an eyebrow. She looked dubious.

"I had that dream twice, Lillian," I explained with a sigh.

"Twice?" repeated Lillian.

"The night they attacked. This time I saw them closer, and I knew somehow that they were close. That they changed their plan."

"Oh. And you went to find them."

I nodded.

"To get your gem," she stated.

I nodded again.

"Isn't that because of what I told you?" she asked with a somewhat irritated look in her eyes.

"No. I swear it's not," I lied.

Lillian's gaze penetrated me. I could tell she didn't believe me.

"It has nothing to do with you," I told her. "Whether you'd told me that or not, I'd have felt that I needed to go. I've been looking into Victorina Archer,"

Lillian's eyes were unreadable, but I could tell she was listening intently.

"I've read about... I've read about Queen Serena," I continued. "I wanted to know more about why she died. I thought I could find out more about it... or find my gem. Either way, I'd get something from it. That's what I thought."

"Did you?" Lillian asked, raising an eyebrow.

I shook my head. "No. And it was stupid."

Lillian stared at me a while before she gave a slight nod. "Good," she said. "Don't do anything stupid. I don't want to take responsibility for stupid things you do."

I smiled. "I won't."

Lillian turned and left, obviously displeased.

Robert and Sophie arrived shortly. Both of them, who normally looked very well contained—with properly buttoned shirts and straight collars—stood in the doorway with flushed faces and widened eyes. They embraced their kids, and then everyone else, with flustered relief and cries of gratitude. Only after hearing a detailed account of the battle—from Calleigh and from a couple more soldiers—did their composure return to them.

The house soon came back alive with noises and movement. Calleigh had set to work in the kitchen, preparing food and drinks, and Sophie followed suit. Robert was standing at a corner with another officer, nodding seriously. I had so many questions to ask, but knew I needed to wait my turn. I shuffled over to join Calleigh and Sophie, but Calleigh let out a tiny shriek and jostled me out of the kitchen. For a while I wandered around, studying paintings, returning to my room and trying to get some packing done, getting out and wandering some more—until I found that Robert was no longer in sight.

This was the chance. I knocked on the door to his study. The door was dense, and my knuckles felt numb. I waited patiently, going over the things to say.

"Come in," said Robert's voice from the other side of the door. I opened the door and let myself in.

It was an old fashioned study. The walls were lined with bookcases full of old books, rows after rows of dusty red covers and faded green spines. A window at the far corner with a rounded top let in rays of sunlight on which danced fluttering specks of morning dust.

Robert looked up from his desk. It looked as though he had lost half his weight, his eyes sunken and his skin stuck gauntly to his bones. But amidst the fatigue I could see a morsel of peace, something we had all earned from the morning's battle.

"Can I have a minute, Robert?" I asked.

Robert looked up from the pile of papers, and proceeded to pull a chair to his desk.

"Sarah. Good to see you well. Have a seat."

I took a seat in front of the desk.

"What is it that's troubling you?" asked Robert with a kind smile on his face.

"A lot of things. There's many things I don't understand."

"Why don't we start with the simplest?" Robert suggested.

That seemed reasonable. "Why did they disappear?" I asked after a minute of reflection.

"From all the details, it looks like they've gone to save themselves."

"Save themselves?" I repeated in disbelief. "From *us*?"

"Yes. Although more specifically, it may have been from you. Each of the Xentrios is believed to have a weakness. Victorina can't affect gemless Enrici, Cuper's easily distracted—but Darius' weakness was unknown up to now—but I think you might have uncovered it. His own strength is his very own weakness."

I was completely dumfounded. "But how could they disappear?" I asked.

"Benefits of being what they are. They have an inborn ability that we aren't gifted with—except for those of us with certain gems—and they can take shortcuts through space."

I frowned. That didn't add up. "I feel like they could use that to kill us. Why didn't they?"

"It weakens them immensely. When they disappear like this, it means they've given up on further assault. At least, for the time being."

"Has this ever happened?"

"In the past, yes."

I pondered.

"But when you say..." I began after a while, when a flash of something crossed my head. "When you say benefits of being what they are..."

Robert looked at me with round, patient eyes. I was reminded somewhat of Calleigh, except that I couldn't quite picture her waiting in silence for me to speak.

"What are they really?" I asked finally. "I mean... I mean fundamentally. What Calleigh's told us this one night was a lot of information, but it wasn't everything. I've been meaning to find out about... about Serena's killer, and I came across nothing. It was like someone was trying to hide all this from us."

Robert sighed.

"It's a long story," he said. "Do remember the story of how Enrici came into being?"

I nodded. "Some sort of flux of energy from the star Alpha Enrica. Kind of like the solar wind. They bring us into a new state, where we have another, well, *phase* or something," I answered briefly, not sure if I'd used anything close to the right words.

"Yes, quite like that," Robert replied. "There's still much to learn about our enemy, but it seems they've been blessed—or cursed—with a similar fate. Long before the First Original came into being, there's said to have been a power so dark and so great—it's called by many names: The Evil, The Dark, The Haze... and its nature, in its own way, mirrors the essence of what gives us our second forms: the Star. It's closely related to the star, and to the radiation-like energy that it emits. It's what brought them into existence, and it has something to do with how the Knife functions. A lot of researchers have been trying to philosophize about the origins of these creatures, and they've never come to an agreement; but for now we'll simply put it this way. What powers them is the *mirror opposite* of what powers us."

I did not understand a word of his.

"As for why you weren't able to find much information on it, well—this is strictly classified, but I feel we've already crossed that line when you had that dream."

I looked at him intently.

"Some Enrici are gifted with gems that predict the future," Robert explained, drawing a careful sip from his jug of coffee. "And with that being said, there had been some prophecies in our world. It told that Queen Serena was to put an end to the evil."

I swallowed.

"And yet, as you probably already know—"

My mind went wild a while—did he know that I had been reading Princess Rena? I thought back to when Calleigh had snuck me the book. Perhaps he'd known what was going on.

"—she failed." Robert said matter-of-factly. He did not seem to care much whether I'd been prying through banned books or not. In fact, his expression was very tired, as he continued: "What institution would want their people to know that their hope had failed, that the only one capable of destroying their enemies had in fact been slain by those enemies? Naturally, the government had to keep it to themselves. Gradually they destroyed the books that told these tales, erased the evidence that those prophecies existed, that those battles happened, and that these foul creatures live among us, hidden somewhere. And the world forgot, and they believed. It doesn't take much to fool a society. Memories are more flexible than you think, and less people pay attention to truth than to how sentimentally appealing something is. A house could have windows on all sides, always wide open—and still conceal its secrets, perhaps do so even better. In less than a century, no one spoke of the Xentrios anymore, or of Queen Serena's death."

I sat there, silently gazing as this sank in. From outside the window a soft, dusty light fluttered in, tenderly touching the corners of the study, the walls and desk, the books and shelves and jugs full of pencils that sat like an old patchwork of knowledge and time. I imagined a wall from centuries ago, patched with rocks old and new, a mixture of young and aged. What Robert had said seemed a lot like this. If all those words had been a book, it would have been one that took more than a decade to write.

"I see," I breathed at last.

"I know this isn't much of an explanation, but I hope this answered your questions," Robert said conclusively. But I could not let the con-versation come to an end, at least just yet. There were so many questions left unanswered.

"But these Xentrios," I spoke tentatively. "They've been around for centuries, haven't they?" I retorted indignantly. "How can we know so little about them?"

"The universe has been around for billions of years, even before the existence of humans and civilization, and yet we know very little about it," Robert said softly.

"But not anymore," I retorted, thinking back to my physics classes, and to books I'd read. From how ordinary objects worked to mind-boggling concepts about big and small, fast and slow things, I was sure we knew way more than we knew about these hazy figures in my dream. "We know quite a lot about the universe. This is different."

Robert smiled, taking off his glasses and rubbing his face. "A lot about the universe, you say? You'll learn how far we still have to go. It could be a wonderful journey. But yes, this is different, this is a threat that looms upon us, it's something we should duly know more about. And yet we don't. I don't have anything to say to excuse this, Sarah. We were just wrong. We failed in every assumption. We were just wrong too many times, and for far too long."

I stayed silent. His eyes seemed tired and old. It seemed like he'd aged ten years in a single day.

"I... Can I ask you one last thing, Robert?" I asked .

Robert wearily pushed up his glasses, and nodded. "Sure," he replied.

"This dream. Why did I have this dream?"

Robert looked thoughtful for a moment, running his hand over his stubble.

"Concerning the dream, Sophie doesn't think this is a sign of a gem. There aren't any newly detected lapidary sources," Robert said sternly.

I had already known it wasn't anything like a gem, that it was something, something akin to a deep connection, that I was meant to find. Nevertheless hearing it again reminded me of the hollow that persisted in my chest.

"But it's happened in the past, and it's happened irrelevant to gems. There were several reported cases of Enrici having dreams or visions of the Xentrios, especially known and powerful ones, when they were either close or growing powerful. I believe it has something to do with with the Entanglement."

"The Entanglement?" I repeated with a frown.

"Do you recall the Haze we had talked about—the thing that existed before Darius? Between our essence and theirs, there lies a deep connection, a sort of balance between the two."

"But how does that relate to the dream I had?" I asked impatiently.

"I have to admit it's a mystery we weren't able to understand quite yet. There was one mastermind who had come close to understanding this profound matter, and that is the late queen. But we believe a lot of that knowledge passed with her."

"Why me, though?" I breathed.

Robert looked at me, his eyes gaunt and hollow, as though saying *'that wasn't one question, Sarah.'* I looked back at him, apologetic.

"Same as before," he said. "None of us know the exact answer to that, Sarah. But it had happened before, and it has happened again. I like to think sometimes, when it's most needed, the world seeks someone who can help. That it's a vast thinking being—the world, the Enrici, Alpha Enrica... and finding you at that moment was its way of saving us."

I stared, a bit dumbstruck. It was not exactly the answer I'd expected, and also not the answer I wanted.

"That... doesn't explain anything," I retorted.

"I believe that sometimes it does, Sarah. Better than anything else," Robert replied with a warm smile.

"Whatever it was, I don't think you have to worry about it. You did great. Not just as a young Enricus still on her primary courses, but historically. You deserve to be proud, and you deserve to take a break from these matters. I hope you wouldn't, for all the curiosity, yearning or even a very misleading sense of responsibility, take part in anything like this again. It's what *we* do, Sarah. Those of us like me and Sophie, and the XTM. That's what we're for, keeping Enrici, whether old, or young like you kids, all safe and well," Robert said assuringly.

And something told me this was all he would tell me.

"Thank you for your time," I said politely, to which Robert smiled warmly and said, "Anytime."

Then I left the room.

Well, it wasn't the easiest thing to do, but if that's what the expert says, I could as well leave it be and let it go. It was not a night I wanted to live through again, but we were out of it, and we were out of it alive and well. And so I decided to bring my mind off it and onto everything else; the sound of morning, the sound of the world waking again as it did every day—the plans I could make for the remaining holidays... and the kiss.

It had been a long day, and I felt I could collapse at any moment—but my heart began to race again, and I could feel a tingle rush through my body to the very tips of my hands. I found my feet carrying me forward, as though dreaming, to the guest room.

Here we are, I thought to myself. *There's one thing left to do. One thing I was waiting for.*

There were worlds, that no matter how cozy and ordinary, scared you more than battles in the forest. This was one of them, for I wasn't one to excel in everyday life stuff. But now it was time to give it a try. I drew a deep breath.

I raised my hand to knock.

Chapter 15
Mock Carnival

The Carnival was just as I remembered it. Beads of light were strung around lamp posts and railings, filling the night with sparkles. Wooden bridges and archways connected pavilions, big and small—on some of them were arcades, on some snack stands. On yet another, a group of buskers were singing Coldplay—and the nearby platforms had turned into dance floors, where people swayed and turned in ensembles. The night was sweet and spirited; several girls passed by in animal onesies, offering free drinks in little airplane cups, and a group of boys were huddled in a corner by the punch machines, flinging themselves at the pad like jumping gazelles.

I walked dreamily through the crowd of people, watching their eyes sparkle like suncatchers in the festive lights. Through the crowd I caught a pair of familiar eyes, and the world slowed to a halt—my stomach did yet another somersault as I neared the boy. He too approached me, smiling like a sun—in his hand two ice cream cones; one mint chocolate chip, one strawberry.

"You look gorgeous in that dress," Carlos remarked. His voice was soft, but clearly audible through the laughter and chatter.

I looked down. Underneath a puffy brown coat I was wearing a red cotton twill dress that came down to my knees. I hadn't ever worn it—as I wasn't one to dress up often—and had saved it for an occasion, well, like *this*. "You told me that like five times tonight," I reminded him.

"And I thought that like fifty times," he responded.

I blushed.

"Aren't you cold, though?"

"Freezing," I replied. I could feel the chill slice my skin.

"And you wanted ice cream?"

"Yes," I replied.

Carlos shook his head with a sigh.

"Here, hold this," he said, handing me the ice cream cones. Then he took off his jacket and put it around me. "Here you go, now you're nice and warm."

I beamed. The night was beautiful. We strolled around among the crowds, filled up on food, and at some point Carlos pulled me excitedly to a kicker machine—and congratulated me as I scored just below the high. Then we danced on a little dance floor, where the music melted into the background and voices faded to ambience.

"You know what would be a good idea?" I chimed.

"The Ferris wheel?"

"Yes, how did you—"

"You're staring at it."

And I was right. The carriage slowly rose above the horizon. The lights of the Mock Carnival, along with the lights of the homes, disappeared into one sparkling picture beneath our feet. It felt good to know how brilliant the lights were in a city we had just saved.

As in anyone's dreams, we kissed when we reached the top—and didn't stop until the ride came full circle. As I felt the warmth of his lips on mine, and a coolness of metal on my collarbones, my thoughts enveloped affectionately around a little memory from that morning—the morning that seemed like days ago, perhaps even weeks. It was in the guest room, where the air was hot, and my heart was racing, and my mouth was fumbling:

"Okay," I'd replied, back in the guest room. I was sure I was blushing like a ripe strawberry. "And I'm leaving now. I'm done."

"Not so soon," Carlos said. "I was waiting to get some time alone with you."

I blushed terribly.

"I mean, not—I hope it didn't come off as, well, you get what I mean," he sent on. I found that Carlos' ears had turned bright pink.

"Is your..." I reached for his ear as his bandage caught my eye. "Does it hurt?"

Carlos winced. "Disgusts me more than hurts me," he remarked.

"That *bitch*," I cursed. Carlos seemed a little surprised at the word that left my mouth.

"Thank you."

"I'm sorry about that," I said. My fingertips brushed his bandaged ear ever so slightly when he flinched, inhaling sharply.

"Sorry," I apologized.

"No, don't, I wasn't—no, never mind," Carlos fumbled.

We looked awkwardly at each other a while, my eyes darting around the room, desperate to find something else to talk about. I caught glimpse of a soft almond-colored hoodie lying on the edge of the bed. I reached for it.

"Uh, nuh-uh," Carlos blurted uneasily as I buried my face in it. "I didn't wash it."

It smelled like Carlos. I knew this scent. It would drift into my feline nose right after we'd both changed, a lingering residue in the air left by his human body. Come to think of it, I'd always liked it. It had a soft, sweet essence; an opaque bass note, a middle note of bare skin, topped by a subtle balm of nectar. I peeked from the crumpled hoodie, and found Carlos leaning down toward me, his eyes merely inches away. My heart skipped a beat.

"It smells like you," I managed to whisper.

Carlos' ears turned pink. "I think I need to wash it," he said, trying to grab the sweatshirt.

With a mischievous grin I yanked it out of his reach. "I want to borrow it. It's warm. I like it."

Carlos laughed. "Suit yourself," he replied with a smile. "I still think I need to wash it, but just bring it to me when you do too."

I giggled. The sun spilled in through the window, forming a glowing little halo around his face. He looked... nice.

"I'll bring it to you with your jacket," I said. "When do you want your jacket back?"

Carlos laughed. "I don't know, I honestly liked how it looked on you."

I rolled my eyes. "It's oversized as heck."

"That's what I like most about it," said Carlos thoughtfully. "You look like uh, like one of those sea things. Sea lions, rolled up in snow?"

"I think I know what you're talking about," I said.

"Yeah those," he said, a soft smile forming dimples on his cheeks. "Cutest thing ever."

I blushed.

"But I mean, if you don't want it, you can give it to me—"

"Uh-uh," I said, shaking my head. "I like it," I added defensively. Carlos chuckled.

Carlos laughed. "Well, I can let you keep it, but you know how the deal is."

I blinked. "The deal?"

"You give me that." Carlos said, pointing to my hand.

I looked down, baffled, and saw what Carlos was pointing to. It was a yellow dotted scrunchie on my wrist.

I laughed. "Really? A scrunchie?"

Carlos nodded. "It's a universal law. Of uh, trade."

I giggled. I took it off my wrist and reached for Carlos' hand. His broad hand slid into mine. An impish smile crept on his face, and he turned his hand—his fingers wiggling between mine until our hands were intertwined. I blushed. He reached for my other hand, which again he took in his own, fingers between fingers. His hands held me, his firm arms tipped me over, and I sank into a pile of clothes on his bed. His warm palms dug my hands into the bedsheet, and his eyes gazed into mine not more than a couple inches away. My heart began to race frantically.

"Sarah," Carlos whispered softly. "Sarah. Don't do that again."

I blinked. I wanted to ask what he meant, but it was hard. My heart seemed to be pounding in my mouth.

"Don't scare me," Carlos added.

Heat rushed to my cheeks. It took a lot of effort for me to open my mouth and speak; what came out at the end of that struggle was something barely above a whisper.

"I can't make any promises."

"Why did I bother," Carlos sighed. He reached down to deliver a light kiss on the lips.

"Fine, but if you do, steal my keys. Take my car."

A giggle escaped my lips. "What?"

"So I'd know you're up to something," Carlos said softly.

I looked at him, unable to tell if he was serious or teasing me.

"I woke up last night after you stole my car. It was probably long after you were gone, but..." Carlos halted for a second, and his ears turned a shade of pink. "I knew right away that something was up. I thought—I thought I could smell you. In the air."

"Seriously? You could smell it?"

"A little," Carlos replied thoughtfully. "I don't know, maybe not. But I thought I did. Or... I don't know, I *felt* it. Kind of like you could hear me about to change."

I opened my mouth to say something, but was interrupted by the sound of a doorknob turning. We both nearly jumped. Carlos quickly straightened up, but I wasn't as fast—I raised myself sheepishly back up as the door flew open.

Our intruder, as it turned out, was Calleigh. The girl gasped and shut the door in front of her. "I am really, like really really really *really* sorry, guys," Calleigh apologized through the keyhole. "I didn't mean to. I *swear* I didn't mean to. You know, this also happens to be my house, and I mean, this is the guest room normally, right, and it's usually empty, so sometimes I keep my canvases and stuff in there, and I just, walk in, you know. Sometimes I even, just walk into Lillian's room and she doesn't exactly give me hell for it but the look she gives me—"

"Calleigh, stop," I laughed. "It's all right, Calleigh. You can come in. We're just... talking."

Carlos gave me a quizzical look. My face grew hot.

"No, no, no, you guys can just do whatever—uh, you were doing," Calleigh groaned, as though she was simultaneously saying things and regretting them. "I, um, I just wanted to let you know that—just in case, like *just* in case you two are interested in coming downstairs and having lunch I wanted to—yeah. Lunch is ready. And my mom made dessert. A lot of stuff. And there's cake. Chocolate cake with lemon frosting and coconut cream. A giant one."

I looked at Carlos. Although the cake sounded a lot like... *Calleigh*. It was an unfortunate combination of fortunate things—but there was no denying it was made of things I loved. A bubbly warmth filled my chest as I imagined Calleigh, putting together a bizarre shopping list of items in a bowl of dough.

My eyes darted to Carlos. He smiled. I was never the best at reading someone's expressions, but Carlos was different. He was my hunting partner. Without a word, we nodded in agreement.

His eyes—glowing, if that was possible—never left mine as he said: "We'll be downstairs in a minute, Calleigh."

"Oh, all right, no problem, take your time," Calleigh said. "Be safe, kids."

"*Calleigh!*" I cried indignantly.

With a birdlike giggle, footsteps scampered away from the door. Our eyes traveled back to each other's, and a coy smile bloomed on the corner of Carlos' lips.

"What's that minute for?" I asked.

Carlos eyed me, his eyes traveling between both of mine, then over the contour of my face, and onto my lips.

"This," he said softly. Then tore in to kiss me.

Furrowing into my hair, his hands were working something on my neck, but it barely caught my attention. The only thing I could think of was the taste of his lips—and the twirling fervor of my heart.

When Carlos pulled back, he was beaming. A smudge of Chapstick had transferred onto his lips, and I blushed.

"Happy birthday, Sarah."

Oh—my birthday. February twelfth. It wasn't every day that you forgot your birthday.

That explains the cake. For the first time since, well, *birth*, I had been crept up on. I had been preoccupied with thoughts of the Xentrios and whatnot, so much that I'd completely forgotten what day it was. I for one did not know I'd go home later that day and be welcomed by an arrangement of my old stuffed turtles holding a stuffed birthday cake—because obviously, moms think you're five forever—and I for another had not foreseen this little gift. So I froze for a moment when I felt something cold and metallic on my chest; I looked down, startled, to find a little pendant, with thin rose-gold lines forming a delicate outline of a gem.

"When did you—"

"Shh. That's um, classified."

It was a typical February morning, kissed by a light chill which I knew would melt away as the sun climbed higher. It was the last day of the week-long meeting at Vanna Daya; and though I'd already grown fond of Lillian's room and Calleigh's shimmering voice waking me in the mornings, the thought of home welcomed me more than I could ever have imagined. And yet, it was one of those rare moments that I was enveloped by everything I loved, all at once—home was close, and so were friends. There was an absurd cake waiting for me downstairs, and lastly, a gem glistening between my collarbones.

"I love it, Carlos," I whispered. "Thank you."

I planted a light kiss right beside his lips.

Little did I know then, that this was only the beginning of a long journey— peril, gifts and tragedy, answers to yet unanswered questions. But somehow I did know, that through most—if not all—of the journey, I would not be alone.

Epilogue

She ran as fast as she could.

Her long locks sailed behind her, painting a streak of flame red on the dire dark of the forest.

The sound of footfall, the swift rustle of broken branches echoed fatefully beneath her bared feet in the foreboding silence. She glanced back behind her shoulders, her eyes dilated in terror.

No one. No one was there. It was just the still forest. Where they'd played as children, where they'd plucked wildflowers and crafted them into rings and crowns. Where Arynne had died.

What good did it do to run? She believed she was at the very same level as her pursuer, in that she knew what he knew. He knew there was no getting away; that she was running to her death. Or, quite probably, something a lot worse.

She stopped in her tracks, frozen to the ground.

He smiled brilliantly in front of her.

The End of Book 1

Author's Words

Hello, reader.

I hope you enjoyed my little story. I cannot thank you enough for picking up my book and seeing it through to the end. It means the universe to me.

The story has only begun. I hope we'll meet again in the sequels as it unfolds, as worlds are introduced and grand schemes are played out. Your questions will be answered, and at the same time you will be met with new ones. As Sarah's journey progresses, we will meddle with greater topics and notions; of good and evil, of right and wrong; of destiny, of dirty hands, of identity—and of love.

I cannot express in words how good it feels finally to have finished the book I have been working on since I was eleven. Everything of this world, from a couple of eagles circling the sky to major and minor experiences of my own, filled me with brimming inspirations; and ever since I was a little girl I have sought to turn them to creations of my own. I remember starting off the earliest version of this story on a yellow notepad on lazy afternoons after school. I filled it with—mostly in bad prose—suspenseful scenes I'd daydreamed, along with backstories of characters inspired by people I loved. As I grew to feel *'love's keen stings'* my note-pads were then filled mostly with stories of love.

After about ten good years of writing all the scenes that were fun to write, what I had left was four years of torture. In early 2021 I finished my first draft, and the last few hours of it were so terrible—and the very first feedback from a friend so devastating—that I neglected to look at it for another three years. Then after a couple more months of labor, in May 2024 I finished the second draft. In October I began the final revision, which I'd expected to take three days. It ended up taking a couple months, and was equally dreadful. I vowed to write shorter novels in the future so they don't take as long to revise.

There have been many changes in the plots and characters since that early version, and due to academics and procrastination, it has not been until a good fourteen years later—when my friends are no longer the kids with braces that I knew and instead hold fancy titles like *doctor*—that this story met the world. Because of the unfortunately long time it spent in my hands, the book is a patchwork of fourteen years' worth of me. I had to cross out a lot of atrocious sentences along with ideas I'd grown out of, but I am proud to say that the essence of the story, including most of the plot and a lot of my favorite scenes, comes from the mind of a much smaller, much less experienced version of myself. I would like to thank her and let her know that I have finally realized her dream. There is still a long way to go, but I am sure she would be as happy as I am to hear this news.

I have, like anyone, had undeserved enemies. I've had many mean friends and classmates, crappy lovers and more—some of whom tried to plot my downfall in classroom politics, some of whom tried to corrode away my self-esteem, and some of whom did nothing but to toot indelicacy from their sad lips. Now that I have had one of my biggest childhood dreams come true and an audience made of the most wonderful people in the world, I would like to take this opportunity to publicly and formally tell them to [♪] off and go suck a [♪].

Despite the interesting patchwork of background, as you may learn, I realize I have always been an artist. It has been my most natural impulse since childhood, and the thing I enjoy most; in a recent interview I used the phrase 'characteristic action of my existence' to describe creation, and I believe this most effectively defines who I am as a person.

And as an artist I have two goals. One is to elevate my art until they're enough to make one scream a profanity. The other is that my stories, whether written in text or in music, will inspire, heal, and spark hope—that they will keep people expecting goodness from the world, tell them their lives have worth. Life is too short and at the same time too long—so I choose to make a risky little move; I will not comfort you and tell you that dreams are needless. I am going to tell you, through the lengths of my works that will come and go, to dream of the great and unending sky.

I hope that you, dear reader, will see me through this journey.

On Christmas Eve, 2024
Seoul, Korea

Suinne Clara Lee is a Korean novelist and aspiring composer. Rediscovering the love and zeal she has had for music, Lee began to teach herself classical composition in the spring of 2023. These studies had to pause due to academics, but now toward the end of her masters' program, she is searching for a way to continue her musical training.

Since childhood, Lee has been fascinated by the stars. This, long before her journey in music began, led her to physics and mathematics. It was in the later years of college that she discovered her own path toward the stars. The wonder and awe she's fostered for the world and its clockworks nevertheless remain a treasured source of inspiration in her art.

Lee plays the viola and piano, and also has a handful of cherished hobbies. In her free time, she occasionally transforms into a singer, figure skater, and second-dan kenshi.

For more information, visit www.suinneclaralee.com.

Acknowledgements

This book is a patchwork not only of fourteen years of my life, but also of many people I've had the privilege of knowing. I hope this snippet of text does well enough to show how much they mean to me.

I would firstly like to thank my friends, Dr. Scott Sussex, Taewon Kim and Taehyeok Moon for taking the time to read my drafts and share their valued opinions with me. Many thanks also go out to Viviane Egli for her valued insights and interest in my project, and to Dr. Victor Steinborn for his wholehearted support; to Yujin Choi, who with her keen and gentle eyes read and recognized all the pieces of me that longed to be read; to Tyler Wertsch and Virbin Sapkota for their great help in the early stages of research; and especially to my friend and mentor Mary Wertsch, not only for reading through the lengths of my terrible first draft, but for guiding me through my journey as a writer ever since I was a little girl.

My love for writing also owes much to Ms. Marty Miller, my great tutor and refuge back in the days I'd begun to make a second home of St. Louis. I would like to send her my heartfelt regards.

I am also obliged to the wonderful people of Korea University. It was a pleasure and honor to study under my supervisor Professor Seungsang Oh, and many a time I was inspired and encouraged by my classmates, especially my fellow lovers of the arts, Jeong Yoon Yang and Seungeun Lee.

And though I will not name her—as it may go against policies—I am deeply grateful to my former counselor, for being angry, sad, and happy for me. Your words will always give me strength when I am in need, and will push me to continue on my adventure as an artist.

Warm hugs and thanks to Jenny Lee, my friend of twelve years, for sticking around and for never forgetting to gift me flowers on a special day; to Denis Ferster, my brother in crime, if such a term exists—for being my glorious comfort human; and to my precious friend Dr. Yuyeong Oh, one of the most driven and warmhearted people I know—for always being on my side. I love you guys, and want you to know that I am forever on your side as well.

I would also like to express my heartfelt appreciation for some of the people who inspired and influenced me through their works.

Thanks to Julee Rosso and Sheila Lukins, authors of *The Silver Palate Cookbook*, for their inspiration on scrumptious dishes; to J. R. R. Tolkien, J. K. Rowling, Philip Pullman, Elizabeth Kostova, of whom I am a great fan.

Thanks to Professor Kyong-jun Chang of Korea University for letting me audit his course on the history of the Korean language, which helped greatly in vital parts of the writing.

Thanks to Linda Sue Park: you probably won't remember this one talk you gave, where I handed you a note with a question about writer's block. You read my question out loud and said: 'whoever asked this question is already a writer.' It was truly a delightful thing to hear from an author whose works nourished and inspired me throughout my childhood.

Thanks also to everyone in my life who inspired bits and pieces of the characters, including my childhood friends back in St. Louis—who gifted me, along with the golden memories, a second home on the other side of the globe. Alice, Ariel, Mary Clare, and all the other friends I'm out of touch with: I think about you often.

Last but by no means least, many many thanks and endless love to all of my family: including Wandu, my favorite ball of fluff; my beloved mother and father, Professor Kyung-Sook Shin and Dr. Wonmin Lee; my grandmother Young Oak Kim who fed me and taught me to read, my grandfather Dr. Hyunje Shin who was the one to hold my bike (or pretend to hold it) as I learned to balance; and my other grandparents Jeong-im Hyun and Sun-bong Lee, who taught me how loved I am, and are sending me their love from the heavens.

A Cookie

I knocked.

"Yes?"

"It's me."

The door swung open. Carlos stood in the doorway, concealing a smile.

"Hey," I greeted.

"Hey."

"You look... great today," Carlos complimented after a while. "I mean, you always did."

"Probably 'cause I showered," I replied, wondering if I'd always been this bad at conversing.

A smile crept onto Carlos' lips.

I giggled. *"What?"*

"No, I was just thinking about how nice it is to... well, have you here." Carlos said, the smile growing, softly lighting up his whole face... his perfect face.

"In the doorway?" I asked. I didn't mean to mock; I had no idea why it had even come out.

But I felt better when Carlos laughed. He stepped aside, making a dramatic gesture toward the door. "M'lady."

I fumbled into the room. It seemed like ages ago that I'd sneaked into this very room to steal his car keys. I thought of his sleeping figure, the tickle of his breath on my face as I hovered over him, anxious that I might wake him—and my heart began to pound, sending, seemingly, an electric current into my bloodstreams. I stood awkwardly for a couple seconds before I bravely decided to plop down onto his bed—a bit too hard, I guess, because I sat there bouncing up and down, self-conscious, like a rubber ball gone out of control. When the bouncing subsided, and Carlos coughed away his laughter, I stiffly looked around the room, noticing it was littered everywhere with clothes.

"Oh, I'm packing," Carlos said quickly, pointing at his open suitcase. "I'm normally not this messy, as you probably saw when you stole my key."

I pouted. "Look, I'm sorry. Okay? I was going to apologize. That's why I came here."

Carlos grinned mischievously. "You know you don't really need a reason to come see me."

I scowled. "I didn't want to see you," I said indignantly.

Carlos raised an eyebrow. "You didn't?"

"I mean," I breathed. "I mean I did,"

"You did," Carlos repeated.

"I did."

Carlos eyed me for a while before a smile crept onto his face. He was beautiful, with his whole face lit up like a star. I smiled.

"But that's really not why I came here," I explained quickly. I could feel myself blushing. "I wanted to apologize. I'll uh, pay for the repair. Guess I'll have to do some tutoring. Just let me know how much it costs."

Carlos shook his head. "No, you don't have to. It's all right. Also, my car would have ended up far worse if *you* hadn't stolen it."

"But—" I began.

"No, really. The XTM is paying for the repair," Carlos said.

I peered sheepishly at him. "Really?"

"Yeah. Robert told me. They'll write me in a few days and I can get it taken care of. By pigeon mail, actually."

"*Pigeon mail*?" I repeated in disbelief.

"Really, I swear," he replied. "I'll send you a picture later."

I giggled. The jitters had worn off a little, and mellow happiness had begun to take its place. For a while I studied the merry light that came through the windows, then for some reason, the tips of his fingers. I could not bring myself to study his face—I felt like it would bring back the swarm of butterflies in my stomach, something I wasn't ready for.

"Are you going to leave?" Carlos asked with a grin on his face.

"Excuse me?"

"Because you're done apologizing."

I looked at him, confused. "Do you want me to?"

"No, no," Carlos said tenderly, a sweet smile creeping onto his lips. He pulled me into his arms, wrapping them softly around my neck. My face was suddenly buried in his broad chest, the pleasant softness of his red sweatshirt against my cheeks. His sweet scent tickled my nose, and my heart began to race—I was certain he could hear it.

"I'm just teasing you," he added with a smile. "Stay a while. God, why are you like this? This isn't like you, Sarah."

I blushed. "I hate you."

And so I did stay, perched on the edge of his bed like that. I couldn't find much else to say, however, for what seemed like an eternity—until a bold idea appeared at the rims of my mind, and my tongue acted on it before I could stop it.

"There's one more thing I wanted to ask you," I found myself voicing. *What*? I panicked. *Why did I say that?*

"Mm-hmm?" Carlos looked at me waiting, his eyes smiling.

"Mock Carnival." *What am I even doing? It was like I'd lost the ability to speak.* I tried again. "Mock Carnival?"

Carlos' lips bloomed into a full smile.

"Yes," Carlos replied, his voice a semitone lower.

"What?"

"I'll go with you."

I stared at him in disbelief.

"*If* that's what you wanted to ask me," Carlos went on playfully, "well, and if it isn't, I'll ask you if you want to come out with me to the Carnival tonight."

I looked up and we caught each other's eyes; I could see a little spark there. I giggled.

"I'll pick you up. Eight-ish. Is that good?"

"Very," I replied, a smile spreading on my lips.

"It's a date."

Or Two

I gritted my teeth. A sharp pain shot through my head, and the courtyard shifted in and out of focus. I knew I was about to change, and that I need to get myself somewhere safe. I held my breath and ran toward my red Subaru.

"Yo, Carlos," shouted a voice.

I turned and saw Cole holding his skate bag over his shoulders. Right, he did say going on the ice today to try out his new blades. I did a quick upwards nod with my chin.

"Where you off to?" Cole hollered.

I shrugged. I needed to get out of here as fast as possible. "Family dinner," I shouted out randomly. Out the corner of my eyes I saw Cole frown in question.

"See ya at practice tomorrow," I added.

I hopped onto the car, pinned the clutch to the ground and started the engine. Then I shot out of the parking lot and to a spot I knew so well.

I dove into the trees just as the uncontrollable impulse finally grasped me. A spin, fast and dizzy as usual, and I was a panther. I plopped down onto the ground just like that, laying there, panting.

It had been about a week since I'd first begun to feel these uncontrollable urges. I couldn't pinpoint where it came from, or what triggered it. The urge came regardless of my feelings, or whether I was with someone or alone. It was always there at the back, tugging me, and would come from time to time in waves I couldn't fight. And it didn't vanish even after I gave into it. A part of me told me this would get worse, that someday I would lose my control. This wasn't just something that happened every day. It was getting clearer that it was part of something bigger.

I buried my face in the ground. *What do I tell Sarah?* Would I have to stay away from her? If so, for how long? Would it be forever? She still didn't know why I'd avoided her last fall—I shuddered as it occurred to me that she may never know.

I raised myself up onto my feet. After a good five minutes it wasn't hard to change back, and I knew I would be left in peace for a couple hours, even a couple days if I got lucky. I guess I'd just have to wait it out when the storm came again. I'd just have to make it past the hockey cup.

The first game was nearing.